THE GODDESS PROJECT

BRYAN WIGMORE

Proudly published by Snowbooks

Snowbooks Ltd | email: info@snowbooks.com
www.snowbooks.com

British Library Cataloguing in Publication Data.
A catalogue record for this book is available from the
British Library.

Paperback / softback
ISBN 978-1-911390-22-0
Electronic book text ISBN 978-1-911390-23-7

To Ian, for walking down the table.

1

A COIL IN DARKNESS

'There it is,' said Cass. 'Number thirty-eight ahoy.'

With a clutch of nerves in his gut, Orc pushed himself up for a better look, steadying as the fishing-boat smacked through a wave. The white-painted barrel that acted as a marker buoy now bobbed only a hundred yards ahead, and just beneath it, sunlit against the deep, there showed a patch of submerged stone. From this angle it might have been only a shallow reef or sandbar, and for a moment Orc almost wished it could be nothing more, and not the flat summit of a structure no one had entered in thousands of years.

'Thirty feet across, you reckon?' His wetsuit felt tight round his chest.

'That's good,' said Cass. 'One that big, there's got to be something to sell. And we can't afford another blank.'

Orc nodded. Something to sell. Keep it routine. He breathed deep, trying not to let the jinx-thought into his head that a ziggurat that size might be the one they'd been searching for all summer – one that held not just ritual artefacts, but the big focus-stone that could retrieve their pasts, their selves, their lives.

Plus the fortune in gold. That would be handy too.

'You see it, outlander?' called Yorge's thin voice from the stern. Orc looked back along the sailboat, past Ranga lazing along a thwart, to where the old fisherman sat at the tiller with his grandson Esteban. Their eyes met his like dark stones.

'Hard to miss,' said Orc.

'Yes, the water is clear,' said Yorge, 'the sea is light. We'll sail around.'

'What?' said Orc. 'No, we need to get in.'

Yorge's eyes narrowed. 'Into the Dwelling?'

Orc held his gaze. 'The water.'

'No need. You can see from the boat.'

Before Orc could protest further, Ranga groaned and sat up. 'Nothing doing, Yorge. They need to estimate its measurements and count the steps and so on. That's what the museum's paying for.'

'And why does your museum need to know such things?'

'Some new craze called "science". You won't have heard of it.'

'*Ranga*,' Orc whispered. 'Don't piss him off.'

'Oh, don't fuss,' Ranga muttered, turning towards them. 'He probably thought it was a compliment. Anyway, who's paying who?'

'He's already got our money,' said Cass. 'That's the point.'

Their self-styled manager didn't answer that, but looked past them to the submerged ziggurat. 'Ooh, that is big. Yes, thirty-eight could be our *golden* number.'

'Like thirty-seven was,' said Cass. 'And the rest.' But there was a strain to her voice. Orc almost jumped as her hand closed around his knee, fingers squeezing through the spongy rubber.

Ahead and to port, the ziggurat's plateau grew clearer, the topmost of its steps now visible. Yorge swung the boat hard into the breeze, and the craft slowed and began to pitch, its momentum wallowing it towards the white barrel. Esteban hauled in the flapping sail, then stepped nimbly forward with a gaff and a whiff of bare armpit, and hooked the barrel just as the boat bumped. While the young fisherman tied the rope, Orc got their bag from the catch-hold, and he and Cass began to gear up. He sensed Yorge's close attention as the old man crabbed forward from the tiller, on their freediving equipment as much as on themselves. They'd met no one who'd seen its like.

'You swear you'll disturb nothing?'

'I told you,' said Ranga, 'it's just a visual survey.'

'That is well, then,' said Yorge. 'When the Sea Mother is angered, even God is powerless.'

'The who?' Orc glanced up from fastening his weight-belt.

'She whose bounty sustains life, and whose wrath takes it,' said Yorge. 'She wears a calm face today, but that can change in a moment.'

'Hear that, you two?' said Ranga. 'Any old ladies you meet down there, be sure to show them respect.'

Esteban knocked the end of his gaff against the deck. 'You'd do well to show *respect* up here, outlander.' They were almost his only words since they'd left Bazantin. 'Do you know nothing of sea-craft, in your country?'

'My country's the same as yours, *friend*,' Ranga said. 'And yes, I know ships. Torrento harbour's packed with them – steamers and dreadnoughts, not piddling tiddlers like this.'

Yorge spat over the side. 'We'll stay an hour.'

'An hour?' said Ranga. 'We paid for the afternoon.'

'In an hour the winds will change,' said Yorge. 'You truly know nothing of the sea, in your country, if you would argue with those born to it.'

'It's plenty, Ranga.' Cass pulled up the fastener at her back of her wetsuit, and nudged Orc's leg with her fin. 'Come on, Otter-boy. Before we cook.'

Orc needed no encouragement. He perched his backside on the gunnel, inhaled to his limit and rolled off to crash into cool water and a storm of bubbles. As soon as he'd righted himself he finned away from the boat, looking around at a world much clarified by his mask, free of the distorting window of the surface. Ten feet below, sunlight water-danced across the ziggurat's plateau; near the lump of concrete that anchored the barrel, surgeonfish picked at the algae-crusted stone grille that blocked the deep shaft leading down to the chamber.

And there! – his heart leapt as Cass powered from out of the boat's shadow, her body snaking with her double-finned kick. He ducked after her and into a chase, catching her just as they passed over the edge of the plateau – below him the ziggurat's slope dropped away, ledge after ledge, out of sunlight and colour and into blue murk. Lured by depth, he angled into a dive and finned down, skimming the steps. At forty feet his diaphragm contracted, its first warning, and he rolled over to see Cass hanging just above him, her hair fanned out in a halo of gold.

For a moment the beauty, the joy of it, almost burst him – then she pointed upwards, and he grinned and fought his leg muscles hard against the resisting flex of his fins. He took her by surprise, burned up his last air, breached the surface so hard the force of it pushed his mask down over his mouth. Settling back in the water, he moved it back up to his forehead, and lazily finned to keep his head clear, while Cass did the same.

He poked his tongue at her. 'I won that time.'

She back-handed water at him. 'I wasn't racing, idiot.'

'No point splashing me if I'm wet.'

'I wouldn't say you're *wet*. Just a bit pathetic.'

'Ha. So funny.'

Her eyes briefly lidded. 'Anything's funny next to those two. Am I glad to be off there.'

Orc glanced at the boat ten yards away, out of earshot if they didn't talk too loud. The fishermen and Ranga stood at opposite ends. 'Not too friendly round here, are they?'

'Yeah, I've been wondering about that,' said Cass. 'What did you make of that "Sea Mother" stuff?'

'Local superstition, why?'

'Remember those evil looks we got from those other fishermen we tried to hire earlier, and that one who called Ranga "slant-eyes"? And just now, Yorge wanting us to stay out of the water. What if it's all part of the same thing?'

'A local arseholes contest?'

'I mean to keep us away from something?'

Orc's ribs constricted as he caught her meaning. 'Shit, you think it's really here? And they know about it?'

'Maybe there's an old legend about the gold,' she said, an edge to her voice now. 'So don't bring up anything obvious.'

The stone, though – if the gold was here, the stone would be too. He could hide it inside his wetsuit. And use it tonight: only hours away. After months of searching, two years of torment…

He met Cass's eyes and saw it all reflected back at him.

'I shouldn't have said anything.' Her voice was slightly choked.

'You didn't.' His was unsteady. 'Nothing different about this one. Just routine.'

She nodded, refitted her mask. 'I'll go first.'

Her descent to the seabed was plumb-straight, swift, graceful: Orc never tired of the vision of it. Hanging seventy feet above on safety-watch, he could barely see her through the gloom but for her yellow fins as she searched the base of the ziggurat. He was so focused on that depth that whenever he lifted his face to breathe, the contrast shocked him as though he'd forgotten the world of sun existed. A distant steamer's smoke, the hazy brown cliffs of the Kymeran coast, the white houses of Bazantin clustering the hillside above its harbour – that it all could exist so close to the older, denser world beneath, separated by only a surface of water and a turn of the head – that *he* should be the pivot between them – it almost scared him. And each time he put his face back in, to be confronted anew by that man-built mountain in its dim, drowned slumber, he half-feared he wouldn't find Cass again, that he'd lost her to some pull of that ancient dreaming.

But at last here she came, finning powerfully upwards, bubbles escaping the edges of her mask as the air within expanded.

'Doorway's on the north side,' she said, after several breaths. 'Not much silt, about four feet clear. You doing a practice dive?'

'No, I want my legs fresh. I'll just go for it.'

Concern tightened her brow. 'This size, you'll need two minutes at least.'

'I got four-twenty on the way out here.'

'Which means two minutes on a dive,' said Cass, '*if* you're relaxed.

If you're all keyed up—'

'I'm not going to get any *less* keyed up, am I? And we can't come back some other time: paying Yorge cleared us out. It has to be now.'

Cass touched his arm underwater, quickening his nerves through his wetsuit. He glanced at her fingers on the lettering there, the ORCA white against the slippery black.

'Even if this *is* the one,' she said, 'Orc's a better name than nothing. Be careful.'

They swam to a point directly above the ziggurat's doorway, and Orc called to Ranga to time his breathe-up. Cass held him from behind, finning to keep his face clear. Limp in her arms, Orc counted out slow, deep breaths, and guided his awareness away from Cass holding him, focusing his thoughts on Otter's ability to swim into dark places and still see. Count of three in, count of six out, while the swell gently lifted and dropped him, and the sun burnt down, and the fishing boat rocked with the soft slap of water...

'Eight minutes!' called Ranga.

'Ready?' said Cass.

'Hmm,' he exhaled, and kept exhaling, forcing himself empty till his chest hurt. Then he breathed in long, and long, and long, and Cass released him, and he ducked his head under, lifted his feet and drove himself into the dive that might be the most important of his life.

A clean start, no thrashing at the surface: he finned smoothly down, one hand pinching his nose through the rubber of his dive-mask so he could pressurise his ears. The mounting weight of water pushed his stomach wall against his compacting lungs, squeezed his mask against his face; he spent a quick snort of air to restore the balance. As his buoyancy faded, he slowed his kicks to save energy. The ziggurat's lowest terrace resolved from murk as he glided down. A school of pale mackerel lazily spread to let him fall through.

Just short of the seabed, he stalled his descent to hang near-weightless before the doorway, its massive stones carved with serpents and leaves and corn-stalks: eroded outside, but clearer just within the passageway, before it turned black. An entrance to thousands of years –

and to the Otherworld. It was dangerous to think in such terms, but he needed to be on the edge of that world to get the help he needed. He touched his throat, felt the jagged little lump beneath his wetsuit: his own small focus-stone, cousin to the much larger one surely waiting in the darkness ahead.

Right, Otter – let's go.

He opened himself to his animath, mind and body, felt his spine and muscles shift and reform. The blackness at the end of the passageway softened. He kicked through the doorway into suddenly colder water, close to the ceiling to avoid disturbing the silt. In, and in, and the feeling grew of a presence: the nearness of the large focus-stone, it had to be. As he neared the end of the passage, the wall-carvings became visible again, no longer natural shapes but spirals, lines, zigzags. Tension gripped his diaphragm, the urge to breathe mounting with his excitement and nerves.

The passageway opened into the central chamber: twenty feet each side, dimly lit by the shaft in the centre of the pitched ceiling. And its floor—

Crap. It was bare, no sign even of the hole Ranga's source had mentioned. No gold, no stone.

He couldn't believe it, almost refused to. But no time for disappointment; he had to check for the usual artefacts. Lungs already burning, he finned towards the shaft opening. For a moment he saw blood dripping from it, but he shook off the image. Invoking Otter opened himself to other things, too – he had to keep his mind together. But the presence from the passageway felt stronger. And if not the crystal, then what? It felt different now, somehow aware of him: a scrutiny as heavy as the stones that penned him in, and as old.

Stop it.

Beneath the shaft, he glanced up. At the top, the surface glittered between crossed stone bars. The nearness of air pulled at him, but the grille would make it a cage of death. *Relax.* Groping just within the shaft, he found the usual hole on one side. He pulled his head and shoulders into the shaft and reached in.

The first contraction spasmed through his abdomen, his body urging him to breathe.

Relax. Relax.

His fingers touched something.

A shadow fell. He jerked his face up. A body had fallen across the grille, and from it rained blood.

No – he refused the image, and the body was gone, the light returned. Ghosts or his imagination, they were strong here. But the scare had raced his heart. He pulled out the cup he'd found: not much larger than his hand, black with tarnish but whole. Silver.

His diaphragm contracted again. He needed to breathe *now*. He ducked out of the shaft and turned, ready to kick towards the passage. Then his neck prickled, he glanced aside and—

A *face*.

A woman's face staring teeth sharp in the murk and something *uncoiling*—

His air almost blew. He fixed his eyes on the passage and kicked. But got nowhere. He worked his legs madly, and now felt it: the rope of muscle round his ankle. Holding him. Imagination, had to be, but – his diaphragm convulsed – he couldn't move. Panic clawed. *Submit*, came a voice in his head. *Let me have you.*

He struck with his right fin towards his left ankle, felt it hit. The hold loosened; he kicked with everything and shot forward. His diaphragm bucked again as he powered into the passage; and again it contracted, and again after a few more yards, his insides squirming and twisting with need. Ahead, the bright entrance, the open depths – then a seventy-foot ascent; it would take seconds, he could make it. But every moment was pain and his legs were draining of strength; his fins crashed against the walls.

Let me take you.

The backs of his legs scraped the doorway lintel as he swam out into the open. Glittering high above was his next breath, but he had no buoyancy and no strength; his blood was exhausted and his thighs burned with acid. He kicked and it was feeble; another contraction punched through him, then he was grabbed again—

But under his arms. He was rising.

He held on through the agony of the stale poison in his chest, held on with everything. Cass's legs beat against his as she finned, but hers were strong and fresh and the seabed faded below. Orc's contractions came faster. His vision tunnelled into black. He fought against the approaching faint, and the surface rushed and he crashed into purple sky and – air!

'Breathe!' shouted Cass in his ear. '*Breathe!*'

He forced his lungs to work. Blackness dragged at him, but he sank mental claws into the feel of Cass holding him, refused to let it go.

Soon as he knew he'd avoided fainting, he croaked, 'Get out! Something down there!'

'It's okay, you're safe.' She turned him to face her, studied him. 'God, your lips are *blue*.'

'Get out, come on!' He hardly knew what he was saying.

'You're safe, calm down.' She kept finning, holding him up. 'What *happened*? Was it the one?'

He shook his head. Heartbeat mad with fear, he immersed his masked face, but saw no sign of pursuit. A fog of silt had risen to hide the doorway.

'Orc, what are you doing?' She pulled his face clear of the water. 'It really wasn't the one? Why'd you stay so long?'

They both turned at a splash from the boat. Ranga had jumped in and was now thrashing towards them, the fishermen staring after him. 'On my way!' he called. 'Don't worry!'

'What the…?' said Cass.

'Only got a cup,' said Orc, almost surprised to find he was still holding it. 'And why I was so long: something grabbed me.'

'*Grabbed* you?'

'My ankle. Couldn't kick.'

'Your fin must've got caught,' said Cass, still watching Ranga. 'I said to be careful.'

'Everything all right?' gasped Ranga as he reached them, his clumsy swim hampered by his clothes.

'Except with your brain,' said Cass. 'What the hell are you doing?'

Ranga trod water with jerky determination, as though any lapse might send him plunging to the depths. 'Just making sure Orc's all right,' he said loudly, then lowered his voice. 'Get anything?'

'One bit of silver.'

'Well, don't let those peasants see it. All your fuss got them muttering about their precious zig being disturbed. If they guess you've been inside…'

'Ranga,' warned Cass. Esteban was untying from the buoy.

'Hey!' shouted Ranga. 'That was never an hour!'

'The wind isn't set by your pocket-watch,' Yorge called. 'We're leaving. Hurry.'

'Bollocks,' said Ranga. 'Remember,' he told the others, 'we found nothing.'

They swam back, Cass and Ranga loudly discussing measurements, maintaining the surveying act. Holding the cup underneath himself to keep it hidden, Orc started to shiver.

'Everything's fine,' Ranga called up as they neared the boat. 'He stayed down too long, that's all.'

'Why did he shout something was there?' asked Yorge.

'Too much breath-holding can bring on a kind of mental fit,' said Cass.

Yorge studied Orc, his eyes near-buried in sun-leathered wrinkles. Then he nodded to Esteban. Ranga got a foot on top of the rudder and was hauled up.

Cass whispered in Orc's ear, 'I'll go next. Stick that cup in one of your fins, then give me them. I'll put them straight in our bag.'

She handed up her own gear, and struggled on board – Esteban aiding her more gently, Orc noticed, and with a hand placed right on the curve of her rump. Biting his lip, shivering worse now, he pried off his fins one-handed, tucked the cup into a rubber foot-pocket, and passed them up to Cass before accepting Esteban's help himself.

By the time he was seated in the bow with the others, he couldn't stop shaking. The sun seemed to have lost any power to warm him, as though his struggle in the dark depths had chilled him forever. But his fin had caught on something; the rest had been imagination. This was the real world, with Esteban hauling an oar to turn the boat, and Ranga wringing out his shirt over the gunnel.

He looked at Cass, her hair messed by salt and wet, her freckled nose sunburnt. He would be dead, really dead, if not for her.

'Orc? You okay?'

He shied from her eyes, and found Esteban's gaze intent on her tightly outlined figure, before the youth noticed and looked away.

'You sh-should cover up.'

'Oh, don't start this,' she said. 'You're the one who's shivering.'

'I'll get you the towel.'

'I don't need it. Orc—'

'Till we get back.'

'Orc, leave it!' Cass jumped up and followed him to their gear-bag, tugging on his arm, trying to get past. He pulled open the bag, careful not to expose his fins.

'My blouse then,' said Cass sharply. But the shirt she'd worn over her suit from the hotel to the boat was pale linen, and would go transparent while she was wet. Orc picked up the heavy roll of towel.

'*Orc!*' She tried to reach round and grab it, but he shook it open.

Something black thudded to the boards.

He stared.

'Ah!' cried Cass. 'So *that's* where it got to!' She grabbed the cup, snatched the towel from Orc and bundled them together. 'Ranga, I found our salinity calibrator!'

'Thank the gods!' said Ranga. Orc glanced at Esteban. The young fisherman met his gaze with lowered brows. Orc didn't check Yorge's reaction. Face burning, he lugged the bag after Cass back to the bow, where she stashed the wrapped cup.

'Act like nothing happened,' muttered Ranga.

Orc jammed his jaws tight, still shuddering with cold, dreading the inevitable questions. But soon Esteban's oar squeaked and splashed again, and Orc let out his breath. It would be all right. The fishermen had believed Cass's lie.

Or they were unwilling to do anything about it yet. Esteban hoisted the sail, the canvas flapping as it swelled with the onshore breeze. The creaking boat slowly made headway, Esteban's hand on the boom-line, Yorge's on the tiller – and Orc's on the gunnel, gripping hard.

2

LORD FISH-RAT

As soon as the sullen fishermen tied up, Orc muttered thanks and escaped with Cass and Ranga across the hot cobbles to their harbour-front hotel, fending off the same children who'd pestered them on their way out. The Royal Bull was cool inside, though not as cool as the look the owner's wife gave them before returning to her newssheet. Their stay was a grudging trade of necessity: the hotel should have been busy with Kurassians visiting the nearby Lady's Leap Falls as part of the Grand Tour, but hotel bombings in the major cities had kept tourists away from Kymera that summer, and 'Mr Bull', as Ranga had named him, had been desperate enough to rent them two vacant garrets. That had been fortunate, as they'd already been turned away from the town's cheaper guesthouses, whose proprietors had been openly suspicious of them.

'Stupid backwater dump,' said Ranga, as they climbed the servants' stairs. 'I'm amazed the sea hasn't stagnated.'

In the attic the two shared, Orc struggled to peel off his wetsuit, which had got tighter in the last two years as he'd finished growing, while Ranga changed his damp clothes and checked no water had got into the tobacco tin that held his precious map. Orc thought about leaving again. He didn't want to be near the cup that had almost got him killed. But nor did he want to wander the small town alone.

By the time Cass had joined them from her room next door, Ranga was seated cross-legged on the rug, prying off the cup's thickest tarnish with his knife. 'Worth three hundred, maybe,' he said. 'If there were any rich tourists to sell it to.'

'Shouldn't we telegraph the museum?' asked Orc. 'Gregal said to.'

'When we had another *collection*, he said.' Ranga scraped and gouged. 'He won't come all this way out for one cup. And we need money right now – we're down to our last pennies. You saved our arses finding this thing.'

'Before he nearly lost it again,' said Cass.

Orc's jaw dropped. 'Oh, come on! How was I supposed to know it was in the towel?'

'By listening to what I was trying to *tell* you?'

'But why was it even in there? The towel! Someone was bound to use it.'

'It's been months,' said Cass. 'The only reason *you* wanted it was some stupid idea about covering me up, because of course men find nothing more attractive than a girl with a big mask-line across her face and a nose full of sea-snot.'

'Children!' said Ranga. 'Orc, the bowl?'

Orc rolled his eyes, then filled the washstand's enamel bowl from the ewer and set it before Ranga. From his bag, Ranga took packets of salt and baking powder, and poured carefully judged drifts of each into the water.

Tiny bubbles fizzed with the cup's immersion. Each time Ranga took out the vessel to examine it, more tarnish had given way to detail. Orc peered closer. A row of bulls jumped over corn-sheaves, and the bowl of the cup was ringed with robed figures holding snakes – or with snakes for arms, he couldn't tell. The unwelcome thought came to him that for thousands of years, those images had been concealed. Now, thanks to him, they were once more being exposed to air and light. To the world.

And the world was being exposed to *them*...

It felt suddenly an effort to breathe. He moved to the open window for more air, and looked out over a harbour bathed in late-afternoon sunlight. People haggled over fish on the quayside, boats bobbed and jostled; on the harbour mole, the long barrier of jumbled rock that bent round from further along the shore as protection from the open sea, children fished from its inner edge of dressed stone, or urged each other to jump from the steamer jetty that stuck out from the far side.

All solid, all ordinary. But still the air seemed to resist the draw of his lungs, as though it carried some of the darkness and pressure of that deep-sunk chamber. He couldn't shake off the feeling that time itself was being stripped away with the cup's tarnish: that as the images emerged and clarified, the modern world around him would fade, was already beginning to.

'Well, that's as valuable as it'll ever be,' said Ranga. 'Last look at your find?'

Orc turned – Ranga was about to toss it. 'No!' He stepped back, and his head cracked against the sloped ceiling beside the window. He clutched his skull, stifling his yowl.

Ranga laughed. 'I wasn't going to throw it *at* you.'

'Yeah, it's just—' Orc sat down on his bed, seething with pain and embarrassment. 'I've seen it enough.'

'Evidently.' Ranga wrapped the cup in a yellow polishing cloth, and stood. 'Wish me good fortune, then. A chance meeting with a rich drunk should do it.'

'Shouldn't one of us try?' said Cass. 'After what that fisherman called you this morning?'

Ranga looked displeased to be reminded of the *slant-eyes* comment. 'I won't be hawking it to fishermen, will I? Anyway, you don't look any more local than I do.'

'We look like Kurassians, and they're used to those here. I just think—'

'One man's foreign is another's exotic,' said Ranga. 'A richer man, more cultured; the two go together. The town mayor, perhaps.' He

19

checked his spiky black hair in the mirror. 'Or his wife.'

'Oh, whatever.'

'It doesn't matter who to,' said Orc. 'Just sell the bloody thing.'

When the creaks from the stairs along the landing had faded, Cass sat on Ranga's bed. 'You all right?'

'That thing with the cup?' said Orc. 'Just worried I'd drop it.'

'Ooh, convincing.'

Orc lay back. He hated lying to Cass, hated getting caught even more. 'Okay, the thing spooks me.'

'Because of what happened? Your fin getting stuck?'

He frowned at a crack in the ceiling plaster. 'If that's what you think happened.'

'Well, what else? Nothing really *grabbed* you, did it?'

If she mocked his lying, she could have the truth. 'A woman.'

Cass broke out laughing. 'That fishermen's legend?'

'I saw her!' He sat up. 'She grabbed my ankle – an old woman with snakes for arms, or tentacles, or something.'

'Oh, like the figures on that cup?'

'Yes. I mean, no, that was all crusted up – I couldn't have seen them before.' He swung his legs off the bed. 'Okay, my fin got stuck. Hard to do when you're swimming, jam a fin so hard into a gap it takes seconds to pull out, but you're right, it's the only rational explanation.'

'I can't tell if you're being sarcastic.'

'Me neither.'

Cass sighed. 'Orc, I accept you "saw" something. With your Otherworld eyes. I know you have to keep your mind open when you're down there, to get Otter's dark-vision. But the dive's over now. You need to keep it separate.'

'Because if I don't, I'll go mad, won't I, Cass?' He boggled his eyes and brayed out the word: 'Maaaad!'

'Stop it.'

'And even if we find who we are, we'll be no better off, because you'll be looking after a *maaad* person.'

'*Stop* it!'

'Just saying what you're thinking,' he said, but already regretted it. 'Look, I know my senses lie to me down there, but—'

'Then forget it,' said Cass. 'You're not going back to find out, are you? So *assume* your fin *somehow* got stuck, and *leave* it.' She exhaled, and stood. 'I'm going to rinse our gear off, then see about a bath. Coming?'

He snorted a laugh, but thought better of making the joke.

'I meant,' she said, 'they must have more than one bathroom in a place like this.'

'No. I'll stay.'

'It might help, don't you think? Doing something ordinary?'

That needled him. 'I'm going to talk to Otter. He might know what really happened down there.'

'For God's sake, *I* know what happened down there!'

'I need to be sure,' he said. 'Or I'll never be relaxed enough for another zig. No dives, no big stone, no piercing the Shroud – or have you forgotten why we're doing this?'

'But he'll make it worse! One imaginary creature isn't going to be rational about another.'

'He's not imaginary. It's more complex than that.'

'Oh, that's right,' said Cass. 'I forgot what a childishly simplistic view of reality I have.' She snatched up Orc's wetsuit, fins and mask from the damp floorboards. 'Have fun with Lord Fish-Rat,' she said, and slammed the door after her.

When he'd calmed down from the stress of her, Orc shut the window against the quayside noise, pulled the curtain closed, and jammed a chair under the door-handle. He took from his neck the rawhide thong with his focus-stone, and bound the fang-shaped crystal round his middle finger to make a claw. With its tip, he pricked his face in the precise ritual pattern, dots making up whorls, point after point of pain and fire summoning the tattoo-mask to the surface of his skin.

Then he mentally readied himself for what he was about to undergo. He could never do this within a couple of hours of a meal. He'd been sick before. There were other methods, Geist had said. *'But you don't have the temperament for meditation, so we'll try a more... aggressive approach.'*

He curled on the floor, clutching the focus-stone so hard it dug into his palm. He began shivering, mimicking for now. He drew painful memory like a flame of illness. He was cold, and scared, and hungry. He'd been shut in the cave for two weeks, with no food, only drugged water. The floorboards became damp stone – he convinced himself, made his senses deceive him; it only meant changing the present for a stronger past, an eternal past, the past that was the focal point of his broken self and which always lay only a little beneath the surface.

The memories stole back through his famished body. There was danger to this Little Death, Geist had warned him. That danger made the fear real. He began to whimper, to cry with terror at the monstrous forms that bled from the darkness. The shivering was genuine now. The cold was real, and the stone of the cave floor against his naked skin, and the mad, beautiful destroying dance of the serpents drawing nearer just beyond his senses, which he might find again if only he loosened the ties of his sanity.

He pushed himself towards that point, and when he sensed something start to slip, to break in his mind, he whispered, 'Help me.'

And help came: he sensed it with warm relief. Sitting up, he half-opened his eyes to the darkened room, which seemed less substantial than before. Before him was the same set of markings he'd awakened on his face, but dye-pricked on a bone mask worn by a sleek brown animal. A familiar musky odour mingled with the hotel's aroma of dust and tobacco-smoke.

'Classier digs than usual,' piped Otter, standing to look about. 'High time you treated her. But you won't get anywhere smelling like that.'

'I'm not trying to "get anywhere".' Orc leaned carefully against the bed. 'And smelling like what?'

'That fake seal-skin: you reek of it.' Otter's nose searched, whiskers twitched. 'And salt! Not good, bruv. Otters need to rinse the salt from their fur.'

'Well, I'm not *actually* an otter...'

'Never a truer word spoke!' Otter jumped onto Ranga's bed. 'You dive too deep. If I'd dived deep with that burning brand in my teeth, where'd you humans be now? Sitting round a pile of sticks wishing you weren't so flippin' cold, that's where.'

'Fine,' said Orc. 'I won't dive so deep any time I'm stealing fire from the gods. Can we get on without you pointing out all my faults?'

'Something's made you thin-skinned,' said Otter. 'I won't ask.'

'Thanks. Now—'

'Is it her?'

Orc groaned. 'No. Not in *that* way.'

'It pains me,' said Otter. 'You're a young dog, you got a young dog's needs. To see you all twisted up inside, when all you need is a good—'

'No!' said Orc.

'I'd risk it. Either she's your sister or she's not – that's an even chance.'

'It's *not* an even chance! I don't want to talk about this.' Orc took two deep breaths to calm himself. 'I need to ask you a question.'

'Sheesh,' said Otter. 'Anyone'd think you didn't enjoy my company for its own sake.'

'About the ziggurat today. When I got stuck – what was that?'

'Pfagh!' retched Otter. 'Something rotten: that's all you get down there. The rotten bottom, that's where things fall when they die. Nothing a clean-whiskered animal wants to eat down there – the sunny shallows have fish aplenty. Deep is where the ugly fishes are, the ones shamed of showing their faces. And it's cold!'

'Was that snake-woman thing just my imagination? Can you tell me that much?'

Otter twisted to scratch behind his head. '*Some* might ask that about me.'

Orc didn't rise to that – Geist had warned him not to discuss the soulscape's reality with its denizens. 'Would Eel know?'

'Bruv, what Eel doesn't know isn't worth an idle ponder while you're dumping a spraint. She wriggles and she squiggles into the cracks where the secrets hide, and her children swim from every headwater to bring her the news. She'll know all right – it's you understanding, that's the problem. You want to visit?'

'Yes. I'm ready.'

'Then let's go,' said Otter, and jumped off the bed.

Orc fully closed his eyes, and in his imagination followed Otter to the door, which his mind made ajar. Otter nosed it open and ran to the stairs. Along the landing, Orc focused on asserting the soulscape's primacy, consciously ignoring the bed against which he was physically leaning, and creating in his mind the feel of rugs under his feet.

Otter was clumsy down the stairs, half-falling from one step to the next. He chattered about how much better a mud-slide would have been. They met no one on the descent. The ends of roots appeared through the faded wallpaper; ivy mantled the stair-rail. Down and round they went, until they'd gone several times the height of the hotel, and the walls were damp earth and the steps rough-shaped stone, and water dripped, and the only light came from the landing high above and the Otherworld still far below. As the former weakened, the latter grew brighter, until at last the stairwell ended at a stone arch.

Beyond, thick grass and moss covered the courtyard's paving, and ivy and clematis tangled across the walls. Great tree-branches thrust out, shading the central space. The hotel's hand-pump had been replaced by a well.

Orc's dive-mask lay on the low stone edging. He shucked his clothes and pulled the mask on, drawing on memory to make it as real as possible: the sniff of rubber and old salt, the press of it against his face. He looked into the well. The water was close to the lip, and not far below a dim-lit cave opened out.

Otter jumped onto the lip and peered in. Below the edge of his bone mask, his little pink tongue licked his chops. 'There she is!' he yipped. 'Quick!'

Orc took a deep breath and plunged. Water closed over his head. Below him swam Eel, three feet long and thick as his wrist. A pull of his arms brought him just above her.

He grabbed. Eel thrashed and wriggled, a yard of solid muscle, but

Orc held tight behind her gills and kicked back up to the surface to push the squirming fish onto the lip. Otter sank teeth into her side and gouged out a bite, then Orc let Eel tumble back into the water before hauling himself out.

'Still seems a bit gruesome,' he said, as Otter swallowed his mouthful.

Otter licked the blood from his fangs. '*When* you find a mask for Eel, *then* she'll speak to you straight. Till then, all you've got's my digestion to answer your question.'

Orc focused his thoughts. 'What held me in the ziggurat chamber?'

'Haah.' Otter stood, and swayed from side to side. Orc held his breath again, until the animath gave a soft, fishy burp.

'Ancient terror,' he said. 'Modern error. Future era.' He shook himself.

'That's it?'

'All I got,' said Otter. 'Make sense to you?'

'Not as such. Was it just my imagination? Focus on that.'

'Not an easy question, bruv.'

'But you've just had a mouthful of Eel!'

'And tasty she was. But even guts like mine don't break down bones easy. I'm getting a thought, though: water and earth, and the one not the other.'

'Uh?'

'The bottom of a sea or river.' Otter swayed again, his voice a near-monotone. 'No disturbance for ages, silt settles, the divide is clear. Then something comes along with big fins and starts churning it up. Loads of mud and murk, no knowing where the divide is. Maybe there isn't one any more.'

'But... how does that tell me whether it was my imagination?'

'Who knows?' said Otter, and burped again. 'Maybe that was all just guts-ache.'

3

FACES FROM THE PAST

The light outside the window had faded, along with the quayside noises. Orc lay on his bed, waiting for Cass or Ranga to return.

Otter's non-answer to his question worried him. He couldn't risk entering any more ziggurats without finding out what had happened that afternoon. But if he didn't keep diving, he would never get the large focus-stone, and he knew of nothing else that could strengthen his scaping abilities enough to pierce the wall of shadow that lay across his life two years back. Calling up his earliest memory, he could almost feel the Shroud just beyond it – as though, in that first stirring, he might have reached out with his mind and touched those webs of magic woven by someone still unknown.

That earliest memory was of noise, a series of sharp bangs provoking his awareness. But they hadn't woken him. Something had discouraged him from full consciousness, soothed him, forbidden him. Then silence had returned, a feeling of heaviness, the eternal state re-established after its interruption. Time had passed – he hadn't known how much, unable even to formulate the question – until his blank calm had begun to be intruded upon by worry, a sense that all was not as it should be. He became aware of the possibility that there was a state other than eternal silence and darkness. He became aware of sensation, of a body, of a face, of something on that face, of pressure and heat on that face and it was his *mask* and the *sun*, and something that had been restraining his consciousness released him.

He smelt rubber and opened his eyes. Sunlight through glass blinded him. He groped, pulled off his dive-mask.

What he saw stopped his breath.

A man stood over him, his strong, craggy face weathered and grizzle-bearded and shaded by a wide-brimmed hat, but not so shaded as to hide the whorls of tattoos across it, nor the blue lens over the man's left eye, held in place by a leather patch.

'Easy, there.' Tension in the man's gruff voice. 'I'm a friend.'

Orc, who didn't yet have that name, pushed himself up onto his hip. The man wore a long, thin, light-coloured coat. He carried – Orc almost choked – a gun, a rifle. His boots were covered with sand and dust. A beach of sand and flat rock stretched behind him, a hundred yards to a natural barricade of driftwood, and behind that, trees: skeletal, bare, crumbling, a forest of decay mounting in ridge after ridge to disappear against the vicious sky.

All dead.

He glanced to the left, and jolted: a second man lay there on blood-soaked sand, a gaping redness where half his face should have been. An out-flung hand clutched a revolver.

Dead.

Frantic, he looked the other way and saw *her*, lying there, on her side. He tried to reach her but things on his feet hampered him – *fins* – he scrambled to her on hands and knees. She wore fins too, and a *wetsuit* like his, and a mask, but she lay still, and she couldn't be dead, couldn't be. *Blackout*, the word surfaced from somewhere deep. He tore her mask from her and blew on her familiar face and urged 'Breathe!' over and over but she didn't stir, didn't—

'She is breathing,' said the man. 'I checked.'

And now she did move, as though some hold on her had released.

She pushed herself up on one arm. Her newly opened eyes met his, blue-green, piercing, but there was panic too because she was starting to realise as he was starting to realise, and worried-looking dreamy-looking she reached a hand to touch the hair above his ear, as though it was something she often did, but—

She cried out as she looked past him to the corpse. 'Who—?'

'Doesn't matter,' the man said. 'What matters is that I stopped him killing you.'

The words shocked through Orc. 'What? Why would he?'

'Forget all that.' The man's mouth shifted into what he might have intended as a smile. 'Kurassian, are you?'

The word meant nothing. Same for the girl, her knotted brow told him.

'Well, where are you from, then?'

The panic grew. 'Can't—'

The girl shook her head, scared-looking now. 'No.'

'Can't *remember?*' said the man. 'What, did you both hit your heads or something? Was there a boat accident?'

Accident – his eyes clenched as something roared in his mind, like sea trying to break through a barrier, but the man's gruff voice kept speaking and he couldn't get to the sea because the barrier was being rebuilt, strengthened.

'You have a northern look: your hair, your skin.' The man went on, 'And your gear, those outfits, what is that? Some kind of gum or rubber, like an auto-carriage tyre? I've never felt anything like it.'

Felt. He'd touched one of them.

'Something new by one of those big chemical factories? Come on, this must be bringing up something. Those words on them – *Orca, Picasso* – what are they?'

'I don't *know.*' He clutched his head. 'There's *nothing.*'

'Nothing? But – what about her? Your sister?'

His head jerked round. Realisation and shock knitted his gaze with the girl's. Faintly came the thought, why had the man said that? Why the strained tone?

'I don't think…' The girl's voice resonated somewhere warm behind the barrier, somewhere in that troubled sea that couldn't break through. 'I mean, the way…'

Sister. It hadn't occurred to him. And yet.

He turned to the man. 'Is she?'

'You don't know? I just thought, you look so alike. You could be…'

The man trailed off. Orc looked at the girl, half-shy now. He felt she was about sixteen, seventeen; he should know exactly, but he didn't. It occurred to him that they were about the same age.

'Are they?' The man wasn't addressing them – he seemed to be talking to the sand near his feet. 'Is that what you meant? The gate to power, to reshape the world?'

'Who are you talking to?' asked Orc, nervous of madness.

'Hush,' said the man. 'A bird.' A few seconds later he made a noise of frustration. 'Right,' he said to them. 'You can't remember who you are, let's find out.'

His free hand drew a sheath-knife. The girl yelped. Orc ripped his fins off and scrambled to his feet, fists clenched.

'Easy!' the man said. 'I need some hair from you both, that's all.'

'Hair?' Orc said. 'For what?'

'Divination. Magic. Consulting the invisible archive, if you prefer.'

It felt like a sick joke. But it pulled everything into focus: the strange beach, the corpse, the dead forest, the blankness where his life should have been. That was where he was, with a tattooed man who had a rifle and a knife and a lensed eye-patch and who wanted to do magic. That was what he had to deal with. He couldn't let it overwhelm him.

He told the man he would cut the hair himself. He demanded the knife. The business end of the rifle twitched, but the man breathed down the irritation in his gullied face and handed the blade across. Orc's scalp hurt as he cut, then he moved to the girl. 'You can't believe him?' she whispered, her well-marked brows lowered over worry. Orc could do nothing but shrug. He had to be strong.

The girl's wetsuit, like his, was so close-fitting and pliable that it showed ribs and collarbones, even, faintly, her nipples. Orc didn't want the man to see those. It angered him that the stranger had wanted to cut the girl's hair himself. When he did it, careful as he could, the girl seemed nervous of him touching her. He knew he'd touched her before, perhaps even... no, he couldn't remember in what way, it was in that sea that couldn't break through the barrier, whose noise was fading rather than building. A boat, perhaps; an accident, maybe; and her.

'Hurry.' The tattoos on the man's face seemed fainter. Orc gave him the hair, then the man led them away from the corpse for a few tens of paces, along the edge of the gently lapping sea, and told them to sit and be quiet. He sat stiffly cross-legged a few paces from them, rifle resting across his knees, their locks of hair held in his closed hands.

'Fly, old friend,' he addressed the sand again. 'Fly to the Tree Beyond the World. Find and swallow the ash-key that holds the seed of the knowledge I seek, and return with its secret.'

The girl laid a hand on Orc's leg. He thought of grabbing hold and running. He wondered if they could make it to the dead forest. He tried not to look back at the killed man. He tried not to think about a rifle bullet slamming between his own shoulder blades. But even if they made the trees, where then? There was no way out, so he turned his thoughts inwards. He sought anything that might be a chink through which the sea of his past could pour. But he was nervous of trying to make that chink, nervous even of talking to the girl about it, because something out in that sea was not good.

He tensed as the man spoke. 'They are? Who by?' A pause, then the man huffed out and said, 'By all the gods devised by man, what a pain in the arse.'

'We are what?' asked Orc, leaving aside how the man might have learned anything.

The man pushed himself to his feet. It took effort; he was approaching old age. He was an old man who talked to an imaginary bird, and who had a gun, and who had already killed. Every muscle in Orc's body strained with readiness.

'You said, "They are?" What did you mean? We are *what*?'

The man removed his lens-patch. His tattoos had faded almost to nothing. 'You're dead, if I leave you here – it's four days back to the nearest village. Now let's get moving, before those who sent that gunman send another.'

'Who did send him?' Orc demanded.

'Save your breath for walking,' the man said. 'I've spare boots on my mule in the trees, and clothes. You, girl, you can ride: we'll carry some of the baggage. You any objection to me calling you "Picasso" for now?'

'None,' said the girl.

'What do we call you?' said Orc, who guessed what his own name would be.

'When there's no one to hear, you can call me Geist.' The man tugged his hat-brim lower. 'When there are, you'll call me sir.'

It was dark when Cass came back, wearing her one surviving summer dress. She didn't ask how his scape had gone, only whether there had been any sign of Ranga.

'Think he might be in trouble?' said Orc.

'If he's sold the cup and started drinking the proceeds, he will be,' said Cass. 'Trouble of the painful kind.'

'Cass-tration?'

That got a laugh. 'I'm amazed his bits haven't rotted off anyway,' she said. 'Come on, let's find him.'

Orc would have forgiven Ranga a little embezzlement as long as the cup was gone; just the thought of it disturbed him. Outside the Bull, the night felt strained, airless – as though the darkness upon the world had been caused not by the sun going down, but by a light-swallowing flood rising from the deep chamber of the disturbed ziggurat. He tried to counter that feeling by looking at the few catches still being unloading on the lamp-lit quay. There were a couple of species he couldn't name and wanted to ask about, but the fishermen's glances weren't friendly. Nor were those of the men eating fried baitfish and playing draughts outside the taverns. *Outlanders*. Nowhere else along the coast had it been made so obvious.

It wasn't long before they spotted Ranga, sitting at a corner table in the third tavern eastwards from the Bull, Ospinar's – and he wasn't alone. Opposite him, with his back to the entrance, was a portly, balding man in a cream linen jacket, a satchel and hat resting by his elbow. As Orc and Cass approached through the fug, Ranga looked up. His companion turned, and Orc halted in surprise.

'Mister Gregal!' said Cass.

'Ah!' The man rose, his beaming smile quirking the ends of his waxed moustache. 'The intrepid trio is complete!' He took Cass's hand and pressed it with his lips, much too firmly for Orc's liking, then pumped Orc's hand with both his own. 'Join the party!'

They pulled chairs from a nearby table. Orc glanced at Ranga, who rubbed his fingers together and darted a glance towards Gregal's bulging satchel. *Thank God*, thought Orc. He seated himself as though within striking distance of a live snake.

'We were talking about you only this afternoon,' said Cass. 'What on earth brings you here?'

'The gods of good fortune, it would seem,' said Gregal, and chuckled. Then he called across the serving girl and ordered the best wine. She made to remove Ranga's beer-mug, but Ranga placed a hand on her wrist and smiled.

'Did I say that was empty?'

'It must be,' she said. 'By now.'

'I was savouring it,' said Ranga. 'Every sip was so intense, through the sweetness of the hand that brought it to me.'

'Not the *sweatiness* of the one that raised it to your lips?' She gave him a pointed look. Ranga jerked his hand back, and she swept up the mug with a smirk of triumph. Ranga stared after her.

'I happened to be searching out dig sites just inland from here,' Gregal explained. 'A hazardous enterprise: lawlessness and banditry everywhere.' He poked a finger through a hole in his hat. 'That was too much for my guides, the quitters. So I gave up my plans and came to catch tomorrow's steam-packet for Torrento. Imagine my surprise when I sought ease in this house of refreshment and recognised this handsome fellow.'

Ranga visibly suppressed a wince.

'You found him already in here?' Cass turned to Ranga. 'Before you even sold it?'

'Where else would I meet potential contacts?' Ranga said. 'And if I hadn't been here, who says I would have met him at all? You rather we stayed broke?'

Orc barely held back from snapping at them; he felt tense enough without their bickering. He wished Gregal would put his satchel under the table. Luckily the barmaid forestalled any further argument by arriving with a bottle and glasses. Ranga thanked her as though the order had been his.

'Call me when you need another,' she said. 'If we're still open by then.'

'I'll down it like water, to bring you back more often,' said Ranga.

'You'll get nothing but a sore head,' she said. 'And my father's thanks.'

Her slight emphasis on *father* raised Ranga's eyebrows. He laid his hands folded across his chest. 'A sore head would be less painful than this aching heart.'

She laughed, shaking her hair as she walked off. This time Orc followed Ranga's gaze, watching the sway of the girl's hips. His knee jigged under the table.

'How sweet, Ranga,' said Cass. 'Is she another one who reminds you of your "true love" back in Torrento?'

'Never hurts to be friendly to the locals, Cass.'

'They were "peasants" earlier.'

Ranga scowled, but Gregal had poured out the wine. The four of them knocked their glasses together. Orc was about to empty his down his throat when he noticed Ranga's stare.

'Oh, splendid,' said Ranga. 'Don't turn round.'

They did. Orc groaned as he saw Esteban in the doorway.

'A friend?' said Gregal.

'He hides it well,' said Ranga.

Esteban weaved between the tables so clumsily, Orc thought he must already be drunk. He looked dressed up in a shirt and waistcoat, his hair slicked back.

'The jolly fisherman,' said Ranga, as he reached them. 'If you've come to buy us a drink, you're too late.' He raised his glass.

'You were going about the town earlier.' Esteban's voice was low, but still clear against the suddenly quiet background. 'Trying to sell an old cup.'

Shit, thought Orc. This was it, what he'd feared on the boat. And now Esteban had a whole tavern-full of his fellow fishermen to call on.

'An heirloom.' Ranga attempted a smile that didn't quite come off. 'Been in my family for generations. We were short on funds.'

'Until more could reach us,' said Cass. 'From the museum. Mister Gregal here represents them.'

Gregal half-rose from his seat. Esteban ignored his proffered hand. 'My uncle's catch was poor this evening. The fish shunned his nets, or were scared away.'

'So?' said Ranga.

'We saw plenty being unloaded earlier,' said Orc.

'*My* uncle,' said Esteban. '*My* family. They suffer because we took you where you should not have gone. Because you stole what was not yours. I saw that thing fall on the deck.'

'We explained what that was,' said Cass.

'We believed you,' said Esteban. 'I let myself trust you. But then my uncle's catch…'

Ranga leaned back in his chair and pushed his arms above his head, exposing the knife at his belt. Orc prepared to grab the wine-bottle.

'Bad luck happens, friend,' said Ranga. 'Blaming others without evidence will get you in trouble.'

'If there's trouble,' said Esteban, 'it will hit you worse.'

Gregal coughed. 'I hope that wasn't a threat. There is a constable in this town, I believe.'

Esteban exhaled hard, and turned to Cass. 'I wish to speak with you alone.'

'No chance,' said Orc.

Cass glanced at him critically, but said, 'Right. Say it to all of us.'

Esteban took a breath. 'What is your life?' he asked her. 'Disturbing sacred places, measuring things that should be left alone. To feed people is good work, sacred work, but you waste your gift.'

'Gift?'

'You swim like a dolphin.' Perspiration glazed his forehead. 'You could find the fish and drive them into the nets. Fishermen would honour you, sing songs about the Daughter of the Sea. That would be a good life.'

'I have a good life now,' she said.

'She's not interested,' said Orc. 'You'd better go.'

Esteban turned to him. '*You* will not live a good life. Those who disturb the Sea Mother pay a heavy price.'

He turned and lurched back out, bumping tables. The background chatter grew as most other patrons returned to their food and games, but many eyes remained on their corner.

'Just superstitious crap,' Cass said in Orc's ear.

'Thanks for letting me know.' But he felt slightly sick.

'Not an ounce of civilisation in that one,' said Gregal.

'Might be an idea to head back to the Bull,' said Ranga.

'Yes,' said Orc.

Gregal downed his wine. 'I'll return to my lodgings too. Are you leaving tomorrow?'

'The evening boat,' said Ranga. 'To Carnega.'

'Ah, intrepidly westwards, as ever.' Gregal tucked his satchel under his arm. 'Look me up when you're back east. Good luck.'

There was no sign of Esteban outside, but to Orc the night pressed even harder than before: like a heavy mist coming off the sea, but a mist that was clear. Between glances back over his shoulder, he kept an ear out for trailing footsteps as they walked back towards the hotel, but near at hand he heard only the scraping of boats' fenders against the quay, the slap and bob of dark water in the harbour. The voices from the taverns across the cobbles seemed muted. If he hadn't seen Gregal walk off with the bulging satchel, he might have been convinced Ranga had stolen it back. The cup seemed to weight the darkness.

'What did he pay?' said Cass.

'Two-fifty,' said Ranga. 'Damn good, considering. The other offers were barely scrap value.'

'He had all that on him?' said Cass. 'At Correlon and Arguse, he had to wire Torrento.'

'Wages for the guides who ran off, probably.'

'I suppose,' she said. 'It's just… doesn't it seem strange that we keep running into the same man, the only one who's keen to buy our finds, and always when our money's about to run out?'

'Coincidence happens,' said Ranga. 'The word wouldn't exist otherwise. Anyway, what's strange about a museum man him wanting to buy our finds?'

'Maybe. I guess it's the money that counts.'

'Exactly,' said Ranga. 'It'll get us to Carnega with plenty to spare, and I've a good feeling about that place.'

'So have I,' said Orc. 'Because it isn't here.'

Ranga laughed. 'Quite so. Decent-sized town, locals not inbred fish-worshippers. Four sites near there, too – bet one of them's ours. Remember, the odds get better each time.'

'That's assuming one of the zigs on your map really is the one,' Cass said. 'Don't you ever worry this "source" of yours might be wrong?'

'Nope.'

'But *how*…' began Cass. 'Oh, forget it.'

Orc knew what she'd been going to ask: how could Ranga's mysterious source know there was a large focus-stone and a fortune in gold in one of the sunken ziggurats, but have no idea which? But they'd posed the question many times since first meeting Ranga in Torrento, and he'd always shrugged them off with the excuse that their spit-and-handshake contract didn't oblige him to tell.

'If you'd rather give up and herd fish into Esteban's nets,' Ranga said, 'feel free.'

'No one's giving up,' said Orc, looking again over his shoulder.

He hoped his dread would fade in the more modern surroundings of the hotel. But the dining room was near-empty, and somehow if felt as though the tourists had stayed away not because of the city hotel bombings, but because of the darkness outside, that he had stirred up like silt. Its pressure stifled conversation. After dinner, they went to the lounge for backgammon. But after only a few increasingly fractious games, Ranga suggested retiring early: 'Since we'll be most of tomorrow night on the boat.' The others agreed. The sooner he slept, Orc thought, the sooner daylight would come.

But when he and Ranga were in their garret, Ranga seemed in no hurry to get to bed. 'I'm not that tired after all,' he said, checking the mirror. 'Think I'll pop out for a bit.'

Orc rolled his eyes. It wasn't the first time Ranga had suggested an early night so he could slip away without Cass seeing, and so avoid her barbed comments.

'What, back to that barmaid?' He slid beneath his sheet. 'Yeah, she was keen. Don't make too much noise when you get back – in ten minutes.'

'Don't be so sure,' said Ranga. 'Her eyes and mouth were playing different tunes.'

Orc wanted to scoff, but he suspected Ranga was right. He wished that just once, Ranga would return with a black eye. But no, of course the barmaid would be waiting for him, her ample chest heaving with lust. More sex for Ranga: more fantastic, guilt-free, amazing sex.

'Piss off then. We'll get your body in the morning, if we can find where Esteban's dumped it.'

'Oh, he's no danger.'

'Huh? *You* were the one who said to come back here.'

'To protect *you*. You're the one he's got it in for – Cass being the one he'd like to get it in *to*.'

'Ha so very ha.'

'I reckon he's got a chance,' said Ranga, prinking his hair. 'Did you see her face when he said she'd get songs written about her?'

Orc chilled inside. 'Come off it…'

'Seriously, women like that kind of thing. I've already composed one.' Ranga cleared his throat. *'There was a maid who dived in rubber, her face behind a mask of glass. Her suit worked like a layer of blubber, but didn't hide her shapely –* hey!' he cried, as the pillow hit his head.

'Accident,' said Orc.

Ranga threw it back at him. 'Save it for fighting off the Woman Beneath the Waves when she comes for her cup back.' He chuckled as Orc made a face. 'Have a good night with your goddess. I shall with mine.' He made to shut the lamp off.

'Leave it!' said Orc, too sharply. 'I mean, we're not getting charged extra for paraffin, are we?'

Ranga shrugged.

After he'd gone, Orc dimmed the lamp, but only a little, and lay stiffly in bed. His heart sent tremors through his body. Ranga's parting comments had been a joke fuelled by Esteban's superstition; it didn't mean Ranga had picked up on anything. But as minutes stretched by, his ears became taut with the sense that out in the windless night, the water in the harbour was rising, flowing across the quay to pool around the hotel, slowly climb the walls. At last he dared the window, and found the scene just as before. But back in bed, his fear changed to one of premonition. He tried to assure himself such a flood was impossible: the near-landlocked Shallow Sea had a tidal range of only a few inches. But it must have risen greatly in the distant past, to drown the ziggurats. Might it not do so again, if some long-dormant power were disturbed?

He tried to distract himself thinking about the serving girl at Ospinar's, but couldn't finish. He started to worry about Ranga: he imagined him lying face-down in dark water. Ranga had handled the cup. The water would seek it. And the cup had been in this very room: this was where the tarnish keeping its power at bay had so foolishly been removed...

Ranga wasn't back in ten minutes, nor even the two or three hours that passed before tiredness at last pulled Orc into sleep.

4

NIGHTFIRE

Her bulk blocked the exit passage. Her eyes gleamed through dark water. *Mine.*

Orc's lungs were spent. Terrified, he looked for escape. Up the shaft was a disc of skylight and hope. He kicked his fins into movement.

You are mine. You cannot.

But he was, he was escaping, up towards—

The grille. It formed across the light like a grid of bones, trapping him only feet from the surface. Lungs in agony, he tried to break through the encrusted bars. His hands tore. The water clouded red.

His body overcame him and he inhaled the sea. Pain exploded in his head and he lurched upright, his lungs fighting – and found air.

And air, and more air. He filled the cramped tightness of his chest over and over. His skin was wet from his drowning – or was it night-sweat? Reality flittered away from his attempts to grasp it. He couldn't focus. Something was calling him.

The floorboards felt strange to his feet. Beyond the window, the water had retreated as though it had never risen. Night entombed the world. No lamps lit the quay; only the green beacon glowed at the end of the mole. A sea smooth as black oil stretched out to the horizon, where a small cluster of lights showed.

A ship. *The* ship, he knew – the one that waited to take him.

With that realisation, the shadow-room vanished. He stood at the ship's prow as the vessel raced over miles of dark sea. Three islands approached: near the largest rose the tip of a huge ziggurat. *Her* presence filled the moonlight, the sea, the land. Cold stone chilled his feet. On an altar suddenly before him lay a large flake of blue-tinted crystal, its edge glinting.

The knife of sacrifice.

He would do what had to be done, and complete what he had started.

He reached for the knife, but it receded before him, as though pulled by the drag of an outgoing tide. He leaned his hips against the altar's edge and pushed forwards, his arm stretched—

Something banged behind him. 'Orc?'

He frowned, almost recognising the word. It troubled him to see that the altar now occupied the same space as a window-sill. The false world was intruding, overlapping. He put a knee on the sill and stretched through the open casement. The knife was out there; if he could only—

'Orc!' Fingers dug into his shoulder. He swung round to face a young priestess in a short white robe, her face taut with fear. He blinked. Why was the girl here? What had gone wrong?

She backed off a couple of steps. 'You trying to get yourself *killed*?'

Her voice, he thought he knew it. Her face, from somewhere.

'C—' Yes, it was: 'C-Cass…'

The world refocused: faint lamplight, floorboards, beds – and her horror.

'What the hell were you *doing*?'

'Nothing, just—' What *had* he been doing? 'Wait—' He stepped across to the corner and grabbed his trousers, pulled them on. 'Nothing, honest.'

'Don't talk crap. What's going on?'

'Why does anything have to be "going on"?' Then he saw how scared she looked, the erratic heaving of her shoulders. She wore nothing but her short nightdress, the one she'd bought for the hot nights after they'd sold their first lot of finds to Gregal in Arguse. He'd only ever seen her with a shawl over it.

'What's wrong?' he said, guiltily fighting his attention away from her skin. 'What are you doing here?'

'Checking you're all right.'

'Why wouldn't I be?'

'You were half out the *window*.'

'I was just – I thought – I heard something.'

A sob burst from her. 'You fucking *liar*.'

'Cass, what—' But she'd turned from him, her whole body taut. She gasped in, and her crying came as if she'd held it back for months.

He made the two steps to her, touched her, and she pushed hard into the cage of his arms as though that were the purpose for which they'd been made. He enfolded her, tight; all his soul was in his skin that touched her, in his hands pressed against the heat and pliant firmness of her heaving back. 'Cass, babe,' he murmured into her hair, wondering that he was allowed to do this at last and hating that it had to be because she was in tears. His own tears stung; he wanted to crush whatever had dared upset her. But the memories of strength seemed a lifetime ago, when he'd held her in a high field under the stars and had not been broken.

He waited, patient, absorbing her heat, the movements of her distress. As they ebbed, so did his fear for her, replaced by a longing to hold onto everything he could of this moment that might never come again. He rested his cheek on her head. The urge pulled at him to kiss it, since he didn't dare kiss her wet freckled face, or her ear, or her neck; but he tightened his self-restraints, kept his hands from stroking down her thinly clad back and cupping the rounded muscles at its base.

'Cass,' he murmured, trying to ignore his packing hardness. 'What is it?'

Her grip on him eased a little. 'I thought you were dead.' Her cheek moved against his collarbone.

'What?'

'I watched you drown.' Her voice trembled. 'I had a nightmare. You were under that grille, and I couldn't get to you.'

Orc's breath caught. His own dream…

'Then I woke up, but everything was confused and I thought… I couldn't remember how, but I *knew* you were—'

'I'm not.' He caged her tighter. 'I'm alive.'

She nodded into his neck, uttered a little wet laugh. 'I can feel.'

His erection. But she didn't seem offended. He hoped they could pretend it was just a physical quirk, like a pulled muscle, and he could keep to himself the delicious, infuriating pleasure of having it trapped against her heat.

So slightly, as though an accident, she moved her hips and belly. 'Would it matter?' she whispered.

God, he so wanted – but he made himself break from her, gentle as he could, knowing he should have done it sooner. She held on at first, then removed herself, taking her warmth from him, leaving the wetness of tears cooling on his chest.

Exhausted, he sat down on the end of his bed. Cass took the room's only chair. Her damp face shone with the dim light. She dragged a forearm across her eyes.

'So…' Orc said. 'That was what you were all upset about? A nightmare?'

She exhaled hard. 'And why do you think I *had* it? Don't you remember this afternoon? What nearly happened? If I hadn't been down there already, rather than waiting up top like I was meant to…'

He flinched. 'I know.'

'There wouldn't have been time—'

'I *know*! Don't – talk about it. It's this place, it just… I'll be more careful in future.'

She stared at the floor between her bare feet. 'I'm sick of it, Orc. How do you think it feels, watching you go into those holes, knowing what might happen?'

'You think *I* have a jamboree going in there? If you know another way to find the stone, let's have it.'

She looked hopeless with defeat. Orc ached to hold her again, to cling to her, to let the kiss happen this time. Why couldn't they have found the big focus-stone already? Why couldn't they *know*?

Understanding bolted him. 'God!'

Cass looked up.

'I know where it is.' His mouth felt dry. 'I've *seen* it.'

'The stone? How?'

'You sneaked a look at Ranga's map once, right? You said all the zigs were marked with red crosses?'

'Uh-huh?'

'Were there any out in the sea? Way out from the coast, near an island?'

'No. But what—'

'It's not on there! We've been following him and his bloody map for nothing.'

'For fuck's sake,' said Cass, 'tell me what you're on about.'

'Just now.' Orc drew a deep breath. 'It was some kind of half-awake dream – I went to an island, with a massive ziggurat sticking out of the water. The *stone* was there, a big chunk of blue crystal. I was reaching for it when you came in.'

'*That's* what you were doing?'

'Yes!'

'But, a dream? How can you—'

'It was *more* than a dream! Almost like a scape. There's a connection between this place and that big ziggurat – I felt *her* there as well. The Sea Mother.'

'No!' cried Cass. 'Get that out of your head. Can't you see what you're doing?'

'Trying to get our lives back?'

'Or lose yours.'

'What?'

'You were right, earlier,' she said. 'Getting a fin stuck, that'd be a million to one.'

'So you think there really was—'

'No, there was no Sea Mother. What trapped you there was *you*.'

He almost shied from her gaze, she looked so sick with worry.

'You saw a shadow or something,' she said, 'and because your dark-vision is… I don't know, but it's not properly *real*, is it? So you see things that aren't there; you can turn a shadow into a fisherman's legend you've heard of. You imagine her grabbing you, and you're in that Otherworld state so you *feel* it too – and you're so convinced it's real, so convinced your leg's caught, your muscles lock. You can't escape.'

Her meaning chilled him. 'I did escape.'

'This time. Just. But what if we find this big ziggurat and the same thing happens? You're already convincing yourself she's there too. And what about just now? What if I hadn't come in?' Her voice fractured. 'You didn't even recognise me. You weren't *here*. Did you even know there was a twenty-foot drop?'

'I wouldn't have fallen. Why would my imagination try to kill me?'

Her eyes fixed him. 'I want you to give it up, scaping, all that.'

'You're not serious.'

'At least until you know how to stay in control.'

'I *am* in control. And it's not about control: Geist said—'

'*Geist said*!' Her cry shocked him. 'For fuck's sake, the man *poisoned* you; he made me think you were *dead*, and then he… what he brought back…' She choked off.

'I mended okay.'

She shook her head. 'And it's getting worse. Now it's not just when you scape that you blur what's real and what isn't, it's when you're half-awake too. How long before it's all the time?'

He hugged his chest, tightened his muscles, stared at the floor.

'I want you to stop it,' she said.

He almost hated her for that. 'I can't. It's who I am.'

'It's not who you *were*.'

'So? We change. We grow. And it will take us to the stone. I saw the *stone*, weren't you listening?'

'Yes, I listened.' She got to her feet. 'And when they find you spread over the quayside in the morning, I'll know you died true to who you are. I'll try to be happy for you.'

She banged the door open and crashed it even harder behind her. Five seconds later came the sound of her own door closing.

Orc let out a hard breath. 'Bloody hell, Cass, can't you ever leave quietly?'

Shaken, he went to the window. The curtain was open – he must have done that himself, though he couldn't remember. He leaned on the sill and took a few breaths, but the night air was barely cooler than the room.

Then he ducked. The quay was no longer empty: a man stood staring up at the hotel, one with Esteban's build, though it was too dark to make out a face. Orc wondered if he was contemplating breaking in. But after a couple of minutes, the figure turned and walked slowly off, and soon after, Orc slid into bed, his thoughts on the girl who lay on the other side of his bedroom wall, doubtless as far from sleep as himself.

Such a mess. He understood why Cass had been frightened for him. But now he understood the danger, he could be more careful – he should have told her that. And the stone was worth the risk. It was worth any risk if it could help him find out what he and Cass were to each other. Parents, home, even his real name: these were things he'd become used to living without. But he could never get used to not knowing who she was, the girl whose mystery haunted him every day because she was there, every day.

And now the touch of her hot skin, the smell of her hair…

'Would it matter?' He must not, he told himself, dwell on how she'd moved against him. He must reject even fantasy, in case it seduced him into asking himself the same question – because it *would* matter, if he and Cass ever went too far and then discovered they'd done so in error. The warning felt deeper than his own thoughts, as though it had been sealed within the core of him by a god. Such a mistake would destroy them.

Something would destroy them.

***

A whooshing hiss of blown-off steam made him scramble out of bed and wrench back the curtain, his bleary mind convinced it was the packet-boat and he'd slept all day. There was indeed a smoke-fuming ship lying alongside the crowded jetty beyond the mole – but not a mail steamer, not with those guns. Apart from its slender length, that was all Orc took in before familiar voices caught him through the quayside noise from below. He looked down. The morning sun brightened Gregal's straw hat and linen jacket, and gleamed in Cass's hair.

Not putting it past the archaeologist to invite Cass off somewhere for breakfast, Orc threw on his clothes and ran downstairs. The hallway was busy, all the maids polishing wood and brass under Mrs Bull's supervision. 'Took her child as his own,' Mrs Bull was telling them as he squeezed past. 'One of the newssheets said she was a princess.' Orc rushed outside, fumbling to button his shirt.

'Mind if I join you?'

'Not at all!' said Gregal. 'I was just urging the young lady here to take care. Some unsavoury types about, trying to take what's not theirs.'

'Yes,' said Orc. 'There are.'

'Well, ah…' Gregal seemed to Orc as though he might try to kiss Cass's hand again, but he touched his hat-brim instead. 'You'll excuse me. Matters to be attended to, and all that.'

As he walked off, Cass turned. Her eyes were bruised with tiredness. Orc wondered if she'd slept.

'He was burgled earlier.'

'The cup?' said Orc, jolted by the unwelcome reminder.

'Nothing taken, he said. But someone went through his room. That's what he was warning me about, with all that money he gave us.'

'Gave Ranga. Let's hope he's still got it. He's still not back.'

Cass glanced along towards Ospinar's, but only briefly. 'I was going to have a look at that ship. Mrs Bull reckons the captain's a hero – rescued his wife from a burning palace, or something.'

Orc frowned. 'You think it's safe?'

'Oh, you care about safety now.'

'I meant, if it's come from Torrento.'

'I knew what you meant,' said Cass. 'And the Kaybees can't have a spy on every ship. Even Geist didn't think there were that many.'

'Okay, let's go,' said Orc – there would be time afterwards to scape and ask Otter about his half-dream. 'But try not to draw attention.'

They walked to the landward end of the mole, and from there along its paved, inner edge, past abandoned fishing rods and half-mended nets and squabbling gulls, while the smell of coal-smoke strengthened. Despite the bright sunshine, Orc felt the previous night hanging over him, and not just the residue of his half-dream. Now he'd once again experienced holding Cass against him, the urge to repeat it felt an intrinsic part of his limbs, the overriding impulse of his muscles. His long-practised repression stoked old, sad fires of anger and frustration, which he could only try to grind out with his will.

Across the harbour from Ospinar's, a gap in the heaped boulders of the mole allowed the walkway through to the seaward side, and the jetty. The warship's arrival seemed to have provoked an impromptu holiday. People thronged the planking; an accordion-player busked next to a coffee cart; a photographer took people's pictures with the ship in the background. 'Mind whose portrait you're wrecking!' he called as Orc and Cass walked behind his subjects.

The extent of the townspeople's excitement surprised Orc. The ship looked slim and fast, but less than half the length of the Empyreal dreadnought he'd seen from the steamer out of Torrento, and a fraction of the bulk. Though the jetty was only three feet above the water, his eyes weren't far below the bridge's side windows. A man held up a small boy to look in – 'Can you see him, son? Is he there?' – though the boy seemed more interested in the platform that roofed the bridge. Two guns were mounted there, barrels ten feet long. It was the closest Orc had stood to artillery, and he puzzled over what he could see of the mechanism until Cass pulled him away.

Forty yards on from the ship's bridge, past the four smoke-stacks and a third gun, a gangway had been lowered to the jetty. A sailor stood there talking to two men, one of whom Orc recognised as Mr Bull, perspiring in a tight-buttoned suit. As they neared, the sailor crushed out his cigarette and boarded. Mr Bull's companion, grey-bearded and wearing a cap bearing the name *Saguna Steam Packet Company*, turned to face them.

'Ah!' His gaunt face brightened. 'Know what this is, young fellow?'

'A ship?' said Orc.

'*Nightfire*, that's the point,' the packet clerk said. 'A heap faster than anything you lot have.'

'Us lot?'

Doubt pursed his face. 'You're not Kurassian?'

'I said I wasn't certain,' said Mr Bull.

'We just look a bit like it,' said Cass. 'Apparently.'

'Shame.' The packet clerk scratched the back of his neck. 'The only chance I get to rub their noses in it, there's none around.'

'Rub their noses in what?' said Orc.

'Last summer's fleet review, of course,' said Mr Bull.

Orc let his blank expression speak for itself.

'You never heard?' said the clerk. 'When the High Prelate came down from Bismark with that younger one, what's his name…'

'Siegfried Astrasis,' said Mr Bull.

'That's him, the odious bugger. Well, this lady was still being fitted out – no guns, hardly any bridge. She shouldn't even have taken part, but Captain Seriuz – you've heard of *him*, I assume? – he steamed her right through the Empyreal squadrons just as they were doing some fancy manoeuvre. Made them look like lumbering turtles. Ten knots faster than their best cruisers!'

Orc whistled, impressed.

'Top speed of thirty-six, by every god going!' said the clerk. 'And the best thing is, that wretched treaty that gives them our best harbour and hobbles our shipbuilding says nothing about giving them our inventions. They never thought we'd come up with anything they'd want – and then we did, and they can't have it.'

'Their spies'll get it sooner or later, though,' said Mr Bull.

'Maybe so,' said the clerk. 'But that won't change the fact that we've finally taken our place in the modern world. Ah! The man himself.'

An officer had appeared at the top of the gangway: a tall man with a lean face and deeply tanned skin. Scattered applause came from the crowd, and quickly gathered strength as he walked down to the jetty, followed by a fresh-faced lieutenant. Despite the captain's weathering, his greying temples and the scar-tissue in the hollow of his left cheek, Orc guessed he wasn't much older than Ranga, maybe not even thirty. The shape of his eyes seemed suited to melancholy, but Orc felt something assertive, almost hunting, in the way they looked over the gathering – though his gaze seemed to pass straight over him and Cass.

When both officers were off the gangway, the accordion struck up the jauntier section of the national anthem. At its close, Mr Bull saluted.

'Captain Seriuz, sir!'

'Easy, my friend,' said the captain. 'Saluting isn't required of civilians.'

'Of course, forgive me.' Flustered, Mr Bull lowered his hand and thrust it forwards. 'Frederic Maratt, at your service. On behalf of our little town, I'd be honoured to extend to you and your officers all the hospitality of the Royal Bull Hotel.'

'Most generous.' Seriuz accepted the handshake. 'Appreciated.'

'And of course, we'd all be thrilled to hear a first-hand account of your seamanship last year.'

'Yes, indeed!' said the packet clerk. 'Bravo for wiping the smiles off those arrogant Empyreal faces!'

The captain's eyes now looked both tired and amused. 'I'm sure Mister Juneau here would love to recount the tale. Regrettably, I have to go and relate another, and to a less appreciative audience. My "seamanship" might soon be wiping smiles off faces at the Admiralty.'

'Not your fault, sir,' said Juneau.

'As far as our masters are concerned, it will be,' said Seriuz. 'We anchored overnight in the bay,' he explained to those gathered, 'but this morning the anchor snagged and we had to slip the chain. Now I must visit your post office and telegraph for advice.'

'I'll give you advice.'

Orc turned with the others at the gruff voice.

'Leave these waters as soon as you can,' said the bearded, thick-set man at the front of the crowd. 'The sea is angered.'

'Nonsense,' said Juneau. 'It's like a mill-pond.'

'Not the surface,' the man said. 'Beneath.' Something in his face reminded Orc of Yorge, despite the difference in build. 'Did any here sleep easy last night?' the man asked, casting his dark gaze around the crowd. 'If the sea felt no anger, what troubled our dreams?'

A chill flashed down Orc's back. The packet clerk and Mr Bull scoffed loudly, but uneasy murmurs came from others nearby. Orc felt Cass touch his elbow but didn't turn to her; the man's eyes pierced him from beneath heavy brows.

'She disturbed our dreams because of *him*. She cries out for what was taken from her.'

Seriuz turned to Orc. 'What's this about?'

Orc swallowed. 'We were surveying ruins, underwater. But nothing else.'

'Nothing else?' said the man. 'My father and my sister's son took them to the Dwelling. These two stole a cup, then foxed my nephew with their lies. But after the dreams, my nephew knew they'd lied about the theft, and this morning he told me what they'd done. Then I knew it was no bad luck that my evening's catch was so poor, just as it was no bad luck you lost your anchor, Captain. It was the Sea Mother's anger made it snag.'

'Rot!' said the clerk. 'Your honour, pay no attention. It would be generous to call some of these people backward-thinking.'

'And what do you incomers know?' growled the man. 'The Sea Mother cares nothing for packet-ships and telegraphs. Only those with roots here know the truth of the waters that nourish them.'

'Captain, your anchor,' said Cass. 'How deep is it? Maybe we can help.'

Orc had started to feel sick, and this sudden swerve in conversation didn't help.

'I can't see how,' said Seriuz. 'It's in twelve fathoms.'

'We can get down there,' said Cass. 'Even if we can't free it, we can see what the problem is.'

'*You* two are the problem,' said the bearded man. 'Go beneath the waves again, and you might not rise back up. And then, perhaps, the trouble will cease.'

A hard exhalation came from Seriuz. His jaw visibly tightened. 'If you again express yourself desirous of the death of a young lady,' he said, '*I* shall be your problem, and your trouble will not cease until you are greatly contrite, understand?'

The bearded man scowled, and walked off. A thinner, lank-haired man followed.

'Well said, sir,' muttered the clerk. 'That Pettor Jarano might have stepped from a thousand years ago. You should hear the things he says when he's drunk.'

But others in the crowd seemed of a different opinion, and broke off to talk in low voices. Their glances discomfited Orc. He wondered if they'd all had dreams, and of what nature.

'If you can make good on your offer,' Seriuz was saying to Cass, 'I'll be in your debt, Miss…?'

'Strandborn. Cass.'

'Captain Martin Seriuz, at your service.' He lifted Cass's hand, not quite touching her knuckles with his lips. The precise grace of this courtesy made Gregal's equivalent seem like fumbling lechery, but if anything, Orc disliked it even more.

'And your companion?'

'Orc,' said Cass. 'Also Strandborn.'

'Your brother?'

'Cousin,' said Cass quickly. 'We'll just fetch our gear.'

Orc walked beside her along the jetty, glad to get away. When they'd gone far enough not to be overheard, he slowed. 'Why did you say we'd do that?'

'A good turn is its own reward,' said Cass, a hint of mischief in her voice. Orc thought of the captain's kiss.

'I don't trust that Seriuz. There's something wolfish about him.'

'Wolfish?'

'You know, like some hunting dog thing.'

'Orc, he commands a fast gunship: he's not going to have something of the baa-lamb about him.'

'Did you see how he pretended not to notice us?'

'Pretended? Why *should* he notice us?'

'Because we stand out here like sheep in a field of cattle!'

'Oh, come on,' said Cass. 'He's from Torrento. There are loads of Kurassians there.'

'Exactly! He comes from Torrento, and he's going back there, and even if he's not a Kaybees spy himself, he'll report that two Kurassian-looking divers in strange black gear rescued his anchor. Who's going to see that report? Who's going to come after us and finish off what that guy on the beach tried?'

Cass frowned. 'No, I don't think he'd tell. He's too embarrassed about losing his anchor.'

Something itched at the back of Orc's mind. *'We anchored overnight in the bay...'*

He shook it off. 'When we find the big stone, we'll know who wanted us dead, along with everything else. Till then we keep away from the authorities, like Geist said. I'm going back to the hotel, to try to figure out what that half-dream was trying to tell me.'

'Right,' said Cass. 'So you want to know where that ziggurat with the stone is, but when I come up with an easy way of finding out, you're not interested?'

He'd half-expected her to start up about his blurred reality again. 'Easy what?'

'I don't trust your half-dream thing, but I can see it's worth checking out. You said that big zig was still partly above water? Near an island?'

'Uh-huh.'

'Then it would be on charts, yes?'

'Oh...'

'Like the charts you'd get on, I don't know, a navy ship? A ship whose captain might soon owe us a big favour?'

Orc had to laugh; he forgave her smug look. 'Yeah, I'll give you that.' Then he remembered. 'The lights!'

'Lights?'

'It was *that* ship! Last night, I saw its lights out on the sea. And in my half-dream, it took me to the island.'

Cass's brow tightened. 'You think he might even give us a ride there?'

'Even if he doesn't, don't you see? It was a *sign*. The ship's vital to us getting there – and that *proves* the half-dream was telling me something real.'

Her eyes widened. 'Then—'

'We're really going to find the stone,' he said, and the sudden certainty made him breathless: it expanded to fill the whole harbour town, to light its painted boats more brightly, to tune the gulls' cries with a joyful excitement. He grabbed Cass and squeezed her. 'We're going to find *us*.'

5

WANTED

Not a white-painted barrel this time, but a bright orange sphere, the buoy sat on a sea even calmer than the day before. Or maybe that was because he was seeing it from higher up, Orc thought, leaning against the gun-platform railing. 'This is how to do it,' he said. 'We should hire one of these to take us out to every dive.'

'Sure,' said Cass. 'If you prefer the smell of smoke to fish.'

He laughed. 'And you don't?'

'Yeah, okay,' she said. 'And it is faster, of course. But is it really *that* fast? From what that clerk was saying…'

It was fast enough to stir her hair, Orc noticed. 'Only the first two stacks are smoking, look. He's just too stingy to take her up to full speed.'

When Seriuz called up that they might like to get changed in his cabin, they climbed down to the small bridge, which felt crowded even with only a handful of officers and men in it, and followed the captain along the ship to a hatchway behind the rear gun. The cramped corridor below hummed with engine noise, and was lit by the first electric bulbs Orc had seen since Torrento. Aft of the ladder was a door marked *Wardroom*, while forward were two cabin doors each side.

Seriuz opened the second on the left.

'Ah, one moment,' he said, and slipped round the door, shutting it behind him. Orc barely had time to exchange a questioning look with Cass before the captain came back out.

'Sorry about that: I'm afraid there are things on a warship not meant for civilian eyes. Miss Strandborn?' He stood aside to let her enter, then squeezed past Orc. 'I'll be on deck.'

Orc leaned against the painted cork wall of the corridor while Cass changed. He tried not to think of her behind that cabin door, shedding her clothes and pulling her tight-fitting suit over her body, transforming herself for the private world they shared – but he didn't try very hard. He wondered how it might feel for that world to be truly private, for them to be able to dive just for the joy of it, with no Ranga or sailors or fishermen around. When Cass emerged, the sight of her sent a hot ache through him.

'Wait for me here, yes?' he said, watching her walk to the ladder. 'We'll go up together.'

She turned. 'I suppose you want me to wear my blouse over the top too?'

'No, just wait.'

She rolled her eyes. 'Quick, then.'

As soon as Orc shut himself into the cabin, he felt a strange, prickling sensation that somehow reminded him of the stifling darkness along the quayside the evening before. An antique cabinet in one corner seemed out of place amongst the grey functionality, and needled his attention as he undressed. Suited up at last, he looked at it more closely. Its doors were mounted with oil-painted boards, dulled and cracked with old varnish, featuring a tall woman in white with one breast bared. Her left hand rested on the head of a black bull, whose hoof pinned a defeated lion. The bull's tail became a snake that twined about the woman's leg and disappeared head-first up her dress. In the background, the horns of a crescent moon enclosed a dull red sun.

Unsettling as the imagery was, Orc sensed it was more the cabinet itself that was tugging on his instincts – the instincts Geist had said to always be alert for. And now he remembered what Seriuz had said about keeping things from civilian eyes.

Things like naval charts?

The doors were stuck. Locked, he realised, spotting the keyhole. Then he noticed a corner of yellow cloth protruding from beneath the doors, similar to the polishing rag in which Ranga had wrapped the cup. He made to touch it – but suddenly his mind plunged back into the darkness and terror of the ziggurat, and his hand jerked back.

Get a grip, he told himself. It couldn't be Ranga's – Gregal still had the cup. He wasn't sure why he'd tried to touch the cloth anyway.

He left the cabin, and swore under his breath as he found the corridor empty. Reaching the top of the ladder, he saw Cass showing Seriuz her mask, watched by several of the crew.

'I see it uses the same principle as a copper dive-helmet,' Seriuz was saying as Orc joined them. 'The air-space limits the refractive effect of the water, so your eyes can focus, and because it also covers the nose, you can equalise pressure with the breath. Ingenious, and remarkably compact. I'm not familiar with this type of rubber – is it new?'

Orc jumped in: 'We just use them.' He noticed Cass's weary look. 'Shall we get on with it?'

'By all means,' said Seriuz. 'Everything's ready.'

After a short briefing, which told Orc nothing he couldn't have guessed, he and Cass were lowered in the ship's gig, along with a couple of oarsmen, and rowed to the orange buoy that marked the captain's best guess as to the anchor's location. Orc tried not to let his nerves be affected by his previous day's experience, but after forcing himself to plunge in, he righted himself as fast as possible to make sure nothing was reaching up for him.

Nothing was that he could see, but the water was slightly deeper than at the ziggurat, and the sea floor too indistinct to spot any features from the surface. He and Cass took turns finning halfway down the weighted line that descended from the buoy, then striking off in different directions to quarter the area as efficiently as possible. On his third dive, Orc found the heap of chain thirty yards to the east. Cass then followed it to the anchor, and returned to report that one of its drags had become jammed in the remains of an old wall. Diving on it from directly above, Orc saw it had been pulled a long way before getting stuck: the furrow ran across the seabed silt, out of sight. Deep enough for his weight-belt to sink him, he knelt beside the wall and wriggled the drag from its trap, freeing it just as his lungs began to hurt. That left Cass to take down a line and tie it on.

When the ship's capstan pulled the anchor clear of the sea, a cheer erupted from the crew. Clambering dripping back onto the deck, Orc and Cass were surrounded, their hands shaken, shoulders patted and backs slapped as though they'd saved the ship from sinking rather than mere embarrassment. At last, Seriuz called for his men to disperse.

'You've made quite an impression,' he said.

'Glad to have helped,' said Cass.

'It wasn't that tightly stuck, though,' said Orc. 'If you'd tried pulling from different sides, it probably would've come by itself.'

Seriuz's smile tightened. 'Remiss of me not to think of that. But one's vision is always clearer looking back, no?'

'He didn't mean it like that.' Cass gave Orc a frown.

'There are clean towels in my cabin,' said Seriuz. 'When you've put your wet things on deck, I'd like you to join me in the wardroom. I think our talk will be to your advantage.'

Orc nudged Cass as they went to the hatch. '*Re*-ward-room,' he whispered. 'Island coordinates coming up.'

The space they entered ten minutes later stretched the twenty-foot width of the ship, but was narrow front-to-back. Seriuz had already poured three drinks from a crystal decanter, and now invited them to join him at the long table.

'Before we toast your skill,' he said, 'I'd like to make you an offer, and I hope we'll also be able to drink to your acceptance.'

'If it's a reward,' said Orc, 'we'll be happy with a look at your charts.'

Seriuz paused, about to hand them their glasses. 'Charts?'

'We're interested in maps,' said Cass. 'Sort of a hobby.'

'Ah,' said Seriuz. 'Impossible, I'm afraid. Admiralty charts are restricted to naval personnel.'

Orc hadn't expected that. 'We won't tell. We'll sign something if you want. Won't we?' he said to Cass, who nodded.

'I didn't use the word *impossible* lightly,' said Seriuz. 'I'd bend the rules if I could, after what you've done, but there are data on those charts that might be valuable to a foreign power. I'm sorry, it's out of the question.'

Orc bit down a protest, and tried to think of an argument round this obstruction.

'I meant what I said, however, about this talk being to your advantage.' Seriuz pushed the glasses across to them. 'I believe I can gain you greater benefit from your diving than you currently enjoy. Am I correct in thinking your equipment unique?'

'As far as we know,' said Cass. 'Why?'

'When you showed me your mask earlier, I didn't get the chance to ask how you came by it.'

'A curio shop,' said Cass. 'The seller didn't know where all the stuff was from originally.'

'Your outfits too? They have your names on, don't they?'

Orc bit his lip.

'We had them put on,' said Cass. 'To mark them as ours.'

'And now you use your abilities to survey sunken ruins. Does it pay well?'

'We get by,' said Orc.

Something of the hunting wolf had returned behind Seriuz's gaze. 'Maratt told me you'd taken his cheapest rooms, and only then because he'd offered reduced rates. Did you never consider applying to the navy? Our current divers wear helmets and canvas suits so cumbersome, swimming is impossible. Even the simplest task needs an air-line and compressor setting up – checking a fouled screw takes hours. With your equipment, it could take minutes.'

'You want us to join the navy in case your propellers get tangled?'

'I'm sure we could find many uses for your skills,' said Seriuz.

'And, Miss Strandborn, don't assume your sex would place you at a disadvantage. We might lie under the shadow of our Empyreal allies, but we're not bound by their rules. I shall propose to the Naval Board that you both be made sub-lieutenant, with commensurate pay and quarters.' He lifted his glass. 'Shall we?'

'No thanks,' said Orc. 'We like things as they are.'

'I need hardly point out that joining up would allow you access to the charts.'

That was a cheap bribe, thought Orc. Or blackmail. And they might well learn the island's location, but they'd have no say in the ship going there. 'No.'

'Miss Strandborn?'

'It's a flattering offer,' she said. 'But Orc's right.'

'Perhaps if I detailed the pay…?'

'That doesn't matter,' Orc said, annoyed now. 'We need to be free to go where we want.'

'A shame.' Seriuz set his glass back down. 'I'd prefer you accept a commission, but a moment's thought should tell you it's your equipment I really want. I'm sure there are some in my crew it would fit.'

The air left Orc's chest. 'It's not for sale.'

'Mister Strandborn, this isn't a trade between private individuals. I am a captain in the Republican Navy, and I may commandeer whatever I need for the effective running of my ship.'

'Don't you dare!' cried Cass.

'Miss—'

'Don't "Miss" me!' She was on her feet. 'Bloody hell, we came out here to *help* you, and we didn't even ask for a reward except a look at your stupid maps, and now you want to steal our living! What a dirty trick. People in town think you're some kind of hero – I thought you were a gentleman at least, but you're nothing but a thief!'

Seriuz looked taken aback. 'You don't—'

'I understand perfectly well! You've got a ship full of men and we're a mile out at sea and you think you can do whatever you like. Well get on with it then, steal our equipment, or "commandeer" it if you think using a posh word makes it less immoral. Follow your pirate navy rules. At least I'll have the satisfaction of being proved right.'

She stood leaning on the table, face sharp with anger. Orc tightened with readiness in case Seriuz reacted badly. But the man's face betrayed nothing.

'Quite correct,' he said. 'Please, forgive me. I assure you my threat was merely a crass attempt to give my recruitment proposal greater leverage – though its emptiness makes it no less reprehensible.' He looked annoyed. 'Let me at least toast the help you have, as you rightly pointed out, so freely given.'

'And then you'll take us back?' said Cass, resuming her seat.

'You have my word.'

They drank. The brandy burned Orc's throat. He couldn't wait to get to shore.

'Stay here if you like.' Seriuz stood. 'I'll get things under way.'

When he'd gone, Orc laughed shakily. 'Cass, you were fantastic.'

'Look at me.' She held out a trembling hand. 'He could've done it, too. What if he'd just taken off with us on board? How could we have stopped him?'

'Let's check he's not doing just that,' said Orc. 'And I want to make sure our gear's where we left it.'

Their wetsuits were still drying on the torpedo tubes. Having turned them over, he and Cass leaned against the deck rail and watched the coastline. The engines had started again.

'So what about the charts?' said Cass, as the ship swung about. 'Where else could we get them?'

'A city, I guess,' said Orc. 'Carnega might be big enough. But the answer should be *here*, on this ship: that's what the half-dream was telling me.'

'It might have been wrong about that.'

'I don't think so. I had a feeling in Seriuz's cabin that there was some connection with this whole thing. Even if he won't show us his charts, I bet he knows where that island is.'

'You think we should just ask him?'

'But carefully. Casual. We don't want him thinking there's anything valuable there, not if the navy has divers too.'

'It's worth a go,' said Cass, 'if we can find an excuse to chat to him. Shame we can't come clean with Ranga. I'd love to tell him his source was rubbish.'

'Actually, his source wasn't. There *is* a ziggurat with a big focus-stone inside. What's rubbish is his map.'

'I don't think I'll let the distinction bother me.' Cass leaned over the rail, staring down into the water. 'You know, this is beginning to seem real. I'm not keen on how you found out, but I've got a kind of tingling about it. It's like I can almost smell the old world, the normal world, somewhere over the horizon. Oh, please, let it be there.'

Orc risked a hand on her neck, where it curved into her shoulder, its warmth. 'It will be,' he said, finding it hard to speak.

She placed her hand over his. 'It'll be weird getting used to your real name.'

Orc glanced at their drying wetsuits. 'Wouldn't it be strange if they *were* our names? If what you told Seriuz was what we really did?'

Cass laughed. 'Actually, I've always thought that if we heard our real names, the recognition would break through, Shroud or no. Don't you agree, David?'

'Ha. I don't know, Justine.'

'*Justine*—?'

'Why not?'

'There's no *way* I'm a Justine.'

'No, you're right,' he had to agree. She was a Cass, for sure.

Ten minutes later, when the ship moored alongside the crowded jetty, they still hadn't made up their minds how best to get Seriuz into conversation. Then he walked up with his two lieutenants and answered the question himself.

'We've decided to avail ourselves of Mr Maratt's hospitality. I'd very much like you both to join us for a late breakfast, as a token of my gratitude, and by way of apology.'

'We most humbly accept,' said Cass. Orc grinned at her as he shouldered the gear-bag.

Seriuz was mobbed the moment he stepped off the gangway, but answered the crowd only by saying the anchor had been recovered without any show of divine wrath. That brief statement didn't satisfy many, and a group accompanied them all along the mole, shouting questions or asking Seriuz to intercede in disputes or help with personal tragedies. Uncomfortable with some of the looks he was getting, Orc made sure he and Cass stayed near the officers.

The mob swelled as they reached the quayside – Orc thought he saw both Esteban and Pettor's lank-haired friend, but lost sight of them quickly. Several people tried to come after them into the hotel, causing the burly porter to stand blocking the doors. Mr Bull professed himself delighted that Seriuz had accepted his invitation – as he ushered them into the dining room, Orc heard him whisper to a maid to run for the photographer – though the hotel owner's smile tightened at the news that Orc and Cass were to be counted among the officers, and began to look rather forced when Seriuz told him to open two bottles of Caustillard.

A round table was quickly laid. Orc dumped the gear-bag in a corner, before Seriuz directed him to sit between him and Tomas Juneau, the fresh-faced gunnery officer. Cass was given the captain's other side, with moustached First Officer Karsten Lyle on her right. After the waitress left with their orders, Mr Bull and his wife stood awkwardly by and asked Seriuz polite questions about Torrento politics, as though he had a high seat in government.

While Orc was waiting for a chance to redirect the talk, Juneau leaned towards him. 'So, Mister Strandborn, what do you think of my three sisters?'

'Uh... sorry?'

'You must have noticed them: Yanika to starboard, Purtha to port, Agatha to the rear?'

'The guns?'

'Spot on,' said Juneau. 'Twelve-pound charge, seven-mile range, fifteen rounds a minute with the right crew. The captain named them from an old epic poem. Unceasing, Grudging, and Avenging: the Furies. Quite why – well, that'd be better coming from him.'

'He seems to have a thing for legendary women.'

'Ha!' laughed Juneau, then frowned. 'Uhm, what do you mean exactly?'

'His cabinet, with the painting?'

'Oh. Yes, full of symbolism, that. But he'd be the best person to explain it.'

'Explain what?' said Seriuz, breaking off his talk.

'The Saucy Serpent, sir.'

Seriuz's face became stern. 'I doubt that's a fitting subject for the breakfast table, Mister Juneau.'

'Do you like old stuff, then?' asked Orc.

The captain's face seemed to freeze for a moment, his brows halfway to a frown, then he coughed. 'Antiquities, you mean? Anyone with a stake in his country's future should take an interest in its past, wouldn't you say?'

Orc saw a chance. 'Then you know about the—'

'And such interest is not hard to cultivate, when one belongs to a nation that was once the most civilised in the world.'

'Kymera was?' Mr Bull looked dubious.

'Indeed,' said Seriuz. 'Our humble land once possessed a culture more advanced in some respects than any other of the time. More even, some might say, than our current example.'

'With respect, can that be true?' said Mr Bull. 'The Book tells us that after the Fall, Elok and his wives turned the world into a terrible place. Human sacrifice and all sorts.'

'The truth is being revealed by the science of archaeology,' said Seriuz.

'Ah,' Orc tried to break in, 'we know a—'

'It remains to be seen how its findings accord with the Book,' Seriuz went on. 'But evidence shows the ancient culture of Kymera to be one in which war had been extinguished, the excess energies of men being turned to art and sport.' He sipped his fizz. 'One might hope for such a moral civilisation to come again.'

Mr Bull looked unconvinced. 'Then you'd be out of a job, Captain.'

'Shouldn't any warrior desire his role unnecessary? But a navy would always be needed, if only to police the sea. What I wish brought to an end is the practice of one state interfering in another. An impractical dream, perhaps. But imagine it: an empire of peace, in which all peoples could decide how they wished to be ruled. Ancient Kymera was one such, I believe. The proto-type.'

'They built the ziggurats?' said Cass, slipping in before Orc had even spotted the opening.

'Buildings are only the most visible aspect of a culture,' said Seriuz. 'What matter more are its intangible structures: its ethics, its moral purpose. This was a civilisation, for instance, in which men and women were held equal.'

'Then we need look no further as to why it became extinct,' said Mr Bull.

Lyle scoffed a laugh. Cass audibly exhaled.

'Not quite extinct,' said Seriuz. 'The Kingly Bull, after which your establishment is named, is an emblem of that culture.'

'I meant no offence, sir. But Golgomera is ruled by women, and you'd hardly call that a civilisation.'

'Perhaps your wife has an opinion?' said Seriuz.

'The Holy Mother is my example,' said Mrs Bull. 'Whether she is equal to a man, I shouldn't presume to say.'

'But she is part of the Empyrean faith,' said Seriuz, 'a Kurassian introduction. Some would say a modification of an older idea.'

Her face hardened. 'The Lord Empyreus is not an "introduction", sir. Unless you mean an introduction to the world by God, His father.'

Seriuz looked uncomfortable. 'I intended no offence. I merely...'

She turned. 'I'm needed in the kitchen.'

'Isabel!' called Mr Bull, but the kitchen door shut behind her.

'My apologies,' said Seriuz. 'I seem to be offering them a lot this morning.'

'She's a conscientious churchgoer, sir,' said Mr Bull. 'Unlike most in this town. It hasn't been easy this year. With no tourists, the church has been largely empty.'

An awkward silence fell. Orc decided to break it.

'These ziggurats, we wondered if there were any that weren't—'

He cut off as commotion erupted in the hallway. 'Yes, I know who they're with!' came Ranga's voice, followed by something muffled but insistent from the porter. 'I'm a guest here too. This is important.'

The door burst open. Orc drew a sharp breath: Ranga's expression verged on panic; the ripped knees of his trousers were dark with blood.

'This is a private function,' said Mr Bull. 'Breakfast for other guests has ended.'

'We need to talk.' Ranga looked from Orc to Cass. 'Now.'

Mr Bull stepped between Ranga and the table. 'I believe I just said—'

'And I just said I *need* to talk to them,' said Ranga. '*Both* of you, come on.'

Orc pushed back his chair, Cass the same. 'If you'll excuse us?' she said to the frowning Seriuz. 'We'll be back as soon as we can.'

Ranga fetched the gear-bag from the corner. 'Might as well take this upstairs. We'll talk there.'

The porter gave Ranga a dirty look as they left the dining room. Ranga led Orc and Cass along the corridor to the back stairs, then straight past and out to the empty courtyard.

'Where the hell are we going?' said Orc.

'Out of here.'

'What? Get lost!'

'Shut up and listen,' said Ranga. 'Ospinar, that barmaid's father—'

'Fuck off!' cried Cass. 'If your prick gets you into trouble, *you* deal with it.'

'Don't be stupid!' hissed Ranga. 'Her dad's one of the constable's deputies. The constable came a couple of minutes ago. I heard them talking. A telegram came about a young couple pretending to be Kurassian, scouting out sites for hotel bombings. He's got to arrest them and hand them to the nearest military officer, to be sent to Torrento.'

'That's nothing to do with us,' said Cass.

'Of course it is! The constable thinks they're you. He's gone to fetch his other deputy and then they're coming here. You've got to run or our whole plan's stuffed.'

'No one could believe we're *bombers*,' said Cass. 'And we've never said we're Kurassian.'

'But you *look* it.'

'So Seriuz questions us, so what? He's an intelligent man.'

'No,' said Orc. 'Ranga's right.'

'What?'

'He'll want backgrounds, families. He won't believe we can't remember, he'll think we're hiding something. If he hands us to the Torrento police and they investigate…'

Cass's face showed she'd caught his meaning. 'We don't know Geist was right about the Kaybees.'

Orc remembered a beach, a revolver clutched in a dead man's hand. 'You want to risk it?'

Cass frowned, then closed her eyes, shook her head.

'Thank the gods,' said Ranga, 'whatever that was about. Now let's get moving.'

He hustled them through the courtyard and almost pushed them through the gate. The back-street beyond was hot with sunlight, empty but for a faintly familiar mop-haired boy sitting on a step a few houses down.

'I'll get your other bags,' Ranga said. 'Go up to the edge of town – there's an olive grove with a ruined hut with a red door, me and Zina were there last night. Hide in the trees, and don't come out unless you hear me. *Go!*'

Dry-throated, heart pounding, Orc shouldered the heavy gear-bag and started along the street. They took the first turning, up a narrow alley that ran towards the top end of town.

'I don't believe this,' said Cass.

Orc didn't either. Such a stupid, kick-in-the-teeth coincidence –

two other people resembling Kurassians. They'd seen hardly any in months. 'I was just about to ask Seriuz about the ziggurat, too.'

He stopped, clawed inside by frustration. On the run, having to leave this place where they'd come closer than ever to finding answers. And with Ranga, who got a third of their takings only because of his map, which probably didn't even have on it the one ziggurat they needed to reach.

'Orc, come on.'

Looking back, he saw the boy had followed them as far as the corner. Now he knew where he'd seen him before – he'd helped tie up the boat on their return from the ziggurat.

'That's Esteban's cousin.'

'So?'

The idea rose, urgent. No time to dither or think. He started back down. The boy watched his approach nervously, but didn't move.

'Orc!' whispered Cass, following.

'We need to see Esteban,' Orc said when he reached the boy.

'Orc, what—?'

'Quick, do you know where he is?'

The boy nodded.

'Bring him here. Tell him the Daughter of the Sea wants to talk.'

The boy nodded again, then ran to the junction with a wider street and disappeared.

'What the hell are you doing?'

'We *can't* just throw it away.' He moved into shadow, pulling Cass with him. 'Esteban knows about the Sea Mother, and there's some connection between her and the big ziggurat. He might know where it is.'

'But Seriuz, and the constable—'

Orc watched the junction. 'Come on, come on…'

'This is insane. Esteban's got no reason to help us.'

'He likes you.'

'Oh, fantastic! What are you going to do, offer him my hand in marriage?'

'Don't be stupid.'

'Orc, *think*, please. If you have any sense of reality left, come *on*.'

That hurt, the dig about reality. Cass tried to pull him away, but he anchored himself with his strength. 'I *saw* it. The connections lead from here. If we run, we'll never find it.'

Cass groaned. Orc worried she would go anyway, and didn't know what to do if she did. But then Esteban appeared at a shambling run, shoes flapping, followed by the boy.

'What do you want?'

'The ziggurat,' said Orc. 'There's a bigger one, out to sea, by an island. Part of it still out of the water. You know it?'

Esteban frowned, then asked Cass, 'You want to be taken there?'

Excitement spiked Orc's chest. 'You *do* know it?'

'What will you pay?' said Esteban.

'A lot,' said Orc. 'There's treasure inside. But only we can get it. Take us there and we'll split it three ways, understand? How far is it?'

Esteban blinked at him. 'Treasure?'

'A fortune. In gold.'

'Beyond the horizon,' said Esteban. 'With the afternoon breeze, it will take until nightfall.'

'Just you, though,' said Orc. 'Not Yorge or your uncle, no one. I can help sail.'

Esteban nodded. 'The boat's drawn up in a cove to the east. Tulpi will take you. I have to go home, to give a reason to be away. I'll bring food.'

He jogged back round the corner. 'Grandfa's boat is this way,' announced the boy, pointing up the hill.

'*Up* the hill?' said Orc.

'This way!'

Away from the harbour, there seemed no real street layout, only gaps between houses joining in a haphazard network. Dust-tracks soon replaced the cobbles of the harbour area. Only half-naked children and dogs sprawling in the sun witnessed their escape.

'See?' said Orc. 'I take it you don't still want to leave?'

'I feel trapped,' said Cass.

Orc didn't ask what she meant.

On reaching the olive grove with the ruined hut, Tulpi turned east along a dirt path. Soon they came to the rutted coast road, which had climbed from the harbour-front to the root of a small headland. Now Orc understood why they'd gone uphill to reach the boat. After following the road a short distance away from Bazantin, Tulpi guided them onto a narrow path leading down into a little cove, which the headland had screened from the town. Yorge's boat lay grounded in the shallows. Gulls flapped up from the gunnels as they stepped onto the beach. The air in the cove was still and hot, silent but for cricket-song from the thorn bushes in the cliffs above.

Tulpi ran to the boat and made a show of inspecting it. 'This is perfect,' said Orc, when the boy was out of earshot. 'No one will find us here.'

'And when we come back?' said Cass.

'Esteban can drop us along the coast. Just think, we'll have the stone by then.'

'Don't you think he's changed a lot?' she said. 'Last night he was saying how evil we were to make his family suffer. Just now he didn't even mention that, or the Sea Mother.'

'I wonder if that *gold* had something to do with it?' said Orc, then noticed Tulpi look up.

Esteban was coming down the cliff path.

And he wasn't alone.

6

SEA MOTHER

Behind Esteban came Pettor, then the lank-haired man who'd been with him on the jetty, and finally Yorge.

'Shit.' Orc glanced around. There was no way out.

'Orc...'

'It's okay. We'll just have to give them all a share. Crap.'

At the bottom of the steps, Esteban moved aside. Pettor halted on the sand three yards from Orc and Cass.

'I am Pettor Jarano, son of Yorge, cousin to Simon here,' he said. 'I declare myself because family and home are my life. Blood is salt, like the sea. Your names I don't need to know, because you have no respect. You stole from the Sea Mother. Listen!' he roared as Orc made to protest. 'I'm explaining to you. You fooled Esteban yesterday, but there will be no more lies.'

'We can't give back the cup.' Cass sounded scared. 'We don't have it any more.'

'We know,' said Esteban. 'But it wasn't in the fat man's room. What's he done with it?'

'The cup is spoiled now anyway,' said Pettor. 'Passed between the hands of thieves and merchants who think they owe the sea nothing.

Its return alone will no longer have the power to calm her.'

Orc swallowed. 'Did Esteban tell you there's a fortune in treasure just over the horizon?'

'No,' said Pettor. 'What is this?'

'Another ziggurat. We need to get something from it, but there's a huge pile of gold there too, and you can all have a share if—'

Pettor came at him.

'No, wait!' Orc raised his hands in defence, but Pettor brushed them aside and punched the air out of him. Orc tumbled, curled up, fighting for breath; then someone landed on him and crushed him against the sand. Cass cried out – he twisted to see Esteban had grabbed her wrists.

'Leave her!' he gasped. He fought against his captor's grip, and caught the worried eyes of Tulpi. 'Get help!' he begged. 'This isn't right, you can see that.'

The boy looked at Pettor.

'All is well, little fish,' Pettor told him. 'You see his hair? He's been crowned with the sun, like in the stories. Now go and help your mother.'

Tulpi ran up the steps.

'So,' Pettor said, turning back to Orc. 'This "gold". You were planning to rob another of her dwelling places, and you even sought our help.'

'Please, let us go,' said Cass. At the fear in her voice Orc struggled, fighting everything into his muscles; but it was no good, he was just bleeding out his strength.

'But she has been disturbed, wheat-haired girl,' said Pettor. 'The dreams showed us. And some were shocked, weren't they, Simon?' he said to Orc's captor. 'Some were surprised to find there was truth in her after all.'

'We won't tell,' pleaded Cass. 'Our friend, he'll give you a reward.'

'Don't worry,' said Esteban. 'You won't be hurt.'

'Hurt? Of course not!' said Pettor. 'We only wish to return to the Dwelling and seek her forgiveness. Then you can go on your way. But there will be no softness, no girlish heart. The ill-will of the Sea Mother would leave our nets and stomachs empty. I would kill you before I let this go unfinished. So you see, it is best for all that you come quietly.'

Cass looked hopeless as Pettor bound her wrists behind her back. After Orc's had been tied, he struggled to his feet, and Simon gagged him with a dirty kerchief that almost made him sick.

They sloshed to the boat, and were made to sit in the bow. Cass had been gagged too. Esteban dumped their bag in the catch-hold, then pulled off his shirt.

'Don't worry,' he told Cass. 'You're safe. Trust me.'

Orc wanted to believe him: why say so otherwise, when they were helpless? But Cass didn't look convinced either.

The men shoved the boat out, jumped in and took to the oars. By the time the headland no longer screened them from Bazantin, the town was at least half a mile away. Pettor set a hard pace, and sweat darkened the men's shirts and gleamed on Esteban's back long before the breeze had steadied enough for sail. Then, with canvas raised, the men rested; the boat bumped over the swell. All Orc could do was move a little to avoid cramp, and meet Cass's eyes from time to time in an effort to convey a reassurance he didn't feel.

After half an hour, Esteban and Pettor changed tack, and looking over his shoulder Orc saw the white-painted barrel ahead.

'Hey, Sun-Crown!' called Pettor from the tiller. 'The sun is hot, yes? Up here, it feels powerful, but down there—' he pointed over the side; 'it stays cold. You know why? Because the sea is greater than the sun. In old times, the sun paid homage to the sea, was eaten by the sea at night and reborn each morning. Everything came from the sea in the beginning.'

The sudden hope struck Orc that all this madness might be down to a misunderstanding. He struggled to speak through his gag. Pettor grunted to Simon, who unblocked his mouth.

Orc spat out the taste. 'That's not true. The earth has always gone round the sun. The sun never came out of the sea – it was around before there *was* sea.'

Pettor laughed. 'You think that is news to me? You think me an idiot? Meaning does not depend on someone saying this is true or that is true. Like you are crowned with the sun. You might say to me: it means nothing, it's just the colour of my hair. But there are truths that cannot be spoken with words, because words are things of fire and air, and not of water and earth.'

'Why do you say I'm crowned with the sun,' said Orc, 'but you called Cass wheat-haired?'

Esteban grunted. 'Because she will live.'

'Hold your tongue!' barked Pettor.

'Why?' said Esteban. 'What can he do now? No one will hear him.'

Orc felt numb. Next to him, Cass struggled, gasping.

'It's true, she wants you.' Pettor looked into Orc's eyes. 'The dreams told us so. She wants back what she lost – maybe the cup, maybe otherwise.'

Let me take you…

'Did you think there would be no price to pay? Or were you happy for us to pay with our livelihoods?'

Orc strained against his bonds, hurt his wrists with trying, a fire of fury and terror streaming into his blood that felt strong enough for anything – but the ropes held.

'We didn't want this,' said Esteban. 'My grandfa warned you not to disturb her.'

Cass pleaded through the gag. It had loosened enough for Orc to make out her words. 'Este-an, mae -is sto. I'll oo any-hing—'

'Don't say that!' said Orc.

'It isn't up to Esteban,' said Pettor. 'Sail!'

He swung the boat into the wind; Esteban and Simon jumped up to furl the slack and flapping canvas.

'Or,' moaned Cass. 'Or, ook.'

He followed her eyes. The harbour was barely visible, *Nightfire* a small dark line billowing smoke. Then Cass's meaning snapped at him: the gap between ship and harbour-front. *Nightfire* had moved off the jetty.

'May-e tha oy.'

Could Tulpi have raised the alarm? But the ship might not be looking for them at all. Maybe Seriuz had just decided to leave. Orc felt sick; he couldn't think what to do, what to say.

The fishing-boat knocked the barrel. Pettor came to the bow with a length of rope. 'Hold him,' he said to Esteban, then to Simon: 'Secure the girl.'

Simon held Cass, despite her struggle. Pettor and Esteban moved up. Fight surged through Orc's body; he lifted his feet and tried to kick, but with bound hands couldn't balance.

'Ump in!' screamed Cass. 'Fwim on -or -ack!'

Desperate, Orc tried to get his feet onto the seat, but his heel slipped and the men grabbed him, held his legs together until a rope was lashed around his ankles.

'Now her,' said Pettor, breathing hard.

'Do we need to?' said Esteban.

Pettor answered him with a clout. 'Question me again and you'll go down with them.'

'With *them*?' said Esteban. 'But—'

'No!' shouted Orc.

Pettor raised his fist.

'You promised!' cried Esteban.

'You think she'll forgive you?' said Pettor. 'Will you keep her in a locked room with her mouth stopped? Fool! They *both* disturbed the Sea Mother. Isn't that so, Father?'

'The girl brought him up half-dead,' said Yorge. 'Stole our lady's prize. Though if my loins were as young as Esteban's, I might speak as he does.'

Pettor grunted; he'd tied Cass's legs. 'Put Sun-Crown's gag back on, and tighten hers. I'm sick of their shouting.'

Orc threatened and begged until the cloth bit again into his mouth. Simon refastened Cass's gag against her thrashing.

'We'll do him first, though?' said Esteban.

'Didn't I say not to question me?' growled Pettor. 'Simon, help me shift her along a bit.'

They picked Cass up, moving her along to the end of the bench that ran inside the bows. Orc stared helpless into her eyes, his own terror and grief shining back at him.

Then Cass looked past him. Kept looking past him, her wet eyes fixed.

He turned. Below her smoke, *Nightfire* barely showed against the coast, a fraction of her former width. She'd turned head-on.

But she was over a mile away.

Simon threw off the tarpaulin in the catch-hold, revealing two concrete blocks with ropes attached. He tied one to the ropes round Cass's ankles.

'Get her over,' said Pettor.

Orc howled through his gag.

'No!' said Esteban. 'Him first!'

'Take this as your lesson,' said Pettor. The two men strained to lift Cass and the block.

Esteban pulled a knife from a trouser pocket and flicked out its blade. 'Leave her!'

Orc stared as Esteban rushed the others. He couldn't follow the short struggle that followed. The men half-dropped Cass, then Pettor's fist sent Esteban sprawling against a thwart.

'Hurry!' cried Simon, as Esteban struggled to rise. 'A ship!'

The men heaved Cass over. A detonation of water wet the boat. Orc tried to get to his bound feet but fell over. His mind was white noise.

Pettor, Simon and Yorge stared over the side. Esteban threw himself at Orc. He sawed at the ropes with his knife. The strands parted easily. Feet first, then hands.

'Pettor!' shouted Yorge. Pettor looked just as Orc's wrists came free.

'Save her!' cried Esteban. 'I don't swim well.'

Pettor and Simon both came at them. Orc wrenched the gag painfully over his chin, clambered onto the seat and jumped, breathing in hard just before he hit the surface – below him was the broad patch of sunlit shallows, the top of the ziggurat, then everything vanished in stinging eyes and water up his nose.

In the blur, he made out a shape.

He pushed his head down, pulled with his arms to dive to her feet

75

and the block that weighted her. He clawed at the ropes but could barely see them without his mask; he would never untie the knots. Picking up the block would let Cass float, but manoeuvring himself to stand and do so was impossible: he was too buoyant.

In desperation he blew half his air, sank to his knees. He hauled the block upwards and raised it to his waist, pushed himself standing, lifted it to his neck. Weakness washed through his body, but he held it as long as he could, to give Cass time to suck in as much new air as possible. His diaphragm contracted again and again and again, a crescendo of pain, until he had to let go and launch himself at the surface and breathe.

He came up only feet from the boat. An oar whacked next to him. He thrashed away from the attack, breathed deep and dived again, down to the blur that became human, anchored in water but now in the boat's shadow. He knew he couldn't lift her again, to hold her as a helpless target. He grabbed her shoulders and positioned himself upright. Putting his face close to hers, he saw her eyes move; their terror powered into him. He trapped a foot under hers, so he could free his hands from her shoulders without floating upwards, and worked the gag from her mouth.

He gripped her shoulders again and put his mouth to hers. She opened as he did, but her lips sucked against his and then the sudden, desperate poke of her tongue surprised him, confused him. He exhaled, and for a moment she seemed not to know what to do, then she twigged and breathed in his air. But not enough: she hadn't emptied first. He let go, swam up at an angle – breached, eyes and nose streaming. The oar crashed down, splashing him; he swam away, fatigue burning, filled his lungs, dived again.

This time bubbles blasted from Cass's mouth at his approach. He emptied his lungs into her and swam away again, at a shallower angle, farther from the boat. When he breached he felt light-headed; he didn't know how long he could do this. Hoping Cass would have enough air for half a minute or so, he tore off his shoes and shirt to swim better.

'No point fighting!' called Pettor. 'She'll have you, it's the way of it.

Don't make it harder for yourself.'

Orc didn't waste breath replying. He sucked air and dived again. This time a strange droning noise sounded underwater; he couldn't tell how far away it was, or from which direction. It disorientated him so that he had trouble finding Cass.

Her eyes were closed.

Fear pulsed through him. He touched her and she bubbled out, opened her eyes, but strain burned in them and he thought maybe this was it, the last one – it might be better to stay with her than fetch air she wouldn't live to receive.

No. He clamped his mouth onto hers, blew out until he was empty, broke away.

The droning was louder when he reached the surface; even when his head hit air he heard it, and its direction. He glanced round.

Nightfire's bow-wave foamed white against her dark hull, now a few hundred yards away. His streaming eyes made out sailors on the gun-platform. But had they seen him?

Three strong breaths. His head swam. A thrown oar crashed into the water inches from him. As soon as he dived, the suddenly amplified thunder of the warship's screws shot him through with the terror that they were inches from him, that he would be churned to blood. He reached Cass; she was crouching to avoid an oar being jabbed down from the boat. In the fog of engine noise he gave her his breath, then clung to her as the sound battered them. Something scraped down his arm, tearing it in pain: the second concrete block sinking beside him. Then monstrous gears clunked, clanked; the screws changed in pitch, whined in a torment of machinery as a titan's shadow darkened one side of the world, and the turbulence of the reversing propellers thrashed at him.

He came up right by the fishing-boat's rudder, gasped at air. *Nightfire* looked huge as a continent, a horizon of steel. Orc glimpsed sailors aiming rifles, a boat being lowered from swung-out davits; the ship was still slowing. He was about to dive again when someone shouted: 'There he is!'

'Cass!' Orc screamed. 'Help her!'

He tried to take in breath but it wouldn't come; he was breaking apart before it was over; he tried to hold it together but he started to shake. *Not now, not yet.* He forced in air, dived again into the roar, but struggled to get under and when he reached Cass he saw the contractions in her abdomen, their rapidity. She took his air but wouldn't open her eyes; he wanted to lift her up again but his own contractions spasmed through him. Seconds from fainting he surfaced, to find the ship's boat right next to him, Seriuz looking down.

Sailors plunged into the water. Orc clung to Seriuz's proffered arm until the sailors brought Cass up next to him, limp, her lips purple.

'C-Cass.' He could hardly get her name out. He blew on her wet face. 'Cass!'

'Mouth-to-mouth, someone!' shouted a sailor. 'Quick!'

'No!' said Orc. 'Not drowned, blackout. Keep back.' He blew again on her face, shivering overtaking him. Blew and called her name again and again. Terror wanted him to scream at her, to shake her, but he kept to his deep-buried training. On the fifth go, she revived – straight away she panicked, gasping breath, trying to break free of the sailor who held her up.

'Cass! Calm down!'

'They did it,' she half-sobbed, seeming barely aware. 'They *did* it.'

'Cass! It's me. You're safe.'

Several more times he told her, and at last, she seemed to understand. She went limp in the sailor's arms, then burst into tears.

'Get them on board,' said Seriuz. 'Mister Juneau!' he shouted up. 'I want fresh towels in my cabin, as many as you can find, and brandy and hot water. And open the heating vent.'

It was a blurred nightmare of shivering. Orc didn't think he would ever feel warm or safe again, or anything other than this shuddering wreck, a half-naked ghost of someone who'd been killed ten times over. The boat bumped against the ship. A ladder came down.

When he'd climbed weakly up, someone threw a coat round him. Seriuz led him and Cass to the hatch. 'My steward's our medic,' said

Seriuz. 'I'll send him shortly.'

As Cass made her careful way down the ladder, Orc turned to the captain. 'How did you know?'

The dark steel of Seriuz's eyes gave nothing away. 'Just be glad I did. Now, I think you should concentrate on recovering, don't you?'

Orc shivered outside the cabin door for a couple of minutes to give Cass time to undress. After knocking, he found her sitting wrapped in towels, a steaming cup in her hands, her clothes lying in a puddle. The cabin was stiflingly warm, and Orc was thankful for it. He slipped off his trousers and the coat – Cass looked away – and scrubbed himself dry before tucking a towel round his waist.

'How's the drink?'

Her head moved slightly, neither a nod nor a shake.

You kissed me, thought Orc. *You thought you were going to die, and you kissed me.*

He pushed the thought away, and poured himself a cup. The brandy scalded his throat, then the rough afterglow spread.

'Orc?' Cass looked thoroughly miserable, like she was going to cry again. 'What now?'

'It's okay,' he said. 'They can't hurt you any more.' But he thought her question a good one, now Seriuz had them. He opened the wardrobe and pulled out some trousers he found there.

Cass gulped from her cup, then put it on the floor. 'Something happened.'

'Well, yeah, I'd say so.' Orc pulled the trousers up under his towel.

'No… when I was falling into blackout, or *in* blackout, or coming out of it, I… I don't know how to tell you.'

She stared at the cabin floor. He yearned to sit by her and hold her until she believed herself safe again, if it took years. But he had something else to do first. They had escaped one death, but the horizon was dark with another.

'In a bit.' He threw off the towel and put the coat back on. 'I have to talk to him.'

Reaching the deck rail, he saw both the ship's boats in the water, the longer whaler right by *Nightfire*. All four fishermen were in the whaler, Esteban at the bow and the others at the stern. Between them sat four sailors on the oars and two more with rifles, and Lyle. The empty fishing boat was tied to the barrel thirty yards away.

Seriuz stood further along the rail, talking down to those in the whaler.

'Since none of you can provide any alternative explanation, I'm forced to accept the version suggested by the evidence.'

'Have we denied it?' said Pettor. 'What we did was right a wrong done by ignorant outsiders. But you will punish us with your outlander laws, made from your outlander lies. Do you sail, Captain? No, the only seamanship you have is ordering coal to be thrown into a furnace. Take us back, then, if you wish. Hand us to the constable.'

'I don't have time.' Seriuz turned towards the bridge. 'Mister Juneau! When you're ready.'

Orc caught the flash in the corner of his eye, flinched at the thunderous crack and the splintering explosion from the fishing boat. A spreading fan of shattered wreckage arced through the air before splashing for tens of yards around.

Yorge wailed. The other fishermen said nothing, only stared. Orc glanced towards the bridge: smoke leaked from the barrel of the starboard gun. A chemical stench burnt the air.

'There's enough floating wood there to keep you up,' said Seriuz. 'It's a two-mile swim back to Bazantin, or a mile to the nearest part of the coast.'

'Swim?' cried Yorge.

'Swim, or drown. If your Sea Mother is so desperate for sacrifices, perhaps she'll take you. But let me say this, in case you survive and wish to contemplate it. You call me ignorant, but you and your ancestors have taken something worthy and warped it into a bloodthirsty, fearful cult. Such worship deserves to be extinct, and it will be. Now, you have ten seconds to get out of that boat and start swimming, or you'll be shot.'

'In cold blood?' said Pettor, angrily mocking.

'My men might not do so, but I wouldn't ask them to.' Seriuz opened the holster at his belt and took out his magazine-pistol. 'I might regret it later, but it would give me great temporary satisfaction to find release for my anger.'

'What of me?' said Esteban. 'They'll kill me!'

'He was tied up, sir,' said Lyle.

'Then swim to another part of the coast. The whole sea is yours! Swim across to Golgomera if you want.'

'Wait,' Orc said. Seriuz turned, seeming aware of him for the first time. Orc had been wrestling with his words; he hardly believed he was about to say them. 'He saved our lives.'

'Is that so?'

'I thought you ought to know.'

'Then I suppose we owe him passage elsewhere, at least. Mister Lyle, the youngest may remain if he wishes.'

'Esteban,' said Pettor. 'If you return with us, you must answer to your family and your people, and I can't say what your punishment will be. Your youth might count for something, or it might not. But if you are coward enough to take this man's offer, this man who denied the Sea Mother her rightful appeasement, who has condemned us to starvation and storm by saving the lives of those ignorant, poisonous desecrators—'

Seriuz aimed; Orc opened his mouth but no sound came out before the pistol fired. Pettor slumped, a red crater in his temple.

The sound of the shot hadn't faded before there came two more. Yorge crashed on top of his son; Simon stood before he was hit, and the impact of the bullet knocked him over the side of the whaler. Seriuz swung the pistol towards Esteban, who stared mute at his dead family. But Seriuz's arm was already wavering, and he lowered the gun.

'Mister Lyle, see that their Mother has them.' Disgust cramped his voice.

Orc couldn't feel his legs. His heart jumped in his chest like every beat would be its last. The thought came to him that the only reason he wasn't screaming was that he was already insane, or dead as the men in the whaler. He almost expected to be shot next.

Seriuz holstered his pistol, walked the few paces to him, his face tight with strain. 'What did you want, Mister Strandborn? You should be in my cabin, tending to your cousin.'

All he could do was stare, and shiver in his borrowed coat.

'Those were the first shots of a war,' said Seriuz. 'And no war is clean, not even a war of liberation.'

Orc looked down at the whaler. Sailors were moving, organising. Seriuz grabbed Orc's shoulder and turned him. 'Would you have pleaded for their lives too? They came within a hair's breadth of killing you both – a crime they were only able to attempt because you fled the hotel. Why did you do that? It was stupid!'

He found his voice. 'Ranga said a telegram—'

'But why run? Guilt? Are you with the bombers?'

'No! But we didn't know you'd listen. Are you taking us back there?'

Seriuz shook his head. 'On balance, I believe you're not the ones the telegram talked of, or perhaps the intelligence was faulty. But I can't ignore it. We've no reason to return to Bazantin. You'll be handed to the police in Torrento.'

No, rang in Orc's head. *No, no…*

'If you're telling the truth, then you've nothing to fear – they'll look into your stories and backgrounds. Once they're satisfied, you'll be freed.'

'But Ranga's still back there,' he said, desperate. 'And the rest of our stuff. We've got to—'

'Your luggage is on board.'

'What?' said Orc, amazed.

'As for your companion, I have no interest in him, nor his relationship with you. You seem not to appreciate the seriousness of your situation, and I'm not in the mood to argue.'

He turned to go. 'Wait!' said Orc. 'Please. You said earlier we'd be useful to you, as divers.'

'I did.'

He tried to swallow. 'If we said yes to that, couldn't you forget the telegram, and the police?'

The grey hunting-wolf eyes regarded him. 'I might think about it.'

'I need to know now. I have to tell her.'

'Is there something you don't wish the authorities to discover, Mister Strandborn?'

He tried to hold Seriuz's gaze, but couldn't.

'As I said, I doubt you are bomb-setters. Now, you'd better get back to your cousin. The shots might have upset her.'

They parted just as the men were climbing up a ladder from the whaler. One sailor carried the gear-bag. Behind him came Esteban. As his eyes met Orc's, his expression animated briefly with something Orc couldn't read, but which was not gratitude.

Back in Seriuz's cabin, Cass had put on her dress. She looked up, her face desolate. Orc tried to smile for her.

'Don't worry about those shots,' he said. 'Just warnings.' He couldn't tell her what he'd just witnessed, nor that Esteban was aboard. But there was other bad news he couldn't hide.

He sat next to her. 'We have to go with him, Cass. At least until we can escape somehow. If we don't agree, he'll hand us to the police.'

She shook her head. 'Like a stain. On the whole world.'

'What is?'

'Before.'

He'd never seen her like this. It worried him. 'Cass, what are you talking about?'

'When I blacked out, I saw something, or... felt something. Us. Our past.'

His breath caught. 'You mean who we are? Our names?'

She shook her head. 'Nothing so...' She fingered her damp hair. 'Like a dark stain, spreading out from us. Like we're so stained, we'll never get clean.'

He didn't know what to think. This wasn't like her, never like her.

The sound of the engines engaging vibrated through the hull.

'Cass, you're the grounded one now, remember? We have to hold it together.'

She covered her face with her hands. Orc put an arm round her, but loosely. He couldn't clasp her; it was as though she were the source of the deep, ice-cold fear rising within him.

'They made us,' she sobbed. 'They *made* us…'

'Made us do what?'

She shook her head and didn't say any more. Orc comforted her as best he could, until she lay down on the bed and fell asleep, or pretended to. He put the coat over her. The ship was moving, away from Bazantin and Ranga, towards he didn't know what.

'At least we've still got each other,' he muttered. 'Whoever the hell we are.'

G: I think it happened at the female's near-death. I
didn't spot it at once, but she's mentioned a stain
spreading out from them.

A: Hell. How could it have leaked? Explain.

H: I don't understand. It seemed intact, unbreakable.

G: We always thought the female subject might have
the stronger ability. It's only luck that (unclear:
possibly Earthdog?) chose the male for initiation.

E: Luck, or chauvinism?

A: Neither. The male broke first, as I knew he would.

G: Either way, if she acquires any ability, who knows
what she might pull from Records? If they discover
the Zhenaii connection, or their origins, they might
become unusable.

A: A stain? Nothing more specific?

G: Not so far, I think.

A: Then we might be safe. See it's patched up.

H: Immediately.

E: Any danger the leak might be detected elsewhere?

A: By whom?

G: There's Highcloud.

E: Twenty-seven Watchers. The odds would be small.

A: But not small enough. I want a scry on the monastery.
And no more mistakes.

7

CRY OF SIN

Tashi shifted his backside for the hundredth time, half-hoping the movement would be enough to disturb his master. It wasn't; Shoggu remained firmly in trance, shrouded in his mantle of lammager wing-feathers. Tashi twitched with frustration. It would be wrong to deliberately rouse the old man, but he'd worn his ceremonial uniform in case Shoggu released him in time, and time was running out.

Light footsteps sounded up the corridor, running. They stopped outside the door-curtain.

'Tashi?' came Aino's hoarse whisper.

He rose, quietly as he could, and put his face to the edge of the heavy curtain. 'What is it?'

'Why are you still here?' hissed the younger boy.

'Because my master is.'

'He isn't at the welcome ceremony?'

Tashi hesitated. To lie was a sin, but getting his master in trouble was worse. 'He's unwell.'

'Is it bad?' whispered Aino through the curtain. 'Can't you leave him for an hour? You'll miss it!'

'I *know*...' Tashi looked round at Shoggu on the far side of the fire-pit's embers. Staying would repeat one of many previous hours of boredom, guarding against a threat that never materialised. And on this day, of all days. He had a duty to Shoggu, but it was also his duty to stand the Knifebridge. They had never conflicted before.

If his eyebrows move, then Gevurah wants me to stay. Lord Gevurah, express your desire through my master's face.

He chewed his lip. In five heartbeats, more than enough time for Gevurah to act, there came no movement of Shoggu's wiry eyebrows, his wrinkled eyelids, nor any other part of his shaved head. Tashi swallowed, made the blessing-bow, and ducked round the curtain into the corridor. It lacked most of its roof, and his eyes smarted after the cell's dimness.

Aino grinned, still breathing hard. 'Come on. If we miss it, we'll kick ourselves forever!'

Tashi trotted after him along the corridor to the smashed gap in the wall, and out of the remains of High Place. The morning air was clear, the snow-cap of Tamfang to the north too bright to look at. They ran down the track, the braids and sashes and belts and scabbards of Tashi's uniform flapping and bouncing and getting in the way – past terraced fields and paddocks, then over the lip in the suddenly steeper slope from where the gorge of the Oar-stream became visible, sunlight glinting on the red-tiled monastery roofs on its far side.

At Two-Bridge Fork, they took the left-hand track to the Knifebridge. The other twenty-five novitiates were already lined along the narrow span at perfect intervals, from the High Place side of the gorge to the Novitiates Door in the new monastery's cliff-like eastern wall. Yulenda stood waiting by the nearer end. Tashi glanced southwards. Nothing moved in the hazy air high above the valley. They were in time.

'Forgive my lateness, Youth Leader,' he panted as he ran up, his inner clothes drenched with sweat beneath his heavy felt jacket. 'My master is sick.'

He feared Yulenda would spot the fib at once, but the man showed no sign. 'I should make you stand at the end as punishment,' Yulenda said. 'But for a Prelate, everything must be done properly. Those left of Hann!' he called. 'Turn and file off!'

The first fourteen novitiates came smartly off the bridge. Tashi adjusted the effects of running out of his uniform, and walked off solid land and onto the ten-inch-wide bridge with eighty feet of air either side. He kept his gaze relaxed and on the stone a few paces in front of him, maintaining the mental discipline and confidence built up over seventy-three standings and thousands of crossings. He took his place a foot from Hann, who was six inches taller and next up in the rankings. Aino come on after him, then the mostly younger ones that had filed off to make room for them.

'Turn!' ordered Yulenda from the edge of the gorge. As Tashi faced south, he angled his feet so neither his toes nor heels stuck over the edge.

'We're honoured you made it,' said Hann. 'Shoggu off chasing Zhenaii again?'

'He's checking how many Qliphoth you gave sustenance to last night,' said Tashi.

'Why, is he worried your count might have been beaten?'

'Careful, Tashi,' hissed Aino.

Tashi held his tongue. Aino was right: such chatter risked feeding the demons. And the Knifebridge was no place to be distracted by bickering. To steady a twinge of nerves, he aimed his eyes into the gorge, the so-familiar sight of the Oar-Stream, with the Petitioners Road on its left side and the sheer wall of the monastery rising directly from the churning current on its right. The water carried his gaze southwards, until in two hundred yards the gorge's sides dropped away, the road turned out of sight, and the Oar-stream left the world in which Tashi had spent all but the first months of his sixteen years, to begin its long, tumbling fall down to the haze from which the visitors came.

Except today's visitor. The thought unsettled him. Today's visitor would not make the long trek up the Petitioners Road, would not pass beneath the bridge to look up and see the novitiates outlined against the sky. It was almost impossible to contemplate.

'What do you think it will look like?' asked Genku, to Aino's left.

'More like an insect than a bird,' said Aino. 'Bare metal or canvas, no feathers. Even lammager primaries wouldn't be big enough, or you'd need thousands of thousands.'

'I think like a bat's wings,' said Genku.

'Will it have a bat's face?' said Cank, even farther left.

'Of course not!' said Hann. 'It's a machine built by lower-worlders, that's all.'

'That's *all*?' protested Aino. 'It must have a completely new type of engine! My master was an engineer in his youth, and he says no steam or combustion engine could make enough power to lift its own weight.'

'Hai!' said Genku. 'I see it!'

Muttering, 'Where?' the novitiates peered into the south.

'That?' scoffed Aino. 'That's a lammager!'

Tashi saw it now – a bonebreaker bird, a holy vulture, soaring at his eye-level but with thousands of feet beneath its wings. The realisation jellied his knees; his gaze flinched back down to the road. Meanwhile came laughter and jeering, muted to the level Yulenda would tolerate.

'It looked farther away,' said Genku.

'It's the best we've had so far,' said Hann. 'This is stupid. What's the point of us lining up here if they're not even coming up the road?'

'It doesn't matter,' said Tashi. 'From above, it will be just as clear how narrow the bridge is.'

'The point of standing is to remind visitors we beat Konstantin's army,' said Hann. 'From below, we look frightening and fearless. From above? A row of easy targets.'

'Targets?' said Aino. 'It's an Empyreal Prelate who's coming, not an enemy.'

'And who was it dragged those cannon up here hundreds of years ago and shot all those holes in High Place?' said Hann.

'That was the Old Empire, not the Empyreum.'

'The one father to the other,' said Hann.

'What's that?' said Paiko.

Everyone quietened. Tashi heard it now, like a faint echo of the Oar, but coming from straight ahead. And there: just as Aino gently nudged his arm. Not a bird, this time. Too big – even from a distance, that was obvious. But from the front, it did somewhat resemble a fat lammager with unnaturally stiff wings.

'Novitiates!' cried Yulenda. 'Backs straight! Keep your eyes forward!' The body of the air-craft was the size of a thumbnail held at arm's length. 'Draw!'

Tashi unsheathed his *dughra* and held it upright in front of his face. He tried to focus on the steadiness of the bridge supporting his feet. The Knifebridge had been shaped from a natural arch; it was part of the substance of Tamfang, the Holy Mountain; it would not sway. But the world around him seemed to shift, to be less stable and solid. In the three days since he'd been told of the air-craft, he'd given little thought to exactly how it might look, or work, or even what such a thing might mean.

The blunt nose of the craft was a glass shell split into many small panes. Behind them, Tashi glimpsed the machine's operator: a man, flying – faster than a lammager, and higher. At the rear of each wing was a rounded pod or tank, bearing something that span so fast it blurred.

The roar grew. *Fear is the defence of the lower self against extinction*, Tashi mentally recited, *an attempt to overpower the will and turn it to preservation of the flesh.* Low on the craft's flanks bulged glass canopies with firearm barrels protruding from them. *It is the flesh that fears. I will not be afraid.* The wings were enormous, and ribbed. Their undersides bore the gryphon insignia of the Empyreal Prelacy.

The roar had become a howl. The sword before Tashi's face looked like a toy made of tin. The craft reduced its speed. A hundred feet up, it dominated the sky like a cross-shaped foot about to stamp down. Faces behind gun-canopies peered at them. Tashi craned his neck as the machine passed over. It seemed to slow further, almost to stand still…

Faintly he heard Yulenda's yell: 'Eyes *forward*!'

At once he realised – he'd tipped back his head too far and overbalanced. He snapped his head level and sought the horizon, fighting the pull of the long fall at his back. Sweat ran in his clothes as his legs steadied. Mutters and cries rippled along the bridge; someone at the far end shouted, 'No!' and Tashi caught sight of falling – but only a sword, sun-flashing as it wheeled point over tip.

The craft's roar changed tone as it passed over the monastery roofs. On Aino's far side, Genku had dropped to a crouch on the bridge to stabilise himself. Others along the span had done the same.

'Disgraceful!' cried Yulenda. 'Off!'

They sheathed their weapons and filed onto less dangerous ground. Tashi's knees shook. He didn't dare think how close he'd come.

'Not just a load of easy targets,' muttered Hann. 'A rabble of idiots.'

A vein throbbed in Yulenda's forehead like a worm beneath the skin. 'Go and change out of the uniforms you have so insulted.' His measured tone stabbed shame into Tashi's heart. 'Be in Battle Court in ten minutes. Prepare to redeem yourselves.'

Ten minutes gave them no time to walk to High Place and back. They set off running, just as the pipes and horns of the welcome ceremony started up from the western gate on the monastery's far side.

'At least no one died,' puffed Aino.

'Not yet,' said Cank. 'I don't know if we'll survive the exercises he'll give us.'

Tashi said nothing. Some*thing* had died – memory, tradition, honour – a rabble of idiots had killed it, and himself one of them. And his dishonour might grow greater still, if Shoggu had meantime emerged from trance-flight and found himself alone. He would then have to face two angers.

So it was with heightened nerves that back at High Place he pushed through the door curtain into the dim cell. But what he saw brought only relief. His master still sat cross-legged on the other side of the fire-pit embers, oblivious to his absence. Things could be worse.

Then detail crashed in on him, and they were.

Shoggu was rocking back and forth, muttering with barely audible distress. His shaved head gleamed with sweat; his hands clawed round his prayer-beads.

Dark-flight.

Panic leapt up Tashi's spine. He fought it down. He knew what he had to do, though he'd never before needed to put this part of his training into practice. Careful not to blunder and jerk Shoggu awake, which risked causing a seizure, he crossed to the medicine chest and opened it. He found the pouch of recalling herbs and emptied a small heap into his trembling palm. Shoggu was now whispering: 'Manifest, manifest...'

Tashi threw the herbs into the embers, releasing a smell of rotting meat and meadow-flowers. He knelt by Shoggu and tried to steady his voice as he chanted:

From dark winds I call you
Return to the calmness
From dark seas I bring you
Return to the surface
From dark woods I draw you
Return to the open
From dark thoughts I pull you
Return to the Mountain

Again and again he recited the rhyme, but no change came over Shoggu. Choked with fear, Tashi shoved aside the curtain and ran to Yaggit's cell twenty yards down the corridor, the only other one occupied in this part of the High Place ruins.

'Aino!' he cried, bundling in without waiting for permission. Aino had almost changed into his loose-fitting exercise clothes. 'Shoggu's in dark-flight.'

'What?' said Aino. 'I thought—'

'He'll die! I can't recall him. Where's Yaggit?'

'In the welcome ceremony,' said Aino, scared.

'You have to get him.'

'But the ceremony,' said Aino. 'How can I—?'

'Don't argue, *get him!*' But Aino only looked terrified, stunned.

'I'll do it then.' Tashi ripped off his belt, threw off his jacket. 'Watch Shoggu!'

'But Yulenda—'

'*Watch* him!'

He pelted headlong down the uneven track to the lower monastery, risking an ankle with every step, ignoring the shouted questions of novitiates he overtook as to why he was still in half his uniform. The memory of his earlier near-unbalancing slipped into his mind as he approached the Knifebridge, but he pushed it away and slowed only a little, throwing out his arms as he ran across, eyes fixed on the Novitiates Door at its far end.

Once inside, he charged down the eastern corridor, dodging servants and neophytes. He swung left outside the chained bronze doors that led to the nursemaid's section, his muscled shoulder bouncing him off the wall. Another fifty yards brought him panting to a side-door in the Great Court.

Peering through the grille, he saw the two hundred monks in their fire-red robes, colours and shaven heads bright with sun. The Abbot spoke from the dais at the northern end, shaded by a wide overhang. Beside him stood a much taller, much younger man, perhaps thirty, pale and fair-haired. Rather than a Prelate's usual purple, he wore a high-collared military uniform bedecked with gold braid.

While the Abbot spoke of the three-hundred-year friendship between the Empyreum and the Thangkaran monasteries, Tashi scanned the kneeling monks. He'd never witnessed a welcome ceremony before, and was surprised to find the yellow-scarved Watchers all to the rear rather than the front, with small, round-faced Yaggit kneeling halfway along the back row.

Easing open the door, he sneaked through, to hide behind one of the wooden posts that supported the cloister. But even with Shoggu in danger, he didn't dare rush into disturbing such a ceremony. Seething with frustration, he waited half a minute, and was steeling himself to fetch Yaggit anyway when the Abbot's voice rose in what sounded like the preamble to a prayer.

'Thus we remember,' his Holiness intoned, 'that any interpretive difference between our two traditions, the one father to the other, becomes insignificant before the Holy Mountain itself – which is for us the place of God, and for our guest the place of God's conception, and thus represents for all of us the route by which we shall one day ascend. Let us now humble ourselves before the Power that has hallowed that place.'

The Abbot turned to face the north wall, and knelt. He and all the other monks bent forward and placed their foreheads to the ground: the monks' to the swept dirt of the courtyard, the Abbot's to a wooden block. The Prelate faced the wall, but did not kneel.

Seeing his chance, Tashi dashed along the back row.

'Shoggu,' he whispered. 'Dark-flight.'

Yaggit stumbled to his feet, almost falling back again before Tashi grabbed him. They crossed quickly to the side-door, whilst the other Watchers shuffled the gap closed. Tashi glanced back at the dais, and found the Prelate looking round at him. Despite the distance, Tashi saw his eyes were clear blue, cold as the waters of the Oar-Stream.

Yaggit closed the door behind them. 'Go ahead. You can run, I can't. Not with this leg.'

Tashi crouched. 'Jump on.'

'What?'

'My back.'

'Gevurah lend you His strength, boy,' said Yaggit as he clambered up. Tashi straightened and stumbled into a run. Immediately he thought he'd made a mistake: Yaggit was small, but still heavier than Aino, always Tashi's rider in mock-battles with other pairs of novitiates. But his legs seemed to strengthen as he hurtled along the corridors, watched in amazement by those they passed.

'The indignity!' said Yaggit. 'Shoggu will owe me for this. Are you sure you're going the right way?'

'Yes,' panted Tashi.

'But the western gate—'

'Quicker this way.'

'You can't mean the Knifebridge? I get dizzy looking down the privy hole!'

'Then close your eyes.'

'How will I walk across blind?'

'You won't,' panted Tashi. 'I'll be carrying you.'

'You're insane!'

'I'm a novitiate.' And with those words Tashi felt a surge of pride. He had failed his discipline on the bridge by gawping up at the aircraft. But standing the Knifebridge was nothing next to his highest duty. He should never have left Shoggu. He prayed it wasn't too late.

They reached the Novitiates Door. Hann and Paiko were just coming through in their exercise clothes. Both mouths dropped open. 'Tell Yulenda I'll be late,' puffed Tashi. 'I'll do as many push-ups as he wants – Aino's share too.'

He went through onto the small ledge before the Knifebridge. His heart raced; the strength in his legs was already fraying.

'Do I close my eyes now?' said Yaggit.

'Might be best,' said Tashi, and stepped forward.

Nandi was just reaching the far side of the bridge. He stood aside, appalled. Tashi walked rather than ran, each foot planted firmly in front of the other, the years of training in balance reaching their apotheosis in this one crossing.

'Oh dear Gevurah,' said Yaggit. 'I looked. I don't suppose you could put me down safely now even if you wanted to.'

'No,' said Tashi. 'If I tried, we'd likely both die.'

'That's what I wanted to know,' said Yaggit. 'The Oar does look particularly beautiful when you can see it over both edges of the bridge at once, but the insides of my eyelids look even better.'

Please don't talk, thought Tashi.

Thirty feet became twenty, then ten, then five, and relief flushed through him as he stepped off the bridge. 'Is that Yulenda's punishment?' said Nandi worriedly as Tashi picked up into a run past him.

Now for the hill. Every step became as hard as two before. Tashi pushed energy into his muscles, pacing himself to exhaust it by the time he reached the ruin. His thighs burned, his calves screamed, tendons pulled and stretched, sweat ran down his nose. He struggled over the lip and there was High Place, cannon-shot by an army of soldiers that twenty-seven of his predecessors had defeated, novitiates like *him* – and yes, they had been Inspired by the holy anger of God, but he was inspired too; he pushed on faster because he would do this if it killed him, if it exploded his heart to pieces – the shattered walls crept closer, taller, then suddenly the distance seemed to close in a rush and they'd reached the hole in the outer wall of the corridor. He buckled to his knees. Yaggit jumped off.

'Come on!' said the monk. 'You're not done yet.'

Tashi could barely walk; he couldn't have overtaken the limping Yaggit now if he'd tried. When they reached Shoggu's cell, Aino looked up at them, mouth agape with fear.

Shoggu was worse, his back hunched, his hands in spasm. Tashi had never seen him look so old. Saliva wet his master's lips, which barely moved as he mumbled.

'Tashi!' snapped Yaggit. 'The call-back, quickly.'

'I tried before,' he panted. 'Didn't work.'

'Try again!'

Tashi dropped to his knees opposite Shoggu and repeated the rhyme over and over. Yaggit delved into the medicine chest and returned with a small mound of different dried herbs in his palm.

'These have a more pronounced effect,' he said, squatting, 'but the quantity must be perfectly judged.' He repeatedly voiced Shoggu's name in time with Tashi's chant, dropping small pinches of the herbs onto the embers. The smell made by these was more peppery than before.

As minutes passed, Tashi began to feel light-headed. Fear hardened to despair. He clung to Yaggit's calmness. Then all at once, Shoggu stopped muttering and began to breathe deeply, as though in sleep. Tashi strengthened his chant, put the force of his will into every word of the call-back. Soon Shoggu straightened his back and loosened his clawed grip on the prayer-beads. Yaggit stilled his voice, and held up a hand for Tashi to be quiet.

'I'm in my cell.' Shoggu's voice was drained almost to a whisper. 'Please tell me I'm correct.'

'You are, master!' Relief pricked Tashi's eyes. 'I'm here.'

Shoggu opened his eyes. They focused. 'Thank you, beloved one,' he said. 'I fear I became over-immersed.'

'Master!' said Tashi. Some desperation in his heart wanted to blurt a plea for forgiveness for his earlier dereliction, but he didn't want to tax Shoggu in his weakened state.

Shoggu put his hand to his forehead. 'Is there tea?'

'Tea?' said Yaggit. 'You've come round from dark-flight and all you can think of is *tea*?'

'It's all I *wish* to think of,' said Shoggu. 'And I'll say no more until it is made. Beloved one, if you would?'

Tashi assisted the old man in standing, surprised and alarmed at how unsteady his master was. He helped off his lammager mantle, and placed the feathered cloak on its mannequin while Shoggu sagged into a chair. Yaggit took the other seat, staring at his friend with intense concern. They made an uneven pair. Yaggit was the much the smaller of the two, but younger: Tashi had decided that Aino's master was about fifty, since it was widely reckoned that the Abbot was sixty. And Yaggit at least looked *robust*, Tashi thought as he began work on the fire. Shoggu was, if anything, older even than the Abbot.

Between them, Tashi and Aino got water boiled. 'Talk if you wish,' said Shoggu. 'Some trivia would be pleasant.' But no one seemed able to think of any, and no words came until all had their bowls of tea. By then, Shoggu looked somewhat better, and had dabbed the sweat from his head.

'Well?' said Yaggit, after his first sip. 'I suspect the Abbot will want to know why you not only failed to attend the welcome for the Prelate, but caused me to be stolen away and subjected to a journey I wish never to repeat. No offence to the transport,' he added to Tashi.

'I have attended enough welcomes for Prelates,' said Shoggu. 'So many, the imprint of my accumulated boredom no doubt lingers there to act as my proxy.'

'The Abbot won't accept that as the reason,' said Yaggit.

'It wasn't the reason,' said Shoggu. 'The facts are these: yesterday, while engaged in flight, a shadow fell upon my mind, an intimation of ill. I wanted to find it again, to identify its source. I deemed such work more important than listening to his Holiness fudge the differences between Gevurah's truth and the Empyrean abomination.'

'Well, hm,' said Yaggit. 'So what happened?'

'I heard the air-craft, that's what. I knew, of course, what the noise must be, and tried to put it from my mind, but something about the sound seemed to resonate with my search for the mind-shadow. I sensed a connection, albeit distant. On a hunch, I tried to use this sympathy. But I was pulled right into the sound.'

'The air-craft pulled you into dark-flight?' said Tashi.

Shoggu shook his head. 'That came later, beloved one. I was first pulled into a symbolic vision. I stood on the very peak of Tamfang, the whole world laid below me as a game-board. Pieces moved on it: men and horses, ships, cannons. The air-craft's sound changed to one mass of noise, it might have been all the engines ever made, all the feet that ever marched. The vibration split the very mountain – and in that moment, my eyes were drawn to the far horizon, and there I beheld a stain, a spreading darkness I sensed would cover the entire globe. And I felt… a disturbance.'

He sipped his tea, the firelight casting the bowl's flickering shadow onto his face. The others waited.

'The only way I can describe it…' Shoggu paused again, as though to make certain of his words. 'Is as a cry of sin.'

Yaggit drew breath. 'You're certain you wish to use that term?'

'I do not do so lightly.'

'Master?' said Tashi. 'What does it mean?'

Yaggit answered. 'In some traditions, the Zhenaii's sins became so great that the Earth itself cried out at what it was forced to birth – and that terrible howl through the Immaterium roused Gevurah in wrath, so that He rid the world of that accursed race.'

'With the Flood?'

'The Flood, the Great Storm, the Cataclysm – its names are many. Shoggu?'

He was sucking his teeth, staring into his tea-bowl.

'Shoggu, tell me what you heard? Be clearer!'

'Heard?' said Shoggu. 'No, it was not audible. Rather, I felt it, as though the world itself had shuddered or retched. Only in the Zhenaii residues that flicker deep within the Immaterium have I felt such *wrongness*, such corruption of Gevurah's creative intent. It was that shock, I believe, that pulled me into dark-flight. In my last lucid moments, I caught an impression of people shouting; there was a large steel machine nearby, with the intent of war in its design; and water, so deep it threatened to suck me down – the sea turned to blood and swarmed with serpents. I remember nothing more until you called me back, beloved one.' He smiled weakly, and reached towards Tashi. Tashi took his hand. He smiled back, but also bit his lip at the frailty in his master's bones.

'You were repeating something, earlier,' he said. '*Manifest*.'

He felt sudden tension in Shoggu's fingers. The monk withdrew his hand. 'That is interesting.'

'Why, what does it mean?' said Tashi.

'It means,' said Yaggit, 'that this whole thing was most likely a result of his…'

'Obsession?' said Shoggu.

'Your *preoccupation*, was the word I sought.'

Shoggu smiled faintly. 'You hear that, beloved one? I am not *obsessed*, merely "preoccupied". The diagnosis has become less serious.'

Tashi's attempt to smile back was unsuccessful. He'd heard the word *obsession* too often from the other novitiates.

'Had I been in a more lucid state,' Shoggu went on, 'I would of course have guarded my perception against the influence of previous theorising. But Yaggit, the disturbance felt too powerful to have been a creation of my own mind.' He frowned again. 'I almost fear to remember it…'

'Then don't, for now,' said Yaggit. 'Tashi, perhaps you would get your master something to eat?'

Tashi nodded, and went to the larder, in one of the few intact parts of High Place that wasn't used as a Watcher's cell, to prepare a meal from cold ingredients kept in jars there. When he returned, Aino had gone – to finish changing, Yaggit said.

'You should get down to Battle Court too,' he told Tashi as Shoggu began eating. 'I'll stay. The two of us might take a walk among the ruins. Don't worry, I won't let him drift off.'

'You mean you'll chatter at me incessantly,' said Shoggu, spitting rice as he talked. 'There's no need to treat me like a fool. I have no intention of flying again until I'm fully rested.'

'Your *intention* isn't what worries me,' said Yaggit. 'Think of Ladro: sitting in his chair, recovering quite happily, then all at once sucked back into dark-flight, and dead. I'll have both eyes on you for three hours at least.'

Aino returned before Shoggu had finished, and brought the gear Tashi had left in Yaggit's cell. Tashi went into the curtained equipment closet and changed for exercises, hanging his uniform on its stand.

'You're sure you don't want me to stay here too?' he asked Shoggu, as he finished tying his red headband.

'Don't fuss!' said his master. 'Yaggit will keep me awake. And you wouldn't want Aino to face Yulenda alone?'

'No,' said Tashi. Since he was the reason Aino had not gone to Battle Court when instructed, that would have been very unfair.

There was no incentive to hurry this time, and Tashi's legs felt drained and stiff. He and Aino made no mention of Shoggu's dark-flight as they walked. Such a thing should never have happened, Tashi knew. He'd disgraced himself with dereliction, and all for the trivial reason of wanting to see the Prelate's toy – he felt furious with himself, and with the air-craft, which was revealed once more as they crested the lip overlooking the monastery. It seemed incredible that life should go on as normal – two of the ordinary monks leading the water-cart up to High Place, others working in the terraced fields – when on the ball pitch beyond Highcloud squatted the winged machine from another world, a giant dragonfly of shining metal.

Aino slowed his walk. 'How do you think it flies?'

'No idea,' said Tashi. 'If Yaggit says it can't be a steam engine or an auto-carriage engine, what else is there?' He had seen drawings of both – and been told, and forgotten, the librarian's understanding of their workings – but he didn't much care what powered the craft.

'Perhaps it uses a new kind of fuel, or an entirely new mechanical principle,' said Aino. 'Yaggit often says how quickly lower-world science changes. I don't suppose they would let us enter the craft to have a look?'

'I wouldn't want to,' said Tashi. 'Didn't you hear Shoggu? That thing pulled him into dark-flight.'

'No, he said—'

'As good as. And it almost got us all killed on the bridge. It is evil, born of an evil idea. Gevurah doesn't want us to fly, not in that way. If they try to fly that thing higher than the Mountain, He'll smash it out of the air.'

'Perhaps the Prelate hopes the Abbot will pray for permission,' said Aino.

'Permission for what?'

'To let him fly to the Land Beyond Sky.'

Tashi was troubled by the excitement in his friend's voice. 'Flesh cannot reach the Land Beyond Sky, Aino.'

'Well… no…'

'To die on the Mountain is the only certain way to get there.'

'Yes, yes. But… to *fly*, Tashi! For real, not just in trance.'

'Listen to yourself, Aino! What would you have done in Zhenaii times, urged them to create more and more abominations? They tried to challenge Gevurah's supremacy with their magic – the lower-worlders try the same with machines. They risk another Flood.'

'Do you think so?' said Aino. 'Would the waters reach here?'

Tashi felt reassured by the edge of fear in Aino's voice. He looked at the soaring peak of Tamfang, and was satisfied by how puny the flying craft looked in its foreground. But he couldn't help remembering how he'd felt on the bridge.

'I wish they'd keep their engineering down there, that's all,' he said. But the monastery soon blocked sight of the air-craft, and there was Yulenda to contend with. As they approached the Knifebridge, the Novitiates Door opened and a stream of exhausted-looking boys filed out, their headbands drenched, their hair clumped with sweat, the knees and chests of their gear dirty with sand.

'He wasn't in a good mood,' said Genku as he passed.

'He might be in a better one now he's made us suffer,' said Paiko.

'Until he sees you two arriving late,' said Hann, with a grin.

8

OBSESSION

Yulenda was still in Battle Court, supervising two neophytes raking the sand floor. He listened to Tashi's story without expression.

'Aino had no fault in our lateness, Youth Leader,' Tashi proclaimed in closing. 'I ask to be given his share of punishment.'

'It is not his share you shall have,' said Yulenda, 'but all your own. Not only were you at fault on the bridge, but it now seems you lied to me when you said Shoggu was merely unwell.'

'I…' Tashi swallowed, flushed with shame, and snapped to attention. 'Yes, Youth Leader!'

'It is for your master to punish you for your desertion,' said Yulenda. 'For your lie, however, the holy stream shall be your atonement. I've had enough today of counting push-ups and shouting instructions. I forgot to tell Nandi to retrieve his *dughra*. Do it in his place.'

Tashi nodded solemnly.

'Aino, your punishment for the lack of discipline shown on the bridge is that you must retrieve the sword if Tashi drowns.'

'Yes, Youth Leader.' Aino sounded relieved.

Once they left Battle Court, he said, 'Try not to drown, Tashi.'

'No one has drowned before,' Tashi said. 'They got Ruman's gear out with no trouble a couple of years ago.'

'They had pole-hooks and wading-boots up to their chests,' said Aino. 'Yulenda was hardly generous with the equipment he gave you.'

Tashi grunted. It would be cold, and wet, and dangerous. But what Yulenda had said was true. He had to atone.

The only safe way into the gorge was the Petitioners Road itself, which ran from the gilded Sun Gate high on the monastery's southern wall, and then sloped sun-wise around the outside of the building. From the western wall, before the road sank into its cutting, Tashi and Aino had a good view of the Prelate's air-craft. The machine was about seventy feet long, its tail tapering until it sprouted two giant fins. Its wingspan looked barely less. At the foot of a fold-out stair that led from an open door in the side of the hull, two men in grey uniforms stood smoking, one with a rifle slung over his shoulder.

'See that?' said Tashi. 'They didn't surrender their weapons.'

Aino frowned. 'They should have given them up at the Sun Gate.'

'They didn't come in by the Sun Gate,' grumbled Tashi.

The craft was hidden from view as the road sloped below ground level and ran beneath the drawbridge from the western gate. By the time Tashi and Aino reached the monastery's north-west corner, the walls had risen to thirty-five feet above their heads. From the turning, the exit at the bottom of the gorge looked a tall slit of light, the passage down to it an ever-deepening crevasse.

Tashi hated it. The cutting was dark and cold and damp: the road never saw the sun. The walls were faced well – there hadn't been a fall in decades – but he couldn't help walking faster and faster, slipping on the dank surface, until he reached the bottom and emerged into the gorge, its bright airiness lively with the echoing chatter of water. He and Aino crossed the Oar on the low stone bridge, and walked the Petitioners Road to just beyond where the Knifebridge cut the sky overhead.

'See anything?' said Aino, peering into the stream.

'We'll have to go in,' said Tashi. 'It won't be far from the bridge – a *dughra* doesn't float.'

'I hope we don't find anything else,' said Aino.

Tashi knew what he meant. There were stories told of the secret dead, novitiates who had fallen and had clutched at their comrades as they fell. Unlike those they pulled down, or those who fell with honour and discipline, their bodies were never recovered, but were left to lie in the Oar-Stream for their bones to be worn away or flushed off the mountain they had disgraced.

'Don't worry,' he said. 'Nothing can stay in that current for long.' He stripped to his breechcloth. Aino did the same. 'This is my punishment, remember,' said Tashi. 'You can stay on the bank. Unless I drown.'

'Maybe I'll just dip my feet,' said Aino. 'They need a wash. Be careful, Tashi!'

Tashi stepped in. The rushing water burned with cold – holy cold, he told himself; it would burn the lie from him, and the Qliphoth that had drawn strength from its telling. Another step. The force of the flow tugged at his knees; the icy flame of the meltwater seared his skin. He bit his jaws shut to keep from gasping, but breath sawed between his teeth.

'Ah!' spluttered Aino, right behind. 'Lovely, warm!'

'*Warm?*'

'Trying to – convince myself!' gasped Aino.

'You should have stayed back.'

'Too late,' said Aino. 'G-get on with it!'

Tashi could barely feel his feet. He had to focus everything on balancing on the slippery rocks, but the pain of the cold made it difficult. Nandi had been standing near the monastery end, so his sword would be close to where the stream swirled along the stonework with which the cliff had been faced. The midday sun dazzled and sparkled on the turbulence, but Tashi caught a steel glint.

'Here—'

He reached back his left arm. Aino gripped his hand; Tashi felt the other boy's shivering. He braced himself, plunged his arm in past the elbow and groped for the hilt while water splashed against his chest, needles of ice that stole breath. As soon as his numbing hand brought up the weapon, he and Aino made for the bank, surging through the treacherous tug with agonising slowness. They clambered onto the dry road, gasping and shivering despite the sun. After shaking their legs dry, they sat on the road and rubbed them madly with their discarded clothes.

'I'd rather do an hour of push-ups than go through that again,' said Aino.

Tashi was trying to rub feeling back into his feet when movement caught his eye. 'Oh, no…'

Aino followed his gaze. 'Witch Mother's tits…'

Tashi didn't even reprimand him, his mind was in such panic. People were emerging from the cutting, into the gorge. Gold braid flashed on the uniforms of the two Kurassians. The Abbot walked with them, two of his attendants behind.

'Quick, out of sight,' said Aino.

Tashi glanced wildly round. 'There's nowhere.' Unless they ran to the end of the gorge, and that would look disrespectful. The men were already approaching – there wasn't even time to dress. Grabbing Nandi's *dughra*, Tashi scrambled to his feet and stood to attention, holding the sword before him in salute. Aino followed Tashi's lead, at first holding his own empty hand clenched before his face, then dropping it to his side. Tashi tried without success to control the spasms beneath his gooseflesh skin.

To the rear was a heavily built Kurassian Tashi hadn't seen before, but in front, now gazing up at the underside of the bridge, was the man from the welcome ceremony. Both were taller than the Abbot, and next to their uniforms, the Abbot's robes and sandals looked like the drab garb of a pauper. His Holiness wore a concerned frown, his eyes bright behind his spectacles. Tashi stared straight ahead as he sensed the Prelate's gaze on him.

'What are you two doing here?' said the Abbot.

Tashi, as the oldest, answered. 'Your Holiness, Yulenda sent us to fetch Nandi's sword. It fell into the Oar this morning.'

From the look on the Abbot's face, he thought perhaps he shouldn't have revealed that.

The Prelate grunted. 'Is this an inspection of troops you have arranged for me?' It was the first time Tashi had heard a Kurassian accent, and its harshness startled him.

The Abbot cleared his throat. 'Not as such, your Grace.'

'Nevertheless, a visiting dignitary must do his duty,' said the Prelate. Tashi jammed his jaws together to stop his teeth chattering.

'One has to be creative when inspecting troops entirely devoid of uniform or equipment.' The Prelate examined Aino. 'This one's loincloth seems slightly askew; there is a little puppy fat that could be trimmed off with hard work. But adequate.' He moved on to Tashi. 'This one's shoulder muscles seem somewhat uneven. Impressive calves for one his age. Is he afflicted with some kind of palsy?'

'I believe he is shivering, your Grace,' the Abbot said.

'What, not used to the cold, living up here?' The Prelate sighed, seeming tired of his game. 'My great-great-grand-uncle came here once,' he said. 'Archduke Thorgeld of Andrarch. He came up the road, of course, as one had to in those days. Entering the gorge, he saw the novitiates lined along the bridge, against the sky. That famous bridge, carved from a natural arch! Those famous novitiates, inheritors of the powers that defeated Konstantin's army! His heart was stirred by the sight, his journal informs its reader.

'And then, as though on cue, one of those novitiates fell. Thorgeld learned later that the boy had been put on a fast as punishment for an earlier infraction, and had become faint. The lad fell, and none of his comrades made a sound or a fuss, but kept standing at their salute. And the boy himself, in all the time he was falling, did not cry out, unlike the Archduke's wife and staff. Now that I'm here, I appreciate how long a fall that must have been, how many screams the boy could have vented had he allowed himself. But he made none. My ancestor had never seen such a display of courage, of discipline, of fearlessness in the face of death. I quote his journal: "In that moment, I would without hesitation have traded a cavalry regiment for the twenty-six remaining".'

He paused, as though for comment. The Abbot made none.

'A hundred years ago,' continued the Prelate. 'Naturally, having read his journal, I was keen to see such discipline and courage for myself. Yet what did we witness as we passed over? Boys looking wildly about them. A sword let fall into the gorge. And now we are greeted by two of them in their under-things, their clothes strewn on the bank of the holy stream. Might I examine that weapon?'

Tashi swallowed. He glanced at the Abbot, who looked livid, but nodded.

'A *dughra*, is this called?' said the Prelate as he took it. 'Short blade, well-balanced, but not much reach. A sabre would skewer your heart, boy, before this could near its target. Have you ever opened a man and seen the horror that lies within?'

'N-no, your Grace.'

The Prelate returned the weapon. 'I fear my ancestor might have been exaggerating, his wits perhaps affected by the long trek uphill. And it begins to seem incredible that twenty-seven such youths could defeat an army.'

The Abbot coughed. 'Konstantin's defeat is a matter of record, your Grace.'

'A record made almost five centuries ago. I should like to see a demonstration for myself.'

'Of a... battle?'

The Prelate laughed. 'One boy will suffice, your Holiness! I wish to see one of your novitiates Inspired.'

The Prelate's words chilled Tashi further.

'Your Grace,' said the Abbot, 'the *Elohim Gibor* are not to be called upon lightly.'

'Then call not upon them lightly. Call upon them with reverence, with all ceremony due such beings. But they serve the same Creator as we, and I am one of the highest of His church. The Lords of Holy Battle have no reason to object.'

'It is not for us to presume...'

'Some would say there has been a deal of "presuming" done recently. But never mind that; I've seen enough here. I've seen the bridge from below, I've walked the spiral road. I have enough material for my own

journal entry, though I fear it was be less *inspiring* than Thorgeld's –
unless I witness something to change my opinion.'

Still shivering, Tashi and Aino stood at attention until the Abbot
and Prelate walked back up into the slot of the road. Then they dressed.

'I hate that man,' said Aino.

'Don't hate,' said Tashi, though he was struggling with the same
feeling. 'Emotions emanate from the lower self, the province of the
Witch Mother.'

'I know, but this time…'

'Hate feeds Qliphoth. You have to remove the emotion from it –
that will leave anger, which is pure and belongs to Gevurah.'

'I'm sorry I showed any appreciation for his craft,' said Aino.

Tashi paused in tying his headband, struck by realisation. 'That
evil machine is the source of the Prelate's pride. He should have been
humbled by the climb, by the approach. But he cheated.'

'Cheated?'

'Imagine you're a visitor, just climbed from the valley,' said Tashi,
enthused by his idea. 'You see the wall, from the stream to the top
of the gorge and beyond into the sky – a hundred and fifty feet, a
fortress! And the bridge above, with us standing on it, our blades drawn
in welcome and warning. You pass beneath us, you look up – the bridge
is narrower than we are! How could you *not* be in awe? And then you
climb the spiral road, starting in darkness and emerging into light,
from the darkness of the lower world into the light of the Mountain.
You go up anti-sun-wise, steeped in sin; you come down sun-wise after
you've been blessed.'

He shook his head. 'All that meaning, lost. The Prelate landed his
craft on the ball pitch and came in by the western gate.' His throat
was taut with the wrongness of it. 'And they kept their firearms. There
have been no guns on the mountain in hundreds of years, not since we
pushed Konstantin's cannons off it.'

'But how can it be changed back?' said Aino. 'Now the lower-
worlders have invented this flying machine, won't they build more?
Soon all visitors will come that way.'

'If I could, I'd make it crash,' said Tashi. 'Then they'd be too afraid to send more. All lower-worlders fear the death of the flesh. That's why we impress them, because they see us standing the Knifebridge and know they could never do the same. But when that air-craft passed over us…' He turned the blade in his hands. 'Nandi dropped his *dughra*. We might as well have all thrown ours after it.'

'Tashi, don't—'

'Was the Prelate right, Aino? The novitiates who gave us our number, hundreds of years ago: could we match them? What if Highcloud is attacked and the Lords of Battle refuse to enter us, because we're not worthy of them?'

'They'll come,' said Aino. 'You heard the voices, as I did.'

Tashi suppressed a shiver at the reminder of the Rite of Acceptance.

'And who would attack Highcloud?' said Aino. 'The Empyreum needs us – they have no one as skilled as Watchers in hunting magicians. The Empyreum would have to be overthrown before any enemy could come here. And who would that enemy be?'

Tashi knew Aino spoke the truth, but the thought of the Prelate as an ally tasted bitter. 'Then if there are no enemies, what's our purpose?'

'The Abbot defines our purpose,' said Aino. 'And our masters.'

Tashi didn't want to discuss this any more. 'Then let's get back to them.'

In Shoggu's cell, both Watchers listened with mounting incredulity.

'He wished to see a novitiate *Inspired*?' said Shoggu. 'As a *demonstration*?'

'It was ignorance speaking, clearly,' said Yaggit. 'What were they thinking, to make someone so young a prelate?'

'It was his pride, more likely,' said Shoggu. 'Physical flight might easily make a man think himself closer to God than he truly is. But if the Abbot refused, I hope that will be an end of it.'

'He insulted us,' said Tashi. 'If he wants to see how strong we truly are, then we can show him by destroying his air-craft. Make him walk home.'

Yaggit grunted. 'Well, leave its engine intact. I'd like to examine it.'

'And I would like it to *leave* intact,' said Shoggu. 'I want to take flight myself, and explore the connections between it and my experience this morning.'

'Absolutely not,' said Yaggit. 'The Prelate's due to leave at sunset. That's much too soon for you to fly again.'

'Tashi will recall me at the first whisper of trouble,' said Shoggu. 'Recent attack makes a guard twice as strong. This is too important a matter not to take the risk.'

'Ah.' Yaggit slurped his tea. '*That* matter…'

'Yes, *that* matter.' Frowning, Shoggu turned to Tashi. 'Beloved one, you're certain "manifest" was the word I spoke?'

Tashi nodded. 'I heard it clearly when I came back after standing.'

Aino gasped, his eyes widened. Tashi had no idea why, and his friend quickly looked away.

Shoggu studied his hands for a while before speaking. 'Taken together with the Cry of Sin,' he said at last, and there was a new tremble to his voice, 'that word can only refer to the Zhenaii ability to manifest changes magically in the Materium.'

'Thus speaks your preoccupation,' said Yaggit. 'But in all your investigations, have you found evidence that any magician has succeeded in manifesting even the faintest breath of air?'

'Lack of evidence does not prove they haven't.'

'Speak sense, Shoggu. Any working that caused the world to cry out as you claim would need power – and such power would have to be learned, and then tested, and mastered over many years. The idea that a magician could suddenly bring about a full manifestation—' he wagged his finger – 'with *no progress* on his path coming to our attention, that is absurd.'

'The first Watchers tasked themselves specifically with guarding against the return of Zhenaii magic,' said Shoggu. 'I doubt they would be pleased to have their fears described as "absurd".'

'You twist my meaning, as you well know,' said Yaggit. 'In any case, our predecessors lived in difficult times, and their knowledge of what is possible was incomplete – must we have this same conversation again? In three thousand years, no one has succeeded in reviving Zhenaii practices, nor will anyone in the next three thousand. We must apply our resources to seeking out those who practise real magic, who send dreams to harm and confuse, who attempt prophecy, who speak with demons and trade for secret knowledge.' He cocked his head as a distant bell sounded. 'Ah, there we must end. Are you recovered enough for noon prayers?'

'Yes, Tashi and I will join you outside.'

Tashi took only a minute to change into his grey uniform. As he pulled aside the door curtain to let Shoggu into the corridor, his master gripped his forearm.

'So, you heard me muttering "manifest" *after you came back from standing?*'

Tashi's heart fell to the pit of his stomach as he realised what he'd let slip. He dropped to his knees. 'Master, forgive me! I – it was the air-craft, I was curious to see it. It's brought nothing but evil – it must be destroyed!'

'You cannot blame a machine for your own failings.'

The word *failings* bit deep. 'If Aino hadn't come for me…'

'Tashi.'

'I asked Gevurah to send me a sign.'

Shoggu said nothing. Tashi stared at his master's feet.

'Master, you must punish me.'

'And what punishment do you think suitable?'

'Something that makes me prove myself. And something that brings me close to death, as my failing brought you close to death.'

'Get up,' said Shoggu.

Tashi did so. The hard slap on his cheek jerked his face round.

'Young fool.' Shoggu's voice trembled. 'You come close to death every time you stand that wretched bridge. You think I could bear anything more?' He turned away. 'We must go.'

Tashi burned with disgrace as he trod the path to the lower monastery. Shoggu seemed even more frail than usual, as though the blow had sapped his strength. Tashi would have given Shoggu his arm, but knew from experience that his master would dislike being reminded of his age. And perhaps, now, he would refuse it for other reasons.

At Two-Bridge Fork, Shoggu and Yaggit turned right onto the track that led to Monks Bridge and round to the monastery's western gate. Alone with Aino on the Knifebridge track, Tashi sensed the younger boy building up to something. Twenty yards past the fork, it came.

'Yaggit says you mustn't let Shoggu fly when the air-craft leaves.'

'He's my master, not the reverse.'

'You must persuade him, Tashi. It's dangerous.'

Tashi didn't need to be told that. 'I'll make sure he's safe.'

'Yaggit thinks Shoggu's dark-flight this morning might have been caused by his state of mind. He thinks it possible all dark-flight is caused by going too deep, through obsession.'

Tashi hissed at that word.

'Tashi, I respect your master greatly, but can you truly say he isn't obsessed?'

'Is it "obsession" to faithfully carry on the Watchers' ancient task?'

'*Ancient* task, yes.'

'Has it been repealed?' said Tashi. 'This laxity is exactly what magicians want. What's Yaggit doing about their plots and schemes?'

'Yaggit has his hands full saving your master,' said Aino as he stepped onto the bridge.

Tashi's lack of application during Book study and prayer raised deep draughts from Yulenda's wells of sarcasm, but despite this added shame, Tashi couldn't concentrate. His mind was filled with dreams of the air-craft's destruction. It was a stain on the world: his master had used exactly that term. If it was allowed to leave intact, then Aino's prediction would come to pass: an endless steam of visitors would arrive, all without having undergone the cleansing effort of climbing the road, all looking down upon the novitiates, all come to gawp at the monastery and the warriors who still used swords instead of guns. Not enemies in the sense of battle foes, but enemies nonetheless.

At the refectory afterwards, they found Yaggit sitting alone. He told them Shoggu had returned to High Place already.

'Without eating?' said Tashi.

Yaggit added another handful of chopped nuts to his own meal. 'He insisted he wasn't hungry.'

'He can't be preparing to fly again?' said Aino.

'No, the air-craft won't leave for another three hours,' said Yaggit. 'And we must all do our best to prevent Shoggu attempting another flight then. It is still too soon to be safe.' He looked at Tashi, who grabbed a rice-bowl and dumped some lentils and beans and flat-bread into it.

'I'll make sure he eats.'

He caught up with Shoggu just after Two-Bridge Fork, and nervously fell into step. He hadn't forgotten the slap to his cheek – doubted, indeed, that he would ever do so – and wondered how Shoggu would react to him now.

'You should eat, master,' he ventured. 'You still need to be further grounded.'

Shoggu took several steps before he answered. 'I cannot fly if I am too heavy.'

'But sunset is three hours away. The food you eat now won't trouble you then, but hunger will weaken you.'

'I do not intend to wait for sunset.'

Tashi frowned. 'Aren't you going to wait for the air-craft to leave?'

'That is what Yaggit expects,' said Shoggu. 'And that is when he will contrive to prevent me. Will you seek to do the same right now?'

Tashi couldn't answer that. 'Were you intending to fly even without me there?'

'I hoped you would find me,' said Shoggu.

Tashi feared to ask further. He wanted to try to persuade Shoggu back to the refectory, but of course Shoggu wouldn't listen to him – his earlier dereliction of duty had proved him untrustworthy, unwise, compromised. To take Yaggit's side would lower him even further in his master's estimation, and his own. The air-craft had dragged him into a position of weakness that risked Shoggu losing his life.

He glanced back. They had climbed high enough now to see the craft shining on the ball-pitch.

'Master,' he said, as the thought came to him. 'The machine is still here.'

'Of course. What of it?'

'If you learn the nature of its evil now, the Abbot will have to order it destroyed! We can make the Prelate and his men walk home, as they should have walked here.'

'The air-craft is not my chief concern,' said Shoggu. 'My quarry is the Cry of Sin.'

'But they are connected. There was something in the craft's sound, something that pulled you closer to dark-flight: you said so yourself. In your vision, it split the Holy Mountain! The Zhenaii's pride was their evil, and that craft is the source of the Prelate's unholy pride. He thinks nothing of us, nothing of Gevurah. Master, if you fly now, you *must* discover the secret of that machine as well. To waste the chance would be...' But he dared go no further.

Shoggu stopped, and looked at him. 'So, you will indulge my obsession if I indulge yours? Is that the bargain you offer me?'

'No!' protested Tashi. 'To pursue evil without compromise cannot be obsession.'

He couldn't read his master's gaze: it was complex, and there was sadness there. 'You are indeed the most devout of them,' Shoggu said. 'Come.'

They spoke no more on the way back to the cell. Tashi left the food outside, as Shoggu said the odour would distract him. After his master's breathing preparation, Tashi helped him on with his lammager mantle, then lit incense. Across the fire-pit he watched Shoggu's thin lips move with his preparatory mantra, his swollen knuckles as his fingers moved through the prayer-beads. When Shoggu passed, still and silent, into trance, Tashi pushed away fatigue and pinned his concentration to every twitch of Shoggu's brow, every tiny movement of his lips, alert for anything that might warn of a return to dark-flight.

Such intense focus stretched time; hours seemed to go by before

Shoggu began his comeback chant. When the Watcher opened his eyes at last, they were clear and focused, though troubled. Relieved by his master's safe return, Tashi put some more wood on the fire, and made tea.

But the knots in Shoggu's brow didn't ease.

'Master? Did you find anything?'

'I do not wish to talk of it yet, beloved one.'

'But the air-craft; did you—'

'Let me rest, as I asked!'

Tashi held his tongue with difficulty. It didn't seem promising: if Shoggu had discovered the evil of the air-craft, they would surely be hastening to the Abbot. But at least the flight had passed safely, and his master had called him 'beloved one' again, both reasons to be thankful. As Shoggu sat in thought, Tashi made his own contemplations. Aino had wanted to look inside the air-craft. If they could do so, they might learn the machine's secret that way, perhaps even be able to prevent its lift-off, or make it crash if it tried. He was so deeply absorbed in these thoughts, he failed to notice the footsteps along the corridor until they were right outside.

'Can I come in?' whispered Yaggit.

Shoggu jerked his head up in alarm, clattered down his tea-bowl, and hurriedly began to shrug off his mantle. Understanding, Tashi slipped round the curtain into the corridor.

Yaggit's face was serious. 'I've just received a message from the Abbot. Is Shoggu able to see me?'

'I could pass it on for you?'

Yaggit frowned at him, then looked at the untouched food to the side of the doorway. 'He still hasn't eaten? He hasn't flown again *already*?'

Tashi couldn't answer. To lie again was unthinkable. But he couldn't admit it, not when his master didn't want Yaggit to know.

His silence confessed for him. Yaggit pushed past him into the cell.

'You forget yourself!' said Shoggu, caught in the act of hanging his mantle on its stand.

Yaggit huffed. 'This morning Tashi and I risked *death* because you took flight unguarded, and now this?'

'I was guarded.'

'And did the results justify such madness? Did you find your "Cry of Sin"?'

'No, I did not.'

Despite the tension, Tashi almost sighed with relief. So that was that.

Yaggit did sigh. 'Shoggu, I worry for you. But you have something to worry about now. The Abbot wishes to see both of us an hour hence, doubtless to discuss the Prelate's welcome. Since I was forced to abandon it to assist you, the burden of explanation falls on your shoulders. You should give it some thought.'

'I shall have something to tell the Abbot,' said Shoggu.

'I hope it pleases him,' said Yaggit.

'He is a man who craves peace and calm,' said Shoggu. 'Therefore, I suspect it will not.'

9

THE BARGAIN

His Holiness received them in his audience chamber above the Sun Gate, and immediately dismissed his assistants, which set Tashi's nerves even more on edge. Perhaps the Abbot didn't want his anger witnessed by anyone other than its recipients; and against that anger, his master had no defence. There had been no Cry of Sin, that was clear now – the arriving air-craft had merely confused Shoggu. Tashi hated that his master had been wrong, but hoped he would apologise quickly, placate the Abbot as far as possible and get the ordeal over with.

'What were you thinking, Shoggu?' the Abbot began. 'It's common knowledge in the lower world that there are twenty-seven Watchers. Did you think his Grace can't count?'

'If he was able to count scarves,' put in Yaggit, 'he couldn't have been very attentive to your address.'

'That's as may be,' said the Abbot, his eyes remaining on Shoggu. 'Fortunately, by the time he remarked on it, Yulenda had already arrived with Tashi's message that you were ill, which put a better light on things. But Yulenda later told me that Tashi was not being truthful, and you were in *flight*!'

'Your Holiness, that lie was my doing,' said Tashi. 'I knew that if I told Yulenda the truth, he would send me back and I would miss seeing the air-craft. I was… curious.'

'From what his Grace said, it might have been better if you'd all missed seeing the air-craft,' said the Abbot. 'Well, Yulenda has punished you; we'll leave your conduct at that. But *your* innocence of that lie, Shoggu, does not explain why you were in flight.'

'No, your Holiness. But it's a good thing I was, given what I discovered.'

'Oh?' said the Abbot. 'My ears are at full attention.'

As Shoggu told of that morning's experiences, of his attempt to follow up on the previous day's mind-shadow and his finding of the Cry of Sin, the Abbot's steepled fingertips twitched with impatience. Tashi cringed to hear his master only making things worse. Since that afternoon's flight had produced nothing, what could be the relevance of that morning's episode? The anti-climax would only annoy the Abbot.

Yaggit seemed to think the same. 'But this afternoon,' he interrupted before Shoggu could draw out his story too long, 'you said you *didn't* find it again.'

'That is correct,' said Shoggu.

The Abbot rolled his eyes. 'Then—'

'It was gone,' said Shoggu.

The timbre of his voice tightened Tashi's chest.

'You mean it was never there,' said the Abbot. 'A mistaken impression.'

'No, that is not what I mean.'

'Then what? Things don't disappear from Records.'

The troubled lines had deepened again on Shoggu's face. 'I found the residue of my own awareness from this morning. Not being in dark-flight this time, I was better able to discern the place: a stretch of coastal sea. I felt the presence of a warship, and a smaller boat. Though all these had previously been distorted by my descent into dark-flight, I recognised it as the same location in time and space. The record of such a disturbance as that Cry of Sin should have been palpable. I searched for it diligently. It was gone.'

Yaggit laughed, but uneasily. 'So history has been rewritten?'

'In effect. Someone has covered it.'

'Impossible,' said the Abbot.

'There is no other explanation,' said Shoggu. 'I should have been able to name the ship, at least its country, but there was a vagueness to everything, as though that part of the Immaterium had become blurred. Someone, or something, has interfered with Records.'

'But...' The Abbot was clearly struggling. 'But there is no evidence that such a thing is even possible. If there really were magicians capable of... of concealing...'

'Precisely,' said Shoggu. 'They could hide from us the evidence of their own learning. We Watchers would be blind. They could recover the full power of the Zhenaii and we would have no warning until it was unleashed. They might already have done so – Tashi said that in dark-flight I was muttering the word "manifest".'

'No, that's too incredible.'

'You mean too terrifying.'

'You must be mistaken.'

'If you still think so, then listen to this.' Shoggu leaned forward. 'In an effort to be precise as to the physical location of the Cry of Sin, I tried to get around the blurring by going further back in time. And I did learn the location: a pre-Zhenaii temple, now lost beneath the sea. I was able to identify it, but only by its ancient name, which is unlikely to appear on any map. But that is not all, nor even the most important part, for in searching for this information I chanced upon the mind-shadow from my original flight yesterday. And this time, I perceived its nature: a disturbance in the barrier between the Immaterium and the physical world.'

'A manifestation?'

'Partial, at least. Possessing both female and serpentine qualities.'

An image jumped to Tashi's mind: the Witch Mother and King Serpent combined into one horror. It couldn't be true. But Shoggu's voice possessed a strength of belief and an urgency Tashi had rarely heard before.

'But how were you able to find it,' said the Abbot, 'if Records has been changed?'

'This earlier one was left unhidden, I think,' answered Shoggu. 'If the manifestation were only partial, its creator might have thought it wouldn't be noticed. Which strongly suggests that the concealed one was *more* than partial.'

The Abbot stared at his hands. 'But... but if this is true...'

'You must order a Conclave at once,' said Shoggu. 'If we act while the trail is fresh, our combined efforts might pierce the obfuscation.'

The Abbot shook his head. 'No. That cannot be done. Not yet.'

'But your Holiness!'

'I cannot exhaust the Watchers on this. I need to keep them fresh.'

'Why? We are hardly stretched.'

'We might soon be very much so.' The Abbot looked from Shoggu to Yaggit, every fold of his skin looking more heavily weighted.

'His Grace is not here on a pilgrimage to the Holy Mountain. He has come from the Valkensee with a "request": that I officially acknowledge the divinity of Empyreus.'

The monks gasped. 'They cannot dare!' said Yaggit. 'They know that's impossible.'

'Whether they think it impossible or not, they have dared.'

'You cannot agree!' said Yaggit. 'That... that gibbering head! Your Holiness, there has been too much sitting on the fence. The Prelates are pushing for this because they believe us weak, because no Abbot has declared the worship of Empyreus an error, as should have been done at the beginning.'

'If we had wished to be destroyed, that is indeed what we should have done.' The Abbot took off his spectacles and studied the lenses. 'Now you see, Shoggu? When his Grace departs, he will ask for my answer. I will delay, of course. He will give me a deadline. And before that deadline arrives, we shall have to determine the truth about Empyreus, as should indeed have been done long ago. And for that, we shall need the Conclave.'

'Your Holiness,' said Shoggu, 'if there are magicians already practising advanced Zhenaii magic, it might be too late to worry about whether Empyreus is the Son of God.'

'I must take that risk.'

'That can only mean you don't believe me.'

'You might be mistaken. No one doubts your ability, Shoggu, but it is known that you—'

'I am *not* obsessed! Your Holiness, if you truly cannot spare the Conclave, let me go into the world and investigate.'

Tashi's eyes stretched in alarm. He glanced at Aino and found the same horrified look.

'Out of the question,' said the Abbot, to Tashi's relief.

'But closer to the source of that Cry of Sin, its nature and exact location might become clear.'

'I cannot spare you,' said the Abbot. 'I need the Conclave at full strength. Even one missing member might weaken it to the point where it can learn nothing.'

'Your Holiness, I implore you—'

'And I *order* you, Shoggu, look past your preoccupation. The Valkensee's "request" is the gravest crisis we have faced since Konstantin's attack. This discussion is ended.' The Abbot tremblingly replaced his spectacles. 'And in view of the necessity of being diplomatic to his Grace, I insist you apologise to him before he leaves. You too, Yaggit.'

'Where is he now?' said Shoggu.

'In the library. But the apology can be made when he boards his craft.'

'Then for the time being, I might be about my work?'

'Yes, go. But not a word of this, understand? And your novitiates, of course, will obey your own instructions not to speak.'

'They will,' said Shoggu. He turned to Tashi. 'You will obey me, won't you? Your duty is to me, above all.'

'Yes, master, of course,' said Tashi, confused by the tone. *Above all?*

'Then come.'

Shoggu turned and led him out of the Abbot's office, along the corridor, down the stairs.

'Where are we going?' Tashi had never known Shoggu walk so fast; it was as though all the effects of his old age had previously been a pretence.

'The library.'

'You're going to apologise to the Prelate now?'

'I will say whatever is necessary. But *you* say nothing unless one of us addresses you directly, understand? Do not let your face betray your thoughts, whatever those might be. And know that I love you dearly.'

The words made Tashi's heart clutch with a fear he couldn't place.

The Prelate was with the head librarian at the far end of the great room, in an aisle permitted solely to Watchers and the higher monks. Tashi's unease only increased at being surrounded by shelves of titles forbidden to him, gold-leaf names of demons and kings, treatises on alchemy and the hidden sciences.

The Prelate looked up as they approached. 'Ah, the stream-bather. And, I assume, his master.'

'Your Grace, may I have a word?' said Shoggu. 'Alone?'

The librarian frowned darkly. 'His Grace and I are engaged in research. And you know novitiates aren't allowed here.'

Shoggu kept his attention on the Prelate. 'Your Grace?'

The Prelate considered, then turned to the librarian. 'Why don't you get me that next volume of Karplan's *Voices of the Dead*? If we send this fellow away, my curiosity will be unsatisfied, and I hate to be left unsatisfied.'

The librarian's departing glance at Shoggu suggested he would not be in his prayers.

'The Abbot hopes to please me by having you apologise for your earlier absence,' said the Prelate. 'But I should be better pleased if you had something more interesting to say.'

'Your Grace, I shall come straight to the point.'

'Ah, my mistake – he hopes to kill me with shock.'

'I need passage on your air-craft.'

Tashi opened his mouth, then shut it. The Prelate's eyebrows arched. 'By heaven, that was unexpected. By way of contrast, I shall give a rather obvious answer. No.'

Tashi didn't know what to think. Had Shoggu meant what he'd said, or had it been a ruse to get inside the craft and discover its secrets?

'Your Grace,' said Shoggu, voice lowered. 'I apologise for any offence given earlier.'

'Yes, yes, accepted.' The Prelate returned his attention to his book. 'Now go.'

'I must press my request.'

'Must you?'

'This is a matter of interest to us both. I have uncovered evidence of dangerous magic use in the lower world. The Empyreal charter allows any Watcher to freely hunt down practitioners anywhere within the Empyreum.'

'It does not require me to endanger my craft by overloading it.'

'But it must have burnt fuel on the way up here? And aided by gravity—'

'Are you an aviation expert now you've seen one craft?' The Prelate beckoned the librarian forward.

Shoggu's voice lowered further, edged with panic. 'I can give you what you want.'

The Prelate snorted, but something in Shoggu's tone must have worked on him – the man raised his palm to the librarian.

'You have five seconds to tell me what you think that is.'

Shoggu whispered: 'I believe you wish to see a novitiate Inspired. I will do it.'

Tashi's heart squeezed. The Prelate stared at Shoggu, then turned to the librarian. 'Not that volume: the fourth one!'

When the monk had retreated again, the Prelate murmured, 'Here? Now? I must leave in an hour.'

'Not here, your Grace,' said Shoggu. 'I assume you're returning to Bismark? I shall perform the rite there.'

The Prelate gave Tashi a long look. Tashi tried to be steady, tried not to give in to emotions. Emotions were emanations from the lower self. It was the flesh that feared. His fleshly heart that thumped too fast, that felt like it might break him in tears of fear and anger and – no – betrayal – or make him sick. He willed his flesh to the stillness of ice. He willed his heart to coldness. He met the Prelate's eyes and willed his own not to give away the terror behind them.

'Be at my craft at sunset,' said the Prelate. 'Not too much luggage. Now, go. You have your packing and I have my research. And don't think to cheat me, monk.'

'Never, your Grace.'

Tashi had no words he dared speak. Outside the library, Shoggu turned to him, looking old again, older, like a man who had indeed been through dark-flight and doubt, fear and hunger in too short a space of time. 'Beloved one—'

'Master...' It came out like the bleat of a goat or a child.

'Be brave, be strong.' A pained attempt at a smile flickered. 'If my fears are well-founded, what we embark upon is more important than this monastery and all its history and ritual and learning. Do you understand?'

'Yes,' Tashi lied.

'You know what must be packed?'

He swallowed, nodded. It was a part of his training he'd never expected to use.

'Meet me by the air-craft in an hour. And come back across the Monks Bridge.'

Tashi frowned. 'Master? I am a novitiate. Until a half-hour after sunset I have to use the Knifebridge, unless I'm ill or the safety flags are up.' He didn't understand how Shoggu had forgotten this, unless his master really had lost his mind.

'Beloved one, I said more important than ritual. If you return through the monastery with the pack, you might be seen and stopped.'

Tashi nodded miserably. More important than doing the right thing, the thing that made him what he was.

His crossing of the Knifebridge was one of his shakiest ever. The ruin of High Place was quiet. *Why me?* he thought. *Why couldn't some other Watcher have found that Cry of Sin?*

The reply came easily: *Because no other Watcher is obsessed with the Zhenaii.*

Obsessed, obsessed...

He folded Shoggu's mantle into its cover, which he put into the larger backpack that also took the small medicine chest. From the side-room he fetched his bindings, the complex armour of black leather straps and buckles that had to be worn by any novitiate when Inspired, to prevent the muscles being torn. Handling them made him almost sick. He had only ever worn his bindings so they could be refitted to his growing body; he had attributed to them only symbolic meaning. Now he realised with shock that the refitting, the training, the terrifying Rite of Acceptance beneath the Cliff of Voices, had been for a purpose. The vanishingly distant possibility had become imminent.

His master was going to Inspire him, turn him into a mortal vessel for the holy anger of Gevurah, for the *Elohim Gibor* – not to face a great enemy, but in barter for a journey.

The fear of it, the wrongness of it, stung his eyes. He choked it back. The bindings went in their case. He strapped the case to the backpack, then packed the other things, spare clothes and travelling coats and razors and wash-kit: everything on the list he'd learnt by heart when that, too, had seemed of only ritual significance. His fingers fumbled with the straps that fastened case and backpack into the single travelling pack. Lastly he slotted in the sheathed *clathma*, the larger sword too heavy for his normal strength to wield.

He squatted, put his arms through the straps, and hoisted the pack up like a slightly lighter Yaggit. From the curtain, he looked back at the threadbare rug by the doorway on which he'd slept every night, the pallet against the far wall on which Shoggu had gently snored. The first night, it had seemed so new, so strange, but memory then blurred every night the same. After five years, the cell had become normality, and nothing had intruded to break that feeling. And now he didn't know if he would ever see it again.

When he reached the ball pitch, perhaps fifteen people stood by the air-craft: the Abbot and his assistants, the Prelate and his guard, Aino and Yaggit and Shoggu. The fold-out door to the craft's hull was shut. As Tashi walked up, he saw the Abbot's face lined with a quiet anger. Aino saw his approach, and stared. Soon the others were following his gaze. Tashi's legs felt shaky, as though the load he carried was many times its true weight.

Nothing was said; Tashi sensed words had been exhausted. The inevitable approached. Shoggu seemed to study the ground. Yaggit looked at the craft's outer hull, his brows clenched. Aino turned his face. The sunset painted itself on the high snows of the Holy Mountain, and stained the western wall of the monastery; the air smelled chill with approaching night. Tashi wanted to say something to Aino, but didn't know what, and Aino wouldn't look at him. Was this recrimination? Was Shoggu betraying the monastery, and himself abetting it out of duty? His chest burst out a breath of confusion.

Then came the sound of bolts, and the door swung to the ground to make the stair. Noise started in the craft's hull. 'Go up,' said the Prelate to Shoggu. 'I need a final word with his Holiness.'

Unsteadily, Shoggu climbed up into the craft, given a hand by a crewman. Tashi went to the base of the stair.

'Brother!'

'Aino, stay where you are!' said Yaggit.

Tashi turned, a choking lump in his throat.

'They say you can't come back,' said Aino.

Tashi glanced at the Abbot, who looked away.

'Find it, Brother,' said Aino. 'If you find the evil in the lower world, they'll know Shoggu was right. And when you come back up the Petitioners Road, I'll be on the bridge to salute you.'

Tashi nodded.

'Aino,' said Yaggit, 'come away now.'

Tashi turned. He almost slipped as he mounted into the air-craft. He looked around at the interior, the belly of the monster machine. The space took up most of the length of the craft, but only half its height. Hann would have had to stoop. Above his head was a metal ceiling, with a closed hatchway near the front. Seats and a table were bolted to the floor. Shoggu sat there, grim-faced.

'Did you bring everything?'

'Everything, master.'

Tashi set down his pack on the metal floor. He couldn't make out what the Abbot and Prelate were saying outside, because of the rumble from beyond the metal ceiling. He thought there was a voice up there too, but couldn't be sure.

'His Holiness is even now giving me a last chance,' said Shoggu, when Tashi was seated. 'If we step down from this craft, all will be forgiven. If we leave with it, I will have disobeyed his direct command. He then has the right to take my position from me, and yours from you. I don't know if he will. He has made threats, but he might yet repent of the emotion that drove them.'

He sighed. 'Beloved one, you know I cannot do this without you. If you refuse to come, I will not be able to fulfil my bargain with the Prelate, and it's likely he will put me off this craft. Even if not, I don't see how I can possibly fight the evil at work in the lower world without your strength and support. But I was wrong earlier to say that your duty is to me above all. I cannot with conscience command you to disobey the Abbot, especially when it might mean the loss of what you are. If you wish it, I release you from this task.'

Release. Tashi stared at the table top. To stay at Highcloud, with Aino and the others; to remain a novitiate; to not have to undergo the terror of Inspiration. To not have to go to the lower world that tainted everything holy, that might taint him. And if *he* chose to stay, then perhaps the Prelate wouldn't let Shoggu travel with him either. Everything would be as before.

Except it wouldn't. He would have failed his master's call; he would have sided with those who pronounced Shoggu obsessed. He might sleep in Shoggu's cell and guard his door, but he would no longer be his master's novitiate – not in any way that mattered.

He swallowed, shook his head.

The Prelate and his assistant boarded and the crewman raised the door, darkening the interior. Tashi wanted to see Aino again, was desperate to. Both Kurassians took seats at the table.

'By the way,' said the Prelate, loud above the growing noise, 'I told his Holiness I'd granted you passage because you asked – under the charter, of course. I said nothing of our agreement.'

We cannot come back, thought Tashi. The realisation coursed through him like the vibration that came through the metal hull. He had chosen his loyalties.

A crewman placed a tin cup before him. 'Drink this – it'll ease the effects of take-off.'

Shoggu and the Kurassians had also been given cups. Tashi drank his quickly. It tasted very sweet. The sound of the engines throbbed in his head. He remembered what Shoggu had said about the noise pulling him. The world whirled; somewhere in his thoughts he believed he glimpsed blue sparks and monsters made of wind and fire, and he tried to tell Shoggu—

But all that happened was that his head hit the table.

C: The psychic shield around the monastery makes it
       difficult to be exact. But it seems this Watcher
       detected the first success, and the honourable man's
       ship, as well as the leak.

A: But not Scarab's involvement?

C: No. He believes a magician is involved, but seems to
       have no idea of our agent's identity.

A: Good. Does he know the location?

C: I think not. But I would need more time or resources
       to penetrate the shield and learn that for certain.

A: We cannot spare either. Keep a scry on him for
       now. If we need to take action, it should not prove
       problematic.

D: Eliminating him might bring attention from his
       colleagues.

A: Doubtful, with the other concerns recently thrust
       upon them.

C: Especially so, since they seem to have largely
       disowned him and disbelieved his warnings.

A: A weak old man, alone in a world he is unprepared for.
       If he comes close to interfering, he will be as mutton
       to the slaughter.

D: You can't slaughter mutton. It's the name of the meat.

A: Get on with your work.

10

MEANS OF PERSUASION

As soon as he'd got Orc and Cass out of the hotel's rear gate, Ranga raced up to their rooms and threw their possessions into their bags. He was almost back down at the bottom again when Captain Seriuz stepped across the foot of the stairs.

'Where are your companions?'

'Still up there.' Ranga pressed aside to let the officer pass, but Seriuz didn't move.

'Why are you carrying their bags?'

'We'll be leaving later. Thought I'd bring everything down.'

Seriuz glanced in the direction of the dining room. 'Mister Juneau!'

'What's the matter?' Seriuz's manner made Ranga nervous, but the captain clearly hadn't received the telegram: there was no sign of the constable. 'Listen, I had to give them bad news. Cass got upset. Orc's still comforting her.'

A younger officer had arrived. 'Mister Juneau,' said Seriuz, 'go up and find them.'

Juneau pushed past Ranga and ran up. Seriuz blocked the stairs again.

'Why are you keeping me against my will?' asked Ranga. When no reply came, he tried to squeeze past.

The punch shocked through his stomach. He dropped the bags and clutched the balustrade, doubled over in airless, lung-sucking agony. He'd only just found his breath when footsteps hurried along the corridor, and the constable arrived with his deputies and a third naval officer. At once the constable started jabbering to Seriuz about the telegram, and bombs, and disguises.

'This is timely confirmation,' said Seriuz, when the man at last paused. 'I sensed something suspicious about the divers, which is why I decided to keep them in sight.'

'Rubbish,' gasped Ranga, still half-winded.

Feet sounded above him. 'Empty,' Juneau called down.

Seriuz glared at Ranga. 'Where are they?'

'I don't know,' said Ranga. 'Could they have gone out of the window?'

He flinched as Seriuz clenched his fist again, but the captain held the blow in check. 'I wish only to clear up this business of the telegram,' Seriuz said, coldly polite. 'You must see how hiding incriminates them?'

'If they're not up there, I've no idea,' said Ranga. 'Honest.'

Seriuz turned to the deputies. 'Check the rear entrance. If you can't see them, search the town.'

'With only two men, your honour?' said the constable.

'The coast road, then – both directions. Do you need me to tell you even how to pick your nose?'

The deputies looked sullenly to their chief.

'Go!' commanded Seriuz.

The constable nodded; the men departed. Ranga looked for an opening, but Seriuz and the other officer covered every gap.

'How far to your gaol?' Seriuz asked the constable.

'A minute's walk, your honour.'

'We'll question him there. I wouldn't abuse the Maratts' hospitality by getting blood on their furnishings.'

Ranga hoped that had just been meant to scare him. As the constable handcuffed his wrists behind him, it started to work.

He protested his innocence all the way to the gaol: enough to appear genuine, he hoped, but not so much as to annoy his captors. They paid no attention. Seriuz seemed quietly angry, and there was a nasty look about the moustached officer, Lyle. Ranga kept trying to catch the eye of Juneau, no older than himself and with a more pleasant face. But Juneau maintained a determined expression, and wouldn't meet his gaze.

Whatever happened, Ranga told himself, he could not reveal the divers' location. Orc and Cass would be safe in the olive grove as long as he could hold out. To let Seriuz have them would mean betraying the task Vanessa had set him, and thus betraying her. And that was unthinkable. He'd survived the beatings his half-Thangkaran parentage had earned him in adolescence; he could get through this. He steeled his mind with thoughts of Vanessa's anger if he gave in, on her praise if he held out: her cool hand on his bruises, the revenge she would wreak on his behalf. Not even Captain bloody Seriuz would be spared that.

The gaol was small and dim, humming with flies and the smell of old urine. Pushed through the door, Ranga tripped and crashed to his already grazed knees, then forward onto his chest and the left side of his forehead, his bound arms unable to break his fall.

'Careless,' said Lyle. They hauled him up. His head whined with pain; his knees felt as though spikes had been driven into them.

'I don't know where they are!' he pleaded, as the constable undid his handcuffs. Lyle thrust him into a chair. The constable produced a second pair of cuffs and attached Ranga's wrists separately to the chair arms. Steel bit into raw skin.

'Give Mister Lyle your baton,' Seriuz told the constable. 'Then go outside with Mister Juneau.'

He shut the door after them. Lyle took off his uniform tunic.

'This is insane!' said Ranga. 'Is this what a national hero does to innocent civilians? The newssheets would love this.'

'Would I be a hero to the families of those killed if I failed to prevent a bomb outrage?' said Seriuz. 'Are *they* not innocent?'

Lyle tapped the baton against the edge of the desk, as though to test its weight.

'There won't *be* a bomb outrage!' Ranga felt sick. 'I've been with Orc and Cass for months. There's a man here, Gregal. He can confirm it. We've met him three times.'

'An accomplice?'

'No!'

'Let me hear that from the Strandborns' own mouths,' said Seriuz. 'How can I believe in their innocence when they've run away? You see that, surely?'

'I don't *know* where they are…'

Seriuz nodded, and Lyle advanced.

In panic, Ranga tried to fend Lyle off by kicking. The chair tilted, its feet clattering against the flagstones. A half-smile curled the First Officer's mouth. He didn't strike Ranga's legs; he toyed with him, feinting blows that Ranga tried desperately to block, the cuffs all the time nagging deeper into his wrists. Fatigue ripped at his thighs; only fear kept them up. Then Lyle tricked an opening and the baton's tip smashed into Ranga's hastily tightened stomach, leaving him folded and groaning and fighting to work his lungs, to not die.

'Why do you make this necessary?' said Seriuz, as Lyle stepped back like a fencer after a point.

'Because I don't *know*…'

'If they're as innocent as you say, why not let me talk to them? I'm a reasonable man. I'm not out to hang them on the basis of intelligence that might easily be mistaken.'

Ranga shook his head. 'How many times do I have to tell you?'

'And how many times do I have to ask?' Seriuz nodded to Lyle.

This time, Ranga's legs were tired before they began. He pleaded for mercy throughout his attempts to fend off the blow; he hated himself for it, but he couldn't help it. The expectation of pain was with him all through the build-up, and when it came it was even worse than before. It took all his remaining strength, all his hate, to not cry.

'She'll kill you for this,' he seethed, when he could speak again.

Seriuz snorted. 'Cass?'

Ranga coughed up a laugh. 'You've no idea. She'll make you sorry.'

Seriuz drew Lyle to a corner. The two men talked low, sometimes glancing Ranga's way. Ranga tried to breathe, to recover, but the pain of the blows wouldn't fade, and for all his words Vanessa was hundreds of miles away. He started to wonder if it would be so terrible for the navy to question the divers. Even if they took them to Torrento for interrogation, Orc and Cass were innocent; they couldn't be held long.

But Orc had seemed worried about arrest. Maybe they *were* guilty of something. When he'd found them in that seedy backstreet hotel in Torrento, they'd been wary of the authorities.

He couldn't risk losing them. But to suffer all this, for what might be nothing…

The officers returned from their corner.

'This "she",' said Seriuz. 'Someone you're fond of?'

'That's none of your business,' said Ranga. 'Until she makes it so.'

Seriuz fingered his scarred cheek. 'I was once what you might call a ladies' man. Disfigurement tends to curtail that.'

Lyle tapped the baton against his palm. 'Teeth is it, sir? Or nose?'

'You can't!' shrieked Ranga.

'Your choice, Mister Lyle.'

'The nose first, then.' Lyle looked at Ranga. 'I'll let you decide – to the left or the right?'

'Don't!' The thought of the pain, and Vanessa's reaction, her disappointment, her turning away. 'Please!'

'You can easily stop him,' said Seriuz.

Lyle hit the baton against the desk. The sound cracked through the room. The officer stepped forward, his eyes holding Ranga's as though calculating the speed and angle and force of the blow.

'Wait!'

The baton swung back.

'Hill!' The cry ripped out of him. 'Up the hill…'

He sagged. Lyle grunted. 'Thank you,' said Seriuz. 'Now where exactly—' He cut off at a knock.

Daylight flared as he opened the door. The constable and Juneau had been joined by a panting boy in a post-office cap. The constable handed Seriuz a folded paper.

Seriuz read it, and swore.

'Run to my ship,' he told the boy. 'Fast as you can. Tell them full steam on one and two and make ready, understand? Go!'

The boy fled.

'Come,' said Seriuz to Lyle.

'Your honour,' the constable said, 'what about him?'

'Do whatever you like,' called Seriuz.

Ranga tensed as the constable closed the door, half-fearing things had got even worse. He held the constable's gaze, hoping the man was the kind who enjoyed a quiet life rather than the kind who liked giving defenceless outsiders a good kicking.

The constable eyed him back, as though pondering the same thing, then huffed. 'Arrogant sons of bitches, eh, those navy boys?' He pulled a book from a shelf.

Ranga didn't dare answer, fearing a trap.

The constable sat at his desk and picked up a pen. 'Name and address. Then clear off.'

Still doubting his seeming luck, Ranga gave the same fictitious details as when he'd registered at the Bull. The constable transcribed them, letter by letter. At last he unlocked the handcuffs, and showed Ranga the ledger to confirm. Ranga feigned interest, nodded. Then the previous entry in the log caught his eye.

'Alonso Gregal?' He read across. 'Burglary…'

'Another waste of my time,' said the constable. 'Nothing taken, but Mother Aralla insisted I make a record. You tourists are more trouble than you're worth.'

No one answered Ranga's calls in the olive grove. By his twentieth attempt, he was seething with frustration, his temper worsened by his catalogue of pains and the knowledge of how close he'd come to betraying Vanessa. Where *were* the bloody divers? His instructions had been clear, and Cass especially was too smart to disobey them. And they wouldn't leave him by choice – they needed his map.

He checked his pocket-watch. An hour since he'd seen them. If they'd given him up for lost, where would they go?

He left the grove, deep in anxious thought. As he did so, a *boom* came faint over distance. *Nightfire*'s gun, he assumed, something to do with whatever emergency had taken Seriuz off.

The thought brought him up like a wall.

Why had Seriuz let him go without learning the divers' location? Why not order him detained until he could return? Because the subject of the telegram overrode any interest in possible bomb-setters? Or...

He ran eastwards, along the grove's edge. Reaching a high point on the coast road, he saw above the sea in the middle distance two trails of smoke – one from a ship that could only be *Nightfire*, another from something on the water.

His teeth knifed his lip. *Nightfire* was near the ziggurat, Seriuz had let him go, Orc and Cass had disappeared. No sensible explanation could connect those facts, and yet...

'How?' he shouted. '*How?*'

He stared, and stared, as though his eyes might wring the truth from the distant ship, until he realised *Nightfire* was moving – away.

He ran down to the harbour, along the mole, onto the jetty. None of those staring towards the fading smoke wanted to talk. Word of his arrest had got out, he guessed, and the bloodied state of him didn't help. Only after repeatedly explaining that he'd been released without charge did he learn that Seriuz and his officers had rushed back to the ship half an hour before. *Nightfire* had put to sea even before it had built up enough steam to move fast. There had been no sign, and no mention, of his 'friends'.

The warship's smoke receded further. The accordionist packed up; people drifted away until Ranga alone paced the jetty, willing *Nightfire* to turn back.

'Ranga?'

He turned. 'Oh—' He almost called her *my Lady*. 'Zina.'

'What happened?'

Even in sunlight, there was something about her face: the strength of her nose and bones, the dark hair that fell to her shoulders. Her eyes were too soft; she was still a serving girl. But she was close. Only the harbourmaster's secretary in Arguse had been closer.

'This?' Ranga touched his head: the graze was still raw. 'Captain Scar-face happened.'

'Why did he do such a thing?'

'He wanted my friends.' Thinking it might not be sensible for Zina to be seen talking to him, he glanced back towards the town, but the heaped rocks of the mole concealed them from all but the top floors of the harbour-front buildings. 'You know about the telegram?'

She nodded.

'I heard your father talking about it,' he said. 'I jumped from the window. My friends aren't bomb-setters; the whole thing's stupid. And weird,' he added, thinking of Seriuz's behaviour on the hotel stairs. 'It's almost like he was waiting to arrest them *before* the constable turned up. And then he got another telegram, and he rushed off. Wish I knew what was in it.'

'Truly?' Zina said. 'What would you give for such knowledge?'

'Why? Can you get it?'

'I know the man who works the machine. He'll tell me, if I ask him. But I'll only repeat it back at the olive grove.'

Her smile gave away her meaning. Ranga groaned inside. 'Last night was last night.'

'And today is today,' she said. 'Some say woman is the night and man is the day. I found my pleasure last night; now you can find yours.'

'I don't need repayment, not in that way.'

'It's not "repayment", stupid,' she said. 'You're strange, to give pleasure and take none. Is it because you were disappointed?'

'No, you were beautiful. Are,' he corrected himself. This was why it was never a good idea to see them after the night was over. He'd only stayed in her bed that morning because she'd been at work downstairs. 'It's a vow I've taken.'

'If I truly am a goddess, then you're mine to command,' she said. 'Or did you call me that in fun?'

He sighed. 'No. Not in fun.'

'Then meet me at the grove.' She half-turned. 'And we'll see what offerings you make for my divine wisdom.'

A game, thought Ranga, as she departed. Bored as she must be in this small town, it was hardly surprising. The smoke from *Nightfire* had almost disappeared. He wanted to scream with frustration.

He washed off his dried blood at a water pump, then waited at the olive grove till Zina came. Her smile spoke of success. He pleaded with her, but she refused to reveal her knowledge until they resolved their night's extended foreplay. Ranga tried to excuse himself: his bruised ribs, his still-pained stomach, his vow. She scoffed at these; again she accused him of finding her unattractive. He called that stupid. She got sulky, so he held her, afraid of losing his goal, and holding turned to kissing, and shifting and groping; but when she tried to straddle him, he wouldn't let her. Not even his heart or his tongue were in it now, because it wasn't night and she wouldn't become its queen – and time was passing, minute after minute.

He brought her to a furious squirming. When she was done, he wiped his fingers on her skirt and said, 'Now tell me.'

'Fuck you,' she said. 'I'm not some virgin you can play like an accordion and get applause for it. Even a man who prefers other men could have done that.'

'I don't prefer other men.'

'I've seen nothing to convince me. Tell me of this "vow".'

'No. Tell me the message.'

'You infuriate me!' she said. 'It's the woman's role to be the mystery, but you play it better than any. You're not a man who prefers men – you're a woman who prefers women!'

That made him laugh, despite the stress. She joined in, and for that moment of shared laughter, he glimpsed another life he could have had. He pushed it away.

She sighed. 'Have it, then. It was about a bad harvest.'

'A what?'

'*Dire threat of harvest failure, stop, two miles one-ten degrees, stop, winnow chaff if possible, stop.*' She looked pleased to have memorised it so well.

'Harvest...' But it had sent Seriuz out to sea. Nothing made sense, but somehow he knew it confirmed his fear. 'He's got them.'

'Lucky him.' Zina brushed dust off her hip. 'That man you drank with, he got a telegram too.'

'Gregal?'

'Yesterday. *Seek company at evening and solitude at dawn, stop*: that's all. Arlan said he's never had so many messages.'

Ranga shook his head; he couldn't waste time thinking about Gregal now. His next move, in all its dread glory, was now obvious. 'I've got to go back and tell her.'

'Her?' said Zina. 'Why are you trembling? Is this your vow? Is she a higher goddess than me?'

'When's the Torrento packet?'

'Two this afternoon.'

Ranga took out his watch. 'I'd better get started.'

'If you're going, then go,' she said, and lay back with her forearm across her eyes. 'I'll come and visit you one day. This other goddess and I will make love together. Maybe that will interest your cock at last.'

Since he no longer had to eke out the proceeds from the cup, Ranga purchased a cabin ticket for the two-day voyage. If *Nightfire* were bound for Torrento too, as suggested by its last heading, then its speed might well lead to Seriuz arriving a full day before him, but that couldn't be helped.

Next stop was the hotel.

'I didn't think we'd be seeing you again.' Mrs Bull's tone suggested the surprise wasn't one she welcomed.

'As I'm getting tired of explaining,' said Ranga, 'I was *wrongly* arrested. Not a stain on my character. I've come to pay.'

Clearly dubious, she took out a ledger. Ranga counted out the forty-seven solidos she asked for. 'Now, if you could get someone to bring the bags?'

'Bags?' she said.

'Yes – when I was *wrongly* arrested, I was bringing all the bags down from the rooms. I had to leave them on the stairs.'

'The younger officer came for them.'

The bones left Ranga's legs. '*All* of them?'

Amusement began to rework her facial muscles. 'Yes, all.'

'And he took them on the ship?'

'I've no idea where he took them.'

'But – that's theft!' His bag, with the fetishes. 'And you just *let* him, you stupid cow?'

Her eyes bulged. She called for the porter. Remembering the size of the man's arms, Ranga fled.

With only one solace left to him, he sat inside a dim waterfront tavern, and drank, and smoked, and wondered what he'd done to offend the multitude of gods surely responsible for such a fiasco of bad luck. And he contemplated what awaited in Torrento. Vanessa might not blame him for the loss of the divers; but for the loss of the things he'd kept against just such an eventuality, she undoubtedly would. Her anger might still be preferable to the months of absence he'd endured, but if she was so furious that she dismissed him forever, it would kill him.

He was halfway through his second beer when a cream-coloured jacket caught his eye, and he raised his head to see Gregal pass by outside. Ranga didn't know if he envied him. The archaeologist was also heading back to Torrento, but probably not to face a towering wrath. Rather than being in love with a magnificent beauty, Ranga imagined him married to a mouse-like servant. A peck on the cheek, and he would show her the silver cup. *That's nice, dear…*

His grip tightened on his beer. The *cup*.

Orc had handled it, had almost died fetching it. A strong relationship like that, even a negative one, might be something Vanessa could use.

He left money on the table and hurried out. He trailed Gregal at some distance, following him back from the harbour to a small, deserted courtyard in the angle between a house and its single-storey wing. Ranga recognised the place: one of the guesthouses he and the Strandborns had been turned away from before they'd tried the Bull.

Gregal unlocked a door in the converted outbuilding and went in. After checking for observers, Ranga stole across the courtyard. The man hadn't locked the door after him.

Gregal turned at the sound of it opening. 'Oh!' Recognition softened his expression, but only a little. 'What do you want?'

Ranga deployed a disarming smile as he entered the room. 'Just that cup back, Mister Gregal. I can't repay you straight away, but I can promise that when we reach Torrento, you'll get a higher price than you gave.'

'It's the museum's property now,' said Gregal. 'I'm not at liberty to sell it.'

'Then lend it. I'll pay a hundred sols to borrow it for a week.'

A surprised frown. 'I can't do that.'

'Two hundred, then!' said Ranga. 'Money for nothing! Keep the cash for yourself – no one would know.'

Gregal's face flushed. 'Our dealings are at an end, sir.'

That anyone would turn down so much for so little baffled Ranga. He'd never taken Gregal for a paragon of incorruptibility. But motives weren't his concern. He closed and bolted the door.

'What's this?' said Gregal, and took up a candlestick from the bedside table. 'A fine way to treat someone who helped you.'

'Last night you helped. Now you're obstructing. Where's the cup?'

Gregal's moustache quivered. 'I no longer have it. My room was burgled.'

'Yes, I heard about that.'

'Well, then.'

'The constable said nothing was taken.'

Gregal licked his lips. 'Ah... of course, I didn't tell him about the cup. All those unnecessary questions.'

Ranga stepped forward and snatched the candlestick from the man's hand. 'I know liars, Mister Gregal, and you're a poor one.'

'Search the room, then!' squeaked Gregal.

'I shall. Don't move.'

He went through the man's meagre luggage, then the cupboards. He even lifted the mattress. If Gregal had hidden the cup, he'd done it well.

'You see?' said Gregal. 'Now, we'll leave it at that. No need to let misunderstanding ruin a friendship, eh?'

Ranga nodded. 'My apologies. No hard feelings?'

He offered his hand. They shook. Ranga kept hold. Squeezed, till Gregal gasped.

'*Where*,' hissed Ranga, '*is the cup?*'

'I told you!' cried Gregal, then yelped as Ranga clamped the bones in his hand together. 'No! Ow! *Seriuz!*'

'What?' Ranga relaxed his grip in surprise, and Gregal pulled free.

'I gave it to one of his crew, first thing.'

'Gave it? Why?'

'Because I was told to.' Gregal sat on the bed and nursed his hand. 'And that's *all* I was told. If you want to know why he needs all that junk you fetched up, ask him.'

'*All* that junk?' Ranga thought he couldn't have heard right. 'You're not saying you gave him *everything* you bought from us?'

'No!' said Gregal. But his frightened look suggested otherwise, and truth dawned.

'You were here on purpose,' Ranga said as pieces slotted together. 'Last night, you got a telegram about seeking company. You didn't meet us by chance at all – nor the other times.'

'I'll say nothing more,' said Gregal. 'There are laws against battery, even here.'

'They didn't help me an hour ago.' Ranga stepped towards him. 'I've a beating I'm keen to repay, and I'm not fussy as to who.'

Gregal shrank back. 'You've seen I don't have the cup. Please, go.'

'Seriuz arrested my friends, and you know more than you're telling. Does he want them to get more artefacts? Is he some kind of mad collector?'

'All I know is that poking your nose into this is likely to get you killed,' said Gregal. 'These people are ruthless. Think how many died in those bomb outrages in the cities.'

'Bomb... what? What's *that* got to do with it?'

A sly look had come over Gregal's face, as though he thought he'd gained some kind of advantage. 'You haven't worked it out yet?'

'If you're trying to throw dust in my eyes...'

'Not at all,' said Gregal. 'I'm trying to make you see what you're getting yourself into. You set out with the plan of selling your finds to Kurassians on Grand Tour, correct?'

'Right.'

'But there *were* no tourists this summer. The outrages in Torrento and Saguna proved off-putting to the gentle citizens of the Empyreum.'

Ranga's breath caught at the implication. 'You can't be serious.'

'It's the only explanation that makes sense. Now do you see your danger?'

'You're saying Seriuz organised all those bombings so he could get hold of our finds easier?'

Gregal laughed. 'Seriuz? You think *he's* at the top of this?'

Ranga had the momentary sense of ground turning to deep mud beneath him. 'Who, then? Who sent you that telegram yesterday? And how did they know we had something to sell? Did the fisherman tell them?'

Gregal guffawed. 'The *fishermen*?' Then his eyes widened, his face blanked. 'Oh, gods!' he cried. 'I'll say no more. You made me talk.'

'Who's at the top? You can't clam up now.'

'You hurt me!' Sweat slicked Gregal's brow. 'I couldn't help it!'

'Someone must have recruited you. Someone with a face, a name?'

'No one!' Gregal curled on the bed, breathing heavily.

Ranga repeated the question with increasing vehemence, but to no avail. Something about the man's foetal position smothered thoughts of violence. Instead he went through Gregal's pockets. The man didn't resist, but only lay there, whining and trembling and muttering to various gods, as though ill – play-acting, Ranga assumed. Aside from a little money and a steamer ticket, all Ranga found was the telegram from the previous evening, and Zina had already told him what that said.

Except – he clapped his palm against his forehead. The stupid girl hadn't mentioned the boxes for recipient and sender. In the latter was written *Fusilli*.

'*Mrs* Fusilli?' He flapped the telegram at Gregal. 'From the museum?'

He'd got his ziggurat map from her. But maybe the name was a coincidence.

'Was it her? Answer and I'll go.'

Gregal lay still. Very still, eyes open.

Ranga prodded. A trickle of blood escaped Gregal's mouth.

He stepped back. His heart felt suddenly, horribly vulnerable. He put a hand against his chest. Breath came with effort.

He had the uncanny sense of being watched. In some deep nook or cranny of his mind, he thought he heard, faint and far-off, a peal of laughter.

11

TIME AND THE STARS

The shaft and its rusting ladder went down so deep, Orc thought he might almost have gone through the sea and into the earth beneath. The painted steel walls sweated, and dripped, and boomed to the pulsing of powerful, relentless machines, or the heartbeat of the world. At the bottom, a hatch was set into the floor.

Orc focused his imagination on pulling. Hinges groaned. Distant light from the top of the shaft glinted on water.

'The bilges,' said Otter.

'Great,' said Orc. 'Seriously?'

'You want to know, in you go.'

Orc fitted his dive mask, steeled himself, and dropped – into darkness and the buffeting of engine noise. Right away, he sensed trouble: his dark-eyes didn't work, and he was sinking, fast, away from the hatch and Otter's silhouette, and into a deep that was turbulent with the ship's churning screw-blades.

He jerked round as a long body slipped behind him, long and long and thicker than his own. Eel's size shocked him, but as she tapered into tail, he grabbed her top fin and held fast. She wrenched him through the water, thrashing, trying to throw him. Suspecting a test of some kind, he bent his will on keeping hold, on riding it out.

Then she doubled back on him and – *teeth*.

He flinched to one side and her head passed close by, jaws edged with razors. *Get out*, Orc told himself as he lost his hold on her. But she'd coiled round above him, cutting off the distant hatch opening. Still he sank, dragged down towards the pulsing whoosh and chop, faster.

'No!' His reality-voice seemed to come from miles away. 'Get out!' He couldn't find any sensation in his physical body. Eel curved back down towards him, wide-flexed jaws heading a train of muscle. He fought panic, focused – and there, a foot. He commanded it to move, tapped it against a solid floor. He twitched his calf, and his skin rubbed fabric: dry, real.

Grasping sensation, he tore himself out of his scape and opened his eyes to the cramped space of the officers' toilet.

He stood shakily and leaned on the basin. Sweat gleamed on his tattoo-masked face in the mirror. Remembering Geist's warnings against leaving the soulscape abruptly, he kept his awareness on his pounding heart and unsteady legs, grounding himself in his body before his mask faded.

When he'd recovered somewhat, he went up on deck. The sky was smudged with smoke, the sea churned with wake. He found Cass sitting by the hoisted gig; no one else was visible but a sailor on the gun-platform above the bridge. In the three hours since their rescue, they'd been left to themselves, their only orders to stay aft of the stacks.

'Hey,' said Orc.

She didn't even glance at him. 'Hey.'

'No good,' he said. 'Too much noise and vibration, I think. I'll have another go later.'

She said nothing, as though her desultory greeting had been enough to exhaust her.

'Cass, I'm sure it's not as bad as you thought.' He couldn't keep the tremble from his voice. 'I'm not saying you were being…' He thought better of *hysterical*. 'But a stain on the world? It must have been, you

147

know, stress. Hardly surprising.'

She stared towards the passing coast, but as though she saw nothing. Orc hoped her mood was caused by her blackout vision, because he could do something about that, perhaps – he just had to find the truth and prove her vision wrong. But if her mood was from having been tied up and thrown in the sea to die…

He sat three feet from her until her silence drove him back below deck.

He did try later that afternoon, but decided not to do a full scape, just talk to Otter. He used the officers' toilet again, behind the wardroom: it wasn't ideal, as he had to undergo the Little Death seated rather than on the floor, but at least he could lock himself in.

'Here again, bruv?' were Otter's first words. 'Ship's food giving you troubles?'

'I need to ask something,' said Orc. 'What happened this morning, in the bilges?'

'You didn't come back properly, that's what!' chittered Otter. 'Dangerous! Return with control or leave a piece of your soul – how could you forget that?'

'I didn't have a choice. Eel was different. Huge. She went for me.'

'Ah, but was she guarding something from you, or guarding you from something? That's the question.'

'How about answering it?'

'I'll tell you this much,' said Otter. 'Eel was big because it was dark down there: dark and deep. And the dark depths are where the Big Things lurk.'

'Big things, like big truths? Like what Cass saw?'

'Maybe so.'

'Ah!' said Orc, as an idea struck. 'If Cass really saw something to do with our pasts, was that because the Shroud's weaker? Is it worth trying again, even without the big stone?'

'Get me a juicy chunk of Eel from those depths, and it might be.'

'How, though? If she's always that big where the deepest truths are, how will I ever catch her?'

'I told you,' said Otter, 'she's big because it's dark down there. And what removes darkness?'

'Light,' said Orc, then gasped. 'Fire! And you're one of the Fire Stealers!'

Otter raised himself on his hind legs and bowed. 'And what did we steal, bruv, for your ungrateful kind? What is that fire? Sure, it's the flame you use to burn your sticks and cook your meat, but you can use its light *inside* you, too. Ill-u-min-ate...'

'So if I had light, it'd be less dark, therefore Eel would be smaller and I could catch her?'

'Yes, yes.'

'So how do I use that light?'

'Focus it.'

'Focus... like the stone?'

'Those stones can help, but your own mind would be better, if it wasn't all over the place. Who gave Eel those teeth?'

'What do you mean?'

Otter shook his whiskers. 'So much to learn. I like to help, but it's like babysitting a pup in a pool when we should be racing up waterfalls together.'

Orc tried not to feel deflated. 'Can you teach me to be better?'

'A Fire Stealer doesn't teach, they *is*.'

'So I need a real teacher? A human one?'

'Would help, bruv.'

Orc sighed. 'I don't know if I want another, after the last.'

'Ah,' said Otter. 'But you wouldn't have found me without him.'

Try to remember. Your first experience of the world: him. Even before the gunman and the girl, him: a short growth of beard flecked with grey, a face like a field of scored rock; and in the shade of his wide-brimmed hat, one eye narrowed at you, the other hidden behind a patch with a blue crystal lens. A year on, he would give you your own focus-stone, but at the moment of your waking it was just another weirdness to add to the others.

And then that journey, wearing his spare clothes. A whole afternoon climbing through the graveyard of crumbling trees, the uphill floor soft with rotting needles. Then the road east, away from the slowly spreading deadness that came ahead of the desert. Lands with little government, filled with hiding and thievery. On the road, people displaced by failed harvests: clothes pale with dust, like your borrowed clothes and the hair of the girl who shares the colour of your eyes, the shape of your face, your nose, your lips.

'Your sister?'

You wanted the similarity to be accidental, or simple ethnicity, to make unproblematic the way you felt about her. But there was that deep instinct that there might be more to it, and that feeling you didn't dare ignore.

And every night on that road, the question: what do you remember?

Geist could tell you nothing about yourselves, despite communing every day with a raven you couldn't see. Your memories had been hidden behind a shroud, he told you, and though he couldn't tell who by, he had an inkling who'd sent the gunman. Powerful forces were at work. Did the Kings Behind the World mean anything to you? Geist promised to take you where he could keep you safe from detection, but you could never leave without his permission. If his suspicions were correct, there were almost certainly agents in government who would want you and Cass dead. Coming to the attention of the authorities might be fatal.

At last, you reached Kymera: a name that meant nothing to you. There was no house to call home for long, only a succession of secluded farms owned by people Geist seemed to know from way back. He never told those farmers and woodsmen where he'd found you, though. Not in front of you, at least. Sometimes they stood you and Cass side by side and studied your faces as though trying to read something there.

You were fed, and clothed. And worked: basic labour, ploughing, forestry. In the evenings, Geist taught you geography and politics. Partly to educate, he said, partly in hope of stirring a memory. (Try to remember: who are you?) Sometimes he made you the centre of complex rituals in which he sent Raven to the Otherworld, to try to peck or break through the Shroud. And sometimes people arrived for lamplit meetings that lasted into the early hours and which you were never allowed to hear. You and Cass sneaked a couple of times to listen, but it was mostly about the tensions in Golgomera between the colonial powers, nothing about yourselves.

In the spring, Geist started trying to teach you to break through the Shroud yourselves. They were your memories, he said; perhaps only you could get them back. Breathing exercises, mind-calming, guided visualisations: nothing worked, but he kept you trying until late summer. Then he moved you to Amano's farm, eighty miles from Torrento. He said you would be there some time.

Strange things began to happen. You and Cass went to pump water; you were gone five minutes, but when you returned, the clocks showed an hour had passed. You saw Amano's wife Ellen pass behind a wagon; when she didn't emerge, you went to investigate, and couldn't find her. Later she said she'd been in the village at that time. You woke several times each night. Whose were the voices you heard in the walls as you came round?

Try to remember.

Cass had her own experiences. She told you once how she'd gone into the kitchen to find Amano and Ellen talking gibberish. When she spoke to them, they eyed her as though she were mad. Later, they told her it was she who'd been talking nonsense.

You both asked Geist if the place might be haunted. He investigated, but found nothing. Maybe the strain, a year of not knowing. Who are you? 'Will we ever find out?' Cass asked. You told her yes. 'I hate it here,' she said. 'I'm starting to feel like I don't even know what's real any more.' But there was nowhere else to go, nowhere safe to run to, and you still hoped the exercises with Geist would come through, so you held her tight – brotherly tight, but aware of the delicious, maybe forbidden warmth of her, and said, 'I'm real, Cass.' And she held you tighter. 'You feel it,' she said.

Who? Try.

Geist kept teaching you. The strangeness got worse. Other strains emerged. Sometimes you caught Amano sneaking glances at Cass, glances you didn't like. Geist, too? You would interrupt the two men as they talked together in low voices, and they'd clam up, looking embarrassed. Maybe the voices in the walls were the memories of their conversations, but you could never catch them. At breakfast one morning, Ellen said the father of a friend in the village had died, and you remembered that you'd dreamed someone saying the same thing. You found a dead goat in the woods, but when you went back with Amano it was nowhere to be seen. 'Wolf must've taken it,' he said, But there was no blood. Maybe you'd mislaid the location.

Mislaid.

The strain. Try to remember. But at least you were real. 'I'm real, Cass.' And so was she. But without a name, without a past.

Maybe it was all trying to tell you something.

Maybe you knew no past because there was no past. Maybe it was all a clue, the things you saw from the corner of your eye, faces watching you that turned out to be knots in wood, the impossible things that were gone when you blinked.

You were the one that broke, but Cass was the one who first showed cracks. That day, the constable from the village had come, covered in blood. You and Cass watched through a gap in the woodshed door, because no one from the village was supposed to see you. Heartbeats panicking; whispering to each other to keep proving you saw the same thing. The bloodied constable talked to Geist and Amano and Ellen and their workers as though he wasn't covered in blood, or as though it was normal for him to be covered in blood, you couldn't work out which. That evening, you asked. Amano laughed, perplexed.

'Blood?'

And Cass cried out and ran into the night. You ran after her. She ran to the high field, where there was just enough light from the house and the stars to see. She let you catch her then. She held you like she was drowning and you were the only thing that could keep her afloat.

'I'm real, Cass.'

Try to remember. Remember why you have no past. The world was only a year old. God put the fossils in the rocks.

Remember the stars. Cass in your arms, you lifted your face and the world shuddered beneath your unstable feet. The light of the stars had taken years or hundreds or thousands of years to reach you as you stood in the high field with Cass in your arms. The light from each star had taken a different length of time, but they had all arrived at the same moment. The impossibility of that precision, the giant clockwork of the universe, and you in its centre, under the scrutiny of all those stars, the scrutiny which had been set in motion hundreds or thousands of years before.

The giant clockwork. Wheels and wheels within wheels, the wheel of the sky and the earth under you and Cass in your arms and you her support, her pivot. Wheeling, the sky and the earth and Time. Stars waited millennia to watch you. You became too aware, more aware than you wanted, of Cass, her body, her skeleton, the transience of it. In the length of time the stars had waited to watch you, it was nothing. You couldn't save her. It was as though your perception had jumped the tiny distance of a hundred years and she was already dead. Her warmth, her bones, the solidity of her, they were all there; but you could detect nothing by holding her that was life, nothing that was Cass, only her skeleton and the muscles that attached to the bones and the skin that covered everything. Not life, not her. Not real.

You were made of ice and starlight and fake warmth. Your mind was clockwork.

It broke. A week later, Geist found you slumped in your room, crying. For days you'd been drawing circles everywhere, circles filled with other circles and shapes, wheels within wheels. Cass had grown scared of you. She'd gone to Geist for help.

Geist said, 'It's time.'

Try not to remember this. Two weeks shut in a dark cave in the hills. No food, only strange-tasting water. It could have been a million years, the life of starlight. It didn't stay dark forever. You saw things – try not to remember. Gods and monsters made real, too vivid next to the pale memories you tried to hold onto. Things came to kill you, and you didn't know if they had, nor how long ago, nor how many times.

When your famished body had been eaten and shed as tears by the greatest monster, all became stars. You saw the wheel of the stars, and they formed the pattern you'd been trying to draw since you were born: the serpents' dance of the great wheel of stars and the great wheel of earth that was one and the same. The serpents' dance of the great wheel of life and the great wheel of death that was one and the same. The serpents' dance of the great wheel of You and the great wheel of All that was one and the same.

It offered to dissolve you, to release you from pain and into the beautiful pattern that held everything in One. Refusal would mean endless fear in the endless cold dark. It would not let you choose such misery. You would dissolve.

But something in you did refuse. As you were dissolving, something inside you said:

'Help me.'

And amidst the great wheeling of everything, in the centre of the pattern whose understanding dissolved your self, you saw a light that wasn't a star. A warm light, not pale pink or blue or silver, but yellow and red. It grew, and became two flames, one a mirror of the other. You focused on them. They focused you in turn, and you didn't dissolve. As they grew closer, clearer, you saw the flames were those of a burning brand and its rippled reflection in water.

A brand carried in the jaws of a swimming animal.

There was no sign of Cass when Orc went back up on deck. At once, his mind jumped to worry. No one was in sight apart from the crewman on the gun-platform. If Cass had fallen overboard, who would have seen?

Or, if her emotions had been even darker than he'd thought…

No, don't even. But when he checked Seriuz's cabin, she wasn't there either, though two bags had been placed on the bed – his and Ranga's, he realised with surprise.

Despite the instruction to stay aft, he went forward to the bridge. Seriuz's frown registered the disobedience. 'Mister Strandborn?'

'I can't find Cass.'

'I put her in the cabin next to mine,' said Seriuz. 'We'll leave the Shallow Sea overnight – the Southern Ocean can be rough, and *Nightfire* uncomfortable for those unused to her. I thought your cousin should get some sleep now.'

'Fine.' Orc turned.

'You're not planning to disturb her, I trust?' said Seriuz.

'The cabin she's in. Just one bed?'

'Two berths.'

'Then I might get some sleep too.'

'Your cabin is opposite hers,' said Seriuz. 'You can fetch your luggage from mine.'

'It's okay, we'll share.'

'You normally share a room with your female cousin?'

'She's in a bad way,' said Orc, 'if you hadn't noticed. I don't think she should be alone.'

'You've already left her alone in the past few hours, and for long stretches.'

Orc fought anger at the dig – he'd been trying to help – but there was nothing to say.

'If she wishes to see you when she wakes, she can find you,' said Seriuz. 'From tomorrow, she won't be alone in any case.'

'Meaning what?'

'That cabin is assigned to an engineering officer, Thera Malchis. She'll board again at Torrento. And there won't be a spare bunk in your cabin, because we're also taking on a civilian. The only sensible arrangement is for the two women to share, and for the civilian to berth with you.'

Orc sucked his teeth. 'We're staying on board? Aren't we meant to be clearing propellers and so on?'

'Not every incident will happen in Torrento Grand Harbour,' said

Seriuz. 'Our speed puts us in an ideal position to attend vessels in difficulty: that's what I'll propose to the Naval Board when I discuss your terms of commission.'

Orc's stomach sank.

'Don't let the cramped quarters put you off,' said Juneau. 'It's a privilege to crew this ship. The captain has his pick: everyone wants to serve under him.'

Seriuz cleared his throat. 'I believe you'll find it's *Nightfire* herself that's the draw.'

'And not only members of the Republican Navy,' said Lyle, staring at Orc. 'We've become very skilled at winkling out Empyreal spies since the fleet review. And dealing with them.'

'I'm not a spy,' said Orc.

'No? Yet here you are, wandering into areas you've been told to keep out of.'

Orc rolled his eyes, but turned to go.

'One last thing,' said Seriuz. 'I ascertained that your cousin did hear gunshots this morning, and that you told her they were warnings. I told her we destroyed the fishing boat and fired a few rounds to frighten its occupants into swimming. You'd agree, I trust, that nothing would be gained by contradicting that story?'

'What about Esteban? Did you tell her he's on board?'

'No. Nor will she find out. Until I decide what to do with him, he'll be held in the forward crew area, not given the run of the ship. On which subject…'

'Okay, okay,' said Orc. 'I'm leaving. Sir!'

He walked back aft, his gut prickling with worry. As if he didn't have enough on his plate, Seriuz had added to it by reminding him about the commission proposal. Agreeing to work for him had avoided a police investigation, but recruitment papers bearing their descriptions and skills might also get noticed by agents of the Kings Behind the World, if Geist had correctly estimated their power and the extent of their infiltration.

It was impossible to know, that was the trouble. But he had to trust

Geist's warnings. The dead hand clutching the revolver had been real enough.

No noise came from Cass's new quarters, disappointingly: he'd wanted a reason to check on her. Seriuz had been right, they'd always taken separate rooms where possible. But this separation felt imposed, and wrong. Entering Seriuz's cabin, he suppressed the urge to vent his hurt on the lock of the painted cabinet. At least when he and Cass were recruited, they'd be able to study the charts he felt sure were within. When they'd learned the island's location, they could escape. Or desert, as he supposed it would be.

Before taking his own bag from Seriuz's bed, he searched Ranga's, since there was no chance now of being found out. Apart from clothes, there was a bag of toiletries and some books, most of poetry. An Empyrean prayer-book with a metal hasp felt oddly light for its size. He unfastened and opened it.

And frowned. The block of pages had been hollowed out, and the space housed two small bundles wrapped in tissue. The larger contained a mass of golden strands.

'What the...?' A memory made him cringe: Cass having her hair cut short, just after they'd started their trip with Ranga.

But Ranga had never shown any real interest in Cass.

Never *shown* any...

Disturbed, but thinking this might at least provide an excuse to knock on Cass's door, Orc unwrapped the second tissue. Its contents looked similar, but the strands were shorter, and with hard, pale crescents mixed in.

Nail cuttings – one from a big toenail, cut across its width in one piece.

He swallowed. Cass's nails weren't that size. But his own...

He scrunched up the tissue bundles and stuffed everything back. Ranga keeping Cass's hair out of secret infatuation might have been something to laugh about with her; but this... this could only be magic, witchcraft.

On deck, he waited until the sailor on the gun-platform was

looking forward, then hurled Ranga's bag over the side. At least one positive thing had come from this horrendous day. Ranga was out of their lives for good.

12

IMPURE

Tashi's head throbbed with the rattling and roaring; his body bumped and jolted. After a moment's confusion, memory returned – the air-craft. They were in flight!

Then a horse's hooves sounded nearby, quickly passing. And wheels, shouts, cries.

His newly opened eyes found only darkness edged with faint light. He lay on a padded leather bench, facing the angle between seat and back. Before he could decide to move, the Prelate spoke behind him.

'It's the women you'll have to watch out for.'

Tashi had barely begun to consider what possible response he could make, when Shoggu's voice came from beside the Prelate. 'I have every faith in him, your Grace.'

'The parents of our young gentlemen doubtless feel the same,' the Prelate said. 'Even so, many who travel there lose their moral path for years. It's imperative we overturn what passes for Kymera's religion, but most women there stubbornly refuse to take the Holy Mother as their example. Too close to Golgomera, of course – one can practically smell the odour of the Witch wafting up from the foetid south.'

Tashi felt disturbed, not just by the Prelate's words but by the realisation that he was in an auto-carriage; and that, together with the terrifying volume of humanity suggested by the noise, meant they were in Bismark.

The lower world. Halfway to Hell.

'But the Charter will be observed there, your Grace?' said Shoggu.

'Even if anyone remembers it, it will have no official force,' said the Prelate. 'Kymera is a Protected Ally, not a Dominion. What do your investigations concern?'

'I believe there are magicians engaged in reviving Zhenaii practice.'

'Zhenaii? Truly?' The Prelate might have been either disbelieving or intrigued, Tashi couldn't tell. 'What manner of practice?'

'I'd rather say no more just yet. I hope to be proved wrong.'

An engine roared nearby, followed by cursing from what must have been the auto-carriage's driver in the front. Tashi tried to summon the courage to show he'd woken, to confront this new world that smelt of burnt metal and soot and whose air was too thick.

'I shall give you a letter,' said the Prelate, 'emphasising my support for your mission. If nothing else, it should gain you some assistance from our naval force in Torrento.'

'That's very generous, your Grace.'

'In return, you'll report to me here before returning to Highcloud. If you can capture one or more of the malefactors for questioning, so much the better – I wouldn't want to remain ignorant of any such activities within the Empyreum's sphere of influence. Agreed?'

'Just so, your Grace,' said Shoggu.

Tashi had by now steeled himself. He moved his shoulders, and sighed.

'You're sure he won't panic?' said the Prelate.

'He will not,' said Shoggu.

Tashi pushed himself into a seated position. Darkness and light and movement assailed him through all the windows of the auto-carriage's compartment. His bench-seat faced rearwards; Shoggu and the Prelate sat either end of the seat opposite. Both watched him intently.

'This is Bismark,' said Shoggu. 'Nothing to fear.'

'I am not afraid, master.'

But he was. *It is the flesh that fears*, he reminded himself, but it was not his flesh that felt under threat from the harsh lights he knew must be electric, their wheel-shattered reflections in the rain-wet road, the horses and carriages, some vehicles twice as high as a man. The city was so much greater and more terrifying than the impression he'd gained from the books in Highcloud's library.

'I almost envy him,' said the Prelate, 'seeing it for the first time. And you, monk? You said you've visited Bismark before – does it still impress you?'

Tashi frowned: Shoggu hadn't mentioned any previous visit.

'Of all human endeavours, it is certainly one of the more remarkable.'

'Not merely human,' said the Prelate. 'Our Lord granted us the latest developments in electrical generation and distribution, and the principles that power the new air-craft.'

'Ah...'

'It might not have occurred to your Abbot that our advance has surely been too rapid for mortal ingenuity alone. You should mention that to him before he decides how to answer the Valkensee's request.'

'I have my task to perform first, your Grace,' said Shoggu.

Endless-seeming, the streets passed, tall facades of buildings channelling the traffic like a gorge. Tashi couldn't see how everyone avoided each other. He seized on the reassuring regularity to the shapes of the buildings, and reminded himself that although this was the lower world, and over it stretched the shadows of King Serpent and the Witch Mother, the Kurassians still dwelt within the wider congregation of Gevurah, even if they had abandoned His name and believed a man to be His son.

But whether ordered or chaotic, the city's activity at this late hour puzzled him. Did no one sleep? Did the whole of the Empyreum's might rest on a population so stimulated by worship that they could never rest? Was this their own form of Inspiration?

The thought came as an unwelcome reminder.

Over the next couple of miles the streets grew wider and quieter, thoroughfares lined with large houses rather than the taller buildings of commerce and industry. Many of these were set back from the road, glimpsed between high railings and trees. At last the auto slewed through a gateway onto a wide space of gravel before a three-storey palace. As it halted, men came forward to open the passenger doors.

'Follow me.' The Prelate stepped out beneath an umbrella.

He led them through a succession of airy rooms in marble and dark wood and gold, drawing the curious gazes of men in high collars and neckties or in military dress. After he'd deflected several who wished to speak with him, the Prelate took Tashi and Shoggu up two flights of grand stairs and along a corridor to a pair of panelled doors with gilded handles.

'I'll have your luggage sent directly, and breakfast brought to you at seven.'

'We shall be fasting,' said Shoggu. 'Plain water will suffice.'

'There's as much as you can use within,' said the Prelate. 'We call it "plumbing". Be ready at nine; and naturally, tell no one about the demonstration.'

The room's décor bewildered Tashi. The bed looked more like a pillared shrine, and was large enough to sleep five or six. On examination, one of the two doors off the room led to a smaller bed-chamber – 'For a personal servant, I assume,' said Shoggu – and the other to a washroom whose walls supported a seeming maze of copper pipework. Shoggu showed Tashi how the hot and cold taps worked, and the raised latrine-pan whose contents could be flushed away by pulling a chain.

'Yet there is a room for a servant,' said Tashi. 'Why would one even be needed?'

'To fill the bath,' replied Shoggu.

'These people can't even make twisting motions with their own hands to make the water flow,' said Tashi. 'Master, let's not do this, what the Prelate wants. People who need servants to fill baths for them, when there isn't even water to be carried, they know nothing of Gevurah. They don't deserve to be shown His power.'

Shoggu looked away. 'I made a bargain.'

'Gevurah would not object to you breaking a bargain with these people.'

'It is not for you to tell me what Gevurah would object to,' said Shoggu. 'I made a promise. For better or worse, I made it.'

For worse, Tashi felt certain.

His pack arrived soon after, and he set about practical tasks. He didn't ask Shoggu whether he wanted to sleep in the big bed. Since Shoggu had become familiar with plumbing during his never-mentioned previous visit, it was possible he would, but Tashi didn't want that to be true.

The mattress was too big to move, so he took the one from the adjoining servant's chamber and laid it near the fire. He would rather have lit his own fire in the middle of the room, but there was no smoke-hole and it would only cause trouble. He divided the bedclothes, laying some by the door for himself to sleep on. Above the mantelshelf he fixed the scroll-painting of the Holy Mountain: Shoggu's own work, from when he had first become a Watcher. Tashi remembered how proud he'd felt when he and Aino had secretly compared their respective masters' scrolls, and Aino's crestfallen expression at the clear superiority of Shoggu's work.

But beautiful as the scroll was, it wasn't the real Mountain, which in mere hours had become many hundreds of miles away. Tashi felt the distance as though it were a knife cutting at the threads of his soul.

The fire had died to a friendly glow, but Tashi turned over and over, tangling in the blankets, throwing them off, piling them on again. Evidently Shoggu couldn't sleep either, or had been woken by Tashi's restlessness, for after a couple of hours he said, 'What is it, beloved one? You should rest before tomorrow. I don't believe our sleep on the air-craft was good sleep.'

'So he drugged you too, master?'

'Yes. It seems they keep that narcotic for passengers who become unnerved, but in our case he decided to pre-empt that. And yours was the stronger dose. He said afterwards he wanted no chance that you would wake and panic whilst the vehicle was in flight.'

'I would not have panicked.'

'As I told him.'

'I would have liked the time to think about what is coming.'

'You have it now,' said Shoggu. 'It sounds as though you have been using it.'

Tashi stared into the ember-softened darkness. 'Master, what if the Lords of Battle were called into a novitiate who was unworthy?'

'You are not unworthy,' said Shoggu, quiet but firm. 'You were chosen, and raised, for just this purpose. The Cliff of Voices proved you worthy.'

'But that wasn't Inspiration.'

'Not in itself. But you were accepted.'

'But can't a novitiate *become* unworthy? I lied to Yulenda. And I abandoned you in flight.'

'Your sins are small. The rite of purification shall cleanse you.'

'Will *they* see them as small?' said Tashi. 'The Lords of Battle are timeless. They are the same as when the first twenty-seven won their victory, but are we? Those novitiates needed no rituals; they did not need to be purified.'

'The manner by which the Lords came to those twenty-seven isn't known,' said Shoggu. 'The records were lost, or never made. Battle is a furnace in which new metals can be made, new alloys forged. It was afterwards felt that the bond that was formed in that heat should be cemented, so that in future the Lords might be called upon *before* things got so desperate.'

'And this is indeed one of those not-so-desperate times,' said Tashi. 'How can they not feel insulted when they are called just because a chief of a heretic church wishes to see their power? And if they are insulted, what will they *do* to me?'

He could hardly breathe. With every second of Shoggu's silence, he felt more certain that his master was trying to think of a way round the answer, *They will destroy you.*

'You must not doubt,' said Shoggu. 'You must have confidence and fervour. If you *feel* yourself unworthy…'

'What?'

Shoggu hesitated. 'There was one such case.'

'What happened?'

His master sighed. 'Put away such thoughts. We do not call the Lords merely to satisfy the Prelate, but because by that bargain we can pursue our task in the lower world, and that *is* the task for which the Watchers were constituted. The Lords will understand.'

Tashi wanted to feel reassured. But just as Shoggu had criticised him for claiming to know what Gevurah would object to, he doubted Shoggu could know what the *Elohim Gibor* would understand. It was not Shoggu's mind that their flame had touched years before.

Dawn found him already awake. He performed the rite of purification with complete mindfulness, determined no trace of his sins should remain. After the half-hour ritual, Shoggu helped him put on his bindings, then they waited in silence for the Prelate.

The theocrat arrived accompanied by two guards. 'Fascinating,' he said, looking Tashi over. 'I've seen him near-naked, and now dressed in a hundred leather belts. Are all those straps necessary?'

'They're to prevent the novitiate's body being damaged by the influx and exercise of divine strength, your Grace,' said Shoggu.

'Well, throw a blanket over him, he looks too strange. Has he a weapon?'

'Will he need one?' said Shoggu.

'Oh, we'll give him something to hack at: a log or such. Wouldn't be much of a demonstration otherwise.'

Tashi belted on his swords, *dughra* at his side and *clathma* at his back, before Shoggu draped a blanket round his shoulders. The Prelate led them out, two guards falling in behind them.

Following the Prelate along mostly empty corridors, Tashi tried to clear his mind of everything but the words of Inspiration, but found it difficult. The hundred-and-fifteen leather pieces of his bindings creaked beneath the blanket; they felt strange to move in, and the wide choke-collar at his throat made swallowing awkward. His under-suit of fine-knitted silk, worn to prevent chafing, was soon soaked with sweat. At first, the palace corridors were well-maintained, but several turnings and narrow staircases, both up and down, brought them to regions where paintwork and paper had been neglected, and the few works of art were dingy portraits in tarnished frames. Beyond a heavy double door, which the Prelate had to unlock, the walls were bare stone, and the lamps gas. 'Part of the old castle,' the Prelate said. 'It predates Our Lord, but not my family.'

He unbarred another, even weightier door, and led them out onto a circular sand-floored arena thirty yards across. Beyond the six-foot wooden wall that bordered the sand rose several tiers of seats. A roof sheltered the seating, but left the floor open to the overcast sky.

To Tashi's left, the wall was interrupted by a higher block: a kind of balcony for the most important audience members, he guessed. A faded coat of arms decorated its front. On the other side of the arena, a portcullis barred an opening.

'We have Mordograd the Lame to thank for this splendid space,' said the Prelate. 'He loved to hunt boar, and when he became too gout-ridden to go to the boar, he had them brought to him. He threw spears from the royal box while the sons of those who'd fallen foul of his temper tackled the beasts at ground level. It's only used for amateur dramatics now. I trust today's performance will be more interesting than Aunt Hilde's last verse romance. Wait here, I'll take my seat.' The bar slid heavily back across the door as he and the soldiers left.

Tashi wasn't familiar with the phrase *amateur dramatics*, but he'd sensed its meaning. The Prelate could hardly have chosen a place more insulting. He wanted to protest to Shoggu, but a novitiate was forbidden to speak between purification and the Inspiration ritual, in case an inadvertent lie made him sinful again.

'All will be well,' said Shoggu softly. 'Have no fear.'

The Prelate entered the raised box at its rear, and took his seat. 'Proceed.'

Shoggu lifted the blanket from Tashi's shoulders. 'Are you ready?'

Tashi nodded: a small lie, but perhaps it wouldn't count. His mouth was dust. He hoped his bindings were perfect. Of the twelve novitiates who had survived the battle against Konstantin, ten had been crippled by torn tendons and ligaments and muscles.

He fixed his gaze on the far side of the arena. Instead of the tiers of seating, he tried to see Tamfang, its towering ice ablaze with sunlight.

The effort Shoggu put into voicing the first question made clear both his age and his nerves. 'Who are you?'

'*Teshui Lanathara,*' Tashi replied, the name he had been given during the Rite of Acceptance.

Again came the question, and again his response, twenty times more.

'What do you seek?' said Shoggu.

'*The strength of the Lords of Battle, the many-in-one.*'

'What is your purpose?'

'*The defence of what is holy in the sight of Gevurah—*' And there it was, the lie, undeniable. As the words left his mouth, their wrongness struck him like a blow, a travesty made of his highest calling, a compromise when Gevurah did not compromise. It didn't matter that this was in service to a greater good. He and Shoggu should have refused and taken the consequences, or escaped, or fought their way out. He should halt this now. But it had gone too far, and perhaps it would be all right.

'Have you been cleansed?'

'*I have been cleansed.*' Except that his lie might have stained him once more.

'Have you been bound?'

'*I have been bound.*'

Shoggu took hold of the protruding strap of the choke-collar, just enough for Tashi to feel.

'What are your eyes?'

'*My eyes are vessels for the holy light of Gevurah.*'

'What is your heart?'

'*My heart is a vessel for the holy fire of Gevurah.*'

'What are your lungs?'

'My lungs are vessels for the holy breath of Gevurah.'

'What is your voice?'

'My voice is the vessel for the holy anger of Gevurah.'

'What are your limbs?'

'My limbs are vessels for the holy strength of Gevurah.'

'What is your sword?'

'My sword is the vessel for the holy justice of Gevurah!'

The collar tightened. Tashi breathed in hard past the obstruction.

'I am their vessel,' he said, emptying his lungs with the words. He breathed in hard again, and spoke the line again, and again, with mounting fervour and light-headedness: ten, twenty times, and when he'd breathed out for the twenty-first time Shoggu pulled the collar *tight*.

Tashi's lungs fought to inflate, to pull air past the choking strap. He could feel it coming, the world tunnelling into blackness, but behind sang the fire, the light on the mountain-top. They had not refused him, despite his lies. He tried to say 'Tighter' – he wanted Shoggu to pull with all his strength, so the severity of it might burn away the compromise.

He fell to his knees as blackness closed in, a roar in his ears. But it stopped just before oblivion. It pushed him to the edge of himself – and where his self had been was fire.

A bright, fierce light burned within him and behind him, like the rising sun on mountain snow. His own thought was faint; the light broke through and overwhelmed it. Trying to think for himself was like shouting into a storm.

The hold on his collar slackened. His body stood: it was no choice of his, and he could not have stopped it had he wanted to. He sensed the unrestricted potential of his muscles, waiting to be used. But not for his use.

His mouth opened.

'WHY ARE WE CALLED?'

The words tore his throat, spent his lungs; the voice filled the arena. Behind him, Shoggu whispered, 'Gevurah forgive me.'

The Prelate stood, gripping the edge of the box. 'My Lords,' he called down shakily. 'I welcome you.'

'WHY ARE WE CALLED?'

'As one servant of God to another – to others, rather – I crave your indulgence.'

'WHERE ARE THE ENEMIES OF WHAT IT HOLY?'

'I thought you might appreciate the chance to limber up, as it were.'

Bestial squeals and grunts came from behind the portcullis. Chains clanked. Through the opened gateway trotted two boars, tusks yellow and manes bristling, the hair on their flanks in places matted with blood.

'You cannot!' cried Shoggu. 'Your Grace, this is… recall them, I beg you.'

'Where is your faith, monk?' called the Prelate.

Tashi watched the boars as though they were no more than moving pictures. But his eyes were focused hard, and he sensed the intensity of attention, as well as the fire's disdain, its growing heat.

'WHERE ARE OUR ENEMIES?'

'I doubt these brutes will want to be friends,' said the Prelate. 'They've been somewhat provoked.'

The fire moved Tashi as though it had inhabited him all his life and knew every nerve, every sinew. He felt the binding straps both aiding and controlling movement as his arms drew the *clathma*'s steel weight with a smoothness he could never have managed unaided. From the edge of his own mind, he sensed the fire's connection to the even greater light behind, and through it to battles hundreds of miles and thousands of years apart, to all weapons, all warriors.

The boars were snuffling, grunting heavily in pain. One trotted a few paces towards Tashi.

The fire flared in readiness. It set him with his knees slightly bent, balanced on the balls of his feet. Tashi shared the fire's awareness, its assessment of the beast's weight and power, its sense of the other boar's position not far behind.

The first boar spurted forwards. The fire shifted Tashi's stance, calculated speed and momentum, raised his sword.

The boar's swerve took him by surprise – the beast dodged to one side and then flung itself forwards, trying to ram its head under his guard. But it did not surprise the fire. Tashi's perception blurred; muscles contracted in a violent contortion of movement, all reflex – his awareness lagged too far behind even to observe. Shock jarred up his arm.

Vision stabilised. The boar lay on its side, its spine severed halfway down its bristled back.

Again Tashi's muscles shocked into contraction – even as the second boar charged Shoggu's cowering form, the *clathma* hurtled through the air. The flat of its heavy blade crashed into the boar's head, knocking it aside. Squealing, the beast fell to one front knee as the weapon slid across the floor beyond.

The fire threw Tashi forward, propelling him three paces. Before he'd reached the boar, his hand had drawn the *dughra*. The boar surged back up, tusks lowered to meet him. As the beast rammed its head at him, Tashi's legs danced him aside; his arm whipped down.

The point of the *dughra* pierced the boar's eye, the thinner skull of the socket, the brain. The boar completed its head-butt against empty air, and collapsed.

Sand soaked red beneath the two animals. Shoggu remained on his rear, backed against the door. Tashi's lungs fought to channel enough air, his heart to channel enough blood.

'By God,' said the Prelate.

The fire placed Tashi's foot against the boar's head. His hands gripped the hilts of the *dughra* and grated it free of the skull.

'My Lords,' said the Prelate, his voice unsteady between hard breaths. 'You have blessed me with a vision of your true power. All doubt is purged from me.'

'THERE IS NO ENEMY HERE OF WHAT IS HOLY,' roared the fire and light through Tashi's mouth. 'WE HAVE BEEN FALSELY CALLED.'

'But might not an enemy also be fought with wisdom and

knowledge?' said the Prelate. 'It is said that the highest servants of God know all that passes in the mortal world. Might I, also His servant, be allowed to question you on some—'

'WE ARE NOT INVOKED TO GRANT KNOWLEDGE.' The fire behind the voice intensified. 'HE WHO CALLS US FALSELY IS THE ENEMY OF GEVURAH.'

The Prelate pointed. 'It was the monk!'

Tashi's arm flung the *dughra*. It stuck point-first in the centre of the painted crest on the royal box as the Prelate ducked out of sight.

The fire turned Tashi to face Shoggu, now prostrate. Tashi's arm picked up the *clathma*. As his body approached the Watcher, the fire strengthened further, hot with outrage at lies told, compromises made, ideals corrupted, separations inflicted.

'My Lords.' Shoggu's voice trembled. 'Forgive us, please. I know the calling was not – not ideal, but it was for the greater good. My mission. To prevent a greater sin. You must understand.'

Tashi's sword-arm extended. The tip of the *clathma* touched Shoggu's neck. Boar's blood ran down the blade's edge and dribbled down Shoggu's wrinkled skin. Tashi tried to focus all that remained of his mind, to fight his way into the fire and take control. But the fire's anger was too strong.

'My Lords!' begged Shoggu. 'I must live, to do Gevurah's work.'

Shoggu's grovelling terror burned him. Contempt scorched him.

'YOU ARE NOT WORTHY.'

'There is no one else! My Lords, I pray you, have mercy. Depart in peace from this novitiate. Return him to himself.'

'HE HAS NO SELF BUT WHAT YOU HAVE GIVEN HIM, AND YOU ARE A WRETCHED WEAKLING, A BARGAINER, A DECEIVER.'

'Beloved one—'

The sword raised. Tashi redoubled his fight, pushed into it everything he had left of himself. And the sword did not fall, and with the sickening knowledge that it had been meant only to terrify, to express contempt, Tashi turned away. The fire was gone, the bright light behind him extinguished. He fell to his knees with the overwhelming rush of exhaustion.

Then came the pain and the cramp, muscles burning with a thousand needles. He curled up, breath squeezing between gritted teeth, hissing and seething as tears of agony and shame stabbed at the backs of his eyes.

By midday, the pain had abated. He limped with his left leg, he'd pulled a muscle in his right shoulder and he ached all over, but it was bearable. Packed and ready, they awaited the Prelate. Shoggu had said little, and Tashi even less. He felt numbed, his mind as hurt as his body.

When the Prelate came, it was with the officer who'd accompanied him to Highcloud, and the sound of booted feet taking up position in the corridor spoke of other help the theocrat could call upon. Tashi fought to calm his emotions, but barely restrained himself.

'Very instructive,' the Prelate said. 'I see now how twenty-seven of you managed to defeat an army. A *small* army, equipped with swords and pikes.'

He handed Shoggu an envelope. 'The letter I promised. An auto will take you to the station. The Aldersburg train leaves in an hour. You'll change there for Torrento. I look forward to discussing your findings on your return.'

They had the auto's passenger compartment to themselves. Bismark was even busier during daylight, but Tashi found its apparent chaos affected him less. He felt almost as he had during battle, that his own self was not really involved, or as though the auto-carriage were stationary and pictures were being paraded past its windows. Perhaps, he thought, the mundane world would always seem insignificant now he had experienced the divine. But he didn't know how to feel about what had happened. He had fulfilled his highest function as a novitiate, and had survived; but the fact that his soul had not been destroyed for daring to call the Lords of Battle for such a trivial reason felt almost disappointing, as though the *Elohim Gibor* had revealed themselves to be less uncompromising, less holy, than he'd believed.

He almost hoped they would refuse to come again. But instinct told him a hook had been placed in his soul. Perhaps they would even come more readily now. Perhaps they *desired* a vessel, a means of expression in the world, imperfect as he was.

'Master…' It was the first time he'd spoken since embarking the auto. His dry throat still hurt from the strain of giving the Lords of Holy Battle a voice. 'When I said… what I said, about you. It wasn't me.'

'I know, beloved one,' said Shoggu. 'They are not renowned for their kindness.'

Tashi watched the Lower World go by. Within him, where the fire had spoken, was only ash.

Clairaudioscope transcript 14:33 23-8-336
Known voices: A,B,G

G: They now present a clear danger. Should we shroud all
    our activities to do with this project?

A: We cannot spare the energy. The monk acts alone. He is
    unlikely to divine Scarab's identity or involvement.

B: More likely than others, perhaps.

A: Meaning?

B: I have investigated this Watcher's history, to the
    extent possible. Some years ago, he was unknowingly
    exposed to the stolen key of the Orb of Archive.

A: This is the artist?

B: Indeed. It seems the exposure caused nightmares, and
    he has developed a preoccupation with validating the
    fears that arose from them.

A: This project is only tenuously linked with the
    Zhenaii. Connection with the Orb alone is unlikely
    to lead him anywhere.

G: Should we at least tell Scarab?

A: No. He should not be distracted.

13

DETECTIVE WORK

The *Dahlia* chugged at walking-pace up the busy mile of Torrento's Civic Harbour, past wharves and waterfront offices, through the noise of churning water and crane gears and stevedore cries. Passengers standing near Ranga at the steamer's railing chatted in the relaxed tones of those back from holiday. Ranga was on his third pack of cigarettes. He felt slightly sick as he looked towards the looming, fortress-topped Crag, on whose western slope lay Rosewater Street.

After four months, he was returning in failure. His only hope was that *Nightfire* would turn out to be moored in the Grand Harbour a mile to the east.

The moment the gangway was lowered, he cried excuses about a sick mother, shouldered aside the first-class passengers and raced for the docks exit. A half-mile struggle through traffic brought him to a turning onto the quiet road up to Castle Terrace, and after a stiff climb that aggravated his bruised ribs, he emerged onto the stretch of grass and wind-blasted shrubbery that bounded the foot of the fortress's southern wall. The place was deserted, apart from the two Empyreal marines stationed to enforce the ban on photography.

As he hurried across to the viewpoint, the landscape below opened up to him: first the fortified headlands either side of the Grand Harbour entrance two miles south, then the split into the East and West Deeps, the immense horseshoe of anchorage that bounded the promontory jutting out from the Crag. The sweat of his climb chilling in the sea-breeze, Ranga leaned against the safety railing and scanned the West Deep, home of the Republican Navy.

At first he saw only outdated cruisers and auxiliary vessels lying alongside the quays and pontoons on the inlet's western side. Then he spotted a low, slim warship at a mooring buoy close to the near-deserted eastern edge, and his breath released.

Not only was *Nightfire* in harbour, the sun-awnings spread over her gun-platform and rear deck suggested no plan to leave soon. And the ship's isolated mooring, meaning nobody could come or go except by tender, suggested a desire to keep something secret – or stop someone escaping. Not hard to guess who.

But finding the divers only got him so far. He couldn't rescue them himself, and the authorities wouldn't believe his tale of kidnap without more evidence. Thanks to the previous year's fleet review, Seriuz was as much a hero to his navy as to the public.

But there was one power to whom Seriuz was emphatically *not* a hero…

He turned his gaze to the great two-mile curve of the East Deep, leased home of the Empyreal Southern Ocean Fleet. There massed the structures of Kurassian naval industry and manpower: coaling cranes, dry docks, shipyards, the barrack-rows of Little Bismark, the military railway terminus. There hulked the almighty battleship *Empire's Peace*, and the only marginally smaller dreadnoughts *Iron Tiger* and *Prince Zellant*, and around them cruisers heavy and light, and monitors and torpedo-boat-destroyers and supply ships by the dozen. Hundreds of stacks and chimneys fumed into the sky above the yards.

The Empyreal Navy would welcome an excuse to seize *Nightfire*, Ranga felt sure, both in revenge for the humiliation of the fleet review, and to discover the famously secret source of the vessel's speed. And once they'd seized the ship, Orc and Cass would be released – and the bastard who'd had him beaten up and made him betray Vanessa would be disgraced forever.

The plan was foolproof, and Ranga was no fool. All he needed was a reason for the Kurassians to board Seriuz's ship. But first things first, he had to confirm his hunch about the divers. With a newly purchased notebook and pencil, he went to the West Deep dock gates, and claimed to be a reporter hoping to interview Seriuz. The guard told him to write to the captain personally: there was no hurry, he said, as *Nightfire* was due to rest in port for a week. When Ranga asked if the suspects had been taken off, the Bazantin bomb-setters he'd heard Seriuz had arrested, the guard was incredulous. There were no civilians on board, none had come off that he knew about, and in any case the navy didn't do police work.

'We've enough of our own,' he said. 'Now go away and let me get on with mine.'

Satisfied that Seriuz was indeed keeping Orc and Cass hidden even from the rest of his navy, Ranga retreated to the smoky but largely empty Powder Keg, the nearest pub to the dockyard entrance, and sat with a beer to plan his next step. The logical move would be to follow up Gregal's claims about the bomb attacks. If Seriuz was indeed involved in the murder of Kurassian tourists, the Empyreum would have every right to board his ship.

He pulled out the telegram and read it again. He remembered the blood dribbling from Gregal's mouth.

'Poking your nose into this is likely to get you killed.'

Perhaps the logical course wasn't best after all. Gregal's claims had been pretty wild, and he might easily have been mistaken about the bombings: it was something the man had deduced for himself rather than being told. And if Gregal *had* been mistaken, then the activities of Captain Seriuz along the coast of the Shallow Sea could well be a red herring and a waste of valuable time – Ranga needed to give the Kurassians a watertight reason to board *Nightfire*, and he couldn't see how the captain's obsession with bits of old silverware would link to an anti-Empyreal plot.

No, a convincing construction would be more useful than an irrelevant truth. But it had to be based on real evidence, something Seriuz had done, or said.

He rubbed the heels of his hands in his eyes, sick with weary anxiety, his brain fogged by lack of sleep on the *Dahlia*. Only a mile away lived the one person he could have relied on to figure a way out of his mess, but she was closed to him, and that knowledge made things worse. He needed a scheme so brilliant that rather than destroy him for losing the divers, Vanessa would marvel at his success in retrieving them.

The barman took his empty glass. 'Another, friend?'

'Why not?' said Ranga. 'Say, you know *Nightfire*? You ever get her crew in here?'

The barman grunted as he poured. 'Barely a penny out of them this time. Captain's keeping them on a short leash, maybe for punishment. What he forgets is, he punishes honest tradesmen too.'

'He ever come in here himself?'

'An officer like him, in here? No, there's a club. Or he'll have gone home to his wife. Or his mistress.'

'He has a mistress?'

'Need to have, wouldn't you say?' The barman topped off the pint. 'You know about his missus?'

'He rescued her, didn't he? And her kid?'

'She's in a wheelchair,' said the barman. 'And a man has needs, know what I mean?'

Oaf, thought Ranga, as he dug for loose change. 'His crew ever talk about him?'

'Not much. Strange bunch. What's your interest, anyway?'

Ranga put an excess of money on the counter, and leaned closer. 'I heard they're planning to strike another blow against Empyreal arrogance,' he said in a low voice. 'Like the fleet review last year. And I want to be there. I'm a reporter.'

'Is that right?' The barman looked him over more carefully, and his face hardened. 'Well, I've got a quote for you, stranger.'

'Hang on.' Ranga got out his notebook, readied his pencil as the barman leaned forward.

'Piss,' said the barman, 'off.'

Dawdling through the city afterwards, Ranga berated his own stupidity. Four months in fishing villages, talking only to those who'd barely even heard of school, had dulled his wits. Of course the barman wouldn't have confided rumours about Seriuz, not to him. He didn't look Kymeran, he looked Thangkaran, and even ignorant cretins like that barman knew Thangkara lay within the Empyreum. It was only natural he should be taken for an Empyreal spy.

So infuriating! – to be treated with mistrust in his home town when Seriuz, a kidnapper happy to have innocent bystanders beaten, was placed above suspicion. But even if Torrento *was* still his home town, Ranga felt he'd lost his footing here. The city had become a mixture of the familiar and the changed: the Bull Market was being knocked down; workmen were setting rails for electric trams in Unification Boulevard; the Empyrean Church in Maddoz Square had acquired a spire like a spearhead pointed at the sky. And even where the streets remained the same, Ranga felt subtly unused to them. When he'd last been here, he'd felt like someone close to the true centre of power, above the muddle of gods and governments. Now he couldn't get close to that centre of power for fear of her wrath. He was nobody, a man who'd slept the last two nights in his clothes and who made fuddle-headed gambits in clumsy bids for information.

Panic threatened him. He shouldn't have drunk that beer. He needed sharpening up.

He went down into a nearby sunken shrine to Enshamah, Lord of Replenishing Rains, and put his head under the flow from one of the stone pipes that stuck from the wall. Ignoring the giggles and comments of the women washing clothes at the tank, he let the headache of cold water burn away the drowsiness of beer and insomnia. Determined to keep his head under until he came up with an idea, he tried to think – how could he find dirt on Seriuz? Who would tell him, apparently an Empyreal citizen, anything that might implicate Seriuz as the Empyreum's enemy?

It was the state of the shrine that led him to it. Tilting his head to even out the discomfort, he noticed that Enshamah's statue had been broken from its pedestal, and now lay in a dusty corner of the sunken enclosure. Clearly no acolyte had attended in a while.

'People think gods are forever,' his father had once said, *'but they come and go like everything else.'*

The idea struck so fast, he had to rationalise it more slowly to ensure he'd grasped it. Though Thangkaran-born, his father refused to have anything to do with the worship of Gevurah, or even to discuss it, and had declared he would turn away any Thangkaran monk who came to the guesthouse. But from overhearing other Thangkaran guests, Ranga knew how firmly they held to their version of God, even though their land lay within the supposedly unified, Empyreus-worshipping empire.

And *that* would be his plan, his cover.

'Any deity listening, please accept my thanks,' he said, and removed his head from the torrent of icy pain.

'If you're that devout,' called one of the women at the tank, 'why not strip off and jump in here?'

Ranga bowed, his hair dripping. 'Ladies,' he said, 'I fear even *I* might prove slightly disappointing in a bath that cold.'

He walked from the enclosure smirking at their laughs and provocative calls. He was back.

After getting himself a Thangkaran-style haircut, he hiked across the city to his father's favourite menswear shop and bought a traditional collarless shirt. Thus transformed, and with a strong coffee inside him for good measure, he walked to the Holy Garden, where among the hundreds of minor shrines and statues stood an old stone bust, unidentified but looking something like Vanessa, at which he'd often poured out his devotion, or recited a poem he'd written.

'My Lady,' he said, kneeling, 'though I can't let you know of my failure, or even of my nearness to you, grant me your aid in righting my mistake. Make me worthy of you.'

He looked around – a few people at other shrines, but none looking his way – then dared to press his lips against the cold, lichen-covered stone.

'I wonder if you can help me.' He adopted his father's accent. 'I'm looking for articles on Captain Martin Seriuz.'

The library assistant's spectacles shrunk her slightly too-round eyes. Judging her look to be intrigued, Ranga deployed a smile.

'Anything in particular?' she said.

'I'll start with the famous fleet review, if I may?'

The young woman suggested he try the illustrated weeklies published at the time, and led him to the section. 'If they're not enough, I'll search the archive for you.'

Skimming the magazines at a desk, Ranga found the tone of the reporting matched his memory of the general mood – for though it galled him now, he too had enjoyed the nose-thumbing Seriuz had given the Empyreal Navy a year before. Along with his mother and sisters, he'd joined the crowd on the headland west of the harbour entrance, to view the warships spread over miles of sea – so distant that only those with spyglasses had been able to identify *Nightfire* when she appeared, or relate any idea what her captain was doing.

Precisely what Seriuz *had* been doing, embarrassing the cream of Empyreal sea-power with a demonstration of superior speed, had only become clear with that evening's newssheets. But as to *why* the captain had so decided to embarrass an official ally, those same newssheets seemed reluctant to even speculate.

'Did you find anything?' the assistant asked on his return.

'Afraid not.' Ranga glanced about him, as though fearing to be overheard, and leaned closer. 'I was hoping to learn why Seriuz acted as he did. But according to these, his comments only echoed the Admiralty's line. You know, "high spirits in accordance with the celebratory nature of the event".'

The girl stifled her laugh at his impersonation of one of the stuffy upper-class. But her eyes were suspicious. 'You think there might have been something else behind it?'

Ranga nodded seriously. The girl's mistrust sprang from the same source as the barman's, he guessed. But this time, he'd counted on it.

'It's hard to believe a man would risk his career because of "high spirits", even to restore his navy's fallen pride. There must have been some real passion in him, a burning fire in his heart. He has inspired so many others.' He loaded the words with sincerity. 'I wish to know what inspired him.'

The girl looked slightly taken aback. 'Forgive me, but I'm surprised anyone from so far away would be interested in such a local matter.'

'Not so "local" any more, Miss… it is "Miss"?' He smiled at her nod, as though at a stroke of good luck. 'Seriuz is much admired in my country. That's why I came to Torrento to study. In many ways Thangkara is very different to Kymera, but in one respect very similar.'

He glanced around again, then lowered his voice. 'Both are in danger of being swallowed, digested to form merely a part of the Empyreal body. Even our name for God is threatened by the Empyrean church, which claims He can have no name. To us, Seriuz has become a symbol of defiance against Empyreal bullying. We hope he might inspire a "Seriuz" of our own. Hence my presence here.'

'You mean… you…?'

A half-smile: gratitude for her belief in him, tempered by knowledge of the dangers ahead. 'If fate permits. My aim now is to write an article that can be published in my own country, if possible one that sets out the thoughts and story of Martin Seriuz.'

'I'm so glad you told me,' she said. 'When you started asking about him, I thought…'

'That I might be an Empyreal spy?'

'Well…'

'A pity the Kurassians didn't think so.' He tightened his stomach muscles and briefly lifted his shirt, exposing his ribs. The girl looked shocked, breathless. 'They gave me those bruises to warn me off,' Ranga said. 'But they can't put the brakes on the steam-train of freedom.'

He winced inside at the unconsidered metaphor, but the assistant only nodded earnestly, and Ranga knew he had her. Even those Kymerans who accepted the benefits of alliance with the Empyreum possessed a streak of romantic independence a mile wide.

'There is another event that might help you,' the assistant said. She went off for ten minutes, then came to his desk with several magazines and newspapers six years old. 'Have you heard of Lamurna?'

'No,' Ranga lied, doubting a true Thangkaran would have done.

'It's a port in Essaid,' she said, 'on the north coast of Near-Golgomera. But I'll let you read for yourself – I've put markers in the relevant pages.'

Ranga searched carefully for links with the fleet review. He'd been in Bismark at the time of the Lamurna Incident, and knew only those details he remembered from the single monthly magazine his mother had posted him. The background, though, was familiar enough. There had been Kymeran enclaves in the coastal cities of Essaid for centuries; but twenty years ago, Essaid's government had collapsed through tribal in-fighting, and Kymera, in an uncharacteristically expansionist move, had taken control, a move that led many Kymerans to settle there.

All was well until a Murmedon army spilled without warning from the Golgomeran interior and seized the capital, Lamurna. With other ports too weakly garrisoned to help, the city's governor sent a plea for aid, which Kymera answered with two heavy cruisers and a contingent of marines. The marines retook the city, but only captured the palace after *Resolute* had shelled it.

HEROISM AND TRAGEDY: KYMERA'S COLONIAL ADVENTURE IN FLAMES, ran the headline in the *Messenger*. Below was a photograph of *Resolute*'s gunnery officer, twenty-four-year-old Lieutenant Seriuz, carrying an injured woman from the smoking rubble, her dangling hand clutched by her young son.

Six months later, the same newssheet featured Seriuz's wedding to the woman: the governor's daughter, it transpired, whose parents and husband had died in the fighting. 'A rose from the ashes', the romance was called.

Ranga skimmed three versions of the story, increasingly frustrated.

'He's a true hero, clearly,' he said as he returned the papers. 'But I can't see how Lamurna might have led to his actions at the fleet review.' *Unless he just got a taste for public adoration.*

The assistant sucked a plump lower lip, then glanced around the room. 'There are things in the archives,' she said, hushed. 'Only… we can't show anyone.'

Ranga's nape prickled with excitement. He couldn't let her take fright now. He dared to take her hand, felt her stifled shock. So much depended on it, he wanted her to believe. The freedom of his whole country. 'I implore you…'

She nodded, then indicated a desk in a quiet corner. 'I'll bring them.'

She returned with a volume of maps, and stood over him as he turned its cover. Within were concealed loose sheets: handbills and pamphlets. EMPYREAN SPIRES RUN WITH THE BLOOD OF LAMURNA, read one headline. The accompanying text was no less incendiary:

> *The lengths to which Kurassia will go to crush opposition was made clear by the deaths of the Lamurna innocents. Our weak, toadying government maintained too small a garrison, and took too long to outfit the meagre rescue flotilla, under Empyreal pressure and in full knowledge that many citizens would die. The reason is clear. The Empyreum knew the population of Lamurna believed in freedom, and the Empyreum wished to stamp out that aspiration. While we cannot with certainty say that they incited the Murmedons, we know this: blood is on Empyreal hands, and on the Republic's. Restore the Prince!*

The pamphlet was signed *The League of Restoration*. So were they all, Ranga found as he flicked through. And in the most recent, he spotted something.

> *While we do not condone the murder of Kurassian tourists, we are wholly clear that the upstart government's puppying to the Empyreum*

is to blame. Had the Kurassians any sense of perspective, they might
find it ironic that in seeking to make our country a miniature copy of
their own, they have made it unsafe for themselves.

His chest tightened around his breath as he saw the implication. The monarchists had expressed support for the hotel bombings. If he could find some way to link *them* to Seriuz...

'This first pamphlet,' he said, 'talks about the Lamurnans' belief in freedom. Freedom from what?'

The assistant leaned closer, as though to help him find something. He caught the scent of her hair and skin. He knew the risk she took, showing him these things. He almost despised the ease with which he'd deceived her, but he also admired her courage. She deserved to know the world that lay outside this smoke-stained room and its books. Had his heart not already been taken...

'It's said that most who emigrated to Essaid did so because they disliked the growing Empyreal influence here,' the assistant said in a hushed voice. 'Some believe that if not for the attack, Essaid might eventually have grown strong enough to declare itself independent from Kymera, and would have installed our deposed royal family as its own.'

'The Empyreum would never have allowed that. The rebels would've been crushed.'

'Not if they'd had help.'

'Who from?'

'Prince Harnfell – our exiled ruler – his wife is a sister of the Shahan. Crowning him in Essaid would have gained them the Sundaran Commonwealth as an ally. That would have threatened the Empyreum. Some think the revolution thirty years ago was instigated by the Empyreum, meant to stop Harnfell becoming king when the old queen died and tying Kymera and Sundara together.'

Ranga flicked through the pamphlets. 'You've studied these well.'

'There's not much excitement here.'

Hearing the catch in her throat, Ranga felt a heel for not being who

185

he pretended. But he focused on the issue of Seriuz. Might Seriuz be a monarchist, and angry at what had happened to Larmurna? Or at least be made to seem so?

Or... his wife. She had lived there; she might well be a monarchist and a separatist. She might easily have turned Seriuz, Ranga thought. He knew how persuasive a woman could be.

'I don't remember reading his wife's opinion of the fleet review.'

'I suppose she didn't want to get him into trouble,' said the assistant. 'Speaking of which, you will be careful, won't you, in your article? Not to say anything too specific?'

'The vaguest of terms, I assure you. One last thing...' Ranga pointed to the most recent handbill. 'The hotel bombings referred to here. Do you know if Captain Seriuz said anything about them?'

'Why should he have done?'

'It's possible the bombers took the fleet review as a kind of rallying cry.'

'If they did, they were wrong to,' said the assistant. 'He would never condone anything like that. Those poor people.'

Ranga nodded. 'You see clearly the goodness in his heart.'

But then, the bastard hasn't ordered you beaten up.

He neared the town-house as nervous as if it had been Vanessa's residence. If he could charm Tetana Seriuz into saying something indiscreet and incriminating, something to suggest she was still involved in a separatist movement, he would have her husband by the knackers. The Kurassians would be wholly justified in boarding *Nightfire* on the basis that Seriuz might be supporting monarchist rebels overseas.

He pulled the bell-cord, wondering how best to compliment a woman in a wheelchair. But the housekeeper had bad news.

'Gone?' repeated Ranga.

'This morning,' the woman said. 'Young Robert and the servants too. Mineral water treatment. I don't expect them back till spring: that's all I can tell you.'

True to her word, she shut the door in his face when, flustered, he tried to ask about her mistress's past in Lamurna.

'Unbelievable,' he muttered as he rounded the end of the crescent. All his research at the library had led him to Tetana Seriuz – and she'd left the city. For months!

Coincidence?

If not, if Seriuz had got her out of the way, then whatever he was involved in, the reason he'd taken Orc and Cass, might truly be something big. But…

'… *likely to get you killed.*'

In the cool shade of a plane tree, he drew hard on a cigarette and considered his options. Vanessa was out of the question until all other hope was gone. He wanted to sleep on the problem, but his financial resources were sixty-five solidos: not enough to justify paying for accommodation, not when future expenses remained unknown.

That left only home. His mother and sisters would be pleased to see him, at least; but his father's scorn was inevitable. *What, the great treasure-hunter, returned with nothing? And asking for a free bed?*

He ground out his cigarette. Whatever risk Gregal had warned of, it was better than the certainty of humiliation.

When he and the Strandborns had first met Alonso Gregal, the man's link with the private Museum of Kymeran Antiquity had seemed an unremarkable coincidence. Now, as Ranga stopped before the museum's door in quiet Stonebrook Street, the connection felt murky. The snake-haired female mask carved above the lintel, which months before had seemed almost comic, looked down on him with an intense darkness in the gaps of its eyes and mouth.

A guard seated within the door, next to a propped bicycle, glanced up from his paper as Ranga entered. At once he heard voices: one female, the other with an accent that surprised him.

He walked behind a display screen until a gap between panels let him view the information desk, at the far end of the front wall from the door. With Mrs Fusilli were two Thangkarans – he'd been right about the accent. But they looked nothing like any guest he'd ever seen at his parents' house. The bald old man, his robes a vivid red in the sunlight coming through the arched window above the desk, Ranga thought must be a monk. The boy with him, in grey clothes and a red headband, carried a bulky pack that looked to be several bits of luggage strapped together. The boy kept glancing round as though wary of ambush, his face heavy with lack of sleep.

It was possible the two had already been to the Tamfang Retreat and been turned away by his monk-hating father, so he kept out of their sight as he looked round the displays. He found no sign of the ancient silverware Orc and Cass had brought up, which seemed to support Gregal's hints.

Once the Thangkarans had left, the monk carrying a folded sheet of paper, Ranga approached the desk. Mrs Fusilli's chestnut-tinted hair was artfully pinned in a style he recognised: Vanessa had briefly adopted it a year before.

'Oh,' she said as she looked up. 'Are you with the other two? They've just gone.'

'No,' said Ranga.

The curator lifted carefully shaped eyebrows. 'Well, there *are* a lot of people from your part of the world here today.' Then she frowned, as though at a seepage of recognition.

'Gregal's dead,' said Ranga.

She visibly tried to conceal shock. 'I… who? I've never heard of him.'

'"Him"?' said Ranga. 'I never said it was a man.'

Again, she was too slow to cover alarm. 'But-but,' she stammered, 'I assumed… you would have said "Mrs" otherwise…'

He leaned on the desk. 'Not quick enough.' He kept his voice low, so the guard wouldn't overhear. 'What does Seriuz want with my friends? Why does the gallant captain have the artefacts we sold to Gregal? Why aren't they here?'

'I don't know what you're talking about. All I did was sell you a map.'

A cough came from by the door. Ranga glanced round. The guard had risen to his feet.

'Madam? Everything all right?'

'I think so, Sarno. He's just leaving.'

Ranga pulled out the telegram. 'You deny you sent this?'

She glanced at it and shrugged, seeming more assured now. 'It's a common enough surname.'

'You haven't asked me how he died,' said Ranga.

'What's it to me? I said, I don't know him.' But her voice trembled slightly. 'I asked you to leave.'

'Come on,' said the guard, closer. 'Out.'

Ranga noticed Mrs Fusilli's hand had strayed to the base of the telephone.

'And then?' he said. 'Who will you call?'

She withdrew it. 'The police – if you don't go right away.'

'Fine,' said Ranga, though he doubted it had been the police she'd been thinking of. Not when she already had a guard there.

Once outside the museum, he ambled up the street. After ten yards he checked behind him and saw Sarno leaning round the entrance, watching. Then the guard ducked back and the museum door banged shut.

The sills of the three arched windows were just above Ranga's head, and each had both its leaded glass and inner shutters open. He ran to a small eatery just up the street and grabbed a chair from one of the empty tables, and placed this against the wall beneath the third window from the door, the one above Mrs Fusilli's desk. Standing on the chair, he put his head as close as he could to the window without being seen from inside.

He'd guessed correctly as to what Mrs Fusilli would do. Her agitated voice came clearly. 'And if he returns?'

Ranga's heart thumped several times in the pause before she spoke again.

'There's something else. Before he came in, there were two others asking about ziggurat locations. I helped them prepare a map as well. There was nothing that made me suspicious, but – what I mean is, now that young man's been here…'

Come on, thought Ranga. *What about Seriuz? Gregal?*

'No, of course not. Only the coastal ones. I—' Her voice cut dead. 'Thangkarans,' she said shortly. 'An old man, a monk I think, and a boy.' Another pause. 'A yellow scarf. The boy—'

'Hey, you!' came a voice from up the street. Ranga looked to see a man in an apron outside the eatery. 'That my chair?'

Ranga waved frantically, a finger to his lips. The man placed his hands on his hips and stared.

'That's right,' came Mrs Fusilli's voice. 'Do you know them?'

'You want to use it,' called the man, 'you buy a drink.'

'Yes,' said Mrs Fusilli, 'I didn't think I ought to charge a monk, but he made a donation. I think perhaps he liked the look of me.'

The restaurateur strode towards the museum. Ranga gestured for him to go back, but in vain.

'Yes, I see the exact coin,' said Mrs Fusilli.

As the man reached him and was about to speak, Ranga leaned down. 'Secret service!' he hissed. 'You want to get arrested?'

The man looked doubtful, but clearly wasn't doubtful enough to take the risk. 'Just make sure you return it,' he said, backing off.

Ranga put his head near the window again, but heard nothing. Furious, he wondered what he'd missed. Then came the sound of the door, and voices: Mrs Fusilli and the guard. He jumped from the chair, grabbed it and ducked round the corner.

Peering round, he saw Mrs Fusilli emerge, wheeling the bicycle. She looked about her – Ranga ducked back – then mounted the device and set off wobbling in the direction of the main road.

Ranga was about to run after her when Sarno positioned himself outside the door. Ranga decided against trying to run past. Instead, he ran further up Stonebrook Street – he reckoned Mrs Fusilli was likely to take the main road north, away from the docks, so he took the first turning, aiming to loop round and cut ahead of her while her bicycle was hampered by traffic.

But when he got back down to the main road, she was nowhere in sight. In ten minutes of waiting, he saw no sign of her.

She would be back, he told himself. And so would he. But until the next day, he was left with only the alternatives he'd earlier rejected. Steeling himself for his father's scorn, he set off for home.

14

THE WAR ROOM

Orc raised his head from his pillow at the sound of a door closing across the corridor. A few seconds later, the hatchway ladder creaked. Cass and he weren't allowed on deck during daylight, so it had to be Thera who'd left. He slipped from his cabin.

A wary 'Yes?' answered his knock. Cass lay on the bottom bunk with a novel Juneau had lent her. She barely glanced at him.

'Eaten anything?' he asked from the doorway.

'I'm fine,' she said.

He pushed on, despite her prickly tone. 'I'm going to try again, to work out what you saw. Anything come back to you yet, to get me started?'

'Nothing.'

Orc teased his lip with his teeth. He hadn't pressed her before, wanting her to rest. But it had been two days now. 'In Seriuz's cabin, you said "they" made us do something.'

'I *said*, I don't remember.'

'Okay, I'm only trying to help.'

'Then *leave* it. I don't want you looking for it.'

'Uh? You don't want me to look for our *pasts*?'

'If that's what it was.'

'You said—'

'Orc, I was hardly in a coherent state of mind when I said those things. And maybe, who knows, maybe that had something to do with getting tied to a concrete block and chucked in the sea?'

He stung at the reminder, but couldn't think what to say.

Feet sounded on the ladder. Thera's face carried an accusing expression, doing nothing to improve her heavy features, as she squeezed past him into the cabin. 'Bit cramped in here,' she muttered.

'He's just leaving,' said Cass.

By the time he'd roused Otter half an hour later, Orc still didn't understand it. 'Why wouldn't she want me to?' he asked his animath. 'If it was something about our pasts, it'll help us learn who we are, right?'

'Been a long search, bruv,' said Otter. 'And where did it get her?'

'Yeah, I know. But I almost drowned too, and it hasn't made me like that.'

Otter scratched himself.

'It's more than that, anyway,' said Orc. 'They're getting to her: Thera, and Captain Wolfish. He's always coming down to check on her. All that crap about a civilian coming on board – it was just so he could put us in different cabins. That's what wolves do: they split off the one they want to prey on. I have to get her out of here. You have to help me think of a plan. A trick.'

'Tricks don't come quick, bruv,' said Otter. 'Took me a whole winter to figure how to blunt the teeth of the Black Pike. And even the best escape trick isn't going to work if she won't come with you.'

'She will. Once she's away from him, she'll get back to her old self. But the longer it goes on, the harder it'll be. If I can find out where that big ziggurat is, that might make her more—'

He broke off at the voices of Seriuz and another, coming down the ladder. Their speech became a barely audible mumble as a door shut: the wardroom, he thought.

'So, any ideas? Seriuz won't show us the charts before he signs us up, and I don't want to wait, especially if the Kaybees' agents might get wind of us through the Naval Board.'

'Where does he keep them?' said Otter.

'That painted cabinet, I'm sure. I get a kind of prickling from it. That has to be significant, yes?'

'A shaman knows when to trust his whiskers.'

'Exactly. I've sneaked in there a couple of times, but I can't find the key, and I can't risk forcing it.'

'Ah,' said Otter. 'Perhaps you already have the key. Let's go there now.'

'In a scape?'

'The Otherworld's not the only place worth going,' said Otter. 'Borderlands are good fishing grounds sometimes. That cabinet might not be as locked as you thought, if you want hard enough for it to be open. You in?'

'You bet.'

Otter pulled aside the bag Orc had used to stop anyone coming in, and nosed the door open. Orc detached his scaping self from his body. Imagining every step with care, to make the experience as real as possible, he followed Otter out and crossed the corridor into Seriuz's cabin.

He let the memories of the place come, and their vividness surprised him. Clearest of all was the cabinet's painting: it looked new, its varnish clear. As he approached, the woman turned to look directly at him, and smiled. 'It is the young man crowned with the sun,' she said, then closed her eyes and moaned softly. Disturbed, Orc noticed movement in the serpent that had climbed up her dress.

He willed the painting motionless. Then he thought about what Otter had said, about wanting the cabinet doors unlocked. He focused on an assertion that Seriuz hadn't locked the cabinet that time they'd retrieved the anchor. The doors had merely been stiff when he'd tried them before; he just hadn't pulled hard enough; they *were* unlocked…

And yes, they opened at his tug.

But no charts or papers were revealed. On the topmost shelf lay

Seriuz's magazine-pistol, and several loose bullets, all on a yellow cloth. The gun was silver, tarnished black. It felt heavy when Orc picked it up, and cold as deep water. Etched into it were wheat-sheaves, and bulls, and snakes. Similar designs marked the bullets.

'The first shots of a war.'

A sudden pain in his chest made him look down. A hole marked his shirt, charred black. He realised he couldn't feel his heartbeat.

'Things are getting prickly, bruv,' said Otter. 'Time to leave, if you want my advice.'

Orc nodded. He replaced the gun, and went to the cabin door, which had somehow shut again. He pulled it open.

'Ah,' said Otter. 'Not so easy.'

No ship's corridor lay on the other side now, but a vast mire of red mud beneath a red sky heavy with smoke. Bodies and machine-wreckage littered the wasteland: dead soldiers and heavy guns and, insanely, warships grounded in mud, and other machines Orc couldn't identify, and shreds of flags. He wanted to refuse this and return to his body, which he could sense lying on his bunk. But after Otter's previous warning about the danger to his soul, he didn't dare jump straight back.

On the horizon, a door stood by itself. His cabin, he guessed.

He set off for it, struggling through the mud, passing bodies he tried not to look at, but whose details haunted the edge of his vision. Not all were soldiers: women and old men and children lay there too. Some were no more than bone and scraps of cloth; some barely seemed human.

The effort felt horribly real, the mud sucking at each step. He began to fear he would never reach the door. Then an idea came to him. He visualised a road, asserted its existence. And a road came. But instead of stone paving, what pushed up through the mud and the bodies and the wreckage were bones, interlocking to make a trackway.

In silence, apart from the sound of his feet on the bones, and Otter's claws on the same, Orc made his slow, effortful way to the door. But his relief died quickly as he reached it: this wasn't his cabin. On the door's steel surface were screwed the letters WAR ROOM – a faint outline showed the place of the missing D.

'Wrong one,' he muttered bitterly.

'Wrong?' said Otter. 'Bruv, have you a lot to learn about this stuff.'

The door opened, faint voices sounding from within. Curious, Orc entered.

Two men sat at the wardroom table. On the far side, in front of a cabinet whose shelves were lined with skulls, sat Seriuz, his face oddly static – a paper-maché mask, Orc realised. The captain showed no sign of seeing him.

The other man was little more than a blur. Orc couldn't focus on him. Something happened to his vision whenever he tried to concentrate on the man – as though he didn't *want* to see him. The men's voices were no more than mumbling.

'We'll go,' he whispered.

'No need for quiet,' said Otter. 'They can't hear us.'

'We can't hear them either. No point staying.'

'Can't hear them? Don't you know what good ears otters have?'

Like dark-vision, Orc thought. He concentrated his awareness on his own ears, and felt them shrink and move higher on his head.

The voices cleared.

'… her mongrel lapdog.' This was the other man. 'You should have kept him detained.'

'On what grounds?' came a distorted version of Seriuz's voice, from the direction of that unnervingly static face.

'Consorting with bomb-setters, obviously,' said the second man. 'But we now have a worse threat than his amateur sleuthing.' Orc focused harder: the man's visible aspect, too, was becoming less vague. 'You're certain we can't be overheard?'

'As long as we don't shout,' said Seriuz. 'The man above the hatchway will guard against eavesdroppers.'

'Well, then. A Watcher of Highcloud is in Torrento.'

'Gods! Coincidence?'

'We cannot afford to assume so. I traced his recent movements by psychometry. He comes from Prelate Siegfried Astrasis.'

'Astrasis,' said Seriuz. 'He was at the fleet review last year. Could he have sent this Watcher to look into our engine set-up?'

'I think not,' said the blurred man. 'The Watcher seems interested in the ziggurats rather than your ship. The museum curator unwisely gave him a map.'

'Of all of them?'

'Thankfully, she was not quite that stupid.'

'Then is he really a threat?'

'That depends on what he's investigating. His divination ability might be almost the equal of mine. And his novitiate might not be the only force he can call upon. You're familiar with the Watcher's charter?'

Orc had resolved the man now. He seemed to be wearing naval uniform, of a curiously old-fashioned style, but his face was still obscured behind a disc of rapidly spinning air. While the man spoke about the possibility of the monk calling on help from the Empyreum's Southern Ocean Fleet, Orc moved round the table till he stood by its end – but the disc moved too, interposing itself. Sometimes Orc caught a suggestion of features on the spinning disc. And not human features.

'The Empyreal Navy has better things to do than follow up wild stories, surely?' said Seriuz.

'They might still act, if Astrasis has given the monk his backing,' said the other. 'The Prelate made friends of most of the admiral's staff when he was down here.'

'Then what can we do about this Watcher?'

'You, nothing – except be ready to leave at short notice.'

'How short? Do you know how a steam turbine works?'

'You can maintain steam in boiler four without drawing attention, can you not?'

'Well, true. If we're careful.'

'I'll prepare a surprise for our Highcloud friend,' said the man. 'If he's protected by his Conclave, we might have to put to sea fast. If not, you'll read some lurid headlines in tomorrow's newssheets.'

'I don't argue against its necessity, Daroguerre, but—'

'*Don't!*' snapped the man. '*Never* name me during a talk like this.

Names are beacons in the psychosphere. Any attention…'

'I'll remind you that this is my—'

'Stop.' The word brought silence. Orc suddenly felt exposed. 'There *is* an attention here,' said Daroguerre.

'Meaning what?' Seriuz sounded breathless. 'The monk?'

'Wait…'

The man continued to speak, but his words became indistinct behind a swarm-like buzzing. His form, too, became more vague, as when Orc had entered. But the spinning disc grew more solid, and the features on it settled into eyes – three eyes, the third above and between the others. They had heavy black edges and slit pupils. Two curved nostrils twitched in the disc's centre, and below these appeared a mouth with thin, black, somehow feminine lips.

'*Where* are you?' came a hissing voice, as the nostrils snuffled and eyes searched. '*Who* are you? *Tell* me.'

'Scarpering time, bruv,' said Otter, but Orc couldn't take his gaze from the third eye. At the moment it was looking towards the door, not at him. But he sensed that if it did turn his way, he would be revealed. The terror of being discovered was so great that he half-wanted to blurt out, to get it over with.

'*Where* are you? *Who* are you? *Where* are you…' the voice chanted, an insidious monotone worming into his mind. He needed to break that sound: another reason to reveal himself. He stared at the disc's third eye, unable to look away. The words rose; his throat readied.

Pain stabbed his ankle, a battery of needles. His gaze jerked down – Otter had nipped him. He was about to protest when he realised it had pulled his eyes from the disc.

But how to get out? The thing still watched the door.

Otter sprang into movement, ran under the table to its far side and jumped onto a chair. 'Here!'

The disc swung round the man's blurred head to face the animath.

'Here I am, flat-face!' yipped Otter. 'Remember me? I'm back from the dead, tea-tray head!'

Orc seized his chance. Making sure his eyes kept away from the disc's, he slipped back round to the door and out. To his relief, he found himself in the ship's corridor, no red mud in sight.

He was at his cabin when claws sounded on steel by his feet. He visualised the bunk empty, climbed up, merged imagination and reality. His heart was too fast, and he was soaked, clammy-cold. Sweat trickled down his temple.

'Who was that man?' he whispered.

'Couldn't tell you,' said Otter, furred flanks heaving. 'But that thing was Three-Eyes, one of the Sisters. You might remember, I don't have a happy history with her.'

Orc gasped. 'One of *those* sisters?'

'Anyone who bargains with such a being… watch out… outta here.'

Otter slipped beneath the lower bunk, and was gone.

Orc breathed deeply, slowly, trying to ground himself. Outside the cabin's small window, the last of the sunset stained the smoky sky beyond the dockyard cranes. Dark had fallen.

F: I have communicated with Scarab. He had already
      learned of the Watcher. He dared venture no
      criticism, but I believe he feels irked that we did
      not inform him ourselves.

A: There was no need before.

F: He worries that the monk acts with the full support of
      Conclave.

A: Did you inform him otherwise?

F: I acted displeased to be bothered by trivia.

A: Whatever amuses you. The monk is staying in some
      kind of hotel?

F: Indeed. I asked Scarab if he were planning another
      bombing.

A: That would have been my suggestion.

F: It seems, however, he did not guard his springtime
      outrages against an investigation by Watchers. If
      the death of this monk led them to investigate one of
      the earlier hotel bombings, they might trace Scarab
      through his henchmen. That was his stated reason.
      But I believe he also relishes the chance to test his
      esoteric abilities. He has spent three hours making a
      primitive psychic disruptor.

A: Egotistical insect. Does he think we're playing chess
      here?

F: It might be effective. I shall watch with interest.

A: Keep your interest. It galls me to rely on such people.

15

MASTERY

Tashi woke out of homesick dreams into a dark room dim in the glow of embers, the ceiling plaster cracked and stained. He almost groaned as memory caught up and reminded him where he was: Baker's Rooms, somewhere in the heart of Torrento.

He tensed at noise. Muttering, from the corner.

Dark-flight. He threw off his sheet and sat up.

But Shoggu's voice carried no sense of strain. His master was merely talking in his sleep. Tashi lay back down. His own dreams had been of Aino. Reality was a crippling disappointment.

'… beautiful, oh yes…'

He frowned.

'Can't. Not fitting.' A little laugh. 'Such legs, though…'

Unease prickled. He'd rarely heard Shoggu sleep-talk so clearly, and never in such a manner. He remembered the women they'd passed when out to beg food that evening: standing in doorways, calling to them, inviting, mock-pleading, sometimes with laughter. It worried him that Shoggu could be so ill-disciplined as to let them affect his dreams. *He* had not experienced such dreams, and he was of the age when those aspects of the body constantly strove to dominate.

'Quiet as mice. The burrowing kind. Hn-hn.'

Tashi cringed. He wished they'd followed the advice of the station porter and gone to the Thangkaran-run guesthouse. There would have been familiar food, perhaps even a fire-pit in the centre of the floor. Instead, his master had insisted on looking elsewhere for lodging, a search that had brought them to this wretched, dingy street in an area frequented by harlots. The more easily they found charity, Shoggu had said, the clearer it was that they were on the right path. But the charity of a fellow Thangkaran would apparently have been *too* easy.

Could Shoggu have *wanted* to be close to such women? Tashi had sensed a demoralisation in his master since Bismark. The possible depths of it now horrified him.

He jumped at a sharp double-knock. At first he wondered if he'd imagined it, then heard breathing beyond the door. He pulled his bedding away, and opened a crack. The man outside handed him an envelope, and walked back towards the stairs at the end of the landing.

'Who was that?' said Shoggu, sitting up on his mattress.

'The porter, I think.' Tashi closed the door. 'With a letter.' The dying firelight was too dim to read the envelope, so he uncovered the taper and lit the lamp.

To the monk – for him only, was written in a rounded hand. Tashi gave it to Shoggu, who took out the letter and read it several times.

'Master?'

Shoggu folded the paper, then again, and again. 'The museum curator, Elene Fusilli. She is here.'

'In this hotel?'

'Another room. She has information for me.'

'About our task?'

'I assume so.'

'That is good news! It shows we are on the right track.' Tashi pulled on his trousers.

'Not you, beloved one. I must go alone.'

Tashi paused with his hand on his shirt. 'Why?'

'A lone woman is unlikely to be a threat even to me. And someone should watch our belongings.'

'You are more important than our luggage, master.'

'She told me to go alone.' Shoggu's voice had grown harder. 'If I disobey, she might withhold the information. I cannot risk our task being compromised.'

Tashi dragged on his shirt, took a tight breath. 'May I see the letter?'

'It is private. Did you not read the envelope?'

'Please, let me see.'

'You seek to insist?' said Shoggu. 'Do you forget that I am a Watcher, and you a mere boy – indeed, one whose service has recently been shown to be less than flawless?'

Perturbed, Tashi nonetheless held out his hand, steeled it. Shoggu's gaunt face tightened. He clutched the repeatedly folded letter in his trembling fist – then sighed, and seemed to deflate. 'How ridiculous,' he muttered, handing it over.

Tashi unfolded it.

My friend: I could say nothing at the museum, but I have information about the sunken temples that will interest you. I shall be in room eight, on this landing, for the next hour. I will not come to your room, as I wish us to be alone. I have other things that might interest a man of your nature, just as a man of your nature interests me…

Tashi felt faintly sick with dismay.

Shoggu sighed again, and pulled on his robe. 'Together, then.'

Room eight was three doors along towards the staircase, next to the landing's only lamp. The corridor was silent – Shoggu had asked for a quiet room, and the manager had given them one on the upper guest-floor, where no others had been taken.

Shoggu knocked. Tashi stood to one side, praying that the woman would at least be clothed. But there was no response.

Looking concerned, Shoggu checked the number on the door, knocked again. Then he tried the handle. As his master opened the door – slowly, to give an occupant time to protest – Tashi saw the interior was bright with candlelight.

'Mrs Fusilli?' Shoggu looked round the door he'd half-opened – and his head jerked back on his thin neck. His legs bowed as he retreated a step; Tashi feared he might fall.

'Master!'

Shoggu seemed unable to speak. Tashi pushed open the door, and choked on his cry.

A blood-splashed horror stared back at him: half face, half skull: exposed gums and open nasal cavity and staring eyes, mouth split by a gag. The museum curator – he barely recognised her without her nose and lips – had been bound, naked, to a chair facing the door. The scene was a hammer-blow to his mind. She'd been made to sit, slumped, right on the edge of the seat, her ankles tied to the chair's legs to keep her own legs wide open. The chair stood on a sheet, and in an arc before the chair, within the ring of candles, was written in drying blood: THE GREAT MOTHER OF DEATH DEVOURS ALL.

'Gevurah,' whispered Shoggu. 'The magician. A warning.'

Tashi couldn't focus on Shoggu's words. He couldn't keep his eyes on the dead woman, but couldn't look fully away. The blood on her and all over the walls spoke of madness and slaughter. A nauseous, tingling weakness washed through his body from his fingertips, as though his own blood were draining from him, pumped from him by a heart unnaturally fast. His knees had gone. His body had gone, the room, everything.

'Ah!' breathed Shoggu. 'Beneath her...'

Tashi made himself look. What he saw pitched his stomach. The hairy cleft between the woman's legs still dripped blood, the red drops from her dead genitalia falling onto a small, framed painting that had been placed to receive them, propped against a cord tied between the chair's two front legs.

A painting of the Holy Mountain.

He had to act; it was the only way not to break down. He stepped over the candles, trying to keep his bare feet clear of the bloody words.

'Wait!' came Shoggu's harsh whisper. 'Touch nothing!'

The thought snatched at Tashi that this was the extent to which his master had compromised his faith, that he would no longer try to save what was holiest. Keeping his gaze as far as possible from the horrific sexual source of the blood, he grabbed the fouled icon.

'Tashi!'

A shudder travelled through his insides as he picked it up. The smells of blood and flesh seemed suddenly to permeate everything.

'Foolish,' said Shoggu, closing the door. 'But forget that now. Cover the poor woman, at least. Another sheet, Tashi. Help me.'

'In a moment.' Some of the blood had got onto his fingers. His nausea intensified. He tried to exert the force of his mind. Blood was a part of the body, and the body was a tool, not inherently evil. Part of the physical world, yes; impure, yes; capable of corruption, yes, of contagion...

Breath heaving in and out, he went to the washstand.

'Tashi, a sheet—'

'Must clean this.' The woman's fate was beyond horrific, but she wasn't going to get any more dead – it angered and upset him that Shoggu didn't see the importance of removing corruption from the sacred image. His master was too weak to withstand the lower world; he would have to be strong enough for them both. But he felt too aware of his insides, his organs and the juices that ran between, seeping, oozing. He dunked his hand in the ewer.

His wet fingers smeared pink all across the mountain.

The woman's blood, the squalid, contagious filth—

He swayed with a wave of sickness. The picture slipped from his fingers and crashed against the washstand.

'Tashi, are you all—'

The floor hit his knees, his palms. His abdomen heaved, his mouth stretched – and out erupted a violent gout of blood, splashing and splattering, swarming with scraps of rotting flesh. He stared in terror. Another heave choked up a pale, fleshy bag, greyish white and glistening with mucus, pulsating, squirming – it broke open to disgorge a packed mass of worms, more worms than could have fitted inside, red and yellow and black.

'Master!' he shrieked.

'What? Tashi, what?'

The pain of the corruption clawed into his bowels, towards his heart. He stared at the worms as they jerked and spasmed. More were boiling up, breeding in the poisoned organs inside him. His vision was dimmer, clouded, his breathing clogged, lungs and throat choked.

'Must be shock,' came Shoggu's unsteady voice.

'*Look* at them!' Tashi half-gargled with the breakdown of his lungs. The next heave built with the pressure of worms, his body made a factory of breeding. 'Please, help me...' He started to cry, every out-breath a muffled scream. He knew it was already too late.

'Beloved one.' Shoggu bent towards him. 'I see only vomit. What is "them"?'

Tashi howled at Shoggu's blindness. His heart stuttered as its corrupted muscle softened, its tubes clogged. He tried to prepare, but he couldn't be brave about death, not this death.

'Gevurah save us.' Shoggu's voice seemed far-off. 'Tashi! The icon was a trap. It held a spell, an imprint of the magician's will. You must fight it with your own. Fight it!'

But every beat of his disintegrating heart wracked him with pain. He heaved again, jetting hundreds of black wriggling worms slick with his blood.

'Fight it!' urged Shoggu. 'Think of the mountain: the *true* mountain cannot be defiled. Focus on its high snows in the sun, its cold, its clean air. My scroll, wait—'

'Don't go!' shrieked Tashi. He tried to hold onto Shoggu's words. His life was lost. *It is the flesh that fears.* He had to save his soul. If he could focus hard enough on the Mountain, his soul might fly to it even from here. If not, it would be dragged into the Witch Mother's hell.

He tried to push away that thought, tried to ignore the pain, tried to concentrate through the words of Shoggu's trembling encouragement and his own terror. He pictured the high snows, imagined himself trudging barefoot, legs numbed.

Below him were the tops of clouds, and above him that beautiful, unreachable spire of cold.

No! Not unreachable – it mustn't be. But it reared as high above him as it ever had in Highcloud. He was too far below, too impure, stained with lies and sin and weakness. His vision was almost dark, his rotted heart splitting in the effort of its final beats. He sought Shoggu's hand but couldn't find it. The Witch Mother's pit of filth and corruption gaped.

'Gevurah, help me!' But the peak was too far.

Except – with shock, he sensed it: the power – the power that had been there since Inspiration, as though hiding behind the sun. It wanted to save him, was eager to.

No time to think. He threw himself open in surrender – no ceremony, no purification, but the power came as it had before, flooding him, raging through him. It took his awareness, his self, and flung it to one corner of his mind, a distant spectator as the fire burned away his rotted insides and scoured him clean, a blazing power against the dark magic of flesh.

He stayed on his hands and knees as he was remade in agony. He poured sweat that stank of the corruption expelled from him; it dripped from his face and down his legs and soaked his clothes. At last, the fiery pain faded; soon after, he was able to shakily stand. With Shoggu's help, he just about made it back to their room before he collapsed.

When he came round, his awareness was rooted back in his exhausted, shivering body, which was trapped under piled blankets. The fire was gone. His throat felt like sand, and he accepted the cup Shoggu put to his lips. It was cold water, and tasted of bitter herbs.

'How do you feel?' said Shoggu.

Tashi hadn't the energy to think how to express it. His body felt so weak, so fragile, as though it were a new creation, constructed of webs of the flimsiest tissue.

'Master,' he rasped. 'Did you send them away?'

'Who?'

'The Lords of Battle. They saved me.'

'It was meditating on the Holy Mountain that saved you, beloved one.'

Tashi felt too weak to argue.

'I fear to ask,' said Shoggu, 'but can you walk? We must leave before the magician assails us again.'

'With the pack?' The thought made his head reel.

'It won't be far. We'll go to the main road and find a conveyance.'

'To where?'

'I will not speak that aloud. If the magician knew how to find us, it's possible he also knows what passes in this room.'

In a daze of exhaustion, accepting as much help as Shoggu could give, Tashi packed. He tried to draw strength from the fire that had saved him, but he could no longer feel its presence. It took almost half an hour of concentrated effort before they were ready to leave. Forcing his legs and back to endure the pack's weight, Tashi staggered out onto the landing. The door to room eight was shut. He flinched at the memories.

'I went back to cover her while you were unconscious,' Shoggu said. 'And to put out the candles.'

'But why all that?' said Tashi, feeling sick again. 'The candles, the blood, everything? Can he *enjoy* doing such things?'

'I have only studied these matters in theory,' said Shoggu. 'But I believe such horrors are often used to prepare the way for a magical attack, by causing such distress to the soul that it weakens its attachment to the physical body. As for the question of his enjoyment, let's not dwell on it.'

'Do we tell the police?'

'No. He might have influence over the authorities: most magicians seek to do so. We might find ourselves the accused. That might even be his second line of attack.'

Tashi's knees almost buckled on every step. The hotel was silent. Any guests downstairs had either slept through his cries of distress, or had decided to do nothing about it. Checking for the porter, whom

Shoggu thought might be in the magician's employ, Tashi peered round the edge of the office door and saw him at his desk, counting on his fingers. Counting, and counting, the same fingers, over and over...

Most of the street's gas-lamps had already been extinguished, save one at each junction. Tashi scanned the shadows, his newly mended heart pounding: he had no strength to defend if they were attacked now. The city seemed one vast engine of malice, a beast with a thousand heads.

But no attack came by the time they gained the main road, and five minutes later they reached a carriage station. Shoggu woke the driver and hurriedly negotiated a fee. Tashi slipped into unconsciousness several times during the lurching and bumping journey, and had no idea how much time had passed before the carriage rattled to a halt in the glare of electric light, at the gates to the Torrento barracks of the Empyreal Navy.

They waited in the guardroom for an hour before Staff-Lieutenant Wallen returned and gave them back the Prelate's letter.

'I've spoken to the admiral's aide,' he said. 'He's agreed that you be given shelter and a gate pass. Anything else would be at the admiral's discretion – and not even the name of Siegfried Astrasis gets him out of bed at this hour.'

'And the hotel?' said Shoggu.

'I've sent a good sergeant and a couple of men, out of uniform,' said Wallen. 'The Torrento police are scum, and I won't see a Watcher thrown in a cell.'

'My thanks,' said Shoggu.

Wallen called an orderly to carry Tashi's pack, then led them through the barracks rows to a refurbished dormitory not yet reoccupied.

'We'll be safe here from physical attack, at least,' said Shoggu, when the Kurassians had left. 'But tonight, protection from the Immaterium might be just as useful.'

Tashi nodded. Even weary as he was, he didn't begrudge the delay in getting to bed. Seated, Shoggu verbally guided their joint visualisation of a cone of light surrounding the room, blue-white as the snows of Tamfang. For several minutes, Tashi envisaged the light whirling sun-wise to keep away darkness – in this case, both memories of the night's horror and any dreams or other attacks the magician might send.

When the cone had been established, Tashi used the last of his strength to pull a mattress off a bed for Shoggu, then placed folded blankets to make up his own nest by the door. Gasping with weariness, he fell onto this without removing his clothes.

'We shall have to think what to do,' said Shoggu, when the harsh electric light was out.

'In the morning,' mumbled Tashi. 'Please.'

'I did not expect the reality to be so dangerous,' Shoggu went on. 'The magician is very strong. It might be that we cannot defeat him without aid. But I dare not return to Highcloud, or the Prelate, with so little. I will write to the Abbot, but I cannot tell if he will pay any attention. If he does not, and the Kurassians are unable to help, it might be that we will have to abandon this task.'

That roused Tashi from the mire of his fatigue. 'But if we do, we can never go back!'

Shoggu breathed out slowly. 'Perhaps we could live here.'

Tashi sat up, appalled. 'Our home is Highcloud.'

But, the realisation jolted him, what was true for him might not be as true for Shoggu. His master had lived elsewhere before joining the monastery, and perhaps would find it easy to live elsewhere again.

'But could you not see yourself making a life here?' said Shoggu. 'If the Kurassian colonists overcome Golgomera's horrors, a great deal of wealth will flow through Torrento. It would be an interesting time for a young man. You could take a wife, father children.'

'No! Master, what are you saying?'

'You will have to consider your future soon, in any case. Your graduation is only four years away.'

Tashi swallowed. 'I have considered it. I will become a Watcher.'

'Beloved one, the qualities possessed by a good novitiate and a good Watcher are very different.'

'I will study hard,' said Tashi. 'And I'll have you as a teacher. Master, stop this talk, please. You are testing me. No one who follows Gevurah can live in this dreadful city. A single day here is too much. We cannot wait for the Abbot. We can defeat this magician ourselves. We were unprepared earlier.'

'I cannot expose you to such risk again.'

'You gave me the choice in the air-craft. I chose to come.'

'But you did not choose to be raised in Highcloud,' said Shoggu.

'What does that matter?' said Tashi. 'It doesn't matter whether I was orphaned, or my parents could not afford to feed me, or they gave me up to serve Gevurah. What matters is that I serve Him to the best of my ability. As should you.'

He chilled as he caught his own words.

'You think I do not?' said Shoggu quietly.

Tashi knew he should ask forgiveness. His heart cried otherwise. 'What about the Zhenaii practices? The Cry of Sin? Those things are why the Watchers and Highcloud exist, even if the Abbot has forgotten. A few days ago, you thought them important enough to defy him. Now you talk about giving up. The lower world has…' He made himself say it. 'It has changed you.'

'It has shown me reality,' said Shoggu. 'I believed our mission so important, I thought the *Elohim Gibor* would consent to being used in a bargain. That dreadful arena in Bismark corrected me. The Lords of Battle judged our task unworthy. I am just an obsessed old man, whose obsession nearly got you killed.'

'It's true the Lords did not accept being used in that way.' Tashi stung with guilt at how his body and sword had been used to humiliate Shoggu. 'But they have not abandoned us. They saved me, tonight.'

'Beloved one—'

'No, master. They *did* come to me, even without ceremony – as they did to the first twenty-seven.' The implications of his words scared him, thrilled him. 'That proves our mission as holy as the defence of Highcloud. Forget the Abbot. This is the true and ancient purpose of the Watchers, and what happened tonight shows we are on the right track. We will destroy this magician, this monster. Every crime he has committed, I shall return on him a hundred times. Then we shall go *home.*'

He turned onto his side, face to the door. Shoggu said nothing else, to Tashi's relief. He'd never felt so tired, and never had so much to recover from.

And chief among those things was the knowledge of how he had been changed.

It felt sinfully prideful to think the Lords of Battle had favoured him as they had the first twenty-seven, but he couldn't accept Shoggu's claim that meditating on the Holy Mountain alone had saved him. He sensed the physical reality of what had happened. His inner body had been corrupted, then burned away, and a new body had been given him by the *Elohim Gibor*: one that was purer, cleaner.

A thought flicked his eyes back open.

One more suited, perhaps, to their inhabitation.

A: The disruptor failed?

C: The plan failed. The novitiate triggered it instead. It almost induced heart failure, quite an achievement given his youth and health. But the boy saved himself by invoking the same entity as before. He ceded it the power to reorder his body.

A: The elohim gibbor is warrior energy, not healing.

C: I'm no longer certain we're talking about the elohim gibbor, though it belongs to the fifth sefira. I need to do more research.

A: You think klippoth?

C: That time in Bismark, his emotions were confused and unfocused, and the rituals imperfect. It is possible.

A: If he allows it to psychically reorder his body, and his path crosses that of the others, the result could be catastrophic.

F: I'd be quite interested to see what physical form it would take.

A: I'm more interested in not having our work compromised. Contact Scarab if you can. Emphasise the boy as primary danger. Tell him the Conclave is no threat. He should use a bomb this time if necessary.

F: No more vanity magic.

A: Precisely.

16

FIGHT AND FLIGHT

An hour after dawn, an orderly showed Tashi and Shoggu to the barracks canteen, where they found an unoccupied table. Tashi had recovered less strength than he'd hoped – though at least his sleep had been largely undisturbed.

'We must create the cone of protection each evening,' said Shoggu over the canteen chatter: much of which, Tashi guessed from the glances they got, was about them. 'And vary our sleeping quarters if we can. The longer we stay in one room, the more precisely the magician will locate us, and the more focused will be any attack.'

'How did he know we were at the hotel?' asked Tashi, stirring a tenth spoonful of sugar into his porridge.

'We are hardly inconspicuous. Anyone under the magician's influence might have spied us and followed us, perhaps poor Mrs Fusilli herself.'

Tashi stopped stirring. The memory of her made weakness shiver through him.

'Or he might have acquired an object touched by one of us,' Shoggu said. 'I was careless. It never occurred to me that he might also be in Torrento. You recall when I was trying to find him using the map yesterday evening, I was unable to focus on any of the ziggurat sites? I thought my mind kept returning to the city because my skill was lacking or my sight fogged by the lower world. I didn't see that I had indeed sensed the magician, and he was here, already plotting against us.'

'Will he know where we are now?'

'I fear so, beloved one. I kept the icon.'

Tashi almost choked. 'You touched it?'

'It is harmless. You discharged its spell.'

'So you took it to purify it?'

'In time,' said Shoggu. 'For the moment, it serves us better soiled. The magician's presence must have been impressed upon it during its enchantment. It would make a good focus for flight: I might learn much about him that way. But by the same token, he will be able to link to it. We must be careful when we leave this place – and we cannot remain sheltered here. What you said last night was correct.'

'What I said?' He'd been nervously waiting for Shoggu to touch on their conversation.

'I was wrong,' said Shoggu. 'After the Lords condemned my actions in Bismark, I as good as despaired of our task. I neglected discipline; I let myself become susceptible to flattery, and curious about aspects of the world I should have shut myself from. I believe the magician sent dreams to me, and my weakness made me prey to them. And seeing you suffer so terribly on the floor of that room, and fearing I might lose you… that took my last resolve. So I suggested we accept defeat. That was shameful of me. We must either destroy this magician, or find such proof of his evil that all the wrath of Highcloud will fall upon his head.'

Tashi nodded – though he hoped they would kill him themselves, rather than hand the satisfaction to the sceptical and dithering Abbot. 'What should we do, then?'

'Return to the museum, I think. The magician perhaps chose Mrs Fusilli as his victim purely to make use of our relationship with her, but my instinct is that she was in his thrall, and that he killed her in part to punish her for giving us the map. A flight at the museum, where she must have thought about him and perhaps even talked to him, should tell us something about our enemy without having to use the icon – for which I confess myself unready.'

'Will he know we've gone there?' asked Tashi.

'If we can evade any spies he might have outside these barracks, and if I leave the icon here, we might escape his attention.'

'How do we evade his servants? Disguise?'

Shoggu smiled tightly. 'Let's first see if our hosts can help us in a less theatrical fashion.'

An hour later, after several conversations with increasingly braid-decorated officers, they stood before the desk of Admiral Durer.

'I have communicated with Prelate Astrasis.' Durer read again through the letter Shoggu had been given in Bismark, with little obvious pleasure. 'I am persuaded that his Grace intended to afford you the full protection and aid of the Empyreum. However, there is a limit to our powers here. We may not conduct any police action in the wider city without the request of the Kymeran authorities, nor act in any official capacity outside this base and a few other stations. I cannot risk aggravating seditionist sentiment, not without clear instructions from Bismark. If you need help to arrest this man you're hunting, you should ask the Torrento constabulary.'

'All I ask at present,' said Shoggu, 'is a means of leaving here without being seen, and an escort to deter any attack at the museum.'

'You expect one?'

'This magician seems to favour more arcane measures, but his servants might risk an assault if they find us alone. It surprised me that we were not attacked between the hotel and this base last night, but perhaps he was overly confident about his trap.'

'Yes, I've heard about that "trap",' said Durer. 'Dreadful business. Very well, I'll have an escort arranged. They'll find you.'

Another hour passed before a horse-drawn van rattled to a halt outside their dormitory. Still feeling drained, Tashi took a pack holding only equipment for Shoggu's flight. The bearded driver, darkly Kymeran, opened the van's doors to reveal three Kurassians in civilian clothes seated within.

They introduced themselves as marines: a sergeant and two privates. As the wine-smelling van set off, Sergeant Rasmuss explained that it had been delivering to the officers' mess; the driver had been persuaded to drop them off on his way back to the vintner's. It also turned out the trio had been those Wallen had sent to remove Mrs Fusilli's body. They had volunteered to escort Shoggu in the hope of catching the magician responsible for what they'd found.

'I wouldn't have thought there still was such people,' said Breller, a stocky man in a check jacket. 'Till last night.'

'Didn't all that magic die out when Empyruzh came?' slurred his moustached colleague Rhunke, who even in his middle twenties had a mouth filled with badly fitting dentures.

'The coming of Empyreus didn't stop men's hearts being corrupted by the Witch Mother,' said Shoggu. 'Magic is always a temptation to those who seek the deepest congress with her.'

'If *that*'sh what they sheek,' said Rhunke, 'the wife'sh father could put 'em shtraight.'

Rasmuss and Breller laughed. Tashi bit the inside of his lip. He was amazed the Kurassians could still joke about magicians.

'You've got the gear for it anyway,' Breller said to Tashi. 'A pre-Empyreal weapon to fight a pre-Empyreal foe.'

He wanted not to say anything, but: 'At least I *have* a weapon.'

As one, the marines held open their jackets to show holstered pistols.

Rasmuss chuckled. 'Don't take offence, lad. As for your sword, I envy you.'

Tashi said nothing, suspecting this would lead to some other insult.

'I used to daydream of being a soldier of Empyreus,' said Rasmuss. 'I couldn't wait for the Last Battle to come so I could follow Him in the glorious charge and stick old Elok right in the guts, or lop off the Witch's head. Oi, you two, stop sniggering. So I had ambition – it's why I'm a sergeant and you're not. But you, lad, you're living out my childhood dream, in a way.'

'I'm not a soldier of Empyreus.'

'But you fight against the Witch. And it has a kind of nobility to it, the blade – that's why the officers still have them. You used it yet, in anger?'

I threw it at one of your Prelates. 'My larger sword has killed.'

Rasmuss's eyebrows raised. 'How many men?'

Tashi forced himself not to look down. 'Two boars.'

Rasmuss laughed, the other marines following. Tashi's face burned. 'They were full-grown males.' Shoggu's voice was firm, almost angry. 'And goaded. I would rather fight two men bare-handed than have such a battle.'

That killed the laughter. Tashi bent his head, grateful for Shoggu's words. But the praise was undeserved, he knew. His body had not been truly his during the fight, any more than when his sword had been used to threaten his master.

'Well,' said Rasmuss. 'Not merely our defence against the Hell-Queen, but angry wildlife too. I'll sleep easy tonight. Only joking, lad,' he said, and ruffled Tashi's hair, which didn't improve his mood.

Stonebrook Street looked as deserted as the day before. The noise of the main road faded as they walked the fifty yards to the museum. The marines went ahead of Tashi and Shoggu, alert but relaxed, ready for trouble but seemingly not expecting it.

The museum's doors opened to Rasmuss's pull. Rasmuss and Breller drew pistols and entered. Tashi followed them in, while Rhunke waited outside with Shoggu. The large main room looked and felt deserted. The guard's chair inside the doors was unoccupied, with no sign he'd been in that morning, but the inner shutters were all open on the three windows just above head-height along the front wall, and so were the outer glass panes.

Tashi and the two marines checked behind the display cases, and found no one. At the left end of the rear wall, diagonally opposite the entrance, was a smaller door. Through it, a dim corridor led to the right, with several doors on its far side, and a stair immediately opposite. Tashi listened, but heard only the marines behind him.

'Should we search out the back here?'

'The place is deserted, Two-boars,' said Rasmuss. 'If anyone was planning an ambush, they'd have tried when we came in.'

At the all-clear, Shoggu entered and sat behind the curator's desk, showing no unease at occupying a murdered woman's chair. Tashi unpacked the lammager mantle and settled it around his master's shoulders, then lit incense at a corner of the desk. Eyes lidded, Shoggu stroked the leather surface and the objects before him: the inkstand, the telephone, things Mrs Fusilli might have used.

The two marines talked in low voices, from time to time watching the old man. Since Shoggu wasn't yet in full flight, Tashi went again to the door at the back. He didn't want to risk leaving it unguarded: it had a direct line of sight to the desk.

He'd stood there a couple of minutes when metal wheel-rims sounded on the cobbles outside. 'Ices!' called a voice. 'Delicious ices!'

Tashi had seen such vendors the previous afternoon. Ice-cream was one of the few unfamiliar things about Torrento he wanted to experience, even though food was properly only a source of nutrition, not sensual pleasure. He was wondering if this vendor might give one as charity, when from out in the street came a sharp bang.

The mad thought jumped him that Rhunke had shot the ice-cream seller. Then came a cry from outside the museum entrance, and another bang. Rasmuss and Breller ran for the entrance, but the doors slammed shut. Something ground hard against them.

Rasmuss and Breller pushed against the doors, shoulder-barged. They didn't move. 'Rhunke!' shouted Breller. 'You all right? *Rhunke!*'

Tashi swallowed. 'What happened?' But they were still shouting. He was halfway back to Shoggu when there came movement at the window above the desk. A hand appeared and threw something dark and round into the room. It cracked a glass case, struck the floor and rolled near Tashi's feet: a metal ball, something sticking out of it, fizzing.

'Bomb!' yelled Rasmuss. '*Cover!*'

Tashi's legs bunched to throw him to one side. Something stopped him. He dived instead for the thing, grabbed it off the floor and pivoted and threw it through the still-open doorway at the back. It cleared the right-hand jamb by inches, struck the far wall of the corridor beyond and bounced out of sight. Tashi ducked into a crouch.

Detonation punched his ears. The air shook.

When he looked, beyond the doorway was smoke and dust and drifting flakes of plaster. The wall to the right of the door was bowed outwards and cracked.

He jumped up and ran to the window, banged the shutter closed, threw the bolt. Rasmuss was doing the same to the leftmost one. Tashi got to the middle window and slammed the shutters just as a hand appeared. From outside came shouts and cries – '*Throw* it!' – then the muffled *crump* of an explosion some distance away.

His heart had never worked so fast. He was drenched, but his throat was dry; he couldn't swallow.

'Good work,' said Rasmuss, looming in the dimness. 'How did you—?'

'I don't know.' He turned to look at Shoggu, who still seemed to be meditating. 'Master! Are you all right?'

Shoggu nodded.

'Rhunke's shot,' said Rasmuss. 'He won't answer. I don't know where those bastards are. We can't leave the door in case they unblock it and attack that way. You keep guard, right up close – a sword's as good as a gun there. Understand?'

'I – yes.'

Rasmuss clapped him on the shoulder. 'Breller, with me!'

The marines ran to the rear of the room. Rasmuss crouched by the doorway, Breller ducked through. Tashi stood by the front doors, *dughra* in his sweating hand. He didn't know if he could use it; he'd wrenched his shoulder with the violence of his throw.

Gunshots cracked out, from Rasmuss firing along the corridor, and others from within. Two, three-four, five – each one jumped Tashi's heart. In a lull in the gunfire, Rasmuss shouted, 'Get up there! To the window!' and Tashi heard feet that must be Breller's rushing up the stairs. Rasmuss shouted something else, then disappeared. Another two shots came from somewhere in the corridor, then another two from higher up. Breller's voice came faint: 'They're off!' Feet beat down the stairs again, then crashed through what must have been debris in the corridor, and were gone.

Tashi's heart drummed out second after second.

Shoggu still sat meditating.

A minute passed, then came noise from the front, something being rolled away just beyond the door. Tashi readied his sword, but lowered it at the voice: 'It's me. Rasmuss.'

The sergeant opened the doors. 'Didn't get them,' he said. 'Two of the buggers. But I winged one in the arm and they ran off. Go and bolt the back door. I should've done that first thing. Stupid.'

Tashi picked his way through the rubbled corridor, trying not to think what would have happened to him and Shoggu if he'd missed the throw, or followed his first instinct to run. When he returned from fastening the door, he found the surviving marines had brought Rhunke into the main room and laid him out beneath Rasmuss's jacket.

'Bloody mess.' The sergeant picked up the telephone, pressed a lever. 'Empyreal naval base.'

Tashi made himself look at Rhunke's body. After Mrs Fusilli's naked and bloodied corpse, it seemed almost innocuous, but the man was just as dead. Tashi wanted to believe Rhunke's soul would reach the Mountain, and the Land Beyond Sky. But Empyreans believed they were protected from Hell merely by following their so-called saviour, and Rhunke had probably given no thought to the Mountain his whole life. Tashi felt angry at the deceit. Rhunke would be pulled into the Sink, an unjust fate for one who had died in the fight against magic.

'Master,' he said, as Rasmuss started talking to someone at the base. 'Are you all right? We should get back to safety.'

'I'm fine,' said Shoggu, his voice a near-monotone. 'I had to maintain my calm as best I could, lest the excitement destroy it for hours. But we will not leave here. I must still conduct my flight, when we have quiet again. Be good enough to explain that to the sergeant, if he has other plans.'

'I heard you,' said Rasmuss, setting the ear-piece back on its cradle. 'They'll send transport, but it might be an hour. I'll get you your peace and quiet. Whatever it takes to catch the bastard behind this.'

He motioned Tashi towards the front door, past Rhunke's body.

'That was quick thinking with the shutters.'

'Thank you.'

'But throwing that grenade, that was something else altogether. You can't have been trained to do that. And I doubt you've done it before.'

'I just... did it.' He rubbed his pulled shoulder.

'However it was, Two-boars, you've a cool head in a fight. If ever you want to join the marines, I'll put in a word for you.' He clapped Tashi on the back. 'Good work, son.'

Tashi nodded; he felt suddenly so overwhelmed he couldn't speak.

Rasmuss went out the front to join Breller. Tashi took the guard's chair from by the front door and placed it by the desk, and sat on it facing Shoggu. 'I'm here, master,' he said softly. Shoggu nodded, and settled the mantle more fully around himself as he sank into flight.

Watching his master, Tashi examined his own emotions, but detected no trace of corruption in them; they were simply a reaction to what had happened. He felt shaky, upset, worn out, but also euphoric. The horror of another death, but the avoidance of his own. His survival, the sergeant's praise. This had been his battle, his own fight, and he had done well, by himself. The *Elohim Gibor* had played no part.

Unless... the horrible thought intruded that the throw had been *too* fast, his reactions beyond even his training. And if the Lords of Battle had guided him – somehow, even without Inspiration – then Rasmuss's praise had been undeserved, even a lie.

After a few minutes, voices came from outside the front door: Rasmuss and Breller talking to others. Worried they would disturb Shoggu's flight, Tashi listened. It wasn't the transport from the naval base, but policemen, arguing about not being allowed into the museum. Other voices shouted about a bomb, about nearly being killed.

'Someone *was* killed!' said Rasmuss loudly. 'One of my men lies dead in there, and no one goes in if I don't have good reason to trust them.'

The talk repeated itself. An impasse. Tashi watched the occasional twitch of Shoggu's wiry brows for signs of trouble. Half an hour after beginning flight, Shoggu reached from beneath his mantle; Tashi tensed as his master slowly moved wide-stretched fingers just above the telephone's surface. At last Shoggu withdrew his hand, frowning, and soon after began his call-back chant. Tashi sighed with relief. But there was abnormal urgency to the chant, and after only half its normal duration Shoggu opened worried eyes.

'Master?'

'Someone comes.'

'Who, the magician?' Tashi readied himself.

'No, I think not. I was right: it was the map that angered the magician. They talked on this telephone; the residue of Mrs Fusilli's fear is like cold vapour. But their talk wasn't only about us. Someone else was here yesterday, a man I think. In flight, I saw him as the Kymeran demigod Usanes, having a double face: one towards sunlight, the other darkness. In opposition to the magician, but also his servant? I couldn't resolve it. But I had the strong impression that whoever it was, he is coming here, and is almost upon us.'

'I'll warn Rasmuss.'

Tashi reached the front door to find the backs of Rasmuss and Breller. He heard Rasmuss say, 'You with the other two?' and then the marines parted, and before Tashi could shout a warning not to let any strangers in, he found himself facing a man in his mid-twenties. The magician's servant.

A Thangkaran.

17

THE HOUSE ON ROSEWATER STREET

Like a hawk, he rode the high airs, eyes beyond human keenness watching for prey far below. Watching, waiting. Like a hawk, like a... bored hawk.

Ranga lowered the spyglass he'd borrowed from his parents' house. Nothing had happened in the West Deep for over an hour; the first fifteen minutes after arriving now seemed a frenzy of excitement. First *Nightfire*'s awnings had been taken down, suggesting imminent departure: he'd panicked until he remembered the gate-guard telling him the ship was staying for a week. Then one of *Nightfire*'s boats had been rowed across to the quay, returning with three civilians.

And soon after that, he'd been accosted by the two Empyreal marines, wanting to know what he was looking at with such attention. For reasons that now escaped him, Ranga had tried to suggest he was with the Empyreal secret service, hoping to discover the secret of *Nightfire*'s speed. He'd even hinted at a possible promotion for the marines as a reward for their forbearance. They'd told him to keep his spyglass pointed away from the East Deep, and had even laughed as they'd walked off.

As if the humiliation of his father's opinions hadn't been enough.

Distant movement drew his attention. He snapped the glass to his eye, and his breath caught. A pair of crewmen had moved to *Nightfire*'s bow, another pair to its stern.

Now came a spurt of steam, blown off from the pipe on the rearmost stack.

But – he jammed the glass tighter to his eye – there was no smoke coming from the stack.

Or any stack.

The sailors worked at the lines holding the ship to the mooring buoys. The ends splashed. Water foamed at the ship's stern. 'No,' breathed Ranga. 'You *bastard*.' He dropped to his knees and rested the spyglass on the railing.

Nightfire sliced forward, quickly reaching several knots. The air above her fourth stack shimmered with heat. But still there was no smoke. The impossibility of it, the *cheat* of it, made Ranga want to scream. The ship turned towards the harbour entrance, a mile or more away. Seriuz couldn't have permission – the guard had said another week.

Ten knots now. More. The warship's wash bucked smaller boats at their moorings. Ranga didn't know the speed limit in the harbour, but *Nightfire* had to be breaking it. Was Seriuz stealing the ship?

'*Stop* him, for God's sake…' He aimed the glass at the harbour entrance, the titanic sea walls that narrowed the lane from half a mile to two-hundred yards, the headlands either side blocked and terraced with fortified gun emplacements. But even if Seriuz had no permission, the entrance couldn't be closed, and no other ship had any steam up, save two small tugs and an antiquated light cruiser by the coaling cranes. *Nightfire* had a clear run at the entrance, and steamed through the gap only minutes after slipping her mooring. Tiny even through Ranga's glass, a man on the end of one of the sea walls frantically waved a flag as *Nightfire* passed, before the ship headed south-east into the open sea and disappeared behind the eastern headland.

Ranga lowered the glass, and swore as he'd never sworn in his life.

He ran the mile to the West Deep gate in ten minutes. Several armed sailors stood there. Just as he reached it, the barrier lifted and two auto-carriages sped past into the docks, their passenger compartments crowded with bewhiskered, uniformed men. He thought better of trying to follow them in.

'What's going on?' he asked a sailor. 'Seriuz just nicked the ship, didn't he?'

'Don't talk to him!' called a voice from the guardhouse. 'He's a bloody reporter! He was round here yesterday.'

Sailors turned to him. 'Didn't take you long, did it, you vulture?'

'Go on, leg it,' said another. 'I'll give you a story – heroic sailor bayonets reporter scum up the arse!'

Furious, Ranga turned back through the city. He didn't much care what Seriuz was up to; all he wanted was Orc and Cass. Perhaps Seriuz would release the pair when he'd finished with them, but he couldn't afford to sit and wait. The only course was to learn Seriuz's destination. Though Mrs Fusilli hadn't mentioned the captain, Ranga had no doubt the woman knew the bigger picture. This time, he would leave her in no doubt that she would be better off talking.

There was a new and massive pothole in Stonebrook Street, and a crowd outside the museum next to an overturned ice-cream cart. A half-ring of people, including police, surrounded two well-built Kurassians, one displaying a holstered pistol. Dreading what this might mean, Ranga pushed through to them.

'Is Mrs Fusilli in there?' he asked the Kurassians.

'You with the other two?' said the taller.

It sounded like a chance to get in. 'Yes.'

They stood aside. Ranga entered the museum, and found himself face to face with a surprised Thangkaran boy – the one from the day before. Startled, he then saw the monk, wrapped in feathers, seated at Mrs Fusilli's desk.

Even more startling, a man's body lay beneath a jacket.

'Who are you?' demanded the boy.

Ranga swallowed. 'Mrs Fusilli not here?'

'You knew her?' said the monk.

It sounded like an accusation. 'What's happened?' He warned himself to tread carefully, recalling what he'd overheard of Mrs Fusilli's telephone conversation. 'I was just helping her do some research. I hardly knew her, really.'

The monk stood. 'Let us be open. We know who you are. Part of you serves him, part of you opposes him. You must choose between light and darkness.'

'That's being open?' said Ranga. 'I don't have a clue what you're talking about.'

The boy brought up his naked sword. 'Any move against my master, I will gut you.'

Ranga's gaze flicked to the dead man. *Shit*.

'Tashi—'

'He has a weapon.'

'This?' Ranga pulled out the collapsed spyglass. 'Here—'

He tossed the glass. The boy yelled in alarm and as he moved to catch it, Ranga turned on his foot and raced out the door. He dodged round one Kurassian before the shout of 'Stop him!' came from inside. The Kurassian grabbed, but his fingers only brushed Ranga's shirt. Ranga pushed sideways between onlookers. A man stuck out a foot and he stumbled over it, but caught his balance and kept running, teeth gritted against the fear of a bullet in his back.

None came, and he made it to the main road. In another hundred yards he reckoned he was safe.

Safe, at least, until he reached Rosewater Street.

The previous night, he'd lain awake in his old room at his parents' guesthouse, unable to sleep from the knowledge that she was so close, almost able to smell her on the night air. He'd risen in the quiet hours and walked the streets of the city – *her* city – alone with her presence. He'd wanted to go then, to look on her house, but hadn't allowed himself.

Now, at last, he had no choice. He couldn't solve the problem on his own. He'd reached the end of his resources. She would know what to do.

The noise and smells of the lower city faded as he climbed the winding road to Castle Heights. Flowers he couldn't name heaped the high garden walls of the old merchants' houses. The sea-breeze hissed softly in the evergreens.

Finding the wrought-iron gates of Mythe House locked, Ranga sleeved the sweat off his face and clanged the bell that always set his heart racing. A figure stepped from a doorway in the side of the shadowed archway that led to the courtyard. Umelia shuffled forward, dressed as ever in black, her grey hair braided. Five paces from him, her step faltered with recognition. Then she came forward with the heavy key.

'She's in, I assume?' Ranga nervously licked his lips.

'She is in,' said Umelia. She relocked the gate after him.

Led through to the courtyard, Ranga glanced up as he passed the dry and silent fountain, but no one watched from the windows. A door swallowed him into a dim hallway. In the library, the scents of old cedarwood and even older paper mingled with that of the lilies on the table. He wanted Umelia to offer him coffee. She did not. Ranga had never worried before about what Umelia thought of him, whether she considered him an upstart, a usurper, an interloper. Now he felt horribly desperate for her to be on his side.

'Wait there,' she said. 'Sit, if you want.'

Some way to treat your future master, thought Ranga. This place needed proper servants, and more of them. He creamed dust from the mantelpiece with a fingertip. One near-elderly woman in a place this size was ridiculous. Was it just that Vanessa couldn't afford others? He almost panicked at the thought that she was coming. He wondered if he should recite for her one of the poems he'd composed, then found his memory blank of the words.

'Ranga.'

Her voice sent a cold knife of ecstasy between his shoulder blades.

She stood framed by the doorway, wearing a long white dress of ancient style that bared one shoulder and her throat, where hung the small blue crystal. Excitement fired her sharp, intelligent, beautiful face; her dark eyes burned with it.

'You have it?'

He so wanted to see her anticipation flower into joy. To his embarrassment, tears welled. He almost lied, almost told her yes, just to experience that one moment when she would bathe him in triumph, call him darling, grant him that long-elusive kiss. But he knew the pain that would follow deceit.

At his silence, her eyes hardened like bone. His gaze shied to the crystal at her throat: his one-time gift to her, but so meagre next to the prize he had promised.

'Then why are you here?'

He'd begun to tremble. He was falling apart. He needed to be strong, to give his story, to have her accept that it hadn't been his fault. His head fogged with that rare scent that was always about her.

'They were kidnapped,' he managed. 'The divers.'

'*Kidnapped*? By whom? How did you let it happen?'

He didn't know where to start.

'Sit down, Ranga,' she said. 'I'll fetch you a drink.'

Shaking, he perched on the edge of an armchair. She had indeed told him not to return without the large focus-stone, but he'd entertained the hope, stupid as it now seemed, that she would nonetheless be pleased to see him. It had been four months. His mother and sisters had wanted him to promise he had come back for good. Depending on the kind of drink Vanessa was mixing, he might never see them again.

When she returned, she gave him a glass with blue liquid.

'What is it?'

'Ranga, you mustn't treat me so informally. Not yet.'

'Yes, my Lady.' *Not yet* – so it wasn't poison, at least.

'Tell me what happened.'

She seated herself in a pose of refined elegance, but clearly not the least relaxed, and sipped a liqueur while he talked. Some things he glossed over, or kept secret, the women especially. He felt embarrassed to have thought them a substitute.

'A strange mystery,' she said, when he'd told her of *Nightfire*'s unexpected departure. 'I see now that although you might have done certain things differently, I should not be too angry. And we might yet learn where brave Captain Seriuz has taken his stolen cargo. If it is a port somewhere along the coast, you shall speed there without delay.'

Ranga flinched inside. He knew what was coming, and this was one of things he'd glossed over.

'Give me their fetishes.' She touched the crystal at her throat. 'Or have you left them at your parents' guesthouse?'

'My Lady… they were stolen from me too. All my luggage was.'

She gave a short, sharp laugh, then clapped it silent. 'You kept them in your luggage? Did you also keep the map there?'

'No.' He touched his pocket with the tobacco tin.

'Then why do you not still have them? Did you think them any less important?'

He tried not to look down. 'I didn't think we'd need them.'

'So you thought my asking you to collect them a foolish, idiot whim to be indulged? You think me a woman given to petty flights of fancy?'

'No, my Lady, I…'

'Enough. You possess nothing that came from either of them.'

'I tried to get the last cup back, but…'

She exhaled. 'I should have insisted you had them cut their hair *before* you set off. Why did I not? Was it because I believed you to be trustworthy and clever? Oh, perhaps I am a woman given to attacks of faint-headedness after all!'

'You *can* trust me,' pleaded Ranga. 'Circumstances may conspire against me, but I will always serve you faithfully.'

He yearned to declare his love for her, but he held back. He would not do it as a penniless failure. When he came back to her with the stone and a fortune in gold, that would be the time.

'What about the small focus-stones?' he suggested. 'If that was how you found Orc and Cass in the first place?'

'The connection between them soon fades with distance,' she said. 'When you left here months ago, I was unable to follow your progress even beyond a few miles. Think, now: to whom might Seriuz have told his plans? His crew? Would they have told families? The woman at the museum – you thought she might know something?'

'She was keeping tight-lipped. I went to see her again just now, but she wasn't there. But…'

'What? Speak.'

'After I saw her yesterday, she telephoned someone. She said the monk was interested in the ziggurats.'

'Monk?'

'A Thangkaran. He was at the museum yesterday, and again today. Maybe he knows something about this?'

Her brows lowered. 'Was he accompanied?'

'Yes, some kind of follower, or bodyguard. Looked a bit young.'

Breath hissed between her teeth. 'A Watcher…'

The term picked Ranga's memory. 'From Highcloud? The ones who hunt magicians?'

'And his interest was the ziggurats?'

'You think he might be investigating Seriuz? He might know where he's gone?'

'Even if not, he might be able to learn. The Watchers are masters of divination. But why should he pursue Seriuz? Do we suppose the captain's activities involve magic?'

'There was Gregal's death.'

'When a portly man of advancing years is felled by a heart attack during an interrogation, one need not seek beyond medical science to explain it. To magically kill someone at a distance is scarcely imaginable.' She stood. 'But even if the Watcher is not investigating Seriuz, we might trick him into locating the divers. Bring him here. And on no account breathe any whisper of my own small talents, understand?'

Ranga rose too, his legs weak. 'The monk seemed to think he knew something about me. What if he tries to arrest me?'

'Do not dither, Ranga! One might almost think you had no litany of failure to atone for.'

She turned her back. Ranga bowed and left.

Umelia unlocked the gate for him, her faint smile suggesting she knew he would not be her master quite yet. Ranga stepped out onto the street. He had spent over an hour at Mythe House. Would the monk still be at the museum? If not, then where?

With little hope, he started down the hill. But not fifty yards later he stopped, staring amazed at the grey-clad youth alighting from a cab just ahead. The novitiate helped the monk down after him.

Ranga walked forward. 'Well,' he said uneasily. 'This is a coincidence.'

'Not quite.' The monk pulled the spyglass from within his robe. 'I could locate the street, if not the house,' he explained. 'We have come to talk.'

18

THE ZIGGURAT MAP

Ranga invited the Thangkarans in, acting to give the impression that Mythe House was his home. To his relief, Vanessa, who'd removed her blue crystal, did nothing to falsify this. She sat beside him on the drawing-room settee as though claiming this right as his lover, a pleasing fantasy that did something to calm Ranga's nerves. The monk, who gave his name as Shoggu, took a chair alongside his novitiate. The boy's eyes seemed both drawn to Vanessa, and repelled, to judge from their restless darting.

You couldn't handle her, Ranga thought with satisfaction. *You'd have no chance.*

When they were settled, Shoggu turned to him. 'I wished to talk with you because we seek a magician.'

'I'm not—'

Shoggu had already raised his palm. 'Not yourself, of course. Nor do I believe you still serve him, or I would not have dared come here without reinforcements. I believe you once did serve him, but I also felt an opposition, and an element of deception to the service. It might be that he kept his foul nature hidden from you. Even so, I hope you can identify who I mean.'

Ranga held back the denial. If he told the truth, that he knew nobody who fitted those words, the monk might leave, and the chance to find Orc and Cass would be gone.

Orc! His breath caught at the idea.

'How would one identify such a person?' said Vanessa.

Ranga stiffened, hearing her nervousness and wondering if Shoggu would detect it.

But the monk gave no sign of doing so. 'A magician might spend much time alone. He might possess information unavailable through normal means, and have an abnormal hold over others.'

It was too good to pass up. 'Yes,' Ranga said. 'I know who you're after.'

The Watcher tensed, his head like that of a bald, brown bird of prey.

'I travelled with a young man by the name of Orc. He employed me to help him explore certain underwater ruins.' Now for the killer. 'Ziggurats.'

The effect on Shoggu's face was everything Ranga had hoped for. 'And were you with him at one of these ziggurats a few days ago?'

Ranga nodded.

The monk shifted forward. 'Did he achieve manifestation?'

Ranga heard Vanessa's intake of breath.

'I... don't know what that means,' Ranga said.

'You would know if you'd witnessed it,' said Shoggu. 'Of course, he might reveal that power only to his most trusted servants, if anyone at all. But after that, he came to Torrento with you?'

'Separately. But yes, he came back here too.' It struck Ranga that Orc might in truth be the monk's quarry; certainly there seemed minimal deception required. 'As you said, he used to shut himself away. And he said he got information by talking to an otter. I thought he was just messing around.'

'Oh, by no means was he "messing around". He talked with it in his own tongue?'

'I believe so.'

'That is compelling evidence,' said Shoggu. 'Among the nomads of the far north, there is a dread of those sorcerers whose animal familiars use human speech. The bone masks the creatures wear are said to contain demons. But you said a *young* man? I cannot believe a youth could develop the capability we have witnessed.'

'A young-*looking* man, perhaps,' said Vanessa. 'Might not such evildoers assume a false appearance, a glamour?'

The monk eyed her for a little longer than Ranga was comfortable with, then nodded. 'It must be him. Do you know his full name?' he asked Ranga. 'And where he lives?'

'He isn't in Torrento any more. He left this morning, on a warship.'

'A warship? One also present at that ziggurat?'

'Yes, it was.'

'Where is it bound now?'

'I don't know. Even the navy seemed surprised that it left.'

'And was this shortly before we saw you earlier?'

Ranga nodded.

Shoggu turned to his novitiate. 'He scryed the museum attack, and fled when it failed, is my guess. It's encouraging that he does not believe himself so invulnerable. But where did he go? To another ziggurat, to work his magic?' He shook his head. 'Another flight, beloved one. I am exhausted, but it must be done as soon as we return to our room.'

'But there's no need to go,' said Vanessa. 'I've heard something of the Watchers' abilities. Please, conduct your flight here, in comfort.'

'A gracious offer,' said Shoggu. 'But I would have more success with a map, and we have one at our dormitory that shows the ziggurats.'

Ranga jolted at the hand on his shoulder.

'You have one too, don't you, Ranga dear?' said Vanessa. 'Holiness, please use it if you wish. This is our fight too. My darling has been cruelly used by this malefactor.'

'Used?' said the monk.

'Deceived.' Her hand lightly squeezed Ranga's shoulder: it felt as though every nerve-ending in his body had concentrated in that small space. 'The last few months of his life have been a lie, used for evil when he only wanted to help. And the magician stole his share of the money.'

Ranga nodded stiffly.

She removed her hand. 'You have the map, dearest?'

He fumbled it out of the tobacco tin, warning himself not to make too much of Vanessa's touch, and flattened it out on the coffee table.

'But look,' he said. 'I don't know how this works, but *Nightfire* won't be anywhere on this map yet. Even with her speed, she can't have reached the straits into the Shallow Sea.'

'Learning the magician's current position will achieve little,' said Shoggu. 'I seek his destination.'

'You can tell the future?' said Vanessa.

'I am relying on the ship's course having been firmly decided, and communicated to at least several of the crew,' said Shoggu. 'Unfortunately, the process is inexact. There are few rules to searching the Immaterium. One must be creative.'

He leaned forward to study the map. 'Do you possess anything of the magician's? Or a portrait or photograph?'

Ranga shook his head.

'Is that necessary, even for you?' said Vanessa.

'It would aid me. The ship's name would help, if you know it.'

'Better than that,' said Vanessa, and left the room.

'We should prepare, beloved one,' Shoggu said to his novitiate. 'It has hardly been worth removing the mantle this morning.'

The boy unpacked the bizarre cloak of long feathers Ranga had seen earlier, and put it around the monk's shoulders. He also lit some incense, without asking permission. When Vanessa returned after five minutes, her nose twitched, but she said nothing about it.

'There.' She set down an issue of the *Torrento Monthly*. 'There are photographs of Seriuz and his ship, and the text might be useful too.'

'Yes, indeed,' said Shoggu, studying it. 'I remember the fleet review story: we are encouraged to keep up with events in the lower world. This will indeed be useful, lady. You appear to have an instinctive understanding of divination.'

Vanessa's laugh broke out unusually high. While Shoggu opened the magazine, she excused herself and drew Ranga out along the hallway to the kitchen. Ranga wondered if she were about to follow the touch on his shoulder with something more, perhaps as reward for finding the monk. But her face was hard, her eyes unhappy.

'He suspects me. I'm certain.'

'Just then?'

'He already had his suspicions. His eyes showed them. When he has discovered the divers' location, we must remove him.'

'Remove him?'

Her fingertip touched his jaw with electricity. 'My own small practices are harmless, of course, but such a fanatic would regard them as the utmost evil. Even in Kymera, I might not be safe. The Church now has enough power here to have me executed.'

Her words ripped a hole in his stomach.

'And what of Orc himself?' she said. 'What you did was clever, but do you not see the danger if Shoggu catches up with him, believing him the magician? That novitiate is not merely a protector, he is a weapon.'

'He's just a kid!'

'Who can draw on inhuman fighting power, if the accounts are true. The divers cannot retrieve my stone if they're dead.'

Ranga's mind flailed for reasoning. 'But if those two don't leave here, won't others come looking for them?'

'I can protect myself from those who snoop and pry. What proof will they have? If Watchers themselves come, it might go worse, but they seem reluctant to leave Highcloud these days. It must be done. Leave Shoggu to me. You must handle the boy.'

'How?'

'Draw him out here, to talk: something about your shared ancestral home.' She took a jug from a shelf and poured into it an inch of clear fluid from an unmarked bottle, then half-filled it with lemonade. 'Give him a glass of this. The effect is rapid, but not instant. If he feels he has been poisoned, or if he grows suspicious and refuses the drink, the knives are there.'

'But – won't he suspect, if I don't drink too?'

'You will.' She opened a heavy green bottle and measured a small glass. 'The antidote: drink it now. It will last two or three hours.'

He threw it back, bitterness and sugar, trying not to think.

She smiled, but he saw the fear and sadness behind it. 'Dear, sweet Ranga, is it so terrible a thing to stop those who would persecute and murder those you love? You do love me, don't you?'

It was the chance to make his declaration, the one he had never dared. But before he could gather the words to express the pushing-out in his heart, she turned away.

The novitiate had closed the heavy curtains. The incense drove off all other smells. Shoggu sat hunched over the map, feathered, his eyes closed.

'It might help if you described this "Orc",' he said, his soft voice oddly rhythmic. '*Nightfire* and its captain too. Any detail, however insignificant. Don't be afraid to repeat yourself.'

While Shoggu moved his hands gently across the map, Ranga talked about Orc. He mentioned his unfamiliar accent and his sometimes unique words, some of which Ranga confessed he'd adopted, doubtless a sign of Orc's powerful influence; he described Orc's slender build, unnatural-seeming for someone with his appetite; he related his muttering in his sleep, perhaps from a guilty soul. For twenty minutes he grew increasingly aware of Vanessa listening. He feared she would not be impressed with his blather.

Shoggu's brows tightened in a frown. 'No,' he murmured at last, 'I can find no hint of his course. Which is strange: he might have hidden his own self against detection, but a whole ship? I think you were right: his current position is still off this map, and I have nothing to draw upon. Do you have a chart of a larger area of sea?'

Vanessa left the drawing room, and returned shortly with a map compendium. She opened it at a page showing the whole Shallow Sea and part of the ocean to the east of the Navrantine Straits, with Torrento in the upper-right corner.

The exercise was repeated: Shoggu's hands felt across the map, while Ranga kept up his chatter. After ten minutes the monk's hands ceased their movement, and his fingertips began to spasm, in small, clawing motions.

The novitiate motioned Ranga silent. Only fingertips on paper sounded. Then Shoggu began to mutter and hiss.

'Master!' yelped the novitiate, and began chanting a verse. Ranga wondered what was going on. When the boy had repeated the rhyme three times, Shoggu nodded, and his gnarled hands stilled.

'Thank you, beloved one,' he said, opening his eyes.

'What happened?' asked Vanessa.

'I sensed the ship,' said Shoggu, 'somewhere on that map. But there was a force guarding its location, and that force was itself a trap.'

'You will try again, though?' said Vanessa.

'No,' the novitiate said firmly. 'Not if there's a risk of dark-flight.'

'There is a fog set around that vessel,' said Shoggu. 'If I cannot pierce it, I risk being lost in it. The magician has done his work well, and I am tired. Unless I can somehow strengthen my mental acuity...'

Vanessa drew in breath. 'I might have something.' She went to a small bureau in the corner, and to Ranga's surprise, returned with her blue crystal on its silver chain.

'My dear heart brought me this some years ago,' she said. 'The person who sold it him claimed that it aided concentration. I merely thought it beautiful.' She turned to Ranga. 'But didn't you tell me Orc has one very similar, which he uses in his magic?'

'That's true,' said Ranga.

'Even if it lacks any powers of enhancement,' Vanessa said to Shoggu, 'you might find the connection with the magician's crystal useful. And if it does...'

Shoggu took it, studied it. 'We shall see.'

'Are you sure, master?'

'Be attentive, beloved one.'

For the third time, Shoggu went into his trance. For a while he focused with a near-furious intensity, his knuckles white as he gripped the crystal. Eventually he exhaled. His fingertip rested fifty miles south-west of Torrento.

'Here. I was right: I have encountered this vessel in flight before.'

Ranga wasn't impressed. He could have guessed the ship would be somewhere around there.

'I believe I can also sense the other crystal,' said Shoggu. 'And perhaps more than one. I have a sense of them being drawn together, in congregation. The ship's route…'

Ranga craned forward as Shoggu's fingertip tracked through the Navrantine Straits into the Shallow Sea. But it did not then turn towards the northern shore, as he'd expected.

'Not a ziggurat, then,' whispered Vanessa.

Southwest and west and southwest again, the monk's touch divined *Nightfire*'s intended course, until a hundred miles west and three hundred south of Bazantin, and only a hundred north of the coast of Near Golgomera, it stopped. 'Here.'

Ranga peered in the curtained dimness. At first he saw only open sea, then an island – no, three islands, two of them mere dots.

'Hollow Isles,' he read.

Without a word, Vanessa left. Ranga wondered if he should follow. Shoggu was muttering a chant. The novitiate had relaxed.

A cry made Ranga jump up. He dashed to the library, where Vanessa bent over an old book.

'There!' came her fierce whisper.

The gazetteer detailed the Shallow Sea and the countries surrounding it. Ranga read from where Vanessa pointed, halfway down the brief entry for the Hollow Isles.

Amongst the Sahronic-era ruins is the largest step-temple yet discovered. It is also notable for being the only one whose top, now heavily eroded by waves to a fraction of its former size, rises above the surface.

'The largest ziggurat!' fumed Vanessa. 'No wonder scrying for the stone with your map came to nothing – it shows only the coast. You said it showed *all* the ziggurats.'

'But – Mrs Fusilli said it did.'

'And you trusted her. Yes, yes, I see you had no reason not to. The bitch.'

'You think Seriuz is after the large stone? You think he knows where it is?'

'What would a mere sailor do with it? And in any case, it wouldn't explain why he needs the artefacts Gregal bought from you.' She stared at the passage in the book as though trying to squeeze hidden truths from the description.

'There is a brain behind this,' she said at last. 'What if, in sending you to search for the stone with the divers, all I did was provide a means by which Seriuz could collect those artefacts?'

Ranga struggled with the implications. 'You think the stone might have been a *trick*? It might not even exist?'

'That would be bitter indeed.'

'No, you dreamed about it,' Ranga said. 'A large chunk of blue crystal, on a pile of gold, in a ziggurat with a big hole in the floor.'

'There are those capable of sending dreams.'

'But how could it have been false? I hadn't met the divers then – remember, it was only when you were scrying for the right ziggurat that you sensed another crystal nearby. The dream came when we had no possible way of searching the ziggurats. If it was a trick, what purpose could it have served?'

'Ah, yes. True.'

'And just now, the monk talked about the stones congregating. Surely that means the big one is where the ship's going?'

Vanessa closed the gazetteer, and nodded. 'You have renewed my hope, Ranga. Thank you. But I cannot ask the Watcher, not without rousing his suspicious. You must travel to those islands yourself, and swiftly.'

The idea of leaving her again clawed his heart. 'Do ships even go there?'

'A captain bound for Essaid might detour, if paid well.'

'Or he might dump me overboard.'

'We'll consider that later. Right now... you remember what we agreed?' Again, she touched the line of his jaw, with a sad, worried smile that left him only the ability to nod.

When they returned to the sitting room, the curtains were open, the incense extinguished. 'Is everything well?' asked Shoggu.

'I caught my finger on the edge of a page,' replied Vanessa. 'But I found this.'

She showed him the gazetteer.

'Doubtless that is indeed their destination,' said Shoggu, after he'd read the entry. 'Another journey lies ahead, beloved one.'

The novitiate nodded. 'No effort is too great to destroy that monster.'

Shoggu turned to Vanessa. 'Might I borrow your crystal?'

'Alas,' she said, 'its sentimental value is too great.'

'Then we'll trouble you no further.' He made to get up.

'Oh, but you needn't leave yet,' said Vanessa. 'Your exertions have wearied you, and there's something I would ask you. Ranga, dear, perhaps you could take this young warrior to the kitchen for refreshment? It might be pleasant for you to talk to a fellow Thangkaran of your own age.'

Own age? The boy had to be almost ten years his junior.

'Master?' said the novitiate.

Shoggu looked uneasy, but said: 'Go and refresh yourself, since this gracious lady wishes to speak to me alone.'

Ranga's stomach felt both hollow and full as he led the novitiate to the kitchen. He tried to steady his hands as he poured two glasses from the jug.

'We've seen no others here,' said the novitiate, taking the proffered lemonade. 'Thangkarans, I mean. You've been here a long time. I can tell from your speech.'

'I was born here,' said Ranga. 'My dad came a long while back. My parents run a guesthouse.' He hesitated, then gulped the drink. *Look, it's safe, I'm taking it. Come on.*

'A guesthouse.' The novitiate sipped – began to kill himself. 'The railways porter said there was one run by a Thangkaran.'

'Yeah.' Ranga felt sick. *Railways porter* – the idiot. But the boy had something of the look of Saskia, his youngest sister, when he drank, his concentration on the liquid. 'Dad bribes them to send Thangkarans our way. We get a few.'

It was for love, to prevent another death: one even less deserved. The boy might not have harmed anyone yet, but he would.

'I wanted to go there,' the novitiate said, 'but my master said no. So we ended up at a horrible hotel called Baker's Rooms. It was the only place that offered charity. From your father, it would have been too easy, according to my master.'

'Huh! I don't think so. My dad wouldn't let monks stay even if they paid.'

'Why not?' Another sip, a contraction of the brow, perhaps at the unfamiliar flavour.

'No idea.' Some part of Ranga's mind had stepped outside himself to watch what he was doing, carrying on a normal conversation with a boy he was murdering. 'He's never told us. And we've never had one turn up, so it's never been put to the test.'

'Perhaps he was changed by this city,' said the novitiate. 'How could he stand it? To move from Thangkara to here?'

'Nothing wrong with Torrento.' Ranga wanted to hate the boy for the insult, to ease the guilt. He drained his glass, almost able to pretend that by doing so, he must be ignorant of the drink's true nature.

'You wouldn't say that if you'd come from somewhere pure,' said the novitiate. 'And now my master and I will have to go even further south, close to the Witch Mother's land.'

'If you can find a ship to take you.'

'That will be no trouble.' The boy drained his glass, leaned heavily against the dresser. Sweat beaded his brow.

'It won't?' Ranga eyed the knives in their wooden block. The stomach? The heart? What?

'My master has a warrant from an Empyreal prelate. Their navy will take us.'

It took a moment for the words to sink in, then Ranga cried out. 'Gods!' He threw open the cupboard – wrong one – then the next, took out the heavy green bottle. Close to panic, he poured a big measure into the boy's glass. 'Drink!'

'What?' the boy groaned.

'My fault. I didn't think. That first stuff, lovely, but makes you sick if you're not used to it.'

'I do feel – yes.' The novitiate tipped back the glass, made a face, but swallowed.

Ranga ran down the hall to the drawing room. The monk had the gazetteer open on his lap; Vanessa leant over him from behind, something string-like held between her fists.

Both looked towards him as he stumbled to a stop. Vanessa's face was cold with fury as she slipped the knotted cord between her breasts.

'My Lady, great news! These two – the Empyreal Navy will take them!'

The novitiate weakly followed him in, his skin pale. 'Master, I hope I didn't do wrong to tell him.'

'Are you all right?'

The boy nodded. 'I will be. The drinks in this city are as bad as everything else.'

'Well… it is excellent news indeed that you have a means of reaching that island,' said Vanessa. 'I hope your Holiness will not object to Ranga accompanying you? He knows this "Orc" and his ways. He can help.'

The monk considered this, then nodded. 'If the navy agrees. Despite what my novitiate seems to have suggested, we cannot know they will put a warship at our disposal.'

'Oh, they will,' said Ranga. 'They've never found out what gives *Nightfire* its speed. They'd like nothing better than a reason to board it and have a look.'

The monk nodded. 'Then we'll return to the base. Is there a carriage station nearby?'

'A neighbour drives me when necessary,' said Vanessa. 'I'll send

Umelia for him. Perhaps you'll wait in the garden, while I bid farewell to my darling?'

When the Thangkarans had gone out, she turned towards Ranga a face that did not promise the praise he had hoped for.

'You *fool*. We had them in our hands and you let them live. What's to stop them finding out more about me now? Or killing Orc?'

'I can deal with them when we reach the island.'

'You had better.'

'We needed the ship!'

'You yourself gave a perfect reason why the Kurassians would have gone after Seriuz, had they known his destination – and you could have made that knowledge the price of them taking you! Did you not think of that?'

He hadn't. But neither had she, until now. 'I'll make it up to you.'

She turned slightly. 'I hope so, Ranga. I couldn't bear another disappointment. I thought you would do anything for me.'

'I would, my Lady!'

'Yet I gave you clear instructions, and you disobeyed them.'

He felt caught between arguing his case and pleading forgiveness.

'Perhaps you need an incentive,' she said. 'Perhaps this will remind you.'

She stepped towards him, right up to him. Ranga steeled himself for what would come. He had failed. Whatever punishment Vanessa deemed fitting, he would deserve it.

She touched the side of his head, angled it.

She leaned into him and kissed him on the lips.

Just a moment, but he tasted her. Her withdrawal felt it would pull his heart out of his mouth.

'Bring me back the stone,' she whispered, 'and tell me in truth that I need not fear that Watcher, and your reward will be all that you imagine.'

Clairaudioscope transcript 16:03 25-8-336
Known voices: A,C,F,G,H

F: What now? Scarab won't attempt communication at sea.
    We can't tell him the shroud around the ship has been
    compromised.

A: I'm still unsure why it was.

H: We made it strong enough to defeat the monk alone, but
    he used one of the crystal shards. He made connection
    with the others. We couldn't reinforce it in time.

A: The second failure in almost as many days.

H: It won't happen again.

A: And the monk's cruiser?

C: Still being prepared. It will leave tonight. We can't
    warn Scarab about that either.

G: We could use project baffomet to hold it in port.

A: Baffomet is not intended for micro instruction. It
    might rouse suspicion, or at least confusion.

F: Then how do we resolve this crisis?

A: There is no crisis. By going in pursuit, the monk has
    effectively ensured his own destruction. You forget
    what that cruiser will encounter.

G: Of course.

F: (Phonetic, unsure if proper noun or onomatopoeia)
    Kaboom.

19

THE LOST ART

Returning from the officers' washroom, Orc looked up through the hatchway opening. Still no trace of smoke, and no taint of it in the air.

And this time, no sign of the crewman who'd been standing up top to guard against him and Cass getting on deck.

He climbed the ladder to find the sun high on the left. The ship's roll showed him the open sea, restless with a light swell. And he'd been right: no smoke, even though *Nightfire* was steaming faster than at any time during their voyage to Torrento.

Voices, faint over engines and sea-wash, drew his attention. Near stack number four stood the crewman who'd been stationed above the hatchway. As Orc watched, Seriuz and the steward, Bouran, emerged from between the rearmost two stacks, supporting Thera slumped between them.

Orc caught the smell of coal-smoke at last. The fumes were just starting up from stacks one and two.

'Oi!' The crewman had seen him. 'Get below!'

Orc glared at the man, then clambered back down to the corridor and knocked on Cass's door. She opened, looking worried.

'They're bringing back your room-mate,' said Orc. 'She doesn't look well.'

'What's going on?'

'Don't know,' he said. 'But we've changed course. We were going south or southeast before, but just now the sun was dead left of the ship, so we're heading west.'

'I'm sure it's—'

Cass broke off as feet sounded on the ladder. Seriuz descended first.

'What's happened to Thera?' said Cass.

'Nothing that rest won't cure,' said Seriuz. 'Mister Strandborn, would you take your cousin into your quarters? I'll call you both before long.'

Seriuz closed the cabin door after them. Cass sat on the lower bunk; Orc stood by the door, alternately relaxing and bracing his muscles with the ship's roll.

'I still reckon we left without permission,' he said, keeping his voice low and an ear on the corridor.

'I'm sure not,' said Cass. 'Martin must have got an emergency—'

'*Martin?*'

She rolled her eyes. 'Captain Seriuz then, if you want to get all military.'

'No, I don't. We're still civilians. He can't do this.'

Voices sounded in the corridor: Seriuz and others. Orc tried to quietly pull the door open, but it was yanked shut from the other side.

'What does Thera do, anyway?'

'Something with the engines,' said Cass. 'That's all she's said.'

'What do you talk about, then? You do a lot of it.'

'You can hear?'

'Just voices.'

Cass shrugged. 'The rest of the crew, mostly.'

Orc fidgeted with the door handle at his back. 'Us?'

'Not much.'

A knock came. Orc opened. 'The wardroom, please,' said Seriuz.

'You going to tell us what's going on?' said Orc.

Seriuz looked troubled. 'Yes. It's about time I did.'

It had been only minutes since Orc had passed through the empty wardroom, so he was surprised to see someone now seated at the far left corner of the table. The man wore a pale linen suit, with a white shirt and black tie: all clearly expensive, but rumpled. He looked to be in his forties, his oiled hair still dark and thick, his jaw sharpened by a trimmed beard. His skin looked strangely young, but there was a deep tiredness behind his piercingly attentive eyes.

'Sit, please,' said Seriuz. Orc and Cass took chairs near the door. 'This is Mister Lucien Daroguerre.'

Orc's breath caught at the name. This time, Daroguerre seemed unconcerned about it being used openly.

'At your service,' he said, his voice precise, educated, somewhat nasal.

'You're in the navy too?' said Orc, recalling the uniform from his scape.

'An advisor.' Daroguerre met his gaze with an unsettling intensity. 'Please, unless I'm called upon, ignore my presence.' He gestured to Seriuz to continue.

'You're certain this is safe?' Seriuz asked him.

'I have been assured the ship is secure. Proceed.'

Seriuz nodded. 'I dislike subterfuge,' he said, facing Orc and Cass, 'and I disliked having to employ it in your case. While there was any chance of... escape, to be blunt, I had to make you think I wanted to recruit you into the navy. The truth is, I need your aid in a particular enterprise, and I hope you'll render that aid because you agree with its rightness, not because you feel coerced.'

'But if we don't, you'll coerce us anyway?' muttered Orc. Cass kicked his ankle.

'Let's hear it, then,' she said.

'First, a question,' said Seriuz. 'I understand your amnesia leaves you ignorant as to your birthplace, but what are your feelings towards the Empyreum?'

Orc assumed it had been Cass that had told Seriuz about their memory loss. 'Nothing in particular.'

'We've never been to Kurassia,' said Cass. 'As far as we know, I mean.'

'Do you know for what reason the Empyreum maintains its naval base in Torrento?'

'For their colonies in Golgomera,' said Orc; Geist had talked about it often.

'Precisely so,' said Seriuz. 'Kurassia herself has no access to the Southern Ocean, save for a long and dangerous route around two continents.' He placed a map on the table. 'Her industrial centres are on the western coast of the Norgeld Sea, here. That's less than a thousand miles north of us, but any ships from her own yards would have to steam right around Himulth and then Golgomera, coming round its southern point and up its east coast – ten thousand miles of treacherous waters. The dreadnought squadron came that way five years ago, and lost *Indomitable Will* on route. The passage has not been attempted since, to my knowledge.'

'What about their other ships?' said Orc.

'All built in Kymera,' said Seriuz. 'Thirty years ago, a treaty ceded control of most of our shipyards, and Torrento Grand Harbour, so the Empyreum could support its Golgomeran colonies. And though I'm tempted to say the treaty was forced on us, our government probably saw mostly benefit, with increased trade and shipyard work. But they did not, I think, foresee the scale of Empyreal ambitions, nor their likely consequence.'

He indicated a peninsula a thousand miles to the east of Kymera. 'Historically, Sundara here has been the dominant power in the Southern Ocean. Its ancient trading commonwealth extends eastwards and southwards around the rim—' He swept a finger across a mass of countries and islands – 'but apart from a few short-lived occupations of the Kymeran coast, it has never bothered with the ocean's western half.'

'Until now?' guessed Orc.

'Quite. The Empyreum's determination to colonise the Dark Continent has provoked Sundara into attempting the same. Thus far, neither has gained anything but sections of the coastal strip: the interior is effectively barred to them by a force that induces madness in outsiders who venture further – the Witch, or Golgometh, as the Empyrean church calls it. And now the Empyreum is pouring all its efforts into overcoming that force. If it succeeds, and manages to exploit Golgomera's natural resources and its peoples, it will be able to dominate the world. Sundara's position depends on her preventing that, and her strategy for doing so must be to block Empyreal access to the Southern Ocean.'

Looking at the map, Orc suddenly saw it, as though it were an easy mate in a game of chess. 'By taking Kymera.'

'Which the Empyreum would fight tooth and nail to prevent,' said Seriuz grimly. 'Unlike most of my compatriots, I have seen war. I can scarcely imagine what would happen to Kymera if the two Great Powers were to fight over it.'

Orc remembered the road of bones, the mire of blood-soaked mud. 'How do you avoid it?'

'By removing the need for Sundara to act,' said Seriuz. 'Kymera must regain her independence and stop herself becoming an Empyreal corridor. The treaty must be revoked and the lease on the harbour annulled.'

'This is too big for us,' said Cass. 'We might not be Kurassian, but we're not Kymeran either; we don't belong anywhere.'

'You belong on the side of justice and peace, Miss Strandborn. I'm certain that's what your heart will tell you.'

'But – what happens when you break the treaty?' said Orc. 'If Kymera's so important, the Empyreum's hardly going to leave just because you ask them. What stops them keeping the harbour by force?'

'The goal of this voyage, Mister Strandborn.'

Orc frowned, baffled. 'Which is?'

'First,' said Seriuz, 'I must explain why the Empyreum does not currently fear such a revolt. It dominates Kymera less by armed might than by culture. For all their grumbling, most Kymerans would not wish for true independence, if that meant the removal of Empyreal influence.

The Church has converted many with its attractive certainties. And the Kurassians have brought not only trade, but scientific advancements otherwise beyond us.

'Against this invasion of ideas, Kymera's native culture is weak. We have no religion save for superstitions and gods that rise and fall in popularity, beneath the umbrella of a vague mysticism. Our writers look back to an ethereal age of romance; our government is still obsessed with hunting out supporters of the regime it ousted three decades ago. With no central pillar of identity, our culture is susceptible to erosion. God-days have fallen from observance; children no longer throw flour-bombs in honour of Jonastas, or sneak off to drink Puristo's forbidden wine. Our easy-going nature has been contaminated by the Kurassian ethos of expansion and acquisition, leading to our own reckless attempt to colonise Essaid some years ago – and few have even noticed the change.'

He studied his fingertips. 'But there is still, I believe, a spark of native pride that could be fanned into flames strong enough to burn away Kurassian cultural dominance. The public reaction to last year's fleet review gave me reason to hope.'

'And made you the natural candidate to lead an uprising?' said Orc.

Seriuz half-smiled, but his eyes were sharp with annoyance. 'Your cynicism is mistaken. Alone, I should barely raise enough support to inconvenience the Empyreum for five minutes. Kymera needs an uprising, but one centred on this "pillar of identity" I noted as being missing.

'In past crises, an ancient hero or war-god was raised to the status of figurehead. But such would be inappropriate now, when our aim is peace. And the war-god was still only an image, a thought. We aim to give back to the people a core of identity that is not merely an idea, but which carries a power strong enough to achieve our aims: to force the Kymeran government to revoke the treaty, to drive out the Empyreum and destroy its navy if not surrendered, and to safeguard our northern frontier against reprisals.'

Orc tried not to show his incredulity. The man had to be mad.

'What kind of power?' said Cass.

'One that grows in strength with the passion of the Kymeran people,' said Seriuz. 'A small-scale conspiracy cannot hope to succeed: we need the people with us. But I have no doubt they'll join us when they see what we have returned to them: a pillar of identity that can stand full-square against the living God-Head of Empyreus.'

He seemed about to say more, then looked to Daroguerre. 'Your words here would suit better.'

'Nonsense,' said Daroguerre. 'The language is hardly specialised.'

'I've talked long enough,' said Seriuz. 'And perhaps they need time to digest what they've already heard.'

'No, please,' said Cass. 'We want to hear it.'

'Yes,' said Orc. *Whatever the fuck it is.*

Seriuz nodded, but looked uncomfortable. 'Now it comes to describing it, I can hardly believe it myself; but I'm assured of its feasibility, and I've seen evidence to support it. We plan to make... that is, not really "make", but—'

'We will create a goddess,' cut in Daroguerre.

A short laugh burst out of Cass. 'Sorry,' she said at once, 'I thought you meant...'

'Thought what?' said Daroguerre.

'Nothing. I made a mistake.'

Orc didn't know what Cass had thought, nor was he sure he'd grasped Daroguerre's meaning. The man's tone suggested he was proposing nothing more remarkable than building a giant effigy. But even if such a symbol could rouse the population, how could it repel Empyreal retaliation? Did these people have any sense of reality?

Daroguerre looked disappointed with their reaction. 'To be more specific, we shall physically manifest the ancient supreme goddess of this region, Urshevat: she who was once held to be life and breath and justice and the earth itself, before her attributes were fragmented and scattered across a hundred lesser deities.'

'What do you mean, "manifest"?' said Orc. 'A statue?'

'Don't be ridiculous!' snapped Daroguerre. 'Do you think us insane?

To *manifest* is to draw forth from the psychosphere into the physical world.'

'Huh?' said Cass.

'To make physically real,' said Seriuz. 'And in this case, alive.'

There was silence but for the thrum of engines. Orc felt cold with realisation.

'Impossible.' Cass's voice trembled.

'It's natural you should think so,' said Daroguerre, 'since there's no widely available evidence for it ever having been achieved. The Zhenaii are held by some to have known the practice, but nothing remains of their civilisation but legends. Nevertheless, the art has recently been recovered.' He looked at Orc. 'You appear troubled, Mister Strandborn. You perhaps recall an encounter within the penetralium of the Bazantin ziggurat, a few days ago?'

He couldn't breathe.

'That was his mind,' jumped in Cass. 'His fin caught, or something.'

'A partial manifestation: near-complete, but temporary. And more dangerous than was expected. Fortunately for all of us, Mister Strandborn survived.'

'I understand your scepticism,' Seriuz said to Cass. 'But if you'd seen what I have...'

'Wait!' said Orc, finding his voice at last. 'That thing tried to *kill* me. And *you* created it?'

'No, we did not,' said Daroguerre.

'But you're saying it was *real?*'

'It can't have been,' said Cass. 'Martin, it *can't.*'

Seriuz looked almost apologetic. 'Apparently, it was.'

'If we might maintain calm,' said Daroguerre. 'The meaning of "real" isn't altogether fixed when applied to such entities. One reaches a point in philosophical enquiry when the word becomes useless. But have no fear: we are not about to manifest anything like that horror. I suspect she derived from Skalith, the Destroyer, an aspect of Urshevat dominant during the Sahronic culture's slide into frenzied sacrifice – and it was doubtless your own unease, Mister Strandborn, which gave her that form, by drawing on the later psychotypes imprinted on the chamber. But the artefacts you retrieved had already seen much use before that aspect became dominant, and it's the earlier, truer conceptions of the goddess we shall use when manifesting our living deity.'

'How do you know what happened, if it wasn't yours?' said Orc.

'We've been keeping an eye on your adventures for some time.'

'What, scrying?'

Daroguerre smiled. 'Surely you don't imagine I could manifest a goddess without being a magician of some ability?'

'Fine,' said Cass. 'Good luck with it. Why do you need us?'

Orc realised. 'The artefacts.'

'Yes,' said Daroguerre.

'The ones we brought up?' said Cass. 'We sold them to a museum.'

'After a fashion,' said Daroguerre.

'Alonso Gregal is our agent,' said Seriuz. 'The entire collection is in my cabin.'

'*What?*' said Orc.

'The collection *thus far*,' said Daroguerre. 'We still need the most important pieces, with the strongest psychic imprinting: those from the power-centre of Urshevat worship.'

'Which is where we're headed now,' said Seriuz. 'When they've been retrieved, we'll return to Torrento and make history.'

Amid the bewilderment of plots and ideas, a thought jumped Orc. 'We'll have to dive for them? They're in another zig?'

'The Great Ziggurat,' confirmed Seriuz.

'Off an island?'

He'd wanted to sound casual, but failed. He noticed Daroguerre's eyes twitch narrower.

'The Hollow Isles, yes,' said Seriuz. 'You know of the place?'

Orc shook his head, not trusting speech.

'I think we now truly have given you enough to digest.' Daroguerre rose from his seat.

Seriuz did likewise. 'Stay here if you prefer,' he told them. 'Or you may go up on deck, but again, keep aft of the stacks.'

As soon as the door closed after the two men, Orc whispered, 'Did you hear that? An island! The Great Ziggurat!'

Cass only frowned, troubled-looking, at the table.

'My half-dream!' he added, in case her mind had been too overwhelmed to grasp the significance. 'The stone!'

'Things have got bigger than that,' she said.

'What? Not to us!'

'Their plan,' she said. 'It's not – you can't make things out of thin air. Daroguerre's mad, and he's sucked Seriuz into it somehow. Trying to bring down the government is treason. We have to get them to turn back.'

'Not yet, though!' said Orc. 'When they send me down to get the artefacts, I can get the stone too.'

'We can't let things get that far.' Cass shook her head. 'It's too dangerous.'

Orc frowned, puzzled. 'But we need the stone to find out who we are.'

She pressed her spread fingertips against the tabletop. 'But… do we really *need* to know?'

Stunned, Orc couldn't answer. There *was* no answer, except one so obvious it could never need saying. But Cass was questioning it, denying it. The previous evening, she hadn't wanted him to look for what she'd seen in blackout, and now…

He felt sick, the motion of the ship suddenly too noticeable. He scraped back his chair.

She looked up. 'Where are you—'

'Outside.'

His hands shook on the ladder. On deck, the air stank. A mass of smoke poured from the two forward stacks, but the ship's speed had dropped. He went to the rail. The sea rolled beneath him, impenetrable blue, endlessly deep.

He shouldn't have left Cass alone, that afternoon following the horror. Stewing in her thoughts and what had happened – that must have been the cause of her change. And she was getting worse.

It couldn't be too late to bring her back. It *mustn't* be.

He turned as he noticed movement farther along the railing. Not far from the bridge, Daroguerre was talking with someone else in civilian clothes.

Orc's grip tightened on the rail. Esteban.

He'd forgotten the young fisherman. Why hadn't he been taken off at Torrento? He watched the two converse, his stomach feeling both full and empty, his head bursting with all that had been crammed into it. After a minute, Lyle appeared and grabbed Esteban, and after a short exchange with Daroguerre, took him away.

Daroguerre came back towards Orc, eyes now hidden behind smoked-glass spectacles. It struck Orc then that Daroguerre must be the civilian Seriuz had told him he would have to share a cabin with: the man with the terrible three-eyed ally, a man who might genuinely be mad.

'Mister Strandborn. You contemplate our grand design for peace?'

Orc swallowed. 'That guy you were talking to…'

'Yes, Seriuz appraised me of his reason for being on board. An unpleasant business – but fascinating, for a student of the past such as I, to meet someone who still reveres an albeit distorted version of she whom we seek to return to the world.'

He leaned on the rail next to Orc. 'I guess your thoughts. Either I can do what I claim, or I'm insane, and you're not sure which to fear most. But keep your head down, play your part, and you'll emerge no worse than you went in. Should our plan succeed, you'll be a hero. Should it fail, you can credibly claim you were coerced.'

'Right. I guess.' Orc wished he'd thought of that when talking to Cass.

'In any case,' said Daroguerre, 'I thought at one point in our talk I detected excitement in you, rather than fear?'

'Oh?'

'The chance to dive in another ziggurat seemed to interest you.'

'Well… yeah, it's always a thrill.'

'It has been a while since my own youth, but I dimly recall the relishing of physical challenge and danger.'

Metal flashed on Daroguerre's finger: Orc noticed a ring, its flat circular top etched like a plant with three narrow leaves that didn't quite touch.

Or... three eyes.

'You asked an interesting question earlier,' said Daroguerre. 'Whether I, also, was in the navy. Why should you think that?'

'I don't know,' said Orc, trying to master panic.

'I did in fact hold a naval post at one time. Could you somehow have known that?'

'No, I don't think so. I just... I don't know why I said it.'

'No matter,' said Daroguerre, and moved his hand so the ring was hidden. 'Now, you must excuse me. Even with these smoked lenses, I dislike strong sunlight.'

From the corner of his eye, Orc watched him walk off. The sunlight was indeed strong, as Daroguerre had said, but Orc shivered.

20

NIGHTMARE SEED

After Orc had left the wardroom, Cass returned to the cabin. She didn't want to go after him, nor wait for him to come back and plague her with questions.

'You all right now?' she asked Thera.

'Not so bad,' came the reply. 'How was that?'

'Illuminating.' Cass settled into the lower bunk. 'You know what Seriuz told us?'

'He said he'd be explaining.'

'And it doesn't worry you that no one's ever tried this madness before, and if it doesn't work you'll all be hanged for treason?'

'He must have told you how important it is?'

'But he can't believe Daroguerre can really succeed?'

'Look, can't this wait? I'm knackered.'

Cass was taken aback by Thera's sharpness: a warning sign that their friendship was still too new to be secure. 'From earlier? What happened?'

'Work happened.'

'You still haven't told me what you do.'

'I can't yet, sorry.'

'Even though we're supposed to be working on the same "enterprise"?'

'Look, I'll ask the captain if – *ah*! Bastard!'

'Thera?'

'It's nothing. A pain I get sometimes.' Thera swung her legs over the side of the bunk and dropped to the floor. 'Back soon.'

'Want me to come?'

'I said, it's nothing,' said Thera. 'I won't be long.'

Cass lay on her narrow mattress, staring at the underside of Thera's bunk. Like in a coffin, she thought – a coffin in a ship of madness and secrets, taking her to the last place she wanted to go. Ever since she'd almost been sacrificed to the sea, life had been like a dark dream.

Her actual dreams were even worse.

The foetid, crawling nightscapes had started after her near-drowning. All she ever remembered was something vague about Orc and a tower window, but that was enough – it was atmosphere rather than detail that left the dark stain on her psyche, a tide-mark higher each night. She couldn't believe she'd never thought of the dangers of searching for their past, never realised that the truth might be *better* hidden.

Her nightmares left her in no doubt that Orc could not be allowed to uncover the old bones the Shroud hid. His obsession, his unwillingness to listen, had almost got her killed at Bazantin, and he'd never even apologised. This time, she would stop things getting anything like that far.

Thera returned after fifteen minutes. 'Sorry I was a bit sharp before.'

'No problem,' said Cass, as the mattress above her creaked. 'Everything okay?'

'Better, thanks,' said Thera, though her tone seemed slightly forced. 'I should have realised how difficult it would be for you. Is Daroguerre the first magician you've met?'

'Not quite,' said Cass, relieved Thera seemed something like her normal self again. 'There was Geist. He called himself a shaman. But the only real power he had was to fuck up people's lives.'

'He taught your cousin?'

'Yes,' said Cass, surprised Thera seemed to have been told about Orc's abilities.

'You weren't interested in learning?'

Cass laughed bitterly. 'Not after that, no. He broke Orc's mind with a load of smoke and mirrors, almost broke mine too. Then he shut Orc in a cave for two weeks. He let me think he was dead. And when he brought him back, he might as well have been – all he could do for days was jabber about some serpent-dance, and his new otter friend. No way did I want to end up the same.'

'Serpent-dance?' said Thera. 'What's that?'

'I don't know, just hallucinations, nonsense. But Orc thought it meant everything. I thought he'd never get better. And he never has, not really. A few days ago, I went into his hotel room and he was hanging out the window in some kind of half-dream. He said it was showing him where to find this stone he wants – and yes, it turned out to be right, but being right's no use if you're splattered across the pavement. I spent the rest of the night leaning out of my window, watching.'

'That's awful,' said Thera.

'He just… he doesn't get it. He *can't* get it. It wears me out.'

'This stone,' said Thera. 'Something Geist told him to look for?'

'No, Geist had already buggered off by then.'

It suddenly occurred to Cass that she might, without needing to reveal her fears about her past, recruit Thera's help in preventing Orc getting the crystal.

'He wants it for his magic,' she said. 'There's something he thinks he needs to find out.' Her thoughts raced ahead, making sure her cover story was sound. 'Geist said there was a group called the Kings Behind the World who have agents in every government, and he thought these agents were looking to kill us. They've already tried.'

'You're serious?'

'Geist said he could protect us, because he knew secret places with secret friends, and he made a shroud that stopped people searching for us. Orc believed him.'

'But you didn't?

'I wasn't so sure. But even if these Kaybees do exist—'

'Kaybees?'

'KBWs, sorry. Even if they're real, I'm more worried about Orc completely losing himself to magic. He used to be…'

She almost choked as she remembered being held tight in a field under the stars. *I'm real, Cass.*

'He had confidence before, even though all the moving around with Geist was scary and confusing. He kept saying everything would be fine in the end; we just had to ride it out. Initiation took that away. Like this was no longer his world, and he didn't know what to think, what to believe, how to behave. Sometimes he wouldn't stand up for himself at all, and then other times he'd get all aggressive. He half-killed a farmer Geist left us with. This guy tried it on with me, and Orc hit him with a poker. We panicked and ran. That's how we came to Torrento.'

It felt a relief to talk. It suddenly struck her that in all her remembered life, she'd never had a real female friend, having always encountered a wariness in the wives and daughters of the farmers who'd put them up. 'We tried to get a ship,' she went on, 'but we didn't have enough money, and we had no idea how we'd live – and Orc was on edge all the time about those agents, because we'd lost Geist's protection. It was horrible. I was used to Orc holding it all together, from before. Maybe that's why he broke first, the strain of it. But suddenly it was me who had to plan and work things out, because he'd become useless.

'And one day, this foreign-looking guy got talking to us in the bar of this cheap hotel where we had a bit of work, and it turned out he wanted to explore the sunken ziggurats, because he knew one of them had a heap of gold in it, and a big focus-stone. We thought that stone was the answer to everything, because… well, we'd find out about those agents. Only now…'

'A heap of gold, really?'

'So Ranga said, or his "source". But maybe it was a lie to get us to dive. Maybe this whole thing's just been about bringing up the stuff for Daroguerre's spell. Maybe there's no stone either. Let's hope so.'

'Because then Orc wouldn't lose himself to the Otherworld?'

'Feels like I've already lost him, one way or another.' Cass sighed. 'Sorry, I shouldn't have bored you with all that. We should stay away from my past. I guess you understand. You haven't said anything about yours.'

'You haven't asked.'

'Our pasts shouldn't matter,' said Cass. 'Look… forget all that, just now. I don't want it to change anything. With us.'

Thera's arm reached down. Cass took the hand. A little warmth, a connection.

'Don't worry,' said Thera. 'It changes nothing.'

She decided not to push Cass any further. After several minutes, she complained again about the pain, though this time she was pretending.

In the wardroom, examining papers, sat the man to whom she owed her life. And who had once almost killed her. And who might one day finish the job. As before, Thera went to stand by the door in the corner that led to the small galley and the washroom, so that if anyone came in, it might look as though she'd just been to the toilet.

'Well?' her father asked.

As always, she thought of denying him. But only for a moment. 'You were correct.' She knew he liked to hear this. 'Orc knows the stone's at the Great Ziggurat. He saw it during what Cass called a half-dream: a deep hypnagogic state, I imagine.'

Her father looked displeased.

'You'd've had to tell him about it anyway,' she said, 'if he's going to bring it up for you.'

'It's not that he knows,' said Daroguerre. 'It's that he found out for himself. It seems his ability is greater than I expected.'

'Cass said he saw the Serpent Mandala, during his Initiation.'

Daroguerre's eyebrows raised. 'And survived?'

'Not fully, from what she said.'

'He could be more useful than I thought. Or a greater threat.'

'How a threat?' said Thera. 'There's nothing more he can discover. You've already told him the plan.'

'I was vague about how they came to be involved. I doubt he'll suspect – there's no connection between Vanessa's mongrel lapdog and us, apart from her dream, and it would take an unrivalled talent to trace that to me. Still, better to avoid the chance. It seems clear it was Orc I sensed when speaking with Seriuz last night. He too much enjoys pushing his otter's snout where it's not wanted. We must cut it off.'

Thera saw him stroking his ring. She felt a pang of sympathy for Orc – she knew how it would feel for him to lose his animath. Then again, why shouldn't he suffer too?

'What do you need me to do?'

'In a short while,' her father said, 'the ship will stop, for several hours. The calm spell would be a perfect chance for Orc to try another soulscape journey. If necessary, we might even help persuade him to do so. And when he does, we'll be ready.'

21

STORIES

*O*nce, Geist had told Orc, *when time was the edge of a bowl and not yet an arrow, Lord-Lady Sky-and-Earth kept the sacred fire in a smoking mirror deep in a valley, and to watch over it they set the Precious Night Sisters.*

Raven wanted to be a guardian himself, but because he'd let the first man and woman escape into the world, he was refused. As revenge, he decided to steal the fire and give it to man, so mankind would populate the world and the most sacred thing would become commonplace.

Five animals there were that he persuaded to help. Fox wanted the chance to display his cunning. Hare was too timid to refuse. Otter thought it a great game. Eagle pronounced it a noble endeavour, while Sparrow wanted man to multiply and grow corn she could eat. These five, Raven placed at intervals between the valley of the fire and the Tree Beyond the World, where he waited.

When all was ready, Fox wandered jauntily into the valley, as though meaning no more mischief than a new-born babe.

'Where are you going with that stick in your mouth?' asked the sisters.

'To play!' said Fox. 'Throw this and I'll catch it for you.'

Amused, they threw the stick. Fox caught it and returned it to them, then ran back and waited for them to throw it again. The sisters didn't notice that each time, Fox went a little further round until he was very close to the smoking mirror. When he next caught the stick, he thrust its end into the fire and it burst into flame.

The sisters howled. Fox ran.

Out of the valley he ran, and the sisters pursued him. He tried all his cunning, but they were more cunning still. They caught him where Raven had told Hare to wait. Just before the sisters fell upon Fox and clawed out his tongue and killed him, he threw the brand forward.

Hare caught it. In terror he ran. He was fast, and fresh, but the sisters didn't tire. They caught him where Raven had told Otter to wait. Just before they fell upon Hare and tore off his legs and killed him, he threw the brand forward.

Otter caught it and slipped into Lake Vunar. The sisters made boats. Otter swam fast, but they paddled faster. They caught him where Raven had told Eagle to fly over the water. Just before the sisters fell upon Otter and ripped off his tail and killed him, he threw the brand into the air.

Eagle caught it and flew. The sisters could not fly, but they called upon Lord-Lady Sky-And-Earth, and sky and earth were again made as one. The sisters chased Eagle as she flew high with the brand in her beak. Eagle tired, but the sisters did not. They caught her where Raven had told Sparrow to flutter. Just before they fell upon Eagle and tore out her heart and killed her, she threw the brand forward.

Sparrow caught it, and with all her strength flew to the top of the sky where the holes let through the light of Beyond. Just as the sisters were about to fall upon her, she passed through.

The sisters were too big for the hole. They cried for it to be made bigger, but the wall of Beyond is as a prison to Lord-Lady Sky-And-Earth, and could not be changed. So Sparrow escaped, and flew towards the Tree Beyond the World. But just as Sparrow reached Raven, the sister Three-Eyes shot a bolt through the hole. Speared, Sparrow fell, and Raven caught the brand just in time.

Weeping for his brave, dead friends, by many strange paths Raven brought the flaming brand to the cave of the first man and woman, who were near perished from cold. And so mankind was raised above the animals. And thanks to Raven, some became near as clever as Raven himself.

Three-Eyes – Orc was sure it was the same one. Asking Otter was an obvious next step, but the ship was moving too much for him to scape.

Though its movement seemed less than before. And the smoke had decreased.

As he leaned against the deck railing, wondering what was going on, *Nightfire* turned into the swell. The rolling ceased; the engines died. The ship slowly coasted to a stop, blowing off unused steam.

Handy.

Down in their cabin, Daroguerre sat on the lower bunk, reading papers. 'Take no note of me,' he said, 'if you wish to rest.'

Orc went to try the officers' toilet instead, but someone was moaning inside, clearly unwell. Thera, he guessed: it didn't sound like Cass.

Bugger. He returned to the cabin and lay on his bunk, listening for Thera to come back. Minutes dragged by, scratchy with the sound of Daroguerre's papers.

'You exude restlessness, Mister Strandborn. If you find this cabin too crowded, you might use the captain's.'

'I doubt he'd like that.'

'He won't know,' said Daroguerre. 'He's on watch, and will remain so until night falls and we can run the Straits without risk of being spotted. But leave this door open, and if he appears, I'll find some way to stall him.'

Orc accepted with thanks. Only as he entered Seriuz's cabin did it occur to him why Daroguerre might think he'd want to spend time alone. His face heated, but he pushed the thought away and curtained the small window.

With Cass becoming increasingly strange, the sense of isolation necessary for the Little Death came easier. Alone and scared, he shivered on the cabin floor until the terrible and beautiful dance of the serpents was almost there in front of him, tantalising with its mind-dissolving nearness.

As soon as he called his animath to pull him back, the air was lively with the noise of paws. Otter scuttled around the dim room, standing and sniffing.

'Nasty smell here, bruv.'

Orc carefully moved himself to Seriuz's bed. 'You mean something smells fishy? I thought you'd like that.'

'No time for jokes!' chattered Otter. 'The captain's been de-capped. We shouldn't be here. *He's* been here.' He kept running about, nosing in corners. 'He's worked something.'

'Daroguerre? I need to ask you about him. And that three-eyed sister.'

A shudder ran across Otter's pelt.

'Why would he have her as an ally?' said Orc. 'That story's from the far north, but he's not.'

'He's a thief, bruv! A collector. He takes from anywhere.'

'But does she appear in other stories? Maybe his version has nothing to do with the Fire Stealers. Maybe she's a force for good.'

Otter sneezed in disgust. 'You're looking for a reason to trust him?'

'He was helpful just now. And he wants to stop a war.'

But Otter was up on his hind legs, looking about him. 'Listen!'

At the edge of hearing, Orc caught fluttering. It seemed to come from within the cabin, but to change location. Sometimes it faded completely.

Then came a sharp chirp that sounded like: 'Help!'

Otter shrank onto his haunches, looking wildly around. 'Sparrow!'

'Help! Help!' The chirps came from one corner, then another, always backed by the panicked whirring of a snared bird.

'We have to help her.' Otter darted around, peering up at corners, under the bed. 'We should never have split up. That was the trouble. That was Raven's doing. Help, bruv!'

'How? What's got her?' Orc didn't understand: in the story, the sisters had got Sparrow with a bolt, not a snare. And Otter hadn't taken him to the Otherworld yet; there should be no other entities here.

'Help! Help!' The frantic chirping came from right beneath the bed.

'There!' barked Otter, and darted under.

'Otter, wait!'

The sound of a scuffle, then – a high-pitched squeal that was no bird. Then nothing. And more nothing.

'Otter?'

Orc's blood ran cold. He ducked to look under the bed, then knelt, and groped out two tiny feathers and a small clump of fur.

Fur? It looked like the hair he'd found in Ranga's luggage. His own. Had some of it dropped out and ended beneath the bed?

'Otter?'

But moving so much had disturbed his trance. Worried by Otter's disappearance – even in his least-successful scapes, that had never happened before – Orc brought himself carefully back to reality, and sank his tattoo-mask beneath his skin.

When he went back out into the corridor, Daroguerre didn't look up, and said nothing. Orc climbed to the deck. The vessel seemed becalmed in a faint swell. Cass sat gazing out to sea, a book ignored on her lap. Orc longed for her company, but, nervous of what she'd said in the wardroom, he stood at the opposite railing, looking out to the horizon, trying to raise the courage.

When he looked again, she'd gone.

♋

'Miss Strandborn, I did request you stay aft.'

'This is important,' she said.

Seriuz followed her down from the gun-platform. After handing over to Juneau, he gestured her through the rear door of the bridge, to where they couldn't be overheard.

'What's the matter, Cass?'

She liked that he used her first name in private. She'd liked it ever since he'd asked permission to do so during her convalescence. It made him more approachable. 'I know you're a good man in many ways,' she said. 'I knew it as soon as you backed down in the wardroom that first day, when you wanted our gear. You could have taken it anyway, by force.'

'I could. Which made your challenge to my morals even more courageous.'

'I have to challenge you again,' she said. 'Not your morals, but your judgement.'

She launched into the argument she'd rehearsed for the past half-hour: that the goddess scheme was doomed, that they would be executed as traitors, that those who worked magic, like Daroguerre, were mentally unstable, their claims and promises impossible to believe. 'For God's sake,' she ended, 'back out before it goes too far.'

Seriuz looked disappointed. 'I failed to persuade you, clearly.'

'It's insane.'

'I'm sorry, Cass. It pains me to hold you and your cousin as unwilling participants, but I can't allow any such regret to compromise the mission.'

'You have a family, don't you?'

'My wife and child are the chief reason I embarked on this, not a reason to pull back.' Seriuz looked out to the softly rolling sea. 'You might not know that Tetana was the daughter of Essaid's governor. I carried her from the wreck of their palace after my ship had shelled it – firing on my direction. When I found her and Robert, I had no idea who they were – what mattered was that somebody still lived in the smoking destruction I'd caused. That palace was my first look at death on such a scale, and I do not want to behold worse. I'll strive my utmost to protect you from harm, but you're not the only innocent in this world who stands in danger. I'm sorry if that sounds callous.'

Cass shrugged. 'There's no reason I should mean anything to you.'

'But you do.' He turned towards her. 'I admire you greatly: your skill, your spirit. Had circumstances been different… but, the world is what it is.'

She wanted to examine this unexpected response, but that would have to wait. 'I just can't see why you need those other artefacts. We must have raised thirty or forty of them – how will another couple make any difference?'

'Daroguerre could explain it better. But the gist is, the religious ceremonies at the Great Ziggurat were the focus of tens of thousands of minds, not mere thousands as at other sites. The objects have been impressed with more psychic energy. And because that ziggurat stood at the cultural centre, its artefacts will carry connotations of rulership, which is a quality we must employ if we are to unite the people.'

A thought gave Cass hope. 'And this Great Ziggurat is much bigger than normal?'

'It stands in eighty feet of water, and was originally forty feet taller than that, though the section above the waves has all but gone.'

Excited, Cass raced through the calculations. 'Then Orc can't do it,' she said. 'A ziggurat's twice as wide as it is high. An eighty-foot dive, then a one-twenty swim along to the chamber – even on a good day he couldn't make it back.'

The past was safe from excavation. The relief…

'He should be able to go down the shaft,' said Seriuz.

'No, there's always a grille.'

'Not here. As I said, the top of the ziggurat has been eroded away.'

She gasped as she realised he was right. It felt like a blow she should have seen coming. 'But you can't send him down the shaft,' she said, struggling to order her wits. 'If it's blocked, it might be too narrow for him to turn.'

'We'll see,' said Seriuz. 'The shaft should already have been explored.'

'Who by?'

'I'd rather not reveal that yet.' His tight smile flexed his scar tissue. 'Don't worry, Cass. I have every expectation that all will be well.'

She walked back along the ship, emotionally winded by the exchange. Seriuz had seemed so caring, those times he'd visited her to check on her well-being. She'd dared to hope that he liked her, that she might successfully appeal to that less-military side of him. But he'd ducked or countered all the arguments she could think of – as though he knew the secret reasons she wanted the dive halted and was determined to pay them no more attention than the hysteria of a girl.

'Had circumstances been different...'

What had he meant by that?

Orc was standing at the rail. Cass avoided him and headed back to the cabin, where Thera lay awake. It pained Cass that she couldn't tell her new friend anything about the problem that weighed on her mind. 'Feeling better?' she asked.

'Better?'

She didn't sound it. 'From those pains you were getting.'

'Oh. Those are gone. Just tired.'

'What was it, stomach cramps? I get them sometimes.'

'It doesn't matter.'

Cass had a hunch there was something else. 'Thera, what's up?'

'Gods, can you not *leave* it?'

Cass knew it would be best to shrug off the sting, but it was too sharp. 'Bloody hell – if I can't care about the only friend I've got on this fucking ship, then who?'

Thera hacked out a laugh. She propped herself on an elbow. Cass was shocked by the redness of her eyes.

'You're right,' Thera said. 'And I've been thinking, about what you said earlier. Our pasts shouldn't matter.'

Cass bit her lip, nodded.

'But you asked what I do,' said Thera. 'I'll show you later, if you like?'

'Seriuz gave permission?' said Cass.

'He won't object,' Thera replied.

♋

By dusk, the ship was in noisy motion again. Orc barely tasted his dinner. During the afternoon he'd attempted two scapes in the officers' washroom, but Otter hadn't properly appeared. The first time, there had been no evidence of him at all. The second, Orc had tried to consciously visualise him, but this forced simulacrum had seemed fake, with none of Otter's independence.

He excused himself early. Outside the wardroom, the light-bulbs near the open hatchway had been removed, to reduce the risk of the ship being spotted whilst running the Straits. As he passed beneath the starry space, a voice called, 'Orc!'

He looked up at a dim silhouette. 'Cass?' At dinner, Seriuz had said she was with Thera.

'There's something you need to see.'

He climbed the ladder. A half-moon held the southern sky, its light gleaming on the aft gun and deck fittings.

'What's up?' he asked, nervous; they hadn't spoken for most of the day, not since the briefing. 'Were you waiting for me?'

Cass's moonlit hair danced in the breeze of the ship's speed. 'I didn't want to come down. That man…'

'Daroguerre?'

'I'm not so sure he's insane now. It might be worse. This way.'

She stepped carefully along the silver-washed deck. Orc followed, his eyes now adjusted. Cass led him between the rearmost two stacks to a hatchway surrounded by draught funnels and grille-hoods. Fire glowed as she opened the hatch. 'Quick. In.'

Orc peered down into heat. Near the ladder's foot, Thera, wearing a sleeveless robe, knelt within a painted design made of two concentric circles, the ring between them crowded with glyphs. She faced the opening of the firebox, but there was no sign of stokers or coal.

'Quick!' said Cass.

Orc clambered down. The boiler-room roasted, despite the roaring draught down the funnels. Thera didn't glance at him.

'Look in the firebox,' said Cass unsteadily as she joined them.

Orc got behind Thera and squatted to look over her shoulder. What he saw took his breath. White-hot, its edges flaring yellow, the fire raged deep within the small chamber, shifting and squirming and seeming more alive than any he'd seen. But there was no fuel: it looked to come directly from the bright metal floor. A gas jet? Its bizarrely changing shape suggested a bird with flaming wings, then a toad with a fiery crown. He was about to ask if the performance was somehow Thera's work, when something made him peer closer, squinting.

The floor of the firebox was etched with symbols: the fire burned within the pentagon at the centre of a five-pointed star, itself set within a circle. And at the star's nearest point, embedded in the metal, was what looked like a small crystal.

'Is that…?'

He got round Thera and looked closer into the fire. It was even fiercer now, and its shape more defined, more like a creature. Orc narrowed his gaze through the smarting heat, trying to see if the crystal was anything like his focus-stone. Was this what Cass had wanted to show him?

When he next glanced at the fire itself, there were eyes.

His heart almost stopped at the sight of the lizard-like creature of white heat staring back at him. It had grown larger as well as less amorphous; its head and neck were bent against the firebox's ceiling. A tongue of flame flicked from its mouth. Heat lashed at him; flames licked the opening of the firebox.

'Get back from there!' ordered Thera.

Orc didn't move. Fascination held him, numbing the burning of his face, his eyes.

'Cass, get him out!'

Orc reluctantly let himself be pulled back to the ladder. 'What *is* that?'

'Thee, what's the matter?' said Cass.

'Too much,' said Thera sharply. 'Look at that pressure gauge! Get him back up.' She placed her palms together and began to chant.

'Go,' Cass told him. 'Be with you in a sec.'

Up on deck, the night air and the breeze cooled Orc's skin and his smarting eyes. What he'd seen began at once to feel half-unreal, like a descent to the Otherworld rather than to a ship's boiler room. But despite his shock he felt a thrill, as though the world had cracked open within that firebox and shown him its secret core.

He waited at the railing, watching the shattered moonlight on the water. It was a couple of minutes before Cass joined him.

'Thera got it back under control,' she said. 'It probably got stronger because of your stone.'

'What the hell is it?'

'You know Seriuz was talking about some evidence he'd seen, why he believed Daroguerre's plan was possible? That's the evidence. Mister Burns.'

'Mister...?'

'Thera's name for him. It. A fire elemental.'

He stared at her, but she was looking out to sea.

'They can do it, Orc. I thought this stuff about creating a living goddess was insane, but they can really do it.' She sounded scared. 'How can things like that be real? It feels wrong. I don't mean morally, I mean – yes, I mean morally. But not just our ideas of good and bad, like stealing or killing; much bigger than that. It's like... like the world has gone terribly astray. Do you know what I mean?'

She needed him to agree, he knew. But instead, a wave of delicious, shivering nausea washed through him, so strong he had to clutch the rail. Since his Initiation, Cass had been the grounded one, living in the real world while he flirted with insanity. But now it seemed the real world was not what he'd thought. The worlds of magic and corporeality could be made one. In such a world, he was no longer broken and half-insane, but adapted; in a sudden turnaround, he belonged in the real world more than Cass did. He could be the strong one again, bridge the rift.

'Orc,' she said. 'You mustn't dive.'

Her words hit him like an ambush. 'What?'

'Don't you see? That thing that attacked you at Bazantin. You were right – it *was* real. But why was it there?'

'I don't—'

'Daroguerre didn't make it, and the art's been lost for ages. So why?'

Pieces clicked together, what she'd said when she'd joined him. 'You think my stone...?'

'That elemental got bigger when you got nearer. I thought it might. Those things come from the Otherworld, don't they? The psychosphere. And your stone is a link to that world. And the big stone will link you even more strongly. When you pick it up, deep in that ziggurat, what's going to come out of the dark at you?'

'Shit…'

'You can't do it, Orc.'

'I have to.'

'You *can't*.' She gripped the railing. 'Why do you have no idea what's dangerous? To yourself, to others. Aim for the stone, and too bad if we all die along the way, is that it?'

That wasn't even worth a response. 'I'll ask Daroguerre. It might not even be a problem.' Now her words struck him: *I thought it might.* 'Maybe you just *want* it to be a problem.'

'Meaning?'

He tried to keep his anger down. 'You don't *want* me to get it.'

Her silence answered for her.

'Why?' he demanded.

'Why do you think?' She sounded almost desperate. 'What have the last two years done to us? If we'd just got on and made new lives instead of obsessing about a past that might have been crap anyway, wouldn't we be happier now? It's not too late. We can go on from here, find a… a different way to relate to each other.'

'But we're only a day away!'

'From a dive that might kill you. Or both of us. Like this search nearly did already, or have you forgotten that?'

'That wasn't…,' But he didn't let himself pursue that. 'I don't get it. How can you not want to know? How can you want to jack it in when we're so close?'

'Because I don't want everything to hang on that one chance of you getting some stupid lump of rock to work. Let's choose *now*. Take control. Tell whoever made the Shroud: "Fuck you, we're not playing your game".'

'And whose game *are* you playing, Cass?'

'What?'

'Nothing.' He was suddenly sick of arguing. Nothing he could say would do any good; it would only jemmy the crack open further.

Then cold lightning flashed down his spine.

'A different way to relate to each other.'

Or to not relate to each other at all...

'I'd better get back down there,' said Cass. 'It's hard on Thera, what she does. She could do with the company.'

Orc couldn't speak. He couldn't ask her, couldn't accuse her.

When she'd gone, he leaned on the rail, honing his thought to a knife-blade. The harder he grasped, the deeper it cut. Cass didn't want their past revealed because she was afraid of learning they'd been lovers – because that would bind them together, and she had someone else in mind now. *Keep aft of the rear stack*, Seriuz had told them – told them both – but Orc had seen Cass coming back from the bridge.

From seeing *Martin*.

Only days before, in the hotel, he'd held her in his arms. She'd wanted that, and more. For all their occasional squabbling, the thought that they might actually separate had never occurred to him. Always, they'd had only each other. But though that remained true for him, it was no longer true for her.

For just a moment, all he dared look, he caught a glimpse of life without her, the emptiness of it, the unbearable, useless, lonely, angry, grieving existence. It smacked him hard behind his stinging eyes, it wrung a gasp from his chest, it punched him and kicked him as he struggled to keep from crying.

It couldn't happen. He would not let it.

☌

It was an hour or more after midnight when Thera received the message that they'd cleared the Straits and that the three coal-fired boilers would take over.

She took half an hour banking down and dismissing Mr Burns. By the end she felt as exhausted as after the dash from Torrento. All she wanted was to collapse into bed. She picked up her folded uniform, but risked the walk along the deck in her robe. Orc was slumped near one of the boats, whether asleep or awake she couldn't tell.

Returning to her cabin, she felt the dreaded pain in her chest. She was about to head to the wardroom when she saw the captain's door ajar. Instinct told her to look in.

It wasn't Seriuz she saw, but her father, stroking her focus-stone. He beckoned her in, pocketed the stone, and gestured for her to shut the door.

'I've taken this cabin,' he said. 'Given that my work involves a great deal of thinking time, during which I mustn't be disturbed, it seemed obvious.'

Thera couldn't imagine Seriuz giving up his quarters easily. She wondered if her father had used more than that simple argument to persuade him, and even whether he held Seriuz under the same threat as herself.

'Well?' he asked.

'The elemental did react. About double the power, altogether.'

His eyebrows lifted. 'Did they realise?'

'They thought it was Orc's focus-stone.'

'But it reacted to Cass as well?'

Thera nodded. 'She didn't realise that, of course.'

Daroguerre smiled. 'A doubling of power. I feared we'd gone too soon, but it seems not.'

'Why do they have this effect?'

'My thought is that something about them, perhaps their very presence, acts to corrode the boundary between psychosphere and materiality.'

'Your thought? But you don't know?' Clearly, his masters hadn't told him.

His gaze hardened at her. 'The reason is less important than the implications. Most important of all, Thera, they themselves must not become aware of this quality they possess.'

'They won't. Like I said, Cass thinks it's down to Orc's stone.'

'But Orc has been entering ziggurats for months. Doesn't Cass wonder why Bazantin was the first manifestation?'

'She hasn't said so,' said Thera. 'And remember, she knows Mister Burns is linked to the firestone, so it would make sense for her to think the crystals are catalysts.'

Her father looked displeased to be told what to remember, but nodded. 'Well, say nothing to let her know the elemental stones have a more physical effect.'

'I doubt she'd be interested. She seems preoccupied.'

'Hardly surprising,' said Daroguerre. 'They're about to retrieve the focus-stone they believe will allow them to discover their pasts.'

'Their pasts? Cass said they need it to find out about... agents, or something?'

Her father looked puzzled, irritated. 'Their memories prior to two years ago are shrouded, even from themselves.'

'What, everything?' she said, amazed. 'Who did that to them? And why?'

'I know only that my masters wish the shroud to remain.'

'How horrible,' she said.

'Horrible?' His sharp gaze fixed her. 'I shouldn't rush to judge those who possess such great power. Do you remember that glimpse they allowed you, of the World In Waiting?'

She nodded. She doubted she could forget it if she wanted to.

'Was it magnificent?'

'It was,' she confessed.

'Would you like to have a place of importance in that world-to-come, and be granted what you crave?'

She nodded again. 'I'm sorry.'

'Little use apologising to me.'

'Will they have heard what I said?

'No doubt, if their attention is upon us.'

Her heart quaked. 'Luminous Ones,' she said, 'forgive me, I beg you. I didn't mean to cast aspersions, on your... I only meant, that I imagined what it would be like to have my memories hidden, and...'

Her father cut off her stumbling apology with a wave of his hand. 'You see? Worse fates than yours exist.'

When he released her later, she wondered if it would be so bad to not know her past. For years, her parents had been unknown to her. Bitterly she recalled her excitement on learning her father's identity – and the horror of their meeting, when he'd drained her life almost to extinction to prolong his own, and had only at the last moment reprieved her. Now he could kill her with one incantation, at any distance, such were the bonds between them – and worse, she needed him to replenish her with his magic every month, or her life-force would gutter out by itself. He had taken every part of her except the part no man had yet wanted. He had taken her focus-stone, and now let her call Sparrow only to benefit him. She would live for only as long as he willed, bound to him, unless the magic could be broken. And according to him, even he could not do that.

Restless muttering came from the lower bunk, worse than the previous night. Thera decided against waking Cass. In the cabin light, the girl's freckled face was damp with sweat. Her head twitched from side to side.

Despite exhaustion, Thera didn't sleep at once. For all that she wanted not to, she strained to catch meaning from Cass's sleep-talk.

'What've we done?' The words came sudden and clear, before Cass's voice returned to mumbling, whispering. The noise reminded Thera of the fluttering of a bird's wings, trapped.

'Oh, Sparrow,' she whispered to herself. 'What have *we* done?'

♋

Cass stood gripping the sides of the open window, staring down on streets that seethed with screaming mothers, children, the old, the young: the surging waters pushed them along, ploughed them under. Beyond the failed sea-walls the dark ocean mounted, its growling rumble shaking the city, almost drowning the vast shrill chorus of terror and panic.

But death was better to look upon than the bed-chamber behind. Truth lay there. She refused to turn. She had that much control.

The stonework beneath her hands felt slimy, malleable, as though its substance were corrupted. At her back, she sensed his approach. Liquid flowed around her feet: slow, drooling, staining. It came from her, or from him, or from what they had made, the change in the world.

Her body itched at his nearing. Her flesh was not hers to command. His presence flowed around and within her. She squeezed her thighs together and bit her lip at the craving.

She could jump; she could throw herself into the death she had brought so many others. Better that way. She tried to step up onto the window ledge, but the sticky liquid on the floor held her feet, held her trapped. For him.

A sacrifice.

Clairaudioscope transcript 02:29 26-8-336
Known voices: A,E,F

A: Still no contact?
F: Scarab's water-bowl method requires calm. He must be
        waiting for land. In any case, he would not believe
        contact necessary.
A: And the cruiser?
F: Left three hours ago.
E: There's no need to worry. When Scarab reaches the
        site, he will make contact, and we can warn him then.
        The cruiser will still be a day behind. Plenty of time
        to prepare the three bears to destroy her.
F: And all who sail in her.

22

CHOICE OF WEAPONS

Tashi and Shoggu had been alone in *Archon*'s wardroom for ten minutes when Captain Lansdahl joined them. The armchair they'd left for him looked comfortable. The captain, as he settled into it, did not.

'Gentlemen,' he said, 'we should reach the Hollow Isles tomorrow afternoon. If the magician believes his whereabouts unknown, then we might catch *Nightfire* napping. In that case, the obvious course of action would be to ram it. Know you of any reason I should not?'

Shoggu seemed puzzled to be asked. 'It sounds an extreme course.'

'Presenting our bow reduces the danger from their torpedoes, and ramming will likely cripple *Nightfire* without seriously damaging us – all else being equal.' Lansdahl kept his eyes intently on Shoggu. 'But *is* all else equal? When *Nightfire* left Torrento, it produced no smoke. Our engineers think it must be partly powered by an unknown fuel. If that fuel is flammable or explosive, ramming might be disastrous. You see that?'

'I do,' said Shoggu. 'But why put this to me? I cannot interrogate the Immaterium whilst on a moving vessel. If you think me capable of discovering this fuel, I must disappoint you.'

Lansdahl frowned. 'We made the attempt ourselves, of course, after that damned seditionist's display at the fleet review. The plans we acquired from the Republican Navy's drawing office turned out to be fake. But we later received orders from Prelate Astrasis saying the matter was in hand, and no further espionage should be attempted.'

'Ah,' said Shoggu. 'Astrasis.'

'Last night, Admiral Durer telephoned his Grace to ensure your warrant extended to a warship. His Grace confirmed it, but when asked, would make no comment on *Nightfire*'s propulsion, not even whether he knew its nature.' Lansdahl coughed, as though embarrassed. 'I wouldn't normally ask you to break a confidence, but if Prelate Astrasis has confided it to you, I beg you to speak. Our lives might depend on it.'

'He has not, Captain.'

Lansdahl looked unconvinced. 'Since he'd put a ship at your service, I thought...'

'A sign of how seriously he takes Zhenaii magic, not of the regard in which he holds me.'

Tashi wondered if the secret might relate to the new engineering principle Yaggit had said must power the Prelate's air-craft, but he felt too shy to speak.

'Well, if you can't reassure me otherwise, then ramming is too risky,' said Lansdahl. 'Even drawing alongside might be dangerous – a hothead like Seriuz might explode the ship rather than be taken alive. My question then is, do you and his Grace want the magician captured, or merely stopped? Because if the latter, my inclination would be to shell *Nightfire* on sight.'

Tashi tensed.

'His Grace asked that the magician be taken alive,' said Shoggu. 'And I need proof of his activities.'

'But if the magician were camped on the island, you'd have no objection to my sending that damned ship to the seabed?'

'But how would we know if he were on board or not?' said Shoggu.

'We'll make a judgement at the time,' Lansdahl said, rising to his feet. 'I shall want you on the bridge during our approach. Good day.'

When he was gone, Tashi said, 'He just wishes to destroy *Nightfire*. He doesn't care about our task.'

'He feels humiliated by that fleet review,' said Shoggu.

'How can we stop him? It must be we who kill the magician.'

Shoggu frowned at him. 'Beloved one, did you not hear? We need him alive.'

'For the Prelate?'

'As proof.'

'There will be proof anyway. He will have created abominations, as the Zhenaii did.'

'He might not have done so yet,' said Shoggu. 'Our task is to gather enough evidence to persuade the Abbot I was right, and to send help if needed. It doesn't matter if others deal the final blow.'

Tashi frowned, wondering if Shoggu's courage had again failed him. The priorities of their mission seemed to have subtly changed.

'Vengeance and justice are not the same,' said Shoggu. 'I hope I can persuade Captain Lansdahl of that before he sinks that ship.'

'Slaying the magician will not be to satisfy revenge,' said Tashi. 'It will be to rid the world of a great evil.'

'It would be evil to throw our lives away, if a more prudent course offered success.' Shoggu rubbed tired-looking eyes. 'Why don't you find Ranga? There might be something he hasn't told us, something that might help ensure the magician doesn't escape.'

'You think he hides things from us?'

'Make it your task to find out,' said Shoggu.

Tashi didn't doubt there was a great deal Ranga hadn't told them. The half-blood made a great show of openness, but he'd lived all his life in the lower world, and without even the distorted teachings of the Empyrean church to keep him within sight of righteousness. He was undoubtedly as corrupt as any other denizen of Torrento's festering rat-maze. Why Shoggu had agreed to him coming, Tashi didn't know. He feared Shoggu had formed the idea that because Ranga and he were less than ten years apart in age, they could be friends.

After several minutes of fruitless searching, a crewman suggested he try the aft deck. Tashi took a guesswork route through corridors that smelt of coal-smoke and oil and men, which at one point brought him out onto a gangway above the side-casements. He stopped as he saw dusty-brown land a couple of miles south, and realised it must be the southern headland of the Navrantine Straits. Beyond lay Golgomera, the vast landmass that surrounded the Sink, the entrance to the Witch Mother's Hell.

Even though the Sink itself must be far, far beyond the horizon and round the curve of the globe, farther even perhaps than he had already travelled from Highcloud, still it felt too near. The ship was steaming too close to it, over-confident. The previous night, as *Archon* had passed along the East Deep, Lansdahl had pointed out *Empire's Peace*, its fourteen-inch guns the largest in service in the world. Even larger guns were being tested at Norgeld, he'd said. Eventually, there would be one powerful enough to shell the Tree of Death from the Golgomeran coast – thus would the power at its heart be destroyed, opening the Dark Continent to Empyreal forces. It amazed Tashi that a whole empire could be so deluded as to believe that machines, rather than right behaviour and moral watchfulness, would defeat the Witch Mother.

And now, if Lansdahl had his way, those same cannons and rifles might take his kill.

No – he corrected himself. Not *his* kill. Shoggu was right: he had to be wary of his desire for vengeance, especially so close to the Witch Mother's realm. Her power was greater here, to corrupt him through his bodily emotions, to make him lust for the joy of the sword-thrust into the magician's heart. And he did lust for it, and that was wrong.

And none of that mattered anyway, because even if circumstances demanded he kill Orc, it wouldn't be his own stroke that killed him: not if he was Inspired, as he must surely be to tackle so dangerous a foe. He would have no part in the magician's death except to provide the puppet body through which the *Elohim Gibor* acted, just as when they had contemptuously held the *clathma* to his master's neck. Nothing he could do with that large sword merited praise, not real praise, not the kind Rasmuss had given him. Slaying the magician with it would be a hollow victory. He wanted to be able to go back to Rasmuss and tell him that he, unaided, had killed the man responsible for Rhunke's death; he wanted that hard slap against his back again, to be given those words of praise again, and to know that he deserved them.

But his own wants would take second place to his highest calling.

As they should, he reminded himself.

Reaching the aft deck, he found Ranga out of the wind beneath the rear turret, reading a newssheet. 'I need to question you,' he said. 'About the magician.'

'Eh?' said Ranga. 'Why me?'

'You served him!'

'Oh – yes, but I told you all I know at the house. He kept his abilities secret. I didn't even know he *was* a magician till yesterday.'

'But whatever he wishes to do at this island,' said Tashi, 'it will be on land rather than on board ship?'

'I don't know. Maybe both.'

'Why don't you know?' said Tashi. 'You said you know his ways – that's the only reason you're here.'

'Only reason? I told you, he cheated me. I deserve my revenge.'

Tashi scoffed. 'Revenge isn't yours to take. There are others more deserving. And anyway, we are here to mete out justice – or so we would,' he boiled over, 'except the captain plans to destroy the ship on sight.'

'*Destroy* it?' said Ranga. 'But they need to know how it works!'

'Some Kurassians already know, or they don't care. And Lansdahl hates the captain of the magician's ship.'

'But surely he can't just sink it?'

'It will be *safer*,' explained Tashi. 'That's his excuse. Justice will have no say in it.'

Ranga folded his paper; he looked tense. 'I'll talk to Lansdahl. I'll convince him a quick death is too good for that bastard Seriuz. We'll get him to cripple *Nightfire*, enough to force everyone ashore, and while that's going on they can get a launch to drop me on the other side of the island.'

'You?' said Tashi.

'I know the magician,' said Ranga. 'He doesn't know I've switched sides. When I've worked out where Orc's hiding, his defences and so on, I'll come back and report. Then the three of us can do what needs to be done.'

'No,' said Tashi. 'We'll drive him onto the island as you suggest, and my master and I will go ashore and deal with him.'

'What, you don't trust me?' Ranga looked genuinely hurt.

Tashi couldn't find the right words, so said none.

'Is it because of my father?' said Ranga. 'How he refuses to let monks stay? I don't know why he does that!' He rubbed his temple. 'Don't you think I've wondered what it would be like to live in a proper, godly household? Sometimes I lie awake and feel a pain in my soul, a yearning for something higher. I've wanted to talk to you about such things, but I'm scared it's already too late and I've sinned too much.'

Tashi was surprised. Only the evening before, Ranga had joked about not being interested in any heaven where he would have to leave his 'tackle' at the gates. But it was said that Gevurah's light could shine from the mountain-top into even the darkest hole.

'It's not too late,' said Tashi. 'But to be truly cleansed of sin, you must make a pilgrimage to Highcloud and petition the Abbot. If he agrees, you must climb onto the slopes of the Holy Mountain and bare your soul to Gevurah.'

'And freeze to death?'

Tashi urged himself to be patient: Ranga was showing an interest at least. 'Death is not required. Even so, it is no misfortune. To die on the Holy Mountain is the only sure way to gain the Land Beyond Sky. Here, so close to the Sink, one would need a pure soul indeed to avoid being pulled into Hell. The Qliphoth one creates, the offspring of sinful thought and deed, they gain strength from its nearness. I do not fear death for my body. But that I fear.'

Ranga seemed sobered. '*You* must be pure enough, surely?'

Tashi bit his lip. 'I can only try.'

'What's Hell like?' asked Ranga.

'You lose your mind,' said Tashi. 'Your self dissolves, everything that makes you what you are, leaving nothing more than bodily urges and uncontrolled emotions. The most terrible stage must be when just enough awareness remains to know what's happening to you. Some teach that even when you lose control, a part of your awareness remains, an observer—'

He clammed up at a terrible realisation.

'Sounds grim,' said Ranga.

Tashi shook the thought away. There could surely be no connection between the dissolution of the self in Hell and how it had felt to be used as a vessel by the *Elohim Gibor*. The suggestion of similarity must have come from the Witch Mother.

'Still,' said Ranga, 'if we're already close to this Sink, it won't be so far to chuck Seriuz and his whole rotten crew down into it. That shit Lyle especially.'

'Their Qliphoth will drag them.'

'With help from that big sword of yours.'

Tashi frowned. His unsettling doubts suddenly reached a crisis.

The word fell out of him like a stone. 'No.'

'No?' said Ranga.

'The big one is too heavy for my own strength. I won't use it.'

'Really? What is it, then, a symbol?'

'Something like that.'

It felt dangerous to say so. He feared the Lords of Battle would be offended. But the refusal also felt right. He hadn't realised it before leaving Highcloud, but Inspiration and the novitiate's warrior training were not two parts of the same purpose – they conflicted. A warrior was an armed will, not a mindless tool.

He would kill Orc by his own volition, with full control of his own body, powered by his own anger – he could not bear to have that denied him. It would be revenge for having to leave Highcloud, for the hotel, for the museum. And on his return to Torrento, he would find Rasmuss and get that praise and know he deserved it. And then he would climb the Holy Mountain himself and ask forgiveness.

He had no expectation that it would be granted.

G: Another complication. The Empyreal Navy is preparing a dreadnought and four heavy cruisers to send to the site.

A: A dreadnought? Why on earth? Why?

G: Naval headquarters in Torrento received a telephone call, which I have been unable to trace. Intelligence officials seem to have connected this call with the inability of their network to locate certain Sundaran warships since they left port a week ago.

A: So they know about the three bears?

G: They have somehow deduced their connection with Scarab.

A: The monk's cruiser knows nothing of this?

G: The call was received after it departed.

A: When will the dreadnought arrive?

G: It has not yet left. It will come somewhat less than a day behind the cruiser.

E: This time we must use project baffomet, surely?

A: No. When Scarab makes contact, instruct him. After retrieval of the artefacts, he is to arrange for the monk's cruiser to be ambushed and destroyed, and we will then relay to him an escape course based on the dreadnought's position. He will follow this course out of the Shallow Sea, and resume as planned.

G: If he doesn't make contact?

A: He is under orders to. He must.

23

THE SWIMMER

From the corner of the gun platform, Cass watched the island slowly grow nearer, its rounded outline fuzzy with maritime pines. Spume flickered at the base of its cliffs.

Closer, though harder to see, the top of the ruined ziggurat broke the waters off the eastern end. The largest of the few lumps of reef were only yards across, but from what showed, Cass judged the temple would indeed once have risen forty feet above the waters of the Flood.

The rising, rushing Flood…

She'd woken that morning bathed in sweat, the remembered nightmare clearer than previous ones. Even half a day later, she sensed she could make it clearer still if she tried, but instead she shored up her mental barrier, refused the secret that threatened to emerge. On the other side of the gun platform, Orc stood with Daroguerre. Both were intent on the ziggurat. She felt sick that she hadn't convinced him to give up the search.

The loose bolts on the hatchway ladder banged as Seriuz climbed up from the bridge. Cass wearily gathered herself for another attempt at persuasion. But joining her, Seriuz spoke first.

'You asked who would explore the ziggurat's shaft.' He pointed left of the island. Amid the flashing of afternoon sun on the water, Cass was surprised to make out a low ship about *Nightfire*'s size, two miles distant.

'A Sundaran destroyer,' said Seriuz. 'Its larger companions are behind that headland. They have compressor divers: the type with copper helmets I talked of before.'

Sudden hope made Cass gasp. 'Then you don't need us! They can recover the artefacts.'

'They lack your cousin's acuity in darkness.'

'Couldn't they just grope about down there?'

He frowned as he studied her. 'What is it, Cass?'

She played her last card. 'Thera showed us the elemental.'

'I know.'

'It reacted to Orc's focus-stone. The same reason that thing appeared at Bazantin. And there's another stone down inside that ziggurat: a bigger one.'

His puzzlement seemed genuine. 'Truly?'

'We've been searching for it for months. But we didn't know about the monsters. Even with Orc's own focus-stone, it'd be a risk; but if he picks up the big one too, something will manifest down there, and then... well, he'll be dead and you won't get anything.'

Seriuz thought a moment, then said, 'Damn,' and called Daroguerre across.

The magician showed no concern as Seriuz related the problem. 'I've already discussed that with Mister Strandborn,' he said. 'The solution is to ensure a calm emotional state. He allowed himself to become unnerved at Bazantin; his fear connected with the dark psychic associations in the chamber, and the resulting feedback created the perfect conditions for manifestation. If he prepares appropriately, there should be no repeat.'

'*Should* be?' queried Cass. 'He *should* survive. That's reassuring.'

'I have every confidence no problem will arise.'

'Even with this larger stone?' said Seriuz.

Daroguerre hesitated just a moment. 'Even with that.'

'You knew of it?'

'Of course. It's essential to our success.'

'Then I'm surprised you never mentioned it.'

Daroguerre shrugged. 'It relates to my side of the operation, not yours.'

'But Orc doesn't need to use it?' said Cass, keeping her voice low: Orc looked like he was trying to overhear.

'I imagine your cousin would wish to use it to test your amnesia,' said Daroguerre. 'But I'd hesitate to let an amateur use such a powerful amplifier.'

'And you can promise that?' said Cass. 'You won't let him?'

'I never make promises without good reason.'

'How about me doing your dirty work for months without any reward? Isn't that a good reason?'

'Your cousin has done the same,' said Daroguerre, 'and with rather more risk. Should I reward him by making promises against his interests?' He aimed a look at Seriuz before walking off.

'Please, Martin,' Cass said. 'Promise you won't let Orc use it. You can tell Daroguerre to make sure of that, can't you?'

'I'm not sure I understand,' he said. 'Is it true that it could restore your memories?'

'Yes.'

'Then why—'

'Because I don't want to know!'

'Cass, why on earth not?'

Her throat tightened. She had to tell him something.

'When I nearly drowned, something came into me. Like a… a seed of knowledge, so dense I couldn't make sense of it. A nightmare seed. It buried itself in my mind, but it's sprouted into my dreams. There's something hideous in our pasts, something we shouldn't know. But Orc won't stop looking. I'm worried he'll use this stone to find out, and it'll destroy us. If only I could be sure he won't get the stone, I'd sleep properly again. It's been horrible.'

She hoped he wouldn't ask more.

'Cass,' he said gently, 'if your dreams are trying to tell you something, it might be because your heart understands that you need to know, even if your head resists.'

'No.' But she couldn't put it more strongly without sounding mad. 'Not yet, at least: not while the dive and the goddess are going on. If he drags everything up in the middle of all this...'

'Yes, I see that,' said Seriuz. 'Mister Daroguerre?' he called across. 'Once more, please?'

Daroguerre broke off from Orc, clearly irritated.

'Captain?'

'Please take the stone as soon as Mister Strandborn brings it up, and ensure he doesn't use it for his own purposes.'

'As I said, I've no reason to let him.'

'I wanted to express myself with absolute clarity,' said Seriuz.

Daroguerre raised an eyebrow. 'Is this a request, or an order?'

'The latter, Mister Daroguerre.'

'If it is *your* order, Captain, then of course.' He glanced from Seriuz to Cass as he turned away.

'Thank you,' said Cass. 'He will obey, won't he?' She watched Daroguerre talking to Orc.

'I command this ship, and this mission,' said Seriuz.

Such a relief. Cass almost laughed at her stupidity in not simply getting Seriuz to make such a promise before. She'd been worried that telling him about her fears would lead him to want details of her dreams, but in the end he'd asked for none.

Because he liked her, she realised. He *wanted* to help her. Perhaps he found her attractive.

Orc was looking shocked, staring at Daroguerre as though he'd lost the power of movement.

'Is Daroguerre *telling* him?' said Cass. 'Why would he—'

Orc span away from the magician and almost ran to the hatchway. With one daggered glance at Cass, he scrambled down the ladder as though he didn't care if he fell.

'Oh, God,' she sighed. She felt some responsibility, though not guilt. 'I'd better talk to him.'

She clambered down to the bridge, where Juneau caught her eye and nodded towards the rear starboard door. Orc was leaning on the railing halfway along the ship. His hair needed a wash, she noticed; the armpits of his green shirt were dark with sweat, as though his clothes had lost their power to disguise his body, as though the stain at the root of her dreams had seeped from him. She steeled herself against his baffled, angry hurt as he faced her, reminding herself she had no reason to fear him now. Whatever he said or did, he would not get to use the stone, would not be able to recklessly, stupidly unearth the root of her nocturnal horror.

'You *told* him about it!'

She acted puzzled. 'Is that a problem?'

'He's a *magician*, for God's sake! He's going to want it for himself.'

She shrugged. 'He seemed to know about it anyway.'

'*He seemed to know about it anyway*,' Orc mimicked. 'Oh, God—' He choked off, his face a battle of muscular tensions. 'He says I can't use it, I'm not trained enough. Why the hell did you have to *tell* him?'

He hadn't mentioned Seriuz's order, Cass realised. Maybe he didn't know.

'I told you last night,' she said evenly. 'I was worried about the manifestations.'

'And I said I'd talk to him. And I did – about *my* stone being a problem: he didn't even have to know about the big one.' Orc clamped his hand over his forehead. 'I had it all okay and you fucked it up. Just tell me it wasn't deliberate.'

She could have told him so, could have affirmed his belief that it had only been a stupid, girly mistake on her part. But with a moment's dark thrill she realised she didn't want to.

'But it was, Orc.' The truth twisted a hot fire of joy inside her. 'I got Martin to order Daroguerre not to let you use it.'

His face tightened. It looked for a moment as though he might cry. From being scared of him, she felt now almost fascinated with the childishness of his disappointment. She couldn't believe she'd clung to him in the hotel only days before, that she'd felt the hardness through his trousers with anything other than repulsion. She tried not to recall the craving in her dream.

'You're sick, Cass.' He had trouble speaking. 'I feel sorry for you, throwing away everything that matters just so you can get into his bed.'

'What?' The words had been clear but they made no sense.

'You wrecked everything so you don't have to feel guilty. I hope *Martin*'s a good *fuck*.'

She slapped his face: something she'd never done before, to anyone.

'Ow, *that* hurt,' he sneered. 'That all you got?'

Her jaw tightened almost to shattering.

'Strandborn!'

They turned: Seriuz was coming at them. Cass moved aside.

'Oh, here's a freaking surprise,' said Orc.

'Cass,' said Seriuz, 'could I have a moment with your cousin?'

Orc had stiffened against the railing; there were nerves in his eyes now along with the anger and hurt. Cass wanted him to lash out, and for Seriuz to punch him to a pulp – to punish Orc for almost getting her killed, for inflicting the nightmares on her, for *being* in those nightmares, behind her, the looming, poisonous source of them.

'You're sick, Cass.' The joke of it.

She retreated to near the bridge, only now realising how hard she was breathing, how close she was to shaking. She stood there, glancing round every few seconds to where Orc and Seriuz were talking. Orc looked defiant rather than cowed. At one point he shaped his hand into something like a gun. She couldn't guess what that meant, but it chilled her.

When Seriuz started back, she turned her gaze on the ziggurat ruin, a few hundred yards ahead to starboard, and waited for him.

'He won't upset you again,' said Seriuz as he came to stand at the railing beside her.

'Thank you.' She believed him. He stood closer than usual, powerfully tangible, as though his presence disturbed the air so it moved over the nerves of her skin. She wanted to close up to him, to brush against his uniform jacket. He would be warm, and the darkness where she went at night was so cold.

'I'm sorry he was like that,' she said. 'He's just a boy, really.' Though the presence in her dreams had not felt like a boy. She pushed away the thought, and faced him, smiling. 'Thanks for your promise. If there's anything I can do in return…'

He smiled back, but his eyes were troubled, penetrating. Cass looked back down at the sea-wash along the ship's waterline and waited for a reply, wanting to take back her words and their implication. Or maybe not. After its initial shock, Orc's seemingly ridiculous accusation had cast her own feelings in a new light. *Wolfish*, Orc had once called Seriuz, but wolves could be loyal and noble as well as fierce. And what was Orc but a tiring, untrained puppy, stupidly obsessed with digging up rotting bones? The differences between him and Martin Seriuz were endless. Compared to the mess of her life with the broken boy who might be any relation to her or none, it seemed so simple to want Seriuz to desire her and keep her safe: simple and scarily thrilling. Didn't gentlemen take mistresses? Even an honourable one might do so, if his wife were crippled.

He still hadn't answered. Her legs urged her closer.

'Sir!' came Lyle's cry from the bridge. 'Do you see her?'

Cass looked up, and snatched a breath. Someone stood on one of the wave-weathered lumps of the ziggurat: a broad-shouldered young woman wearing shorts above the knees and a top that left her arms bare. Her brown skin and dark hair gleamed wet in the sun. For an appalled moment Cass thought it might be the goddess, already brought to life by the nearness of Orc's stone.

The young woman waved her arms.

'Full stop, Mister Lyle,' called Seriuz. The young woman dived into the water and swam overarm towards a point ahead of the rapidly slowing ship. She arrived below the bridge just as the vessel's movement ceased. Seriuz ordered a ladder let down.

'Do you know her?' Cass asked, but he seemed too preoccupied to answer.

Glancing around, Cass found Daroguerre had come down from the gun-platform. Orc watched from further along, as did several crewmen. The girl climbed with agile competence, her arms well-toned; her long dark hair was bound behind her head. Cass thought her top might have been a man's waistcoat, adjusted for a closer fit; her bottoms seemed masculine trousers cut off above the knees and tightly belted. In seconds she'd ducked under the railing and stood dripping, breathing hard. Her left wrist was covered by a leather bracer, beneath which showed a lump.

'Welcome aboard, Miss Quallace,' said Seriuz. He extended his hand.

She kept hers at her side. 'And you to the Hollow Isles, Captain. We've been expecting you since early yesterday.'

'Since Captain Rulanza arrived, I assume?'

'Since his men took the *Aurora*'s wheel, invaded our home and confiscated our means of protecting ourselves.'

'I trust he's shown you no discourtesy?'

'Oh no, he's always so polite. Like you.' Her gaze turned to Cass, questioning. She looked with similar intensity at Daroguerre and Orc.

'Some new faces here.'

'Allow me to make introductions,' said Seriuz.

'Later,' she said. 'You'll want to talk to Ferman, to set his mind at rest?'

'Of course.'

'I've come to invite you to dinner. Bring Mister Juneau. And those three.' She pointed to Cass, Orc and Daroguerre. 'Half-six for seven.'

Just as Seriuz was about to speak, she turned and dived off the ship; her entry made barely a splash. Brown against blue, she arced underwater to surface several yards away, and began to swim towards the eastern end of the island.

'Who's that?' said Cass.

'Hana Quallace,' said Seriuz. 'She lives with her adoptive parents on the south side. At a research station, so-called.'

'Researching what?'

Daroguerre answered: 'Matters of which they can only have limited comprehension. Still, if they know the island, a conversation might prove worthwhile. I need to find the most appropriate place for Mister Strandborn to prepare.'

Seriuz nodded. 'Mister Lyle, take her round to the cove, slow.'

'What's that?' said Cass, at a flash of light. Several more came quickly, from the same source. Up the island's steep eastern slope, perhaps two-hundred feet above the sea, she now saw a kind of shelf, or terrace, bare of trees. The flashes kept coming – long ones, short ones, pauses.

'A signal lamp,' said Seriuz. 'The Sundarans have cleared a lookout point.'

'What's it saying?'

Seriuz grunted. 'They wonder why we're early, and if we're pursued. Mister Lyle, return a message: *no enemy pursuit, but a new world follows in our wake.*'

Maybe so, thought Cass. And now she had reason to hope the old one would stay covered.

24

THE RESEARCH STATION

The two hulking warships off the island's southern coast looked to Orc as though someone had tried to replicate Empyreal designs from the memories of a dream. The arrangements of their guns seemed haphazard, the armoured sloping of their hulls almost random. They even had the tall masts and cross-beams of sailing ships. One stack of each vessel trailed smoke, but the spread awnings and full washing-lines suggested they weren't expecting trouble.

Nightfire manoeuvred to a spot between the warships and a cove on the shores of which clustered thirty or so buildings, mostly ruined and overgrown. A steam-yacht showed over the top of the mole that protected the small harbour.

As the anchor chain clanked, Juneau came up to the gun platform. 'On your own?'

Orc stifled sarcasm: he liked Juneau, who had now taken the other bunk in his cabin. 'Those ships,' he said. 'Sundaran?'

'The battleship *Barcuda*, and the cruiser *Tarpon*,' said Juneau. 'That destroyer we passed is the *Makhral* – she's positioned to relay messages from the lookout.'

'Why are they here?'

'*Tarpon* carries pumps and divers,' said Juneau. 'Hopefully they've already made sure the ziggurat shaft is clear. But they're also here for our protection. Outdated they may be, but they'd still see off anything less than a dreadnought. So they'll buy us some time if we're surprised. Not that that's likely this far west,' he added quickly.

His words brought home to Orc what Seriuz had said the day before. These warships expressed the support – clandestine, but support nonetheless – of an empire that stretched round half the Southern Ocean.

'And if a dreadnought does come here?'

'Why should an Empyreal dreadnought be anywhere in the Shallow Sea?' Juneau slapped him on the shoulder. 'Don't worry – we're here to *prevent* a global war, remember? We'll try to avoid sparking one off.'

They watched the completion of the mooring, then were joined by Seriuz, along with a signal-lamp operator. Resisting the urge to leave, Orc watched messages flash back and forth with *Barcuda*. When those were finished, Seriuz turned to him.

'Good news: the shaft is unobstructed. I'll go across to learn more, then we'll join the Quallaces for dinner. There's a cubicle been set up on the wash deck at the stern. I suggest you use it.'

Seriuz then left, with Juneau. A few minutes later, Orc watched as the captain was rowed across to the battleship. He entertained a fantasy of the gun beside him being loaded and ready to fire, boom. Like with Yorge's boat – an episode he'd recently reminded Seriuz of, after that horrible argument with Cass.

'And how would I "upset her again", Captain? By telling her the man she's got a crush on is a cold-blooded murderer?'

'*Hot-blooded,*' had been Seriuz's return, '*as those who anger me discover.*' But unease had dogged his eyes, Orc was sure.

What a mess. He needed Otter's wisdom. Now *Nightfire* had stopped, he thought of trying another scape, hoping Otter would return at last. But there wouldn't be time before dinner, and he needed to keep an eye on Cass and Seriuz. Wisdom would have to wait.

***

Before sunset they were rowed ashore, the boat's progress aided by a gentle swell. No one spoke until the red-gold light was cut off by a shoulder of land that bounded the cove to the west, then Seriuz told them Rulanza's news.

'One of *Tarpon*'s divers got down to the chamber this morning,' he said, over the splashes and squeaks of the oars. 'He tried to feel his way around, but encountered a hole in the floor.'

Orc grunted to himself. The hole: Ranga's sign of the ziggurat containing the stone. The stone everyone now knew about.

'No mere "hole",' said Daroguerre, 'but the very reason for the ziggurat's location. All caves were sacred to the Mother in the dawn ages, but that particular example was considered the entrance to the Mother herself, and retained its significance into the Sahronic era.'

'But it's of no relevance to us?' said Seriuz.

'On the contrary. The sacred artefacts are doubtless somewhere in the chamber, but the crystal was thrown into the hole.'

Orc frowned. 'How deep?'

'Fifty feet down, the tunnel bends to the horizontal. The stone must lie there.'

Orc wondered how Daroguerre could know this with such accuracy, but that thought was overshadowed by the dimensions involved. On top of the eighty-foot descent to the chamber, it made a dive far deeper than he'd ever gone.

'It's too far,' Cass said.

'Not necessarily!' he protested.

'The depth should be no problem,' said Daroguerre. 'Before your own descent, a diver will take down an air-hose and position it so the escaping air becomes trapped in concavities in the rough ceiling. Those pockets will let you reach the deeper cave beneath.'

Orc nodded, impressed. 'A staging post.'

Then he had the idea – and he had to clamp down on his excitement before it showed. If the air-pocket were being continuously refilled, he could breathe down there for hours. It would be cold and uncomfortable, but he could do his scape, penetrate the Shroud, before anyone could take the stone away from him.

He met Cass's gaze and knew she'd had the same thought. He held back a smirk of triumph.

'No.' Cass turned to Seriuz. 'Using air like that – I don't think it's safe.'

Orc stared in disbelief.

'Why so?' said Seriuz.

'It just set off an alarm bell.'

Orc rolled his eyes. Cass had lost, and she knew it, and now she was thrashing to shore up her wretched sabotage plan.

'We have no choice,' said Daroguerre. 'Without the air-pocket, Mister Strandborn has no chance of getting the stone, since he cannot take the most direct route, down the shaft.'

'What?' said Orc.

'But that was your plan,' said Seriuz.

'Originally, yes,' said Daroguerre. 'But new information has come to me since Torrento. It seems Mister Strandborn has developed a magical identification with the Sun-King, the goddess's consort.'

'What, that stupid thing about his hair?' said Cass.

'Not that alone. The dreams of Bazantin's townsfolk showed the wider psychosphere was strongly affected.' He looked at Orc. 'As your own psyche must have been.'

You are mine…

'Meaning what?' said Seriuz.

'Using the shaft would reinforce that identification,' said Daroguerre. 'The shaft was the channel for the sacrifice. At the end of his reign, the Sun-King ritually dismembered himself, casting those parts cut off into the shaft, until he fainted onto the grille and his blood drained into the chamber.'

Orc's face pulled.

'But aren't we dealing with the goddess prior to the sacrifices?' said Seriuz.

'This happened even before the slaughter,' said Daroguerre. 'Throughout the worship of Urshevat.'

Seriuz looked troubled. 'But the goddess *we* create won't require sacrifice?'

Daroguerre flashed a humourless smile. 'You lack an esoteric mind, Captain. Sacrifice can mean many things. Will she require blood? I think not – these days, that would turn the populace against her. But the ancients believed it essential to the continued productivity of the earth. The Sun-King underwent sacrifice willingly, a fact incomprehensible to the modern mind. It was only later, as famine consumed the land, that it was done with increasing frequency to the increasingly *un*willing.

'As to this problem of identification,' he continued, 'I see one way round it.'

'Make him ignore it,' said Seriuz.

'No. That would leave a dangerous psychic vacuum. Remember that he must enter a magical state to see in darkness, and this would make him vulnerable to suggestion from the psychosphere – which, as I said, now contains his Sun-King identification. And to remove it from there would be near-impossible.

'No, we must turn to the king's successor. For, while the outgoing king sacrificed himself, his chosen inheritor entered the central chamber, to encounter the goddess and to consort with her. There he met her in the form of the outgoing priestesses, still virginal, and impregnated as many as he could, while the invigorating blood of his predecessor rained down upon them.'

'Oh, God!' exclaimed Cass. Orc hadn't agreed with her much recently, but he agreed with her about that.

'By entering along the passageway,' Daroguerre went on, turning to Orc, 'you will maintain your role as the Sun-King, but at the moment of investiture rather than sacrifice. If you encounter the goddess at all, it will thus be in her ruling aspect, Urshevat, not her death aspect, Skalith. And with your fear reduced, you will not trigger manifestation, but meet her thought-form at most. And I'll prepare you to negotiate any such encounter.'

Orc nodded. He would do whatever it took. He hoped his wetsuit would keep him warm enough to last throughout a scape; he'd never put it to anything like such a test.

The boat rounded the mole and made its way across the calm stretch to the jetty, alongside which was moored the steam-yacht *Aurora*. The cicadas' shrill noise bombarded from the slopes all around. Orc had the disturbing impression of a single voice projected upwards from the partial funnel of the heights, a hymn to some vast power. As they clambered onto the jetty, Daroguerre carrying a small case, three people emerged from the largest intact building a hundred yards away.

'Say nothing about our purpose here,' said Seriuz. 'Mister Daroguerre and I have the story. The Quallaces have no means of disrupting our work, but I want them given no reason to try.'

Orc noticed Daroguerre scrutinising the pine-covered slopes. 'Feels different to last time,' he said, when they reached the jetty's shoreward end.

'Last time?' said Seriuz. 'You weren't with us then.'

'With you, no.' Daroguerre set off with his case towards a trail that led up the north-eastern slope. 'I'll be half an hour.'

The others made for the house. Orc recognised one of the waiting residents as the swimmer, who he guessed was in her mid-twenties, now with her hair untied and wearing fuller, looser clothes. He wondered if the lump beneath her wrist-bracer was a bone deformity. The couple with her looked Kurassian, their faces pink from sun. The woman's hair was blonde and grey, and what remained of the man's a bold copper.

Seriuz introduced Ferman and Stefanie Quallace, and their daughter Hana, after which Ferman beckoned forward a servant with wine. Orc accepted a glass, but didn't join the conversation, which felt strained, despite the jokily mothering tone Stefanie employed with Juneau. After ten minutes, a series of distant splashes made everyone turn. Men – naked men – were jumping and diving off *Nightfire*, their whoops and cheers carrying across the water.

'Avert your gaze, my dear,' said Ferman.

'First bring me a spyglass,' said his wife, 'so I might know what I'm shielding myself from.'

There followed more laughter than the joke deserved, Orc thought, as though the officers had seized on the first opportunity to lighten the mood. Hana seemed resolutely not amused. When the gong rang, she came in last, and Orc glimpsed her tipping her wine into the dust.

The tableware at dinner surpassed even that at the *Royal Bull*, but the patched-up walls would have shamed the cheapest guesthouse. The vegetable soup was followed by baked mullet, and this in turn by a goat, which Stefanie explained was one of a small population established in the days of the pirates who had built the settlement.

During the meat, Daroguerre returned, his expression troubled. After the small-talk had limped on a little longer, Ferman asked Seriuz exactly why they'd come.

'A naval matter, I'm afraid.'

'But it involves entering the ziggurat?' said Hana. 'I saw the Sundies this morning.'

'They've developed some new equipment,' said Seriuz. 'As well as conducting our exercise, we're recovering artefacts for the National Museum. Mister Daroguerre is their man.'

'I'm surprised about the Sundaran involvement,' said Ferman. 'You didn't mention it, last time you were here.'

Seriuz cleared his throat. 'I assume you've had no recent news from the mainland?'

'Not for two months.'

'Then you'll be unaware of the sudden improvement in relations with the Shahanate. A peace accord has been signed. It's possible the throne will be restored.'

The Quallaces glanced at each other, but didn't respond. The talk dropped. Stefanie ordered more wine.

'You're researching something,' said Daroguerre. 'Might I ask what?'

Ferman looked uncomfortable. 'The past, like yourself.'

'You're an archaeologist?' said Daroguerre. 'You're excavating?'

'Not physically,' said Ferman. 'You might know that this main island, and the Paps to the west, have long had a strange reputation. It was a pirate enclave until the old Royal Navy did for them, but even before, it regularly fell to madness and squabbling, and rumours of ghosts.' He scratched his sun-reddened nose. 'Even I've had strange dreams here, and we believe a sensitive mind might discover much about the nature and history of the place.'

'A sensitive mind?' queried Daroguerre.

'Mine,' said Hana.

'Yes, we're researching the island's effect on our daughter,' said Ferman. 'It's about time the psychic realm was properly examined. Scientific and occult research are not mutually exclusive. My own engineer brother, for example, has invented a revolutionary device, a "clairaudioscope", to amplify voices recorded in the ether.'

'The Church would call that witchcraft,' said Daroguerre. 'Only the Watchers of Highcloud are permitted to engage with the Immaterium, or psychosphere, or whatever you wish to call it.'

Ferman's expression hardened. 'A Kurassian attitude. Which is precisely why we left.'

Over coffee, the two men turned to discussing the island's ancient sites, the stone circles, the megalith-guarded caves. Uncomfortable, Orc kept his eyes from the window, and the thousands of years of darkness that pressed against the house. At last, Seriuz begged his excuses, and the ship's party said goodbye to their hosts. Only Hana accompanied them outside.

The night was brilliant with stars. To Orc, they looked too close, not science's distant balls of gas, but tiny lights on the nearby dome of the sky, part of the goddess's domain. The warships' lights reflecting on the sea reminded him of his half-dream at the *Royal Bull* – his dream of this very island, and the stone that had become a sacrificial knife. The civilisation of dinner seemed suddenly flimsy, with its glassware and chit-chat and the officers' braided epaulettes. It felt madness to have come to this island – as if he'd walked here under the goddess's enchantment.

'I hope we've reassured you and your parents,' Seriuz said to Hana.

She kept her arms folded. 'Are you planning any more dives?'

'As I said, Miss Quallace, the details of the exercise are a naval matter.'

'Why do you ask?' said Cass.

'Because I wouldn't,' said Hana. 'Not with what's down there.' She closed the door.

'Sensitive, perhaps, but unfocused,' Daroguerre said to Orc as they started back towards the beach. 'I learned something from her father, however. One site in particular should suit our preparatory exercises.'

'They'd better be good,' muttered Orc.

At the shore end of the jetty, Cass pulled him back. 'You trust him, do you? You're going to let him mess with your mind, when you know he's been manipulating us for months?'

Orc checked a sigh. So this was her last, desperate angle. 'What are you worried about, Cass? You got "Martin" to promise I couldn't use the stone, right?'

Even in the near-darkness, he sensed the fire in her eyes. 'You really think you can stay down there for minutes?'

'Oh no, of course not, because it's "not safe".'

'It's *not* safe!' she hissed. 'I can't remember why, but you mustn't take air from that line. And don't trust Daroguerre.'

'Maybe I don't trust him. Maybe I'm just using him, like you're using Seriuz – because you can't trust *him*, surely?'

'Why not?'

But now that he'd created the chance to tell her about the fishermen's deaths, Orc hesitated. Seriuz had stopped just along the jetty and was eyeing them. He decided to hold the big secret in reserve.

'Where do you think Daroguerre heard that stuff about the Sun-King and what people dreamed about in Bazantin?' he said.

'He's been scrying us. He said so yesterday.'

'He said he learned it since Torrento. Someone on board told him.' He paused long enough for her to realise she couldn't think who. 'Esteban.'

Her eyes widened. 'No!'

Orc noticed Seriuz start back towards them.

'He's here?' she said. 'How long have you known?'

'Is there a problem?' said Seriuz. He looked at Orc. 'I warned you—'

'He says you've brought Esteban?' said Cass.

Seriuz glanced at Orc, but didn't answer.

'After what he did?' she said. 'Him and his family?'

'I understand he freed your cousin to save you.' Discomfort tightened Seriuz's voice. 'His own people would have punished him. I thought it only humane to grant him passage.'

'You didn't tell me,' said Cass, but with less anger than Orc had expected.

'I thought it would upset you,' Seriuz said.

'What if I'd bumped into him?'

'I took measures to prevent that, and I'll ensure you won't in future. Now, we should return to the ship.'

'See?' muttered Orc, as they followed a short way behind.

'And I should trust *you*, should I?' she retorted. 'You knew Esteban was on board. What were *your* reasons for keeping quiet?'

'The same!'

'Really?' she said. 'If you were so keen not to upset me, why did you just do exactly that?'

Orc's mouth opened, but no words came.

♋

Thera was playing cards with Lyle and three others when the boat returned. Fifteen minutes later, she felt the pain, and folded her hand even though it was a likely winner.

Seriuz's old cabin had, in the past twenty-four hours, become a mess of half-unpacked luggage: books and clothes, the chess-set her father liked to play against himself to relax, his strange wooden puzzles. He now pushed it all against the walls to clear a space.

'Sit,' he told her. 'We have to make a shroud.'

She didn't understand. 'Why? And – I don't know how.'

'I'll instruct you. I want no chance of Orc finding out what we're about to discuss.'

'But how could he? He can't scape properly now: he has no animath.'

'He found the stone's location without scaping. In a hypnagogic state. You told me yourself.'

'How do we do this, then?'

From his pocket, her father extracted – her heart lurched – her focus-stone.

'Sparrow?' she said.

He shook his head as he handed it to her. 'An amplifier only, this time.'

He unlocked the crowded cabinet and took out one of the silver cups, which he placed between himself and her. After she'd meditated herself into a light trance, he guided her in visualising smoke rising from the cup, the smoke of funeral pyres, and swarming clouds of flies, their buzzing mingled with the incantations of primitives. With her father's muttered encouragement, she let her mind find its way into binding the smoke and flies and noise. Her hand sweated against the hard crystal. The electric light in the cabin dimmed; she sensed a presence within the barrier, a guarding female figure, ever-vigilant and with a shield that could be everywhere at once.

And then, worst of all, the sounds of the barrier were joined by a new one: the frantic, endless whirring flapping of a small bird in a snare. She didn't want to listen, but her ears could focus on nothing else. She felt increasingly tense, uncomfortable, trapped herself. Cramped. She was about to beg her father to stop the rite, when he began the call-back.

'That should do,' he said, when they were both returned to normal consciousness. Thera felt weak; she was still vaguely aware of the shield-bearing figure, though it disappeared whenever she looked directly. At least it was facing away from her.

Her father held out his hand and took back her stone. 'That should be effective,' he said, moving to the bed and gesturing her to take the chair. 'Anyone who tries to pierce the shroud will hear that distressed bird and share your terrified fascination with it.'

'Anyone?' she said, still shaken and faintly sick. 'Was that really about Orc?'

He smiled, or his mouth did. 'No.'

He drew in a breath, and released it slowly, staring at his steepled fingertips. 'I said the shroud was intended against Orc because we are, or *were*, being observed, and I wanted to allay suspicion as to why I was creating it.'

He could only mean the Luminous Ones. But she didn't dare venture the name.

'We may speak freely,' he said. 'I wouldn't normally expect a shroud of mine to be effective against them, but in conjunction with the island…'

'Why should you want to?' It scared her, the idea that he might do something he needed to keep from them. 'Did you contact them when you went ashore?'

'I tried, but without success. A force over the island inhibits it.'

'A larger shroud?'

'No. I believe it to be an energy connected with the mother goddess: a store of worship surviving from before the ziggurat, perhaps reawakened by something the Quallace girl has done. The Mother in her primal state is a formless, undifferentiated mass: chaos before it was shaped by language. Hence the energy disrupts the psychic transmission of words. She brings vision, but steals speech. I've ascertained that the force extends as far as this ship. With our shroud as well, we won't be overheard.'

Thera realised this was perhaps the first time in many years that her father had been able to speak with complete freedom. She felt both curious and nervous as to what he would say.

'The presence of this energy also opens up possibilities for the creation of our goddess,' he said.

'But that will happen in Torrento.'

He eyed her. 'Will it?'

'And it's Urshevat you'll create, not the Mother.'

'All goddesses are but masks worn by ancient Mother Night,' he said. 'Even Urshevat hides the sharp teeth of the child-eater behind her stern benevolence. I can use the Mother energy, like an unfired clay figure to which I need only add detail. Can you not feel it, Thera, even from here? It's like a dome of tension over the island, pregnant with power – and I do not use the term carelessly. It would be madness not to take the opportunity.'

'But if you can't contact the Luminous Ones, how will they approve the change?'

'Oh, they will not.' There was challenge in his eyes; the old tiredness seemed gone from them. Sweat gleamed on his forehead. 'The change will be to suit myself, rather than my... *former* masters.'

Thera's heart raced. She remembered the World In Waiting, deep in the psychosphere: the unimaginable technology, the seething swarms of humanity, the *presence* she had felt there. Anything less than total compliance with its rulers seemed madness.

'Two factors I could not have anticipated,' her father went on. 'The Mother energy is one. The second is Orc's relationship, as Sun-King, with the goddess. A psychic relationship with the Mother might also be inherent in him, if he saw the Serpent Mandala with so little training. I believe I can bring him to the point I require. The rewards could be immense. For you as well.'

'Greater than *they* promised? Endless life?'

'I can grant you that myself,' he said. 'When the time is right, I'll teach you. You need a little more maturity in your appearance first, to command true respect.'

She licked her lips nervously. She had hoped she wouldn't have to employ the same technique on others that he'd used on her.

'You cannot be squeamish,' he said, seemingly guessing her thought. 'We who have raised ourselves above the common cattle have every right. The feeble of will are no better than the animals we use for meat and leather.'

'But your method isn't – you can still be killed. What *they* promised—'

'And would they have kept that promise, Thera? And if so, would we be any more than their immortal slaves? They view me with disdain, I can tell. Many of their thoughts and designs they keep from me, who am supposed to be their ally. I also have a plan for this world – why should theirs be the one that becomes reality? And what man of power and vision would wish to spend eternity being forced to admire the creations of others, when his own never had the chance to be given form? No, I am sick and tired of servitude.'

'And how will you make yourself master?'

He smiled. 'By manifesting Urshevat.'

'But that was already the plan.'

'As far as *you* knew.'

'You mean there was another?'

'Yes, Thera, there was another. At the very moment of creating Seriuz's supposed goddess of the people, something was to have "gone wrong". I was to secretly use the latest impressions in the artefacts, those from the time of mass-sacrifice, and so create the destroyer aspect, Skalith. Insatiable, she would have rampaged through Torrento, until doubtless eventually destroyed by modern munitions. Quite a spectacle, and something of a shock for our poor captain.'

'But—'

'I don't know all the plans of the Luminous Ones, nor can I guess what consequences they expected to come from such an act. But they certainly have no interest in establishing a goddess-ruled land of peace.'

She'd had no idea. The power of the revelation was made worse by the casual way in which her father had made it. 'But you do?'

'I haven't yet decided what I will do with Urshevat,' he said. 'And that is the key: the element of control. The Skalith manifestation would have been driven by the destructive energies inherent within the thought-form. The best I could have hoped for was to direct her towards specific targets. But I have seen a way to forge a controlling link with Urshevat through Orc's identification as her consort. It will be delicate work: the trick will be to persuade him to surrender his will to me, such that the rest of his mind falls into the mythic role assigned him. Once he is absorbed into her, I will be able to influence everything she does, through him.'

'But the Luminous Ones. Won't they stop you?'

'They can operate only on the psychic plane, or through human agencies. Once Urshevat is under my control, I will command armies. I'll seek out their desert sepulchre and destroy them.'

Such a bald statement of betrayal terrified her. 'If they can truly do nothing, why this shroud?'

'Because we must be flexible.'

'You mean it could go wrong?'

'I shall need your help,' said her father. 'Try not to think about what I've said: thoughts also imprint upon the psychosphere, though I don't believe even the Luminous Ones could read those of an individual. Try to fool yourself into believing we are still following their plan. I must have absolute trust in you.'

'You know you can trust me,' she said, heavy-hearted. No matter what her father ordered, she could not betray him – not if she wished to avoid what he'd boasted doing to the museum man, Alonso Gregal.

25

PLACES OF POWER

Tiredness dragging at her limbs, Cass climbed on deck to a dawn silence broken only by the slosh of waves against the hull. Her latest dream had been the worst yet. Again she'd stood at the tower window, watching the deaths of thousands; but this time she'd sensed in appalling clarity the stained bed behind her, the swamp of sweat and blood and semen. She'd felt *his* hand on her shoulder, his trembling kiss on her neck.

'It was worth it.' His voice, desperate, straining for confidence. 'It was, Kar—'

He'd used a long name for her. It hadn't stuck in her memory. What had stuck was the feel of his mouth on her skin as she'd stared down at the catastrophe they had wrought.

'It was worth it.'

Seriuz was at the stern, alone, gazing at the eastern crimson.

'They've just left,' he said, looking towards the boat now disappearing round the mole. 'Daroguerre's taking your cousin to go through those exercises.'

Her cousin. But in her dream, she'd known otherwise.

'Esteban too,' said Seriuz.

Cass nodded. It occurred to her that Seriuz had sent the young fisherman away for her benefit. He might do more.

'I crave your forgiveness for his presence here,' said Seriuz. 'I didn't know what to do with him. Things didn't go according to plan. Very little has.'

She barely took in his words. She tried to think how to make her request.

'Whenever I wake these days,' he went on, 'I believe for a blissful moment I'm on normal duty. Then truth breaks upon me, and always my first thought is how to reverse what I've done. It takes all my strength to remember why I'm doing this, to steel myself to continue. The things… the *crimes* I've committed for this cause, can only be expiated by its success.'

She didn't want to hear that. 'Whatever you did, I'm sure it was necessary.'

'Even if so, success or failure will both bring challenges. If we fail, then at the very least I've exiled myself and my crew. If we succeed, then we'll have achieved something not accomplished since antiquity, and the consequences might not be as we hope. They say the Zhenaii were destroyed for similarly trespassing on the gods' domain. It wouldn't be the first time I sought to save something, and harmed it.'

'You can save me,' she said.

The moment's silence that followed wouldn't let her breathe. 'Forgive me,' said Seriuz. 'I've been caught up in myself. You're upset.'

'Orc.'

'I might have guessed.'

'He's planning to use the stone in the ziggurat chamber, breathing from the air-pocket.'

'Truly? He could do that?'

'He's obsessed. You don't know how obsessed.' She felt sick. 'Your order to Daroguerre won't matter. You've got to stop them using the air-line.'

'You said it was dangerous. Is that true?'

'I… think so, yes. But I still can't remember why.'

'Then I'm sorry. Daroguerre says the stone is essential, and your cousin can't reach it without that air.'

'Can't you order a diver to stay down there to make sure he comes straight back up?'

'Even if I did, the diver wouldn't be able to see him. Cass...' His voice was gentle, but firm. 'This memory you fear he'll uncover – it cannot be something that reflects badly on you, I'm sure of it. And if something has happened *to* you, then however painful, it must be brought into the open, to heal. You called it a nightmare seed, but you cannot know what flower might grow from it. Perhaps the time of the goddess's rebirth is also the time of *your* rebirth, from your fears.'

She held back her bitter laugh. She already knew that flower: its corpse-pale velvet petals, its stamens heavy with staining pollen, its sickly scent. The flower of the mortuary. She, and her brother. The thought made her feel ill. Had he forced himself on her, somehow trapped her into it? Maybe for years. And the catastrophe, the ruined city: a symbol, a dream-version of everyone whose lives had been destroyed by their stain of sin. Parents, friends, community.

'Our amnesia.' She swallowed. 'It was to protect us. Maybe we even caused it ourselves.'

The sense of Seriuz beside her had grown almost unbearably strong. She ached for his arms to enfold her, for the warm safety they would bring.

Please, Martin.

His hand on the railing. She placed hers on top.

Please. Her fingers interlocked with his – and to her scared thrill he responded, gently squeezing, though still staring out to the dawn. Her chest tightened around her racing heart. Her hand looked so small against his – paler, delicate – but she sensed she was the one in control. He would make no move without her.

Intuition told her he would not resist, if she moved his hand to her breast. He would want it. Want her. And then – oh, God – they could just go, right now. Leave Orc and Daroguerre and Esteban on the island. Seriuz would be free of his country, his navy, his mad plan. She would be free of her fears.

Her last doubts gone, she lifted his hand—

He pulled it gently from hers, and set it back on the rail.

No word passed between them. Her heartbeat shook the ship. Her blood turned to poison. She warned herself not to over-react. It didn't mean he didn't want her; she had sensed that in his touch. It meant he had his honour, his duty. But that was enough to stop him. There would be no help. No love. No safety.

Except what she could herself make.

She forced her voice to something like normality, as though their hands had never touched. 'When the boat comes back. Can it take me across?'

'Why would you wish it to?' His voice, too, was under strain.

'I want to get off this ship.' Realising how that might sound, she added, 'I'm still not used to it. I'd prefer dry land.'

'You won't do anything…'

She sensed him seeking a word: stupid? Foolish?

'I can't risk anyone's personal fears damaging this mission,' he said. 'My order to Daroguerre yet stands. It will be enough, I'm sure.'

But she wondered if Daroguerre would obey it. He and Orc both used magic: there might be sympathy between them. It would be much better if the dive could be stopped.

'Are you planning any more dives?'

The memory of the voice snapped to her mind.

'Not with what's down there.'

She looked at the cove. 'Nothing stupid,' she said. 'I promise.'

In front of the Quallaces' house, a middle-aged couple were hoeing the vegetable patch. 'Is Hana up yet?' asked Cass.

'An hour ago,' said the woman. 'They'll be working now.' She pointed up the trail Daroguerre had taken the evening before.

The path mounted and twisted between gnarled pines. Since sunrise, thin cloud had closed over the island and for several miles out to sea, and the trapped air felt sticky, as though pregnant with an embryonic storm. Cass sweated; her lungs laboured; her feet struck stones. She'd grown unused to climbing. Even so, it surprised her how quickly she gained height. Below her the sea stretched blue, darkening as its bottom fell away from the island, a serenity marred by the warships' iron jaggedness.

She thought she'd gained about two hundred feet, and gone something like halfway towards the island's eastern end, when the trail met another. One branch carried on east, seeming to run fairly level; the other switched back west, and up. There was no sign which one might lead to Hana, but a hunch persuaded her to carry on climbing. A hundred yards up the western path, she faintly heard a man's voice.

'Drawn!'

Half a minute later, when she was starting to think she'd imagined it, the same word came again.

She stole on. The third time of hearing, she could tell the voice's direction, north of the track. Coming across a little-used trail branching off, she followed it. She'd heard *drawn* five more times when she saw through the pines three standing stones. Ferman Quallace sat against one, facing another. Perplexed, Cass spied from behind a tree as Ferman shuffled a pack of cards and picked one out. Without looking, he held it facing away from him, as though showing it to the other stone.

'Drawn!' he called.

Nothing happened for a while, then a softer voice from farther back called: 'Seen.'

Ferman looked at the card and wrote in a notebook, then shuffled again. The procedure was repeated three more times before Cass felt a subtle prickling on her neck.

'Ferman?' called the other voice. 'Is someone with you?'

The man looked about him. Not wanting to be caught hiding, Cass left the cover of the tree and walked forwards. Ferman pushed to his feet and slipped the cards into his pocket. 'Seems we have a visitor.'

'Please, don't stop because of me,' Cass said.

He offered a thin smile.

Deadwood cracked underfoot behind him. Stefanie and Hana

emerged, Hana finishing with the buttons on her modified waistcoat. Stefanie's smile seemed warmer than her husband's.

'What can we do for you?' she asked.

'I was looking for Hana. But I didn't mean to intrude.'

'Quite all right,' said Stefanie. 'We were almost done.'

'It's meant to be forty every day,' said Hana.

'Hardly matters,' said Ferman. 'The past two days have been wrecked anyway.'

'We'll see you later, dear,' Stefanie said to Hana.

'Oh, you're assuming I want to talk to her?'

'I'm assuming you've manners enough to at least hear what she has to say,' said Stefanie, before she and her husband headed down the track in low conversation.

Cass's courage felt suddenly threadbare. Hana stood with the relaxed poise of someone totally at ease in her surroundings. The half-decade between them felt a gulf.

'Well?' said Hana.

'Last night,' said Cass. 'When we were leaving, you said something about the ziggurat. Like a warning. If you know about a danger, then tell me, please. I need to persuade them to call off the dive.'

Hana folded her arms, emphasising their sleek muscle tone. '*You* need to? Why?'

'Because what they plan to bring up…' But she couldn't hint at her true reasons. 'Thousands of people will die.'

Hana's eyes narrowed in wariness. 'You'd better explain.'

Cass nodded. 'Let's sit down.'

It wasn't hard to come up with a story that fitted her claim; the truth mostly sufficed. She told of a plan not to prevent a war, but to start one: a monarchist plot to push the Empyreum out of Kymera, with inevitable bloody consequences. Clearly mistrustful of *Nightfire*'s officers and their Sundaran allies, Hana took little persuading of their political intent. Having outlined the plotters' objectives, Cass described the means: the fetching up of the artefacts, the kidnapping of Orc and herself – though she omitted any mention of the focus-stones, in case

Hana became interested in them. At last she described the planned goddess manifestation, at which Hana's expression grew incredulous.

'That can't be their plan. Magicians have been trying to manifest things for centuries. No one's ever proved it possible.'

'Daroguerre's discovered a lost art,' said Cass. 'From some ancient race.'

'The Zhenaii? But how? There's nothing left of them, even in Records.'

'All I know is, I saw that elemental in the boiler room. I felt its heat.'

'It couldn't have been a normal fire and a trick of the light?'

'I didn't *want* it to be real,' said Cass. 'And Seriuz wouldn't risk his ship and career if he wasn't sure.'

Hana frowned hard. 'No, I see that,' she said. 'Mother of all – what if they can really do it? To create something outside nature, that's bad enough. But to make a likeness of the goddess and use it as a tool in some political game… it makes me feel sick.'

Cass nodded, encouraged.

'And think about the Flood,' said Hana.

'The Flood?' said Cass, discomfited by the reminder of her dream.

'They say it was because the Zhenaii manifested things. What if the Flood was a natural reaction to the breaking of natural law? The same might happen again.' She made as if to stand. 'I'd better tell Ferman.'

'No, don't tell anyone, please,' said Cass. 'I don't want Seriuz to think I'm making trouble. I don't have any other allies here. Tell me why the ziggurat's dangerous, and I'll pretend I found out by accident.'

'Ah.' Hana's gaze dropped. 'To tell the truth, I was just angry at your lack of respect. I wanted to say something to try to scare you all, get you to rethink the diving.'

'What?' Cass's stomach sank. 'You mean there is no danger?'

'Not to anyone except a sensitive.'

Cass let out a groan of disappointment. Then Hana's last word sunk in. 'A sensitive? Why?'

'Because of what's festering down there.'

'Tell me.'

'You know what that place was meant to be? Beneath the ziggurat?'

Cass remembered Daroguerre's words in the boat. 'The entrance to the Mother?'

'Nice euphemism.'

'For what?'

'You don't know?' said Hana. 'These islands *are* the Mother, or were thought to be. They used to be hills, the only ones for miles on a river plain. This big one is a pregnant belly, and the two Paps are breasts. At the top of this main island is a cave called the Navel. And the other cave, below the belly, now under the ziggurat…?'

'Oh,' Cass said, and coloured.

'The entrance, as you said, and also the exit – the birth canal, and the route by which the seed is planted. This place is all about the union of man and woman – and the *dis*union. That's partly why I'm here, to research that. The ziggurat is where the male energy was supposed to enter, to fertilise the goddess and keep her strong.'

'The Sun-King?'

'Yes, except the ancients didn't understand biology. They thought that just as women lose blood during the menstrual cycle, so the goddess lost blood, and they tried to replenish her strength with the blood of her human husbands. Can you imagine? That's like your lover cutting his penis before sex. It wouldn't make you healthy, and it hasn't made that place healthy either.'

Cass grimaced; the sickness of it reminded her of her dreams.

'And she had thousands of husbands, towards the end,' said Hana. 'The crops failed, so they thought the goddess needed more blood, and so on. More blood, more bad energy, all of it focused on the dark aspect of the goddess, the Destroyer. Her form is still down there, waiting hungrily for her next victim. But only in the psychosphere, of course. Your cousin probably won't even notice it, or he'll just get an uneasy feeling.'

'Unless he is a "sensitive"?'

'A male sensitive would probably last two heartbeats before fleeing for his life.'

'Then we might have something to work with,' said Cass.

Hana stared. 'You mean, he *is*?'

Cass nodded, reluctantly. It was more than she'd originally wanted to let on.

'You too?' said Hana.

'Me? No.'

'You're sure?'

'Absolutely,' said Cass. 'Look – yes, Orc's a sensitive, but that bad energy might not be enough to stop him diving. Daroguerre already knows about the death-goddess. He's teaching Orc some mental exercises so he won't encounter her.'

'But if these exercises fail, so will his dive?'

'I think so.'

'And that will stop them making their goddess monstrosity?'

'Seriuz said they need the artefacts from here because they have more power, or something. Why, do you have an idea?'

'Where's your cousin now?' said Hana.

'Somewhere on the island. Daroguerre took him to some special site this morning, to prepare him.'

Hana thought. 'Not the Navel, we'd have heard them go past. It must be the Spiral. Come on.'

She got to her feet and set off, at a pace Cass struggled to keep up with. Past the junction with the path from the cove, the trail maintained a roughly even height above sea level, slowly curving round towards the island's eastern point. After a mile, Hana led Cass off the path and up onto the spine of the island, then eastwards, gently descending. In a hundred yards the trees ended at the edge of a bluff. Hana crouched by one of the pines, Cass likewise.

From concealment, she looked down a fifteen-foot drop onto a level expanse of bare rock, a kind of terrace seventy yards wide and deep, with nothing visible beyond its far edge but the horizon. A ring of standing stones sixty feet across occupied the centre of the open ground. Within the circle, paving stones formed a spiral pattern.

The bluff sank to the level of the terrace thirty yards either side of them, and to the right, there emerged the trail they'd left earlier. Along from that, near the southern cliff-edge of the terrace, two square tents had been erected, and just past them, two Kymeran sailors sat on freshly cut pine stumps near a signal lamp. The only other person visible was Esteban, standing at the eastern edge looking out over where Cass thought the ziggurat must be. A pistol grip stuck out from the waistband of his trousers.

Cass was about to ask Hana what she planned, when the door-flap of the larger tent opened. Out came Orc, in a thigh-length white tunic that left his arms bare, followed by Daroguerre in a full-length robe of purple belted with red. He still wore his dark spectacles.

'Weird,' whispered Cass.

'Ritual clothing,' said Hana. 'Helps prepare the mind.'

Daroguerre directed Orc to sit at the centre of the spiral paving, then sat facing him. The magician talked, but too softly for Cass to even hear his voice. Orc gave an occasional nod. Minutes passed, the only movement Esteban's slow patrol of the far perimeter.

'Any ideas?' Cass whispered.

Hana nodded. 'I've seen enough.'

She led Cass to rejoin the trail, then back along it, ever faster than before.

'Stone connects,' she said, when Cass pressed her. 'That's the theory behind my father's card-reading experiments. I might be able to reach your cousin through the stone of the island, especially if we're both in places of power.'

'Reach him and do what?'

'He's preparing his mind so he won't encounter the goddess's dark aspect, yes? But what if he's convinced those exercises won't work?'

'He'd tense up,' said Cass. 'And yes, that would kill his breath-hold time! Can you do that? Affect his mind from a distance?'

'Never tried it,' said Hana.

Brilliant.

'In theory, it's possible. It's just not something I've studied. The college I trained with believe magic should only be used for divination.

To try to affect someone else might bring all kinds of unintended consequences, even with good motives.'

'I bet Daroguerre doesn't have those scruples.'

'That's not the point,' said Hana. 'I'm going to try it because if I don't, the consequences might be far worse.'

They passed the turn to the card-reading stones and climbed towards the top of the island. Cass was sweaty and panting with heat by the time the slope levelled off. The trail led between pines and scrub to a pair of squat standing stones a few feet apart, their carvings weathered almost to nothing.

Hana stopped. Cass looked over the scene. The two stones stood at the narrower, eastern end of a depression that was shaped as though a giant egg had been laid on its side and pushed halfway into the earth. Pines struck out from the slopes either side; one on the southern lip had died and fallen long ago, and the remains of its rotted wood littered the whole width of the hollow. A few blocks of carved stone lay tumbled. The trail carried on between the standing stones and down into the bottom of the hollow. In the bank just past this lowest point, where the steeper western side began, scrub and ferns grew around a dark two-foot hole.

'That's the Navel?' said Cass.

Hana nodded. Her face looked flushed, charged with excitement.

'What's in that cave?' said Cass. 'Does it go anywhere?'

'Oh yes. The Abyss.'

'The *Abyss*?'

'Want to see?'

'Don't you need to get on with your… whatever?'

'It won't take long,' said Hana. 'And it might help.'

As they picked their way down into the hollow, Cass quickly found its air uncomfortable and heavy, like water that gained in weight and pressure when diving. As when she'd been climbing from the cove, she thought of the word *pregnant*, and didn't like it. For a sacred site, this place seemed remarkably disordered, cluttered, almost obliterated by nature.

Hana sat in front of the cave and slid her legs into the hole. 'Shuffle down the first bit on your bum,' she said. 'You don't mind those clothes getting dirty?'

'No, I don't have a date tonight.'

Hana laughed, and disappeared.

Following her in feet-first, Cass found the entrance led to a steep slope of loose earth and rock, lumpy but not jagged. Everything was damp, and the cold shocked her after the outdoor heat. Hana's voice guided her down. By the time she reached the bottom, Cass's eyes had adjusted enough to make out a cramped cave, too low to stand in, with a smooth earth floor formed of mud run-off from the depression. The entrance to another passage struck downwards at near right-angles to the first. Within that lay absolute darkness.

'Ready?' said Hana, and crouched towards it.

Cass gasped. 'It's pitch black!'

'At first,' said Hana. 'But there's a secret. Just take it slowly, there's nothing dangerous.'

A secret. The Abyss. How long would this go on for? Cass itched for Hana to get on with trying to frighten Orc. What if he finished his exercises while they were down here?

Hana had gone in feet-first again, so Cass did the same, blindly feeling with hands and heels for the next hold or step. She slipped and bit back a shriek. Behind and above her, what little light there was faded, until a kink in the tight passage extinguished it altogether. Holding her limbs and lungs still, she heard only the rush of her blood, and Hana below.

'I'm there,' came Hana's stone-deadened voice. 'Very careful now. You don't want to miss the ledge.'

'What bloody ledge?'

'Don't worry. Just come slowly.'

Cass eased herself down until she stood next to Hana, who put an arm across her chest. But Cass didn't need this warning, because some vision had returned. What she saw turned her knees to water.

Beyond the ledge, the ground dropped into a black pit – how deep, five feet or a thousand, Cass had no idea. The right-hand wall of the tunnel had also disappeared into absolute darkness, but the left carried on ahead, and after ten feet it met the far wall of the chasm. In that wall was an opening, opposite the one in which she now stood. The tunnel beyond seemed to angle left. From somewhere out of sight came the faintest illumination.

'This is the Abyss,' said Hana.

'No shit,' said Cass shakily. 'How come there's light from that tunnel? We must be fifty feet below ground.'

'Thirty, I reckon,' said Hana. 'I can't work it out. There aren't any other caves round here. Some day I want to get across and see.'

'Get across how? Planks or something?'

'Jump.'

Cass barked an echoing laugh.

'The ancients did it,' said Hana. 'I'm certain.'

'Why would they?'

'To find it: the source. Do you feel anything?'

'Only what you'd expect – terror.'

Hana chuckled. 'I was scared too, when I first came here. But can't you feel *her*?'

'Her?'

'Just let your mind open.'

That sounded too much like something Geist would say. And now Hana had said it, Cass felt a concentration in the air, a stifling quality despite the depth and cold, even more intense than in the depression. As though this place, or perhaps the opposite tunnel with its mysterious light, were the source of it. The pregnancy of it, the building up…

'Let's go.'

'Sure?' said Hana. 'Sensitivity often runs in families. I know you said you weren't like your cousin, but I thought maybe you just hadn't looked for it. If you *were* sensitive, it might help us.'

'I told you, I'm not,' said Cass. 'If that's the reason you got me down here, I could've saved you the trouble.'

She turned, and ignoring Hana's urging to stay a bit longer, she climbed, all the way back out. Hauling herself at last from the cave-mouth, she found herself filthy, but didn't care. What she cared about was that they'd lost time to no purpose.

Hana followed, somehow less dirty than her. 'Well, if you're not going to help, you should stay up past the gateposts,' she said, and led Cass back up to the stones. There she unbuttoned her waistcoat. 'Like your Mister Daroguerre, I find ritual costume helpful. But mine is my skin.' She slipped the vest down over her arms. 'One approaches the Mother as one came out.'

Cass looked aside as Hana took off her sandals and short-cut trousers, then felt even more awkward, since Hana herself seemed so unconcerned about privacy. The islander returned to the hollow, probing each step with her bare feet. Her toned, sun-browned body made Cass feel pale and unhealthy. She almost laughed when Hana stepped on a twig and stumbled like a drunkard.

While Hana knelt on the cleared patch of earth before the cave, facing the darkness, and meditated, Cass sat against one of the stones. After a while, Hana pulled something from beneath her wrist-bracer, and touched it to her face many times, before bending forward into a crouch: forehead against ground, elbows against knees, hands beside her head as though to mimic long ears. Uncomfortable with the sight, Cass found a place where not too many stones dug into her back, and lay gazing at the humid sky through gaps in the pines.

It felt tense enough for thunder. *Pregnant* – the thought-word came again. Recalling what Hana had said about the island's shape, Cass wondered if that was why it had first became associated with the mother goddess, the chance combination of form and atmosphere somehow suggesting pregnancy. It couldn't have been anything real, because there *were* no gods or goddesses, except those made by humanity. Even Geist had admitted so, when she'd cornered him. Though he'd then said that wasn't the point.

But the insistence of the word *pregnant* disturbed her. It felt like it was trying to bring something out of her memory. It sat in her mind like something about to hatch.

To hatch within her.

Like—

She gasped and sat up, the cry strangled in her throat. She wanted to be sick. For a moment, she hung above the horror, awed and dazed by its extent.

The core of the nightmare seed.

His seed. In her. Orc's sperm, her brother's, finding its counterpart, and growing.

'Get out!' she cried. 'Get out, I don't want to know, I don't—'

The squeal snapped her head round. It came again, from Hana, a high-pitched wail of distress that sounded more animal that human.

Cass pushed to her feet. Hana was shrieking like a creature in absolute terror.

Cramming down her own fear, Cass ran into the hollow. Hana shivered crazily; the noise poured from her, impossibly loud and constant for lungs cramped by her position. Cass grabbed her shoulder and Hana jerked up with a panicked start, scrambled to her feet, staggered to one side and then crashed down in a bunch of ferns. Her chest heaved, her face—

Cass stared. Hana's wide-eyed face was patterned with tattoos.

Like Orc's. Like Geist's.

'Get away!' said Hana. 'Go!'

'What?'

'You brought her here! Fuck off!'

'Brought who?'

'Three-Eyes!' It came out as a squeal. 'Mother, help me!' Hana curled up where she sat, her face buried, her whole naked body shaking. 'Mother, Mother!'

'Hana—'

'Get out! You shouldn't have come, none of you! Get out, get out!'

'I'll get your parents—'

'No! Just get *out*!'

Shaken, Cass backed off. Hana's madness reminded her horribly of Orc's after his Initiation, and she wanted away from it. She would fetch

Ferman and Stefanie, never mind what Hana said. They would know how to calm her. She would only aggravate things by staying.

She hurried way from the Navel. Hana's cries faded by the time she reached the junction of tracks. But as she was about to head down towards the cove, she hesitated.

Hana would probably calm down by herself, and going to the Quallaces would take time. Too much depended on Orc not finishing his preparations. The idea of sabotage had been sound. And it didn't need Hana's magic. She could do it herself.

Despite the heat, she jogged all the way to the eastern end, retracing their earlier route to the vantage point atop the bluff. The two sailors and Esteban were by the tents – and yes, she was in time: Daroguerre and Orc still sat in the middle of the stone circle.

She charged her lungs.

'You're *dead*, Orc!'

Orc and Daroguerre jumped up.

'She'll see through your useless exercises, and *you know it*!'

Daroguerre shouted to Esteban, who launched into a run.

'You can't fool her, or yourself – she'll tear you apart!'

No time for more: Esteban had disappeared from view, taking the trail, he could cut her off. Cass turned and ran through the forest, keeping the trail to her left.

'Cass! Wait!'

She glanced behind. Esteban was already among the trees, running full-pelt. She drove her legs into a sprint. She leapt fallen branches, dodged trees, pushed all her strength through each stride. But not fast enough – pounding footsteps closed behind her. She ducked to one side; her blouse collar was grabbed; she pulled free but it was grabbed again and flung her off-balance. A hard mass thumped into her, her limbs tangled, her front smacked the ground and the live heaviness of a body crashed onto her back.

She struggled, but was dazed, too slow. Wet breath filled her ear. A hand clamped her mouth before she could yell. Weight pinned her, crushed her into every knob and knuckle of the hard earth. She squirmed and flexed, tried to bite the hand.

'He said to be silent,' Esteban panted in her ear.

Cass drove all her strength into trying to get free. The ease with which Esteban contained her turned hot outrage to cold fear. His tongue blocked her ear, its rasping shuddering through her. He kissed and licked around it, then her neck. His hips ground against her.

'They might not even find us.' The desperation in his voice scared her as much as his lust. 'We'll have that life I talked about, I'll make sure of it. Oh soft, so soft.'

She tried to scream against the hand, tried to fight. It seemed impossible that all her strength wasn't enough, but it wasn't; every trick of struggle she tried, he countered. Hard thoughts sickened her: that she would have to pretend to agree, to placate him, to beg him to put off what she knew he wanted to do.

'So soft,' said Esteban, between gnawing kisses. 'Soft.' His nose nuzzled her cheek. 'Sweet.'

Then feet – at last, she heard feet, running, but a limping run. Esteban's weight doubled, crushing, as he pushed up off her to stand. Skin crawling, Cass scrambled away a few yards in a half-crouch, and turned.

Esteban stood with his handgun aimed. Orc stood a few feet away, face hot with running and fury, his fists clenched. 'You're dead,' he seethed.

Yes! – she wanted him to break Esteban apart.

Esteban grunted a laugh. 'You begged for my life to be spared before. Now you want it to end? If you save a man, you must look after his needs.' He nodded towards Cass. 'But if she does it instead, it's as good. Stop!' He jerked his pistol as Orc was about to go for him.

Orc glanced towards her, his face tight with pain. 'Get out of here.'

'No,' she said. Esteban might shoot if he had no witness. She had no idea what he'd meant about Orc sparing his life; she just wanted him stopped and hurt. Maybe if she got behind him—

'She wants you to leave, so we can finish,' said Esteban. 'She was excited by it. You know how it feels, of course, to have her move passionately against you?'

Cass almost retched, then saw from Orc's face he was about to go for Esteban anyway. 'Don't!'

'Put it down, Esteban,' came Daroguerre's voice. The robed magician approached, flanked by the two sailors. 'You have no idea what torments await you should you pull that trigger.'

Esteban lowered the pistol. Orc made for him, but the heavier sailor grabbed his shoulders.

'You're letting him get away with it?' cried Orc as he struggled.

'I will not tolerate sabotage,' said Daroguerre. 'I told Esteban to silence your cousin's bizarre outburst.'

'That's not all he was doing,' said Orc.

Cass shrank inside as Daroguerre turned his dark lenses on her. 'Is that true?'

But she just wanted to be out of there now. She shook her head.

'Cass!'

'She'll get you,' she told Orc.

'Silence!' commanded Daroguerre. 'Pisaro, escort Miss Strandborn back. Tell Seriuz what happened and suggest he keeps her on board ship. Esteban, you'll stay in the tent until Mister Strandborn has left for his dive.'

'I want him locked up,' said Orc.

'Do you wish to antagonise me?' said Daroguerre. 'Do you wish to face the goddess unprepared?'

Orc shook his head tightly.

'He'll stay out of sight,' said Daroguerre. 'And you should return to your exercises. I hope there's still enough time for the work, now your cousin has done her best to set us back.'

'It's not her fault,' said Orc. 'She's not thinking straight.'

As the sailor Pisaro led her away, Cass glanced round to see Orc, his face creased with hurt, leaning against a tree and examining his foot. Blood smeared its sole.

Physical pain too. It might be enough.

Clairaudioscope transcript 13:28 27-8-336
Known voices: A,D,E,F

A: Still nothing?
F: He's made no further attempt at contact. We're
     increasing focus through the obfuscating energy, but
     it's taking time, and we can't send unless he's ready to
     receive.
E: He sees no need. He must believe nothing can have
     changed.
A: The instructions given him were clear.
F: He might be waiting until after the dive. When he's in
     possession of the amplifying stone, contact should be
     possible.
A: When is the dive scheduled?
E: Mid-afternoon.
A: And the monk's cruiser?
D: You're not going to like this.

26

THE GREAT ZIGGURAT

The depth was murky; the ziggurat entrance was a monument of shadows within which lay utter blackness, the beginning of a passage twice as long as at Bazantin. But now, on his fourth dive, Orc felt ready. He was the young king-to-be, here for a wedding, not a death: he'd spent hours asserting that truth, purging Cass's attempts to instil doubt. Awaiting him was his queen, Urshevat, she who nurtured wild plants and crops, whose yell was in the clash of battle-spears and whose laughter was in spring rains.

Daroguerre had assured him that whatever psychic quirk prevented him evoking Otter in the soulscape, it would not affect invocation; and indeed, he experienced the changes to his body and vision when he called his animath into him. He swam past ancient rubble from the ziggurat's erosion and into the passageway, trying to ignore the pain of his injured soles as they pressed against the foot-pockets of his fins. He focused on the air that waited at the far end, where in the ritual world also waited the priestesses who embodied the goddess.

But something niggled his memory. The priestesses came surprisingly clear to his mind, as though he'd encountered their image before. Or one of them…

Paleness, far ahead. He calmed the mounting desire to breathe. Plenty of time; he wouldn't have to return this way. But the disquieting feeling grew.

Could he somehow have *met* one of the priestesses before?

The passageway enclosed him: directing him, he felt now, towards a dark secret. But no, he couldn't have met a priestess; his mind was confused. He needed to stay focused.

Further in. Deeper in. Towards—

Memory jumped him: her short white robe, her shocked face.

The hotel bedroom.

He tried to expel it, uncertain and fearful of what it meant. But the intrusion had already done its damage. Confused, his role compromised, hemmed in a dark tunnel without breath, he twisted back on himself and sprint-kicked for the exit.

He came up thirty yards from the top of the ziggurat. *Tarpon* hulked north of the ruin, her air-line trailing into the shaft; *Nightfire* lay to the south. On the eroded ziggurat stood a small cluster of personnel, and Daroguerre and Cass.

Seriuz spotted him first. Orc waved. 'Just needed another practice,' he called, then turned to face away, out to sea.

All through his next breathe-up, he tried to dispel the thought of Cass as a priestess. It had been only a random aspect of his half-dream at the hotel, inconsequential. He steeped himself in his new royal identity, his true self. Daroguerre had urged him to think of his role as a genuine previous incarnation, a past life he must now replay.

When he thought eight minutes had passed, he dived again.

This time, entering the passage, he focused on Urshevat herself, not her priestesses. He sensed her ahead in the cold: mother, wife and war-goddess, the taker of all bodies into her own.

But why *had* he seen Cass in the priestess role?

Because she'd happened to be in the room – no other reason. It didn't matter.

The light grew, and the nagging dread with it. He sensed a flaw somewhere. If the rites weren't performed exactly to the goddess's liking, would she still accept him as consort, or would she become the dark entity who'd sought his death at Bazantin?

Because Cass...

He pushed away the unfinished thought, and emerged into a chamber whose ceiling was supported by pillars almost as wide as the spaces between them. Halfway down the central aisle he saw the shaft's entrance, and the gaping hole in the floor off to one side. No sign of any gold – Ranga's source had been mistaken or dishonest about that, it seemed – but he gave that barely a thought. The goddess's presence filled the chamber: intense, scrutinising, judging. He noted the air-line curving from the bottom of the shaft, touching the floor before bending round towards the far side of the chamber, where it spewed bubbles at the ceiling. But that intrusion from the surface seemed a dream-overlay to the deeper, truer world, in which blood dripped down the shaft, the blood of his forebear.

The image of Cass in her robe wouldn't leave his mind. He sensed her, one of the priestesses, but his image of her radiated horror.

'Orc! What the hell were you doing?'

Because the priestesses had to be virgins.

And if he and she *had* been lovers—

The goddess's rage hit him like a storm. Suddenly, he knew it: he would be torn apart. They both would be. The chamber was filled with blood. He heard Cass crying. The thunder of rage pressed at him from every corner. His diaphragm convulsed.

The goddess was about to manifest.

He almost turned back into the passage, but he would never have lasted its length. He forced himself to brave the chamber – he kicked into the terrifying space with all the strength in his legs and hurled himself into the shaft.

All the way up, fast as he could swim, he expected to be grabbed. Even as he neared the surface he didn't slow. At last he crashed through and seized hold of the stone rim, his legs drained of blood, on the verge of fainting.

The others pressed around the shaft-hole, Daroguerre closest.

'What happened?'

Seriuz echoed the magician's question. Cass was silent.

Orc pushed his dive-mask up. 'I need to speak to you,' he told Daroguerre, still breathing hard. 'Alone.'

Daroguerre asked the others to step back and give them space, then squatted on his heels. Keeping his voice low, Orc related what had happened at the *Royal Bull*, and outlined the possibility that his and Cass's amnesia hid a past in which they'd been lovers.

'Why did you not tell me this before?' said Daroguerre.

'I forgot about the priestess thing till now,' said Orc. 'How do I get round it?'

'By sinking yourself even deeper into the idea of the former life: the one millennia ago, from which Cass was absent.'

'But maybe she wasn't,' said Orc, jumped by a horrible thought. 'What started the whole famine? Maybe one of the new kings fouled the rites by... you know, being with a priestess beforehand, in secret – and the goddess was angry and the crops didn't grow, and they had to kill more and more kings, trying to find one who could get back her favour. Maybe I *was* a king in a former life, and I'm what screwed it all up.' He glanced at Cass. 'Or *we* were...'

Daroguerre straightened up. 'Unbelievable.'

'What's the problem?' said Seriuz.

'Mister Strandborn has imaginatively constructed a disabling fear from the role I gave him to *remove* that fear.'

'I didn't do it on purpose!' said Orc. 'I want this to work as much as you do.'

'Can you hypnotise him?' said Seriuz. 'That can remove fear, I've heard.'

'Mind control?' said Cass.

'*You* were not to speak,' Daroguerre told her, then turned to Seriuz. 'The subject has to be willing.'

'I am if it'll help,' said Orc.

'No,' said Daroguerre. 'Let me think. There must be some way.'

'This is all too unreliable,' said Seriuz.

'It's magic, Captain, not a rifle to be stripped down and greased.'

'Then we'll do without magic,' said Seriuz. 'A diver from *Tarpon* will have to search by hand, however difficult. I assume the tunnel with your stone is wide enough to admit him?'

Dread stifled Orc's breath.

'It would suit us better if Mister Strandborn did it,' said Daroguerre. 'But your plan might be worth a try.'

No. If he didn't fetch the stone himself, he might never get access to it. 'I'll have another go.'

'You will not,' said Daroguerre. 'Not unless we find a solution. I will not risk your fear manifesting a hostile entity.'

'Then hypnotise me, like Seriuz said.'

'Absolutely not. Your free will must remain inviolate.'

'Why?'

Daroguerre didn't answer. Seriuz turned to one of his sailors. 'Ask *Tarpon* to send across her divers and chief engineer.'

Orc's heart raced with frustration. He couldn't go down as he was: the whole Sun-King gambit had brought him too close to the goddess, and he couldn't approach her now except as sacrifice or betrayer. As the sailor walked to the edge of the ziggurat, Orc tried to mentally erase the idea of the Sun-King that Daroguerre had fixed in him. But that might not be enough. The role hadn't been in his head when the Sea Mother had manifested days before. Even before he'd heard of the Sun-King, his uneasy presence in the Bazantin ziggurat had given him that role from the first. Perhaps any human male would have fitted it.

His breath caught. Any *human* male…

His thoughts raced to catch up with the possibility. When he invoked Otter to help in diving, he invited him in, from outside. But what if he'd got that wrong? In the cave of his Initiation, when his self had almost dissolved, only Otter's arrival with the flaming brand had saved him. Otter had saved him from dissolution by rebuilding him from within.

Otter was now the heart of his identity.

He knew that couldn't be the whole truth, but it was a magical truth he needed to assert at this moment, and he threw himself into it. He pushed away the shreds of his human self – and what self could there be with no name, no past? – and into the resulting void he pulled and expanded the core of him, the magical soul that had been there since Initiation. His true self, his animath.

Instinct took him. He wrenched off his fins and dumped them on the stone. Then his dive-mask. He sensed Cass's relief, her pleasure. She thought he was giving up. Tricked!

He took a great breath and twisted round and slipped under.

His secret self filled him, twisting his body within the constriction of his suit. Saltwater was cold on his eyes; his vision was a blur, struggling to focus. He swam down with sweeps of his forepaws under his chest, kicking with his feet, sensing the touch of the shaft's wall as his whiskers brushed against it. He'd gone thirty feet and everything was blue when he realised that he hadn't needed to pinch his nose and blow to pressurise his ears; it had happened by itself.

Deeper he went, down against the fizz of returning bubbles, deeper into the magic as though into a trance. The blue darkened, but he could still see. He followed the air-line into the chamber.

Again, he felt the goddess's presence. Larger than the chamber, than the ziggurat, than the island, she sat enthroned, twin serpents entwined about her arms. Her belly was vast with birth yet to come, her breasts heavy with milk, her legs buried in the vegetation of forest and field. He recognised her as a distant reflection of the Mother who had birthed him and all otters and all creatures: she who had been made something else by human thought and awe, something complicatedly halfway between their own being and the world in which they found themselves. He almost pitied the frightened grappling with existence that had given rise to this power in the darkness.

She awaited a king crowned with the sun, and paid no heed to an otter. He had tricked the Great Goddess herself.

Ignoring the gaping hole in the floor for the moment, he followed the air-line round to where it shot ascending bubbles. Where they collected in a hollow beneath the ceiling, he found an air-pocket. It was as large as it would ever get, the excess escaping up the shaft, but still only a couple of inches deep. Frog-kicking to keep himself in position, heavier than water at this depth, he held his mouth to the air. He hesitated, remembering Cass's warning against doing this. But she had only been trying to stop him.

He breathed in, and his compressed lungs swelled back to their normal size.

♋

When a minute had passed, Cass knew Orc must have made it to the chamber. And if he could get that far…

'What's he doing?' she said shakily – the initial relief of Orc removing his mask and fins, followed by the shock of him diving without them, made the world feel unstable.

'I have no idea,' replied Daroguerre.

'Is it some kind of joke? He can't get to a hundred and thirty feet without fins. And won't the goddess—'

'I don't know,' said Daroguerre. 'My hunch is that he's thought of a way to avoid her, one that never occurred to me.'

Cass tried to breathe down her nerves. She moved to stand closer to Seriuz; she concentrated on the stream of bubbles expelled by the air-line. If the goddess was no longer any threat to Orc, she would just have to hope he couldn't reach the stone, or that the cold would be unbearable. She couldn't believe how much he was willing to put himself through to find a truth that would only hurt them both. To hold himself in a cold place she could barely imagine, sucking air from a rock cavity…

It caught her again: the wrongness of breathing that air. The bubbles breaking at the surface of the shaft reminded her of times she'd watched over Orc when he'd ascended with lazy slowness, letting his growing buoyancy alone carry him – the air he'd exhaled into his mask on the descent leaking out as it expanded again, rising ahead of him, the bubbles growing in size. Something to do with that.

But it was old, buried information. She knew it was very bad, very serious; but she couldn't pinpoint it, the reason he—

The reason he was going to die.

♋

An otter shouldn't be this deep, Orc knew. The weight of stone and water entombed him, a creature of fresh air and shallows. And he needed to get deeper still. Why would an otter need a crystal? He knew he *had* wanted it, but he was now coming to his senses.

'Nothing a clean-whiskered animal wants to eat down there.'

Ah, but there was, he persuaded himself. A fish was down there, the most tasty fish in the world, its flesh like blue-tinted glass.

Even with his previously compressed lungs freshly filled, he was heavier than water here. He stopped kicking to let himself fall from the ceiling, then twisted round and pulled with his forepaws, plunging into the hole to chase his prey down into the chasm, a darkness so deep that even otter eyes were almost blind. He fixed his focus ahead as the rough rock walls closed in on him. He tried to ignore the weight and depth of water, pushed away the awareness of how far down he was. Somewhere ahead—

He saw it.

The stone gleamed against rock so dark that no feature was visible, the blurred paleness of crystal like a faint star against otherwise unbroken night.

He turned in the deep, deep water. His injured feet settled painfully on the rugged stone. The gleam died as he enclosed it in his paw. Somewhere around him, he sensed the tunnel kink to one side and continue deeper into the flooded earth; but he couldn't see it, and was almost scared it would suck him in. Lungs already uncomfortable, he tucked his prize down the neck of his wetsuit, bringing a shock of cold water with it. He pushed himself off the bottom and swam.

Straight away, he sensed trouble. His arms weren't enough. With all buoyancy compressed out of him, he was swimming against the downward drag of gravity. He needed his fins. Each arm-stroke gained him little distance, and most was pulled back again as he gathered his next.

Panic gripped him. His lungs burned with effort. Above, the faint dimness of the chamber showed between the imprisoning rock walls of the chasm. Fifty feet to the air pocket: it should have been easy, but without his fins, and so heavy—

Heavy.

Frantic, he tugged at the clasp of his weight belt. Part of the gear he'd carried his whole remembered life, it dropped around his feet, and he pulled again. This time he made progress; he pawed and pushed, up and slowly up.

His forehead bumped against the chamber ceiling with his eagerness to suck air. He stayed there, breathing awkwardly, kicking, waiting for his heart to slow. But excitement and panic had brought him mostly back to human. Naked of his otter trickery, the goddess would be aware of him: not just the mighty Urshevat, but her darker aspect Skalith, who sat in the congealed blood of centuries. He couldn't help thinking of Bazantin.

He must help it. This might be his only chance to use the stone. But he'd expected to be buoyant with his lungs filled, and even without his weights he gently sank, he didn't understand why, having to kick to hold his mouth in the narrow air-pocket. He pulled the large stone from inside his wetsuit, replaced the air in his lungs with a deep breath, and let himself drop to the chamber floor. He started to prick the tattoo-mask to his face, turning his mind wholly on the task, refusing to let his thoughts wander through the darkness. Just one answer, that was all he wanted: just the answer that he and Cass had been lovers rather than siblings. Different surnames would be proof enough. Everything else could wait.

He couldn't tell if the mask was forming. He jumped up, the force through his injured feet making him wince, and kept himself up by the ceiling to take on more air. He didn't need to call Otter. He *was* Otter. And he was already in the Well.

But that thing uncoiling at the edge of his vision – that wasn't Eel.

∽

'Anything wrong?' said Seriuz.

Cass didn't answer. Maybe Orc was already dead. She tested what that might do to her. She imagined herself distraught, Seriuz holding her, comforting her, tending to her, physical contact at last breaking through the barriers. A new life released by Orc's death.

You cow. You evil bitch.

She hadn't even discovered his name. She would never learn her own. But that hardly mattered next to the fact that the stone and the nightmare truth would stay down there.

Arterial gas embolism.

She gasped at the words, at the sudden flash of old, buried knowledge: a warning, but she didn't know of what. It was too late anyway. Even if Orc wasn't yet dead, no one could prevent it, if it was going to happen. He'd brought this on himself, with his insistence on going for the stone, despite all her arguments, all her pleading, and now his filled lungs – oh God, she remembered – his lungs filled with depth-pressured air would expand past their physical limits as he swam up the shaft.

Be still. Be calm. It's already as good as happened.

The grief would come later. The next Mrs Martin Seriuz. The madness of it. Crying into Martin's chest. Tears of utter hypocrisy. No, it wasn't. She hadn't wanted this. She'd tried to stop it. Until now. It amazed her to realise that there was no external force holding her, keeping her from trying to do something. It was just herself. She looked at his mask and fins lying beside the shaft as though they were grave markers.

And his name on that gravestone: just Orca. That was all. She'd never really known him.

'Wouldn't it be strange if they were our names? If what you told Seriuz was what we really did?'

Her skin shivered at the memory of Orc's words after they'd retrieved *Nightfire*'s anchor, the sudden sense that they held a truth she'd missed. She frowned with the nearness of recognition. Their story, that they'd put their names on their wetsuits to brand them theirs: not quite right, but nerve-pricklingly close. Orca, Picasso.

Not painted on, but—

Chosen.

They'd chosen those wetsuits *because* of their—

'Oscar.'

She broke, pushed past Seriuz and sat at the entrance of the shaft. Her own gear was still on *Nightfire*, but she jammed Orc's fins over her shoes, stuck his mask on her face, wrenched at the strap to tighten it. Ignoring the questions, shaking Seriuz's hand off her shoulder, she sucked air and went.

For the first moment, the crash into water was a repeat of when she'd been thrown in to drown. But there was no room for that fear; she pulled herself round and under and kicked against her buoyancy.

The colder water started only feet down. The chill attacked her held breath, tried to spasm her diaphragm. She struggled to get deep. She swam against the stream of bubbles from the air-line, panicking for speed but forced to slow by the difficulty of pressuring her ears, her tubes tightened by sudden cold and stress. She didn't know where Orc would be. If he'd started up the shaft, he might already be fatally injured. If he was still exploring the deeper chasm, how would she see him to warn him?

She kept going. She hadn't breathed up properly. Her diaphragm had already started its contractions. She could no longer see; she just kept going down into blindness and cold, popping her ears as fast as she could.

Her outstretched hand hit the floor. She turned in the water, confused, immersed in ink.

Something grabbed her. The shock almost burst the breath from her. She felt in front, touched smooth rubber over a firm arm.

She couldn't see him, couldn't talk to him. He tried to swim upwards, holding her. She struggled, tried to pull back down, squeezed his arm in panic.

She looked towards where she guessed his face was and breathed out a little.

He stilled: asking himself why, she hoped. She breathed out again, her diaphragm contracting, and sought his inflated abdomen. She pressed against it.

They'd sunk to their knees now on the chamber floor. She'd started to shiver. She needed to breathe desperately. She tried not to think of the effort it would take to get to the surface, eighty feet, all the air it would burn inside her. She had so little left, and Orc, without fins, couldn't help her. They would die here together – it felt suddenly inevitable, as though it had been meant to happen, had always happened.

But there surely hadn't been time for him to use the stone. They would die with their terrible past hidden, and because of that, and because this was it, she forgave him everything. Shivering harder, she grabbed hold of him, tightened her arms round him, wishing his insulating wetsuit could dissolve for this final embrace. She wished she'd had the chance to tell him her discovery, his name. Now she would never be able to. Several more contractions, and the pain would become intolerable and she would be forced to inhale the sea.

Suddenly she shot upwards. They were floating up, weightless. Orc had jumped – his finless feet had pushed him off against the chamber floor, taking her with him. He grabbed the air-line and began to haul himself up it, arm over arm, an ascent Cass knew would break his lungs – but as the water in the shaft became slightly less than black, she saw bubbles stream from his mouth, a constant, steady release of expanding air.

Her diaphragm spasmed as she now held on, seeing hope. She clung to him as he pulled faster, as buoyancy took them. Light rushed at them until they smacked through the surface.

She let go of Orc and grabbed feebly for the stone lip of the shaft, breathing for her life, flapping away the hands and questions of those who tried to pull her from the water.

Orc gasped, swore as he leaned over the rim of the rock. 'What the hell were you doing down there?'

Her jaw dropped. 'Saving *you*, you moron.'

'*Saving* me? She was forming. She almost got me – got *us*.'

That chilled her. She felt suddenly grateful that she'd been blind down here. 'And you'd have burst your lungs and saved her the bother.'

'I would've worked it out by myself.' But his eyes shied from hers. Infuriating, hurtful.

'How did you avoid her so long?' said Daroguerre.

'A trick,' said Orc.

'You adopted a magical role, but one entirely divorced from the Sun-King?'

Orc nodded. 'I lost it at the end, though.'

'But you gained something?'

'Can we save the questions? Some of us almost died down there.' He put his back to the wall of the shaft and pushed himself out to sit on its edge. 'You'll have to get those divers from the ship, sorry.'

He was sitting curved over strangely, as though trying to hide his front. Cass guessed why.

'Martin?' she said.

'You'll hand over that stone, please,' said Seriuz.

'What stone?' said Orc.

'The one I assume is the cause of that lump on your chest.'

'Hand it over why?' said Orc.

'The stone, Mister Strandborn.'

'You're working for her openly now?' said Orc. 'What if I don't? You going to shoot me in cold blood? Is that the kind of thing you'd do?'

'You're raving,' Seriuz said tightly.

Defeated, his face set, Orc pulled the stone out. For a moment he looked about to throw it into the shaft, but he handed it up to Seriuz. Then he yanked down the zip at his back and peeled his wetsuit off his arms and torso, down to his waist.

Shivering again by now, with relief as well as cold, Cass accepted Seriuz's help in getting out of the water. Seriuz put his uniform jacket around her shoulders. Orc seemed content to be half-naked, his lean, muscled back rounded over his disappointment and hurt. *You stupid boy*, Cass thought. *You've no idea what I'm saving you from.*

'Might I?' said Daroguerre, holding out his hand to Seriuz.

'Wait,' blurted Cass.

Seriuz had been about to give the magician the stone, but retracted it. Daroguerre stared at her.

'The crystal is of little use to the captain,' he told her. 'And I shall need it for the successful completion of our mission, little though you seem to care about that.'

'Not till we get to Torrento,' she said. 'That's right, isn't it?'

His dark lenses fixed on her. 'Not any more. I've decided to create the goddess here, on the island.'

'I beg your pardon?' said Seriuz. 'That would be a matter for discussion.'

'Torrento is too dangerous. That Watcher had wind of me.'

'And have you made any attempt to ascertain the situation in Torrento?' said Seriuz. 'Have you contacted our patrons?'

'It's irrelevant,' said Daroguerre. 'My examination of the Spiral site shows it to be far superior.'

'But transporting her afterwards—'

'You worry unnecessarily, Captain. Creating her on this island will give me greater control. Transporting her will be no problem.' He held out his hand.

No, thought Cass, but Seriuz placed the stone on Daroguerre's palm. The magician's fingers enfolded it with exploratory care.

'You remember my instruction?' said Seriuz.

'Of course,' said Daroguerre. 'For my use alone. I shall begin preparing immediately.'

'And the artefacts?'

'I doubt it would be safe for Mister Strandborn to venture down there again, even were he to be cooperative. Such tricks tend to work only once.'

'So we're back to *Tarpon*'s divers, and a blind search?'

'Not so blind now I have this,' said Daroguerre. 'I should be able to pinpoint the artefacts' location within the chamber by tomorrow. As for the diver, I advise you pick one with a dull mind and no imagination. That shouldn't be difficult: most warships are crowded with such people.'

Seriuz exhaled. Cass felt hurt that he seemed to have forgotten her, even when she'd almost drowned, *again*. Orc was dismally examining the soles of his feet. Some of the cuts had reopened, red streaming freely into the wetness.

Oscar. She tried to figure out if the name suited him. Down in the dark cold of their potential tomb, everything had seemed weirdly simple. She shook away the morbidity, and pushed to her feet.

Things could be much worse, she told herself. The stone had been raised, but Orc didn't have it, and hadn't used it, and couldn't do so as long as Seriuz maintained his control. And Daroguerre's own words the previous day brought some comfort: what would the magician gain by letting Orc use it anyway?

She wanted to believe she was safe. She clutched Seriuz's heavy jacket tighter around her, but it did nothing to calm her shivering. There was no sun, only the lowering, humid cloud. A thousand eyes were on her, on the centre of the ziggurat ruin. A thousand eyes from two warships.

Not wanting to meet the sources of that observation, even at the edge of her vision, she turned her gaze to the eastern horizon, which was nothing but sea and dull grey sky, and wished she could be somewhere so empty.

Except – she frowned.

The horizon wasn't empty after all.

Almost invisible against the cloud was a column of something darker, and beneath it…

'What's that?'

Eyes followed her pointing finger. Moments later a klaxon erupted from *Tarpon*, another from *Nightfire*. Voices cried, calling to stations. She heard Thera's name shouted.

'I'll have our lookouts shot,' Seriuz said, barely audible above the racket. He stared towards the smoke. Though a handful of miles away, the superstructure of the ship was already visible, coming bow-on to them.

'Captain Seriuz, sir!'

The distorted voice came from a sailor on *Nightfire*'s gun-platform, using a loud-hailer. 'It's a bloody Empy cruiser!'

Seriuz paled. He turned an accusing look on Daroguerre before starting at a run across the ziggurat ruins towards *Nightfire*'s boat. As Cass and the others followed, there came an air-ripping shriek.

27

SLAVE OF THE SORCERESS

Tashi jumped at the roar from the forward gun. Through the bridge windows he saw a flash of flame and something streak away at phenomenal speed. He felt light in his stomach, as though about to go into battle himself.

'If they didn't spot us before, they will now,' said Lansdahl, binoculars to his eyes. Tashi needed no device to see the water burst beyond the two distant ships.

'Main gun continue firing,' said Lansdahl. 'Forward casements too. But *Nightfire* only, not the ruin.'

'Captain,' said Shoggu, as the gunnery officer relayed these orders into a telephone. 'Are you certain about this?'

'That civilian in the pale suit must be your sorcerer,' said Lansdahl.

'We can't be sure of that.'

'Seems obvious to me. Don't fret, we'll sink *Nightfire* without losing him.'

Tashi held his tongue, though it angered him that the captain could be so casual about their task.

'They're running for their boat,' said the first officer, also with glasses to his eyes.

Three more detonations came from *Archon*'s guns. The air smelt of burnt metal.

'Flash another message to the Sundi ship,' Lansdahl said into a tube. 'We have commenced our police action against *Nightfire*. Interference will be taken as an act of war.' He turned to the first officer. 'Any new ideas about their presence here, Mister Vandres?'

'Still think it must be a monarchist plot, sir. But why this ruin…'

'If so, they won't want to let us report. What's the likely outcome from a conflict?'

'Odds in our favour, sir. They've hardly any steam, judging from their smoke, and Sundi gunnery isn't the best. We could easily escape any engagement with the cruiser that went against us. *Nightfire* we'd never outrun, but its twelve-pounders would be an annoyance at worst.'

'The Sundi's guns, Jervik?'

'Eight-inchers, most likely,' said the gunnery officer. 'But lower range and punch than ours.'

'Range won't matter if we have to get close enough to arrest the magician,' said Vandres.

'Hm,' said Lansdahl. 'But to fire first on a Commonwealth ship…'

'We're at three-and-a-half miles, sir,' said Jervik. 'About the Sundi's limit. Every hundred yards will weaken our advantage.'

'Damn it,' said Lansdahl. 'Very well: forward casements continue on *Nightfire*. Main gun, target the Sundaran but hold fire and await instruction.'

'Sir,' said Vandres, 'the Sundi's moving.'

Peering across the sea, Tashi saw the larger of the warships had crept forward and turned slightly more side-on to them.

'What the devil is it doing?' said Lansdahl. 'Preparing a broadside?'

'It's putting itself between us and the ziggurat,' said Vandres. 'It's flashing a message. "No intention"—'

'Keep firing at *Nightfire*.'

'—"of hostility".'

The casement guns spoke again. Seconds later, smoke and debris erupted on the ziggurat. Tashi's heart leapt to his throat.

'Captain!' protested Shoggu.

'Keep our fire away from the ruin!' said Lansdahl.

'The civilian is still up, sir,' said Vandres.

The Sundaran cruiser began to slide in front of the barely visible ziggurat, while *Nightfire* moved to position itself behind it. More water-bursts broke the sea.

'*Nightfire*'s trying to screen itself behind the cruiser,' said Jervik.

'Cowards,' hissed Lansdahl.

'Message repeated from the Sundi,' said Vandres.

'Do they truly mean no hostility?' said Lansdahl. 'Or are they waiting for us to close?'

'Three miles, sir,' said Jervik.

'Mister Vandres?'

'As you said, if we've stumbled on a plot to restore the Kymeran monarchy, they'll do everything they can to stop us alerting Torrento.'

Lansdahl drew a deep breath. 'Casement guns also aim at the cruiser, await instruction.'

'Sir,' said Jervik. 'I feel I ought to remind you that no Empyreal vessel has—'

'I'm aware, thank you,' said Lansdahl. 'But Sundi involvement in a plot to destabilise the region is itself an act of war. Ready bow torpedoes.'

'Aye, sir.'

'By the God-Head!' said Vandres, binoculars again to his eyes. 'The Sundi, it's *Tarpon*.'

'So?' said Lansdahl.

Vandres looked slightly to the right. 'That other smoke, coming from the far side of the island.' His voice trembled. 'It might not be from a settlement after all.'

'Meaning? Quick, man!'

'The last we knew of *Tarpon*, it was stationed in Sentilli with the battleship *Barcuda*.'

'Holy Hell,' said Lansdahl. '*Barcuda*'s guns?'

'Elevens, sir.' Jervik sounded shaken.

'*Damn* it…' Lansdahl gripped his binoculars as though his fingers might crush them. Both *Nightfire* and the ruin were now screened by the opposing cruiser.

'Torpedoes ready, sir,' said Jervik, the telephone still to his ear. 'Do we fire?'

Tashi glanced at Lansdahl. Strain tightened the captain's face. Then it seemed to snap. 'No. Gun crews stand by. Heading two-fifty.'

'To where?' said Shoggu. 'What are you doing?'

'We'll go round north and west of the island, and try to spot what they've got on the far side. If it's *Barcuda*, we'll evade, speed north to the mainland and wire Torrento. If there's no danger, we'll carry on round and hope to catch *Nightfire*.'

'We cannot simply flee,' said Shoggu.

'I can't risk tangling with a battleship,' said Lansdahl. 'Once we report, with luck a dreadnought squadron can get to the Straits and bottle them in the Shallow Sea.'

'Won't they anticipate that?' said Shoggu. 'The magician is more likely to finish here and then escape to somewhere on the coast. I cannot take that risk. Return to the mainland if you must, but first set us on the island.'

Lansdahl looked at him, amazed. 'It would be you and hundreds of Sundies.'

'Nevertheless, that is our task. I don't need to remind you whose letter I carry.'

Tashi's heart swelled at Shoggu's courage, even as he thought with dread of being the only warrior against so many.

'It could be done, sir,' said Vandres. '*Tarpon* won't have full steam for ages, and *Nightfire* wouldn't dare come near us. We could drop these people off in a boat as we pass the north side, and no one the wiser.'

'Unless they have a lookout,' said Lansdahl.

'There's a sort of viewpoint up there,' said Vandres, 'but with limited scope. Once round the top of the island, we'll be out of sight.

Lansdahl looked at Shoggu. 'If you're certain.'

'It must be done,' said Shoggu.

The captain turned to Vandres. 'Have a boat prepared.' To Shoggu and Tashi, he said, 'You can row? You'll be on your own.'

'I can do whatever is necessary,' said Tashi.

'Ten minutes, then,' said Lansdahl. 'We'll lower you on the port side.'

As they left the bridge, Tashi said, 'Master, I am ashamed to have ever doubted you.'

'You were right to,' said Shoggu. 'It was you who made me see things clearly again. Now, quickly: prepare.'

Tashi ran to their cabin. He'd left the pack in a state of readiness, and only had to hoist it onto his back. The thing's bulk made it awkward to get back through the corridors, especially with all the activity, sailors getting in his way. By the time he came out into the open, *Archon* was level with the point of the island and *Tarpon* was side-on to them, a mile or so distant.

Someone grabbed his arm, almost pulling him off-balance. 'What's going on?' said Ranga. 'What's that other ship? No one will tell me!'

'I don't have time,' said Tashi. 'We're going ashore.'

Ranga's mouth dropped open. He snapped it shut. 'Yes. Good. I won't let you down.'

'Not you. My master and I.'

Alarm widened Ranga's eyes. 'No, I have to come too. I need to help.'

'I don't have time.' Tashi started towards the ship's boats. Ranga followed, protesting.

'I have to prove myself. To Gevurah. To atone for my life of sin.'

'The proving is on the Holy Mountain,' said Tashi.

'I can't wait. I'll die of shame. You still don't trust me?'

'I do trust you,' said Tashi. And he did: Ranga's turnaround since their talk on the aft deck had been dramatic. In several sessions, he'd almost exhausted Tashi's knowledge on some subjects. 'I know you have changed. But it's not up to me.'

But still Ranga wouldn't stop; he kept up his pestering all the way to where Shoggu waited beside a small boat being prepared by two sailors.

'He wants to come,' Tashi said. 'I've told him he can't.'

Shoggu nodded. 'You were once in the magician's party,' he said to Ranga. 'You might not know how vulnerable you remain to his influence.'

'Praying to Gevurah has utterly changed me,' pleaded Ranga. 'He's given me the strength to resist.'

'We cannot take the chance,' said Shoggu. 'You will find some way to serve Him, I'm sure.'

'I can prove it!' said Ranga. 'I can prove I've broken all ties with those who use magic.'

Tashi stared at Ranga, surprised at the tremble in his voice.

'How?' said Shoggu.

Ranga swallowed, as if to rid his throat of an obstruction. 'Vanessa's one.'

Tashi choked with shock. Shoggu gasped.

'Before I found Gevurah,' said Ranga, 'I was enthralled by her spells.' Sweat beaded on his forehead. 'She made me do terrible things. I almost... no, don't make me say it!'

Tashi felt stunned. They had been in her house, in her power...

'How was I so blind?' said Shoggu. 'Dear Gevurah, there were moments when I thought something amiss, but I refused those suspicions. I did not think it truly possible for a woman...'

He looked at Ranga, intent. 'And she sent you here? Why?'

'She wants something the magician has. That doesn't matter to me any more, of course.'

'You understand,' said Shoggu, 'that when we return, she must be dealt with?'

Ranga nodded heavily.

'You had an attachment to her?'

'That was her enchantments,' Ranga said. 'It's over. I've seen Gevurah's light. Whatever punishment magicians suffer, they bring it upon themselves.'

'Yes,' said Tashi. Everything was going so fast.

'I wish you had said something before,' said Shoggu.

'I was working up to it,' said Ranga. 'But I didn't want to distract you. You must let me join you. Her enchantments have befouled me. I need to cleanse myself with action.'

'Let him, master!' said Tashi.

Shoggu's face creased in thought. 'I can see the sense in it,' he said, looking at Ranga. 'As you said before, you know the magician. And you would not have signed your former mistress's death warrant had you not experienced a profound change of heart.'

'You won't regret it,' said Ranga.

Relief overwhelmed Tashi. It seemed he would not have to fight alone, even without the *Elohim Gibor*. He patted Ranga's shoulder. 'Welcome, brother.'

Ranga looked puzzled. 'Brother?'

'A term of endearment among novitiates,' said Shoggu. But he looked unhappy.

An officer came up, with two sailors carrying bundles. 'We're out of sight of the lookout point,' he said. 'We'll take you close in. These supplies should last until relief comes.'

Archon had begun to slow. Sailors started to lower the boat, and a flight of metal steps. The island neared: Tashi scanned the slope, but saw only trees growing from the honey-coloured ground.

In five minutes the ship had come to a stop. 'God go with you,' said the officer.

The small boat slapped into the sea. Tashi helped Shoggu down the steps to it, Ranga following. They clambered in. The craft's rocking alarmed Tashi; the warship had been bad enough. Sailors shouted down to release the hooks. When that was done, Ranga grabbed two oars and cradled them in the rowlocks, then told Tashi to do the same. Tashi heaved on the oars, but couldn't get any purchase on the water. Without Ranga they might never make shore, he thought miserably.

Archon gradually gained speed again. From this angle, it towered, a floating metal fortress a hundred yards long. Tashi wondered what would happen to the sailors now waving down at them. If he'd understood the talk on the bridge, they might encounter an even larger

Sundaran ship on the far side of the island. It seemed that all routes in this adventure led to possible death.

'At least try to help,' said Ranga, straining at the oars.

Tashi put his back into it, and by concentrating hard on the purpose of these unfamiliar movements, made some progress. By the time they reached shore, *Archon* had rounded the curve of the island, and they were alone.

Tashi lurched out of the boat and splashed into the stony shallows, and wondered what they had let themselves in for.

♋

So that was war, thought Orc. That was how it felt when someone miles away was trying to kill you. It had been sheer luck they'd escaped with only a few nicks from flying bits of stone.

As soon as they were out of the ship's boat and back on *Nightfire*'s deck, Seriuz told them to get below and pack anything they wanted to take onto the island. There was no time to change as well; all Orc could do was put shoes on. When they were called back up again, *Nightfire* had reached the cove. Smoke heaved from *Barcuda*'s stacks.

'What's happening?' said Cass as Seriuz ran down the deck. She still wore his jacket round her shoulders.

'That cruiser surprised us,' said Seriuz. '*Tarpon* should have engaged, but it seems the captain didn't want to risk an incident. Idiot – there already is an incident. My guess is the Empy will make for Carnega to telegraph Torrento. It's possible I can sneak up on her at night by running smokeless and torpedo her.' He clearly didn't relish the prospect. 'But it'll be risky. Hence your remaining here.'

He looked at Daroguerre, who stood at the top of the ladder, taking bags as they were passed up. 'That's everything?'

'All the artefacts, yes.'

'Your men on the viewpoint have a lot to answer for.'

'Regrettable, I agree,' said Daroguerre. 'No doubt their attention was bent more on our activities, and the cloud camouflaged the cruiser's smoke. Though the same could be said of both ships' watches.'

'Those men will be disciplined. As will yours.'

'If I so choose, Captain. They *are* my men, as you say, even if they wear your uniform at present.'

'They disgrace it. I should never have agreed to you bringing them on board, let alone as mine. But we waste time. You're in charge on the island. Do your work with the stone and retrieve the artefacts tomorrow.'

'Of course.'

'If I can't sink the cruiser and they telegraph Torrento, an Empyreal force will likely arrive in three days. At the latest, I expect to return tomorrow afternoon. We'll decide our course then. Damn it, Daroguerre, you said there could be no discovery.'

'I was assured there could not be.' Daroguerre looked uneasy. 'But that was before we sailed. I've been unable to make contact since.'

Orc wondered who Daroguerre had tried to contact, and how.

'Then what else do we not know?' said Seriuz. 'Can we at least assume no other Empies are aware of the Sundarans? Why can't you make contact?'

'An obstructive energy surrounds the island.'

'Then work through it. That stone should help, shouldn't it? We need more information by the time I return. If I don't return, escape to Sundara and carry on from there.'

'Don't say that!' cried Cass. 'You will return. Don't even go. Let the Empyreal ship tell Torrento – we can be gone by then.'

'We need those artefacts.'

'Quite so,' said Daroguerre.

'If we were to run right now,' Seriuz went on, 'we might get the Sundaran ships through the Straits before the Kurassians block them. But without the artefacts, the plan is dead. Don't fear, Cass, I'll do everything I can to return in one piece.'

'Let me come with you,' she said.

'No!' blurted Orc.

Seriuz glanced at him. 'Out of the question,' he told Cass. 'The

Quallaces will look after you.'

'I'm not scared of dying,' she said. 'I've got used to the idea. We might not be safe here anyway. I want to stay with you and Thera, people I believe in.'

'Cass, I couldn't—'

'In other circumstances, you said. What's this if not other circumstances? We might have only days left, Martin! Don't leave me here.'

Orc stared at them. When had Seriuz said that to Cass, about 'other circumstances'? What else? And this time Seriuz didn't counter her mad request. Their eyes were fixed on each other's: Seriuz searching her, as if puzzling over her; Cass looking back up at him in hope, bedraggled wet with his jacket round her shoulders as though she were already his. There was no pretence or disguise left. She moved very slightly towards him; for an insane moment Orc thought the captain would seize her in an embrace. He needed to break this up, but couldn't move, could only watch aghast as the wrongness approached.

'I also said the world is as it is,' said Seriuz.

'But you want to make a new world!'

Seriuz's eyes closed briefly. Then he turned to Orc. 'Keep her safe. And remember my warning.'

'I've been keeping her safe for years, thanks,' Orc said.

Cass gasped out a laugh full of knives.

Turning to Daroguerre, Seriuz said, 'Keep *it* safe, and keep it for yourself.' Then, as if some internal barrier had snapped, he stepped to Cass, touched her shoulder, bent and kissed her quickly on the lips. Her arms moved in surprised response, but he was already upright again.

'Forgive me,' he said, and walked off.

Orc had to look away. He thought he might explode.

All through their journey to shore, Cass wouldn't look him in the eye. Ferman and Stefanie Quallace watched their approach from their house, but Orc saw no sign of Hana. Just as the last of Daroguerre's bags was put on the jetty, Seriuz's voice barked over the water, distorted through a loudhailer.

'Mister Daroguerre! We can't find Thera.'

Daroguerre turned towards *Nightfire* and spread his arms in an exaggerated gesture of ignorance.

'She helped winch the boat up,' said Cass. 'You were talking to her afterwards.'

'That doesn't imply cognizance of her subsequent movements,' said Daroguerre.

'But if they can't find her, the ship won't be able to go as fast, or without smoke.'

'She'll still outrun that cruiser.'

'But not without smoke!' said Cass. 'They won't be able to sneak up at night.'

'You speak as though there were something I might do about it, if only you could convince me of its importance.' Daroguerre turned and walked along the jetty, to the Sundaran marine guarding *Aurora*. Cass turned towards *Nightfire*, clearly agitated.

'For God's sake, Cass,' said Orc. 'They'll find her. She's not *here*, is she? He's probably forgotten to check the bogs.'

The rowers began a swift stroke back out of the cove. Orc picked up his bag. The marine had left his post and was making for the trail.

'I've sent him to get my men,' said Daroguerre, rejoining them. 'To help take the baggage.'

'Take it where?' said Cass.

'You surely don't expect me to wait for the noble captain?' said Daroguerre. 'If my work is successful, I might negate any threat posed by the Empyreal Navy. Miss Strandborn, you'll remain here with the Quallaces. Mister Strandborn, you'll come with me.'

'I'm not going anywhere Esteban is,' said Orc.

'Come now,' said Daroguerre. 'The Spiral makes a good viewpoint.'

'For what? You want me to help spot ships because your guys are so crap at it?'

'They lack your powers of *focus*, Mister Strandborn. Accompany me, and you might find that tomorrow's dawn brings more than the everyday sort of illumination.'

Orc's heart leapt with understanding. Cass gasped. 'You can't let him use it! Seriuz ordered you.'

'You heard him give me charge of the island,' said Daroguerre.

'Yes, and then he—'

'If he returns, you can tell tale on me.'

She looked panic-stricken. 'But – you said yourself, you don't gain anything.'

'And you yourself raised the idea of reward,' said Daroguerre. 'How could I in good conscience deny a fellow practitioner the use of something he risked his life to acquire?'

Orc's chest swelled with excitement and hope. He'd never expected this from Daroguerre, but he hadn't taken account of the bond they shared as users of magic. For once, something had gone his way.

Cass turned to look at *Nightfire* as if thinking of calling for support. Then her shoulders sagged, and something seemed to go out of her. Orc hurt to see it, even if it did show he'd won.

'I need to talk to you,' she said, a finality in her voice.

Orc limped after her, off the jetty and then eastwards around the curved beach of the cove, until the sand gave way to rock near where the mole began – far enough not to be overheard. There Cass sat on a slab, elbows on her knees, eyes aimed down. Orc sat next to her.

'I'm sick of fighting you,' she said. 'I admit it: I've lost. I can't stop you now, not if Daroguerre's going to let you use that stone. All I can do is beg you not to. There is a reason, Orc. It's not that I'm sick, or "not thinking straight".'

'I know,' he said. 'You don't want to find out we were together, because you want to be with him.'

She frowned sideways, at his knees. 'Why would—?' she began, then, 'No, that's not it.'

'Right.'

'Orc, listen. There's something in our pasts, something horrible. I started catching hold of it when I nearly drowned. And it's been leaking into my dreams.'

'Like what?'

She groaned. 'I can't tell you. The more ignorant we both are, the better off we'll be. I don't want to know any more than I already do. If I start telling you even a little, that will make it more real, and more permanent, and it'll make things worse between us. Maybe if we let it lie, it will sink back. I want it to fade away. Like I think we wanted it to originally.'

'We?' His brows clenched. 'Originally when?'

'You never asked yourself if *we* made the Shroud?'

His breath caught. 'That's crazy – how would we know how?'

'Geist said we both had the potential. Maybe we both already knew magic.'

Orc shook his head; he felt like flies of madness were buzzing round it. 'You want me to let everything go because of some bad feeling you got when you nearly drowned? Cass, you were under a lot of stress: it must have screwed with your mind. You'd really be happy never knowing what we were, what we are, to each other?'

'If it means we can stay friends.'

'But we were more than that. I can feel it.'

'Oh, God.'

'I'll prove we were happy together.'

'Happy? Is that what you think?'

'Yes!' The backs of his eyes stung. 'Why can't you?'

She grabbed his wrist, shocking him. But she still wouldn't look at him. 'Orc, please. If you ever had a reason to trust me, trust me now. You do not want to know what this truth is.'

She scared him, the certainty in her voice. But how could she be certain? It was true that Geist had talked about them both having potential, but the idea that anyone could pierce a shroud in a moment of stress and unconsciousness, without training, was hard to believe. And Otherworld information couldn't be taken as fact; it had to be corroborated, examined for the taint of emotions and pre-existing belief. Orc thought of explaining all that, but there was no point – he would be butting his head against a wall.

'Just one more night, Cass. Then it'll all be cleared up. You'll be free of this fear.'

He made to stand, but her grip on his wrist tightened.

'Why could we never answer the question, Orc?' Her voice chilled him. 'Why couldn't we work out which we were?'

'Which…?'

'It's because we were both.'

After a moment's blankness, it struck him what she meant, a hundred blades at once.

'No.'

She nodded, and released his wrist.

'You can't—' he began, but horror corroded his voice. 'How could you think that? No, there's… I'd never do that. There's such a… a horrible feeling. No, never.'

'What, that feeling that if we did it and got it wrong, something really bad would happen? You never thought that's because we *did* do it, and something really bad *did* happen?'

He could hardly breathe. 'Happened like what?'

'In my dreams, it's a city being destroyed. A flood. Some of it must symbolise family, friends: the devastation when it came out.'

He felt like his stomach was turning to ice. That she could even think of believing this made him feel unclean.

'But there might have been more,' she went on. 'I think there might have been a baby. Or the beginnings of one.'

He couldn't speak. He shook his head, kept shaking it.

'I can't stop you uncovering the details,' she said, still not looking at him. 'But if you do, I never want to see you again, because I don't want to see in your face that it was even worse than I thought.'

He choked. 'I don't believe it.'

'Don't argue, please.'

'But it's not *true*! That kiss – that kiss underwater, that's what did this. It made you feel guilty because you weren't sure, and all this crap is from that.' He barked a horrible, fractured laugh. 'Fucking hell, Cass, you don't do things by halves. You want to get rid of me so you can jump into bed with Seriuz, and so you invent this whole buried history nightmare shit – and maybe you don't even realise that's what you're doing! And all because you "believe" in him. That's a sick joke.'

'It's not. He's honourable, moral.'

'You think?' There was nothing to hold him back now. 'You know what happened to Pettor and Yorge and that other guy? Remember those "warning shots"?'

She visibly stiffened.

'That's right. And he did it himself. He could have let them go, but nope: bang, bang, bang. Remember how horrible it was seeing that dead guy on the beach? Imagine what it's like seeing people killed right in front of you.'

'No,' she said. But Orc heard the emptiness in the word. She believed him.

'Did you taste their blood on his lips?'

'No,' she said, and the desperation, the pleading in it made him think he'd gone too far. He steeled his heart against it. 'No,' she said again. 'Oh, God, how did it come to this? How…?'

Orc didn't know. He thought it might have been better if they'd drowned.

Cass started to cry, huddled in Seriuz's jacket. But she was trying to stifle it, Orc could tell, and he knew this was because she didn't want him to comfort her. Not him, not now. He wouldn't have known how, anyway, not from this. He just had to hang on, and hope. With a leaden heart, he got to his feet and limped off to change at last out of his wetsuit.

Offshore, three of her four stacks billowing smoke, *Nightfire* was turning eastwards.

♋

Tashi did most of the work setting up camp among some well-spaced pines just up from the stony beach. He wanted to work, to busy himself with small and manageable tasks, to prevent himself from thinking too much about what must come.

'They could've put in a pistol,' complained Ranga, examining the supplies. 'At least something deadlier than cutlery.'

'The magician's mine,' said Tashi, quiet enough so Shoggu wouldn't overhear. 'Don't forget.'

'You're the one with the pig-sticker,' said Ranga.

By the time they'd finished, two hours of daylight remained. Ranga said he would scout the area. Tashi volunteered too.

'Great,' said Ranga, but with something lacking in his grin.

The island's tree-softened outline belied the ruggedness of its ground. Going in a straight line was impossible, and Tashi worried about finding the way back. As they climbed tortuously between rocks and trees, Tashi also wondered about his new comrade. Calling him 'brother' now seemed rash; he knew so little about him. Ranga seemed so much more confident here than himself. One possible reason made Tashi uneasy: Ranga's familiarity with the Witch Mother's side of existence.

'She enchanted you into loving her?' Tashi asked him. 'Vanessa?'

Ranga looked at him with a brief expression Tashi couldn't read, scorn or pity, before he grunted.

'What did it feel like?' asked Tashi.

'To love her?' said Ranga. 'I felt about her the way I now feel about Gevurah. But I don't want to talk about it. It still hurts, the way she enslaved me. Sometimes she compelled me to her bed and satisfied her desires on me over and over until I was raw. Days, I would lie exhausted afterwards. And the foulness she inflicted on my tongue, which should be an instrument only of holy truth—'

'Don't!' said Tashi. 'Don't talk so, not in a place like this.'

'Like this?'

'Weren't you listening at the house?' said Tashi. 'There's some connection here with the ancient worship of the Witch Mother.' He sensed it, too: the foetid warmth of the air, the secretive insect noise. The island itself might corrupt them.

'Why did Shoggu think it wasn't possible for a woman to use

magic?' said Ranga, ducking a low branch.

'A magician is one who desires congress with the Witch Mother,' said Tashi. 'That's how he gains his power. A woman is closer by her nature, but cannot seek that kind of union. Or so we thought.'

'Some women do. With other women, I mean.'

'Don't speak so, not even to joke.'

'Joke? If you'd seen what—'

'It doesn't matter! Whatever you speak, always ask yourself: is this proper to Gevurah? If it isn't, pray until the thought is expelled.'

'You don't have to keep on,' said Ranga.

'I have to keep on until you have shown that you can keep on to yourself,' said Tashi.

Once they'd passed the island's peak, the air began to smell different, its taint reminding Tashi of *Archon*. The murmur of distant voices came from somewhere downwards. Cautiously tracking the noise, they found themselves overlooking a cove. Two warships lay out to sea, one *Tarpon*, the other even larger. The chimneys of both bellowed furiously.

A much smaller vessel, not a warship, was moored in the cove. Two large rowing boats were drawn up on the beach. Perhaps ten sailors stood there, and several people not in uniform.

'*Archon* must have fled,' said Ranga. 'Maybe *Nightfire*'s chasing it.'

'Is one of those Orc?' said Tashi.

'There in the green shirt,' said Ranga. 'But why—? Ah…'

'What? Is that Orc or not?' It must be, Tashi thought – Ranga had mentioned his fair hair at Vanessa's house. He fixed his gaze on the figure: the end-point of the journey that had begun with Shoggu's dark-flight in his cell at Highcloud, so far away. He stared as though by force of will he could make his eyes as sharp as a lammager's, know every detail of that fiend.

The figure seemed so insignificant. But that, of course, was part of his magic, like his apparent youth. Orc was anything but insignificant. The mutilated woman in the hotel, the bomb at the museum, dead Rhunke: all Orc's doing. If not for that man, he would still be within sight of the Holy Mountain, safe and happy.

He loosened his *dughra* in its sheath. Ranga seemed intent on the buildings and the group that stood outside.

Orc, along with the man in the pale suit and hat, and two sailors, picked up bags and began to climb a track that led from the cove on its far side. Tashi hissed out a breath. 'This could be our chance. There are only four of them. If we work quickly around—'

He made to move, but Ranga grabbed him. 'Don't be stupid. *Only* four?'

'I've slain two boars by myself.' But that had been with help he no longer wished to call on.

'There's plenty of time,' said Ranga. 'Right now, they're jumpy. We need to wait until they're more off-guard – isn't that obvious? I thought you were supposed to be a warrior?'

'Whose purpose is to fight evil,' said Tashi, watching the climbing figures. But he accepted Ranga's point. 'Where do you think they're going? The end of the island, where that viewpoint is?'

'We'll find out tomorrow,' said Ranga. 'For now, we'd better get back before the light fades.'

Tashi nodded. He had a lot to prepare himself for. The next day, for the first time, his sword would shed human blood.

F: Scarab has been in possession of the stone for hours, but has not attempted contact, despite the cruiser's arrival surely telling him all is not as expected.

G: The dreadnought's squadron will arrive about noon. If he makes contact early enough, we can proceed as planned.

A: If. Why has he still not?

G: We cannot guess. Nor do we know why he seems to be planning to let the male subject use the stone.

A: That was specifically forbidden.

G: It might be part of some ruse, but we cannot know without contact. Nor can we warn him about the monk's boy.

A: Enough problems. Give me solutions.

B: Perhaps we should make the best of it. A naval engagement might kill thousands. The energy would be useful.

A: It would not compensate for years of wasted effort. Try sending a dream. No words, just imagery.

B: The dreadnought?

A: Yes. And him being roasted over hot coals.

28

CHTHONIS

Too nervous and excited to sleep, Orc sat with his back against one of the circle's great stones. Within the tents, paraffin lamps glowed, shadowy forms moved. Near the end of the trail, Mord huddled on watch. It felt like the whole world was waiting, restless and weary, for dawn and his scape.

And unless something changed, it would be a scape without Otter. He tried not to let himself worry: magic relied on conviction and assertion, and doubt risked failure. Daroguerre had assured him that Otter's absence should not pose a problem. An amplifier as powerful as the large focus-stone might allow scaping without an animath altogether, or might open other channels – the key was to be flexible. Even so, Orc hoped the stone's power would redress whatever had caused Otter's unsettling absence, and return his companion to him.

It was some time after midnight when a figure approached and stood over him, barely discernable against the stifling cloud. 'May I?' said Thera as she sat down. Orc hadn't talked to her since they'd come across her, soaked and teeth chattering, halfway between the cove and the Spiral.

'Your clothes dried okay?' he asked.

'Yes. Thanks.'

'Wasn't it dangerous? Jumping off a moving ship?'

She hugged her knees. 'Not as dangerous as chasing after one three times its size.'

'What about when Seriuz gets back?'

'*If*,' she said. 'I'll say I fell overboard. You'll back me up, won't you? I can't imagine you'd be on his side.'

'Got that right.' Orc felt troubled by Thera deserting her comrades, but it wasn't his business.

'It's only because Cass feels so lost that she turned to him,' said Thera.

Orc tensed. He hadn't expected to talk about this.

'I've no idea why she doesn't want your pasts uncovered, but I'm sure it would be best if they were. And I know you'll succeed.'

'More than I do,' said Orc. 'What if the stone isn't enough, after all this?'

'It will be. Cass told me you saw the dance of the serpents. And I've heard that whoever sees the Serpent Mandala has the power to know anything.'

That surprised him. 'You know much about magic?'

'Not a lot. I'm what you might call a psychic engineer, not a shaman. No animath, for example. But if I can help, I will.'

'The last couple of times I tried to scape, my animath wouldn't come,' said Orc.

'Well, sometimes things change without us knowing why,' said Thera. 'That doesn't make those changes bad. Go with the flow, is my advice. As we advance, we sometimes leave old friends behind, don't you find?'

Orc shrugged. 'I've only ever had one friend. But... thanks, for being on my side.'

'The unlikeliest people can be allies.' Thera stood. 'That's worth remembering, whichever world you're in.'

Ranga stared down the slope to the dark sea. There was no rush, plenty of time to sharpen his resolve – and to forget the nagging resemblance to Saskia in Tashi's face.

Ever since Mythe House, he'd seen it. Even in this darkness, he imagined it. He must not let such a small coincidence put him off, not when Vanessa's life was at stake. Shoggu would certainly have her put to death. In telling the Watcher about her, he'd left himself no option but to obey Vanessa's instruction to dispose of the pair. It made things easier, in a way, that their killing had become a matter of necessity.

But the manner of it. The poison he'd brought with him would have been easier, but there was so little, and he didn't know what else he might need it for. That left only one option.

The first paleness of the sky warned him the sleeping draught might not last much longer. He drew Tashi's smaller sword. It trembled with his hand.

He knelt beside the boy and put the blade against what might, almost, have been his youngest sister's throat.

♋

By the time Daroguerre emerged, lack of sleep was already making Orc feel half-detached from reality. Without a word, the magician laid the focus-stone at the centre of the spiral paving, then retreated back to his tent. The stone glowed pale in the predawn grey, a pointed flake of blue-tinted crystal five inches long.

As soon as he picked it up, Orc sensed its potential – as though he glimpsed, somewhere at the back of his mind, an infinitely detailed map of the whole world, of all worlds. Kneeling, he used the stone's point to awaken his tattoo-mask. His own focus-stone was attuned to him; this one was not, but he hoped its size would more than compensate. Sure enough, the tattoo-mask came hotly, eagerly, its points not only rising to his skin but sending threads deep to meet in a knot at the centre of his brain.

The sky had grown pink, but was still dim.

It was time.

He curled on his side, the stone's edge biting his palm. The cold of the remembered cave cut through his flesh and his thin robe. He threw himself into the initiatory meltdown.

Straight away it overwhelmed him. The cave was real. He was still trapped in it; his year of life since had been only a hallucination of madness. Images attacked him: a crystal skull smashed by a hammer, a man facing soldiers underground, streets filled with water. An old man in red, a big sword, a woman who was half-snake; a high mountain, a man speared to a tree and another with a patched eye; feathers and fur and a wide lake, and more and more and more and more. Some he sensed were his own memories, some the world's; but he couldn't tell the boundary between, even if there was such a boundary, even if there should be. He'd already gone too far, already forgotten how to keep assembled the fragments that comprised him, how to differentiate them from the rest.

Then he became aware of it: the Serpent Mandala, the wheeling dance that encompassed the world. Its transcendent beauty was almost within reach, the closest he'd ever come to it since cowardice had overcome him and Otter had pulled him away. And now he could reach it, if he abandoned the last traces of the limiting, restricting idea that there should *be* a him—

A harsh noise sounded in his ear, arresting his slide. It came again, a bird's chirp of warning.

He opened his eyes to the early greyness of the stone circle – and a sight that bolted him rigid with shock. A few paces from him stood a woman with bird-like face and wild hair – and a third, vertical eye that rose from the bridge of her strong, curved nose. Her short dress looked made of feathers, and her left arm bore a large, round shield. Her right hung by her side. Her nails were long and curved: talons. A row of animal skins hung from her belt.

Orc shifted his gaze. The tents were still there. Both the real world and Three-Eyes were intensely vivid.

'I know who you are,' he said shakily.

'But you do not know why I am here.' Her voice came strange and wild, something of the male in it. 'I am here to help.'

'Where's Otter? What happened to him?'

'Your need has grown beyond him,' said Three-Eyes. 'Do not fear me. Guardian or thief, it is the fire that is central; the players' roles in the story are superficial. Do you understand?'

Orc didn't answer. It made a kind of sense, but…

'You still hold to trust and loyalty,' she said. 'In the outer world these are commendable, but in magic one chooses whichever tool fits the task.'

'Is that right?'

'Do you know what the fire is?' said Three-Eyes. 'It is the first tool. It is illumination. It separates man from nature, from that terrible, indifferent, nurturing force that was his mother. It separates the dance of the serpents. Watch.'

The paving between them was now a pool of mud. Within it moiled and writhed two serpents, dark and slippery, entwined. Three-Eyes held out her hand. A flame flickered on her open palm. She blew, and sent it shooting at the serpents.

One burst into flame. Screeching, it unfolded wings of fiery feathers and rose into the air above the mud, a creature of coruscating gold, throwing off sparks. Male genitals hung halfway down its metallic body.

'Behold Saeraf!' said Three-Eyes. 'Now observe Chthonis.'

The mud had thinned to water. The other serpent still coiled and slithered, all trace of scales smoothed away. Orc gasped: 'Eel…'

The pool sank quickly, leaving a slippery-walled pit: the descent to the Otherworld.

'Follow,' said Three-Eyes.

'Alone?'

'Go!'

Orc crawled to the edge. The pit sank into darkness, out of sight. He reached into it. There was no sense that he was doing this only in imagination. That troubled him, but he didn't want to think too hard and pull himself out of trance. And surely a scape so intense that he couldn't separate it from reality showed the power of the stone. Daroguerre had been right: it opened other channels. Bereft though he felt at Otter's absence, he had to go with it.

Assuming water lay below, he put his legs over the side and let himself drop.

The pit wasn't straight. It bent round and became a chute, a slide, plunging, careering down until he thumped onto the sand floor of a soft-lit cave.

Shocked, he picked himself up. He couldn't sense his physical body at all. Nervously he recalled his trouble returning from Seriuz's cabin. He'd managed that, but how could he get back to the Spiral? There were no exits but the chute.

The soft light came from glowing crystals in the red-veined rock. In the cave's centre was a pool. Peering in, Orc found the water clear, but there was barely light enough to see Eel moving. She had grown since the surface, and was now as big as she had been in *Nightfire's* bilges. But unlike then, there was no disrupting noise and vibration, and he had the big stone. Otter had explained that darkness made Eel larger. The stone could focus what light there was, and shrink Eel so she could be caught and a piece of her eaten.

But there was no Otter to eat her.

Except himself.

He filled his lungs and plunged in, swam down. The faint light gleamed on Eel's slippery side as she passed him and tailed off.

Movement behind made Orc turn: she was passing again, already disappearing. Again and again, he turned to see her vanish into blackness. The gap was so short, there might have been more than one of her.

He tried to mentally gather what light there was into a beam and shine it at her. But without instruction, he had only instinct, and couldn't make it work. He grew frustrated, out of breath. Eel danced around him as though taunting him. What if Daroguerre only gave him this one try? For months he'd sought this moment, and now—

It struck him. Focus: to a point. A knife-point.

Next time Eel passed, he caught her fin. As she pulled him through the water he gripped tight, and punched the stone into her.

She thrashed, but he held on, stabbed again – the stone was a knife, an otter's teeth, bright and sharp. Through skin and into muscle it cut while Eel jerked and shuddered, blood clouding the water.

At last she weakened, and desperate for breath Orc dragged her to the surface. He pulled the great snake-fish from the pool. She flapped and writhed; her mouth gaped, her eyes stared. The sand beneath was red mud.

'Otter!' shouted Orc. But it was no good: he had to be the otter now. With the knife-tooth, he tried to cut a piece from Eel's side, but she wriggled and thrashed, still denying him, until at last he grabbed her by the gills and plunged the stone knife in again and again until she went still.

Otter would have released her, to let the missing chunk heal. But it didn't matter: if he succeeded now, he would never need to meet Eel again.

He cut through the tough skin, sliced out a chunk of raw, bloody muscle. Nearly gagging, he forced himself to eat, chew, swallow.

When he'd rinsed his mouth from the pool, he knelt with his eyes closed, and put his mind to the Shroud.

He couldn't concentrate. He was covered in blood, kneeling in it.

He opened his eyes. Eel's blood had soaked into the earth, and all he could see was the cratered battlefield of red mud from before, littered with bodies and the parts of bodies, machines and the parts of machines. Faint voices cried around him. His knees squelched free of the blood-sodden earth as he stood.

What was he being shown here? The sacrifices the ancients had made during the famine? Then why the machines?

'Ancient terror. Future era.'

Beneath the red-smoked sky, something curtain-like shifted in a breeze. He took a tentative step. His bare foot sank in gore, but from the ground before him rose again the road of bones. Slowly, his feet tender against the fractured edges, he walked, focused on the billowing curtain. As he neared, he saw it was a sheet of muslin.

Two blurred figures showed through it.

He tried to walk faster, all the time fearing the Shroud would vanish and take the truth with it. His feet in agony, he reached the curtain. If it was attached to a rail, he couldn't see it.

He grabbed the muslin and ripped it down.

'Damn it!'

A stone wall stretched before him, curved, twenty feet high, the edifice of a round building a hundred yards across. He cursed his rashness. He should have cut the Shroud with the knife-stone.

But all wasn't lost. The wall had been laid without mortar. With the crystal knife he worked free a small stone, then another. He pulled them out. Beyond was darkness.

At last, the gap he'd made weakened the wall and it shifted, groaned. Excited, he stepped back as it fell into dust.

'No!' Angry frustration smarted his eyes. 'No…!'

Above him, forever; to each side, forever – he could barely discern its curvature – another wall rose utterly black, utterly smooth. He hit a fist against it. It made no sound. He couldn't even tell if the wall were metal, or stone, or glass, or ceramic. But he sensed it was very, very old.

He gripped the knife-stone so hard its edges almost cut his hand. '*Focus*, you shit!'

Catching his overworked breath, he tried for calmness. A place on the black wall drew his attention. On instinct, he rubbed it with the stone's edge.

A coating like old paint or tarnish scraped off. Indistinct letters showed beneath. His and Cass's real names? It might be enough: the chink by which he could prise open their whole armoured past. He scraped harder, pulled his thoughts into focus, his mind acting with one beam of attention on that small patch of wall.

The tarnish kept growing back. Every effort revealed more of the letters, but most was covered again, and more quickly. The tarnishing was growing harder, as though strengthened by some opposing will. With an effort of concentration, Orc ground the stone into the tarnish and scraped off all the layers at once—

GAI-ENG

—before blackness overwhelmed the meaningless words, and the wall was as smooth and unmarked as before.

Mentally exhausted, Orc realised he no longer stood on bones, but sand. The night sky prickled with stars; the black wall reflected them.

He had the strange instinct that this was a real place. He sensed the distance to his body, almost as though he could pinpoint the number of miles, of thousands of miles. Before he could try, there came the loud chirp from before, this time with whirring wings.

He turned to find on the starlit sand a small brown bird, with a tiny, tattooed bone mask.

'Sparrow?'

She cocked her head. Her mask seemed the most vivid part of her. 'Any luck?'

'I can't do it,' said Orc, and felt suddenly the crushing weight of defeat.

'That barrier is well-made,' said Sparrow. 'But I have come to help. I, who crossed the barrier of the sky. I, who held the brand last and understood it best. Understand this, Otter-boy: Eel is only half the dance. She is the psychic part of the severed world. All shrouds depend on that severing. If you would penetrate it, and *her*, you must travel back to before.'

'Penetrate her?'

'Male arises out of female in embryo, but is inherent from the beginning.'

'I don't understand.'

'Keep up!' she chirped. 'Otter was too slow, even Hare was too slow. I was the only one fast enough.'

Orc thought better of reminding her that she hadn't outrun the sisters, only escaped through a hole. 'Are you my new guide?'

'Only for this.'

'Well… what should I do?'

'You must go back to the dance,' said Sparrow. 'The Serpent Mandala is the whole world in one place and infinite fragments. It is said that one who immerses himself in it can know anything. It is whispered that one who masters it can *do* anything.'

'But it'll destroy me.'

'Perhaps *you* can survive,' said Sparrow. 'Understand this: the Serpent Mandala in its true form is so inimical to the individual will, none can survive there. Disintegration is total, irreversible and immediate. The history of magic is littered with great scholars who have ventured its perils and been turned to dull-eyed cretins.'

'Great.'

'But none has ever assumed the role of consort to the Great Goddess.'

'How would that help?'

'Do you not see?' chirped Sparrow. 'Can you not make the leap yourself? The goddess, too, is the world, the totality of existence. She is a later conception of the Mother, as the Mother is a human conception of the Serpent Mandala. And unlike the Mandala in its true form, she will allow you to penetrate her with some of your identity intact, because that identity is as her consort.'

Orc thought he began to see.

'For a short time,' said Sparrow, 'she will be opened to you. You will have the chance to discover anything you desire to know – and from that state you can be recalled.'

'How?'

'You must give your individual will into the keeping of another, one who can hold it safe. Then I shall call you back and reunite you with it. This is deep magic, but you have the stone; and the stone is intimately connected with the goddess.'

'Wouldn't it be better if Otter called me back?'

'No!' chirped Sparrow. 'The goddess already knows his tricks. You used them in the dive.'

Orc thought that made sense, though he didn't like it. 'And who do I give my will to?'

'Do you know what the brand was?' said Sparrow. 'It was the start of man's individual will, the means by which he separated himself from the world and began to act according to thought, not mere instinct. You have that flame within you, your part of the sacred fire. And who better to keep it safe for you than she who was its guardian before man ever received it?'

Suddenly, there beside him was Three-Eyes. She extended her clawed hand, opened upwards. There was no flame upon it. This time, it was to receive.

Orc opened his own hand. A small flame burned in the hollow of his palm.

He could almost hear Otter's protest. But Otter wasn't there. And Sparrow – another of the Fire Stealers – clearly trusted Three-Eyes, which seemed to bear out what Three-Eyes had said at the Spiral. It was the stone, Orc thought. It had opened him up to deeper layers of understanding than Otter could provide. He had outgrown his old animath.

He wanted to come out of the scape and reflect on what he'd been told, perhaps seek advice. But he might never get to use the stone again; and to not use it again would mean to let Cass's terrible delusion continue. Life with her would be unbearable as long as she believed that travesty. But life without her…

He blew on the flame in his palm. It floated across to Three-Eyes. She closed her talon-nailed fingers around it.

Straight away, he felt different, more vague.

'Come!' chirped Sparrow.

The world changed, and he found himself in dawn light atop a ziggurat. Before his feet was the entrance to the shaft: familiar, destined. He felt as though he had woken from a senseless dream he couldn't remember, back into the world of timeless truth.

'When the sun is at noon, your kingliness will be greatest,' said Sparrow. 'Then shall you immerse yourself within her, and be reunited with her, and find the union you seek.'

The Sun-King nodded at the words, though they had told him nothing new. There was never anything truly new, only the cycle, and what was to come would be the end of his round. His mother and queen would take a new husband, who would also be him, for all were one.

Thus had it always been. Thus would it always be.

A: Scarab didn't sleep once?

B: As far as I can tell, he spent all night in preparation
     to influence the male subject's experience with the
     stone and draw him into trance.

A: Yes, that. Your analysis?

G: Two possibilities. The first, he intends to rescue
     the male subject from dissolution. But that brings a
     strong risk of the subject accessing the knowledge
     he seeks, and if he goes so deep, the shroud cannot
     prevent him.

A: What would Scarab gain, do you think?

G: The male's trust, and knowledge of the subjects' pasts.
     But that is expressly against our instructions. It
     is unlikely he would risk our anger for such a small
     prize.

A: I would dispute small. The second possibility?

G: That he intends to let the sacrifice go ahead.

A: Rendering the male subject a vegetable.

G: Most likely.

A: Also against our instructions. What does that get
     him?

G: The resultant entity might be more powerful, a
     creative as well as a destructive force. And his hold
     on the male subject's identity might allow him to
     introduce some measure of his own will.

E: He wouldn't dare, not without clearing it first.

A: He has betrayed us, that's obvious. He intends to use
     the male subject as a vehicle for his own ambitions.

F: Now it's clear why he made no attempt at contact.

E: This can't be right. He wouldn't dare risk our anger.

G: He might think that if he succeeds, he will be beyond
     our reach.

A: We'll disabuse him of that in time. What we visit upon him will make his treatment of that museum curator seem like pampering.

E: But for now? What do we do?

A: Those assigned to scrying, continue. We'll need a full account of what happens with the dreadnought, with the manifestation, the monk's boy, everything. We others must go dormant to conserve energy. There is no further action we can take.

D: We are in the hands of the gods.

A: I don't appreciate the attempt at irony.

29

CONVERGENCE

Tashi woke to daylight and a splitting headache, still in full clothing, confused that he couldn't remember finishing his watch. Shoggu lay nearby, but there was no sign of Ranga.

Or his *dughra*.

He surged to his feet. The pack had been opened, its contents strewn. And his *clathma* was gone. Where Ranga had bedded down lay a paper, weighted by a stone. He snatched it up.

Regret to say I am not what I seemed, but secret service agent. Vanessa not a magician – only told you that to get onto island. Do not pursue me, but remain where you are and await rescue.

It took minutes to rouse Shoggu. Tashi worried he was in some kind of dark-flight, until he recalled the Prelate's sleeping drug. Ranga must have used something similar.

His master seemed shaken by the turn of events, and needed tea. They hadn't dared light a fire at night, so Tashi gathered deadwood that seemed dry enough to not smoke, and soon had their small kettle boiling. The familiar task steadied him, but did little to lighten the weight of betrayal. He'd called Ranga 'brother'. The teaching not to hate, which he'd barely questioned in Highcloud, now seemed a laughable proscription that took no account of the true nature of the lower world.

'I wonder if it's true,' said Shoggu, reading the note again.

'How can we know?' said Tashi hotly. 'He is happy to lie about anything. He even pretended to find the light of Gevurah, all the time laughing behind his hand. Forgive me for ever trusting him.'

'Trust never requires forgiveness,' said Shoggu. 'Even if it proves misplaced.'

'But I knew the lower world would have corrupted him,' said Tashi. 'I let myself believe in him for my own selfish reasons.'

'Selfish?'

Tashi sipped his tea. 'I wanted not to have to fight the magician alone.'

'But you are not alone.'

'No, master.' He set down his tea-bowl and pushed his fingers through his hair. 'How can I fight without a weapon?' He stood. 'I must find Ranga.'

'Beloved one, no. He is armed, and might be ruthless.'

'I shall return soon.'

'Tashi, I forbid it.'

He pretended not to hear. If he hadn't heard, he couldn't disobey. There was no right way to act now, he thought as he climbed the hill. He didn't feel right leaving Shoggu, but to remain with him would doom their mission to failure. He resented more than ever the Abbot's refusal of help. How could they have hoped to succeed against a magician steeped in years of evil, and traitor naval officers and lying agents of government? Even the warship put at their disposal had proved no use.

He had been stripped of every help, every weapon. He felt naked in the Witch Mother's forest. Even this early, the air felt unhealthily hot. The shadows in the craggy bark hid insects. The shadows among the rocks concealed rodents, scorpions, snakes.

He climbed until he was lost, and far from the previous evening's route. Thirst baked his throat. He wandered directionless across the roof of the island, until he saw, ahead, a pair of squat boulders a few feet apart.

Drawing near, he found they'd been shaped into crude, exaggerated female forms, large breasts resting on rounded bellies. They seemed to act as gateposts for a trail that led into a shaded hollow. His eyes followed it down – and he froze.

A naked body lay before a small cave. Unable at first to make out limbs or head, he feared a worse mutilation than the museum curator. Then his eyes made sense of the sight: a young woman curled on elbows and knees, her rear towards him.

His gaze flinched away. A few items of clothing lay near one of the witch-stones. Heart thumping, he squatted behind the other stone, screening himself from the hollow. The power of the Witch Mother filled the air, the smell of pine needles and heat, of ferment and rot.

He peered round the stone. The young woman's flanks swelled and relaxed, subtly defining her ribs, shades of tan playing over her dusky skin. Except for the terrible sight in Torrento, Tashi had never seen a naked female form, had never even been sure how to imagine one, despite the talk of other novitiates. Warily compelled, he studied how the curves of her rump smoothed into her back either side of her knobbed spine. Apart from the dirty soles of her feet, and the tail of hair that lay between her shoulder blades, she was only a torso. She had hidden her head, her mind. Her body was no tool to be made servant of the will, but something revelled in for its own sake, a hot, pliant mass of the digestive and the sexual.

He knew some of the horrifying organic mess that lay beneath that smooth symmetry, but that didn't stop his eyes being drawn to the focus of her submissive, challenging posture: the darkness between heels and buttocks.

A noise startled his head round, but it was only a bird. His heartbeat shook him. The rest of the island and the world no longer existed: he felt hemmed in this place, trapped by the unwanted hardness of his penis. But having been broken from the witch-girl, he would not look again. He had to deny her. Not doing so was creating Qliphoth; he sensed them swarming, their heat, the lies they told about how he wanted to abandon his control and his training and imagine how it would feel to be gripped and pulled into the wet, slippery dissolution within her. He had to leave.

But he couldn't move. He was failing, even now: even as he trembled and licked the salt from his upper lip, even as he muttered for Gevurah to forgive him, he had to look again.

He peered round the stone—

– *YOUR FLESH IS WEAK*

He crouched against the ground in terror.

– *ADMIT US NOW*

He looked wildly for the speakers. The voices came from everywhere.

– *ADMIT US AND THE RAGE OF THE LORD SHALL BE VISITED UPON THIS PLACE*

Sweat burst from his skin. 'No,' he whispered. 'Gevurah, please—'

– *HE CANNOT REACH HERE*

– *WE GAVE YOU STRONGER FLESH*

– *USE IT AND ALL WITCHES, ALL MAGICIANS SHALL FALL BENEATH YOUR BLADE*

'I don't have one,' he said, desperate to put them off, to give himself space.

– *YOU LET IT BE STOLEN*

– *WE KNOW WHERE IT LIES*

An image flashed into his mind: a hole behind a tree. With it came the certainty that he could find the place, if he let himself be guided. He held himself in a stillness of heartbeat, but the voices didn't speak again. Perhaps, he thought, if he followed his new instinct, they would stay silent.

They had freed him from the spell of the witch-girl, at least. He crept away from the stones and the hollow, and led by a vague, uneasy sense of familiarity, as though he'd hidden the swords himself in his sleep and now had only dim snatches of dream-memory to guide him, he descended the northern slope. Still the voices kept quiet, and though the lash of their disapproval still stung, he began to hope that they had been only a trick of his mind.

But halfway down the slope, he saw the tree he'd been shown, and behind it, concealed by deadwood, lay the *clathma*.

He offered up a prayer, and pulled out the sword. Then he searched the area for his *dughra*. Unease mounted as he looked in vain. The instinctive guidance had gone.

Ranga must have kept the *dughra*, he realised, and only dumped the *clathma* because it was so bulky and because he'd thought it no threat – hadn't he himself told Ranga the big sword was too heavy to use?

He drew the blade and tried a few swings with it. He briefly imagined hacking Ranga to pieces, to show him just how little threat it was. But the truth was as plain as ever: with his own strength, he would be able to wield it only against someone slow and near-helpless.

'I found this,' he said, reaching the camp and his visibly relieved master. He set the *clathma* against a tree.

'Only that?'

Tashi nodded.

'Gevurah guided you,' said Shoggu.

Tashi hunkered the other side of the fire. His master stared into the thin flames.

'I had planned to begin work before dawn,' Shoggu said. 'If you observed the magician heading towards the eastern point last night, I doubt he will have left the island yet. But he might not remain long, not now his presence is discovered. The prudent thing would be for me to fly, to locate Ranga and your *dughra*; but any delay risks losing the magician. I must learn all I can about his whereabouts, his defences, his plans. And you must prepare for Inspiration.'

'Is that truly necessary?' said Tashi.

'To best know the magician's mind, I must connect with him using the icon he defiled. But that might reveal our presence to him. That's why I wished to do this while he slept.'

Tashi exhaled. Another problem Ranga had caused them.

'If I see the magician is alone or vulnerable, I shall send you to destroy him and capture proof of his evil,' Shoggu went on. 'But if he senses me, he might send men against us. In either case, you will need the Lords of Battle. Without them, you cannot use the only weapon you have.'

'Yes, I know.'

'You sound reluctant.'

Tashi stirred the fire. 'I wanted not to call them again.'

'Why?'

'The way it felt, to be an observer. To be helpless…'

'Those boars did not find you helpless.'

'I *meant*, to have my body used by others.'

'By the holiest servants of God.'

It didn't happen to you! He controlled himself. 'Isn't Gevurah's greatest gift our true self, our free will, our ability to refuse the influence of the Witch Mother? Then why does He send servants that take that will from us?'

Shoggu smiled, as though at a child's error. 'But surrender to them is an *act* of will.'

'So they cannot just… take me?'

'No, beloved one. Even the first twenty-seven must have called them in somehow, even if they lacked the precise rituals devised since.'

That steadied Tashi, a little. But remembering the voices he'd heard not an hour since, he wondered how true Shoggu's reassurance was, for him at least. Was if his total surrender in the hotel room had changed the rules?

'And is it also through my will that they depart? Because in the arena…'

Shoggu looked down. 'Do not dwell upon that. Their chastisement of me was an expression of holy judgement.'

'But I was forced to be its instrument,' said Tashi. 'And I'm only human. I carry the shame of those threats and insults – but I can take no pride in any battle I fight when Inspired, because I'm only their tool, a puppet, no more a true warrior than a sword or a stick.'

'Beloved one.' Shoggu was stern. 'You are not a soldier of the lower world, to brag and boast and heap up trophies. Yours is a higher path.'

Until I'm thrown out of Highcloud, if I haven't been already.

'You talk of willing them to depart,' said Shoggu, 'but what reason can there be to resist Gevurah's servants? They express His will, and we exist to enact His desires.'

'They had no right to behave like that to you,' said Tashi. 'Your mistake was made with good intentions.'

'Tashi, do not soften.'

'I am not – not about our task. But they were too harsh. I don't want them inside me!'

In the short silence that followed his outburst, he felt a will bent upon him, a presence like distant thunder.

'Beloved one,' said Shoggu, 'it is the Witch Mother that wants to keep holiness from you, and her influence here is strong.'

Tashi closed his eyes, shamed by a reminder of what he'd lately seen.

'It is she who wants you to fight as yourself,' Shoggu went on, 'to delight in rage and violence rather than acting through righteous anger and the desire for justice.'

Tashi frowned. Had not the voices talked of rage?

'And don't be troubled by memories of that first Inspiration in Bismark,' said Shoggu. 'It was impurely done. This calling of the Lords of Battle, for a correct and holy purpose, will redeem us both for that error.'

The words spiked Tashi with hope. 'Master – you're right!'

'It does happen occasionally.'

'No – it makes sense,' said Tashi, excited. 'The Inspiration in Bismark was flawed. It has stained everything since. If it had been pure, it would have felt ecstatic – how could it not? There wouldn't have been any place for doubts – I would never have wanted to fight my own battles. That all comes from the impurity. This coming Inspiration will wipe it out.'

Including the voices, he felt sure. The *Elohim Gibor* who had come that first time and in the hotel, who had made him threaten his master, who had just now talked terrifyingly of his weakness and of the rage of the Lord, rage which should not even exist – somehow they had been changed by the impurity of that ritual. He did not understand how such beings could be altered by the actions of a human, but it was the only explanation. Their voices were not, he thought now, the same as those he had heard during his Rite of Acceptance years before. A new, correct Inspiration would replace them with the true ones.

'And it will reconnect me with Gevurah,' he said, 'even here on the island of the Witch Girl.'

Shoggu looked at him curiously. 'You mean the Witch Mother?'

Tashi's face heated. 'Of course.'

⌒

By the time it was fully light, Cass had already been sitting on the beach for hours, huddled in Seriuz's jacket for the scant warmth it gave. All night, fatigue had pressed at the backs of her eyes. She had expected to die of weariness and despair.

But she had not. And the coming day had brought with it a slow realisation, one she couldn't have expected.

Telling Orc the truth, or what she knew of the truth, had been an act of desperation, yet it had resulted in her being less afraid of it. Not because the truth was less bad than she'd thought – she couldn't know that yet – but because in telling Orc of her fear, she had stopped running from it. She saw now how much she had been running, how much of what she'd done and said over the past few days had been through fear alone. Even her attraction towards Seriuz had come from the protection and escape she'd thought he could offer, not from any genuine feeling for the complex and contradictory man that must exist behind the heroic mask.

And if she and Orc had been responsible for the Shroud, then its making, too, had been an act of flight and denial.

Maybe she and Orc were cursed; maybe neither of them could ever achieve happiness because of this thing they'd done. But *they* had done it, that was the point. Blaming Orc alone was itself running, and diminished her by casting her as his weak and helpless victim. They had to face it together. Her bond with him had been forged before her earliest memories, and she could not break that bond in ignorance, if at all. The truth was hers, and Orc was hers, with all his qualities and faults, his bravery, his stubbornness, his brokenness.

She watched *Tarpon* steam eastwards, bound for the ziggurat, and made her resolution. If Orc hadn't found the truth yet, she would search for it with him. If he had, she would take her half of its weight.

She pushed to her feet and shrugged off the jacket. Esteban or no, she was going to the Spiral.

Just past the junction of tracks at the top of the climb from the cove – a climb even more tiring than the day before – she heard her name called. She turned to find Hana running down the path from the Navel. She'd seen Hana several times since the screaming episode the day before, but hadn't spoken to her, and assumed Hana felt as awkward about her temporary breakdown as she did.

'What's going on?' said Hana as she came to a stop.

'How long have you got?' said Cass.

'I heard your cousin couldn't get the artefacts. One of the Sundi divers is going down for them.'

'Just about now, yes.'

'So what's Orc up to, if he's not going to dive again?'

Cass frowned. 'What do you mean, "up to"?'

'I went back to the Navel earlier,' said Hana. 'I wanted to...' She exhaled. 'Look, I should explain what happened yesterday, how I reacted.'

'You don't—'

'It took me by surprise. I came up against this thing called Three-Eyes, and it scared my animal helper witless, and he infected me with it. But I wasn't going to let it beat me, so I went back to the Navel before sunrise this morning and tried to connect with the Spiral again. I was more prepared this time. I'm sure I sensed Orc there.'

'He's probably scaping.'

'Scaping? He knows how?'

Cass nodded. She was too tired of secrecy to keep Orc's magic hidden.

'Three-Eyes was there again too.' A wariness had come into Hana's eyes. 'Cass, listen. I had to go and help Ferman with the card-reading before I managed to find anything, but I went back to the Navel again after we finished, to try to work out what Orc was doing. And it didn't feel like he was scaping.'

'How do you mean?'

'I don't know yet. I'm going to the Spiral now, to look. Come on.'

Hana wouldn't expand on her hints as they walked. Cass hoped she hadn't picked up on something terrible Orc had discovered, but she found it hard to think otherwise. They crept to the top of the bluff from which they'd observed the Spiral the day before. As she lay prone, Cass thought she heard a twig crack nearby, but she saw no one among the pines, and the scene at the stone circle put it from her mind.

Orc wore the short white robe from the previous day, and knelt with his head bowed, not sitting back on his heels but awkwardly upright. He was surrounded by artefacts, which Daroguerre in his long purple robe was placing around him. The arrangement of these silver cups and bowls seemed random, but clearly wasn't: as Cass watched, the magician moved one a few inches, then scrutinised the one in his hand as though moving the other had somehow altered its qualities. His left hand held the focus-stone.

'What are those things?' whispered Hana.

'Everything we brought up from four months of diving,' said Cass. 'Is Orc's position normal for scaping?'

'Not in my experience,' said Hana. 'We need a proper look.'

To avoid Pisaro, on guard at the end of the trail to the south, Hana led Cass down to the northern side of the bluff. There, the trunk of an enormous pine had split. The weight of a lower bough had brought it to rest on the ground, creating a living archway through to the northwest corner of the terrace.

They reached the stone circle before Daroguerre saw them. His obvious irritation was quickly covered with a tight smile. 'Miss Strandborn – and a friend, how charming. Welcome.'

'This isn't your place to welcome us to,' said Hana, clearly uneasy.

Orc hadn't reacted at all. Cass stepped over the silverware to a point in front of him. His eyes were closed, his breathing slow.

'Orc? It's me, Cass. Hello?'

'I'm afraid he can't hear you, Miss Strandborn.'

'What's happened to him—'

'Don't touch him!' barked Daroguerre. 'That could be dangerous. He's in a special kind of trance. We have already begun our great work – something I was hoping to discuss with you. If you wouldn't mind giving us a little space to talk, Miss Quallace?'

At Cass's hesitant nod, Hana walked to the edge of the circle, frowning as she looked about her. Daroguerre gestured Cass to the other side of the ring.

'I gather,' he said softly, 'that yesterday's sabotage attempt was not due to antipathy to our work as such, but a desire to prevent your cousin recovering your pasts.'

'Is that what he's doing now?'

'No. The Shroud proved too strong, so you needn't worry about that. As I said, he is engaged on the greater task.'

Cass looked at Orc, annoyed that he'd agreed to help Daroguerre without talking to her first. But her annoyance was less than her unease.

'He's all right, though?'

'Do you find his trance-state alarming? You're welcome to stay and keep an eye on him. The best way to do that would be to help in the culmination of this enterprise.'

'You're really going to do it? Here?'

'Not ten minutes ago I sent *Tarpon* a message giving the exact location of the final artefacts, which I was able to ascertain with this focus-stone. And we have another, even more potent artefact, one I hadn't anticipated. Your cousin, by his various encounters, is himself imprinted with the energy needed for the creation of the ruling goddess. She will arise on this very spot. And your contribution might be crucial.'

'What contribution?'

'That of priestess,' said Daroguerre. 'Merely in a symbolic sense, of course.'

'And that's the price of being able to stay? Becoming part of your magic ritual?'

'You dislike the idea, clearly.' Daroguerre met her gaze with his dark lenses. 'But understand this: the project will go ahead with or without your help, and the gallant captain will take the goddess back to his homeland. If she is powerful enough, his victory will be assured. If she is created with less than her full power, his revolution might fail, with many lives lost, his own included.' A smile twitched the corner of his mouth. 'He would be *most* grateful for your help, I'm sure.'

Too late for that, you slimy git. She looked at Hana standing outside the circle, shoulders tensed as if with the urge to run. 'I'll think about it.'

'Not for too long,' said Daroguerre. 'Return within an hour. And don't listen overmuch to what your friend has to say. Like her parents, she fails to understand what she's dealing with. I, however, do understand it, and the proof of that will change the world for the better.'

Hana readily agreed to go. As they left, Cass caught sight of Esteban peering around one of the tents. He glared at her with what looked like sullen hunger, then ducked back.

'I don't like it,' said Hana, as soon as they were out of earshot. 'There's complex energy there, all dark and manipulative. And did you feel *her*? Three-Eyes?'

'I don't know who that is.'

Hana shuddered. 'Like she was just waiting to spring out at me.'

'What about Orc?' said Cass. 'Daroguerre said he was just in a trance.'

'And you trust him? I knew there was something wrong when I did my last scape. I'm sorry, Cass. I think Orc's trapped somehow.'

'Shit.' It was something she'd feared ever since his Initiation. 'How do we get him out?'

'I don't know,' said Hana. 'But I don't think Daroguerre was lying when he said it would be dangerous to try to break him out of it. I've heard of people wrenched too suddenly from deep states. They can have seizures, heart attacks.'

'And Daroguerre made him like that?'

'He must have. My guess is he needs Orc in that state to create his monstrosity, but I don't know how it all works.'

A terrible thought came to Cass. 'What if he's trying to make Orc a…' She forced it out. 'A sacrifice? Would that help manifestation?'

'Like one of the goddess's husbands?'

'I can't explain it all, but Orc has a psychic connection with the Sun-King.'

'The man's blood was meant to strengthen the goddess,' said Hana. 'Maybe Orc's blood will be the physical trigger, the catalyst.'

Cass felt panic-sick. She'd hoped Hana would dismiss the idea, not confirm it.

'But the man was supposed to sacrifice himself,' said Hana. 'Why would Orc do that?'

'I don't know. But yesterday, on the ziggurat, Daroguerre said Orc's free will couldn't be harmed. What if that's part of the magic, Orc sacrificing himself willingly?'

'Maybe,' said Hana. 'And I don't think we have long to get him out of it. When I was scaping earlier, I got an instinct that midday might be important. If he's the Sun-King, that'd make sense.'

'Seriuz won't be back till early afternoon. What do we *do*?'

'I've got to go back to the Navel,' said Hana. 'Try another scape. Now I've been to the physical Spiral, I should be able to connect better.'

'And me?'

Hana eyed her. 'Look, you're *sure* you're not a sensitive?'

The denial didn't come readily, unlike before. That, too, had been running in fear, and her fear had led to this mess.

She braved it. 'I don't know. Geist said—'

'*Geist?*' blurted Hana.

'A man we knew. Orc's teacher. He—'

'*Geist*?'

'Yes! Why?'

'Mother,' said Hana. 'He was my teacher too.'

Cass gaped. 'What, with the beard? And the eye-patch?'

Hana nodded; she looked stunned. 'How…? No, it doesn't matter, not for now. Does Orc have an animath?'

'Otter.'

'Should've guessed. This could change everything. What were you going to say? Geist said what?'

'That we both had magical potential.'

'Then why the hell didn't you say so yesterday?'

'Orc wasn't about to *die* yesterday! Look, magic scares me, okay? A lot of things scare me. But not as much as him getting killed.'

'All right,' said Hana. 'If you're not trained, it'd probably be no use anyway.'

'I'll go back,' said Cass. 'Daroguerre asked me to stay. There might be something I can find out or do from there.'

'Asked you to stay why?'

'To be priestess, or something.'

Hana bit her lip. 'Don't let him use you for anything you're not sure about. He'll use tricks – I bet that's how he got Orc into that state. But I know some tricks too. When I've found something, I'll come back and make a bird noise.' She cupped her hands round her mouth and voiced a series of shrill cheeps. 'When you hear that, find me.'

Cass nodded. 'Hana… we have to save him.'

'Believe me,' said Hana, 'if saving him puts a stop to this abomination, I'm as motivated as it gets. Stop Daroguerre doing any magic if you can.' She broke into a run towards the junction. 'Good luck!'

♋

While Shoggu prepared, Tashi rigged the canvas sheeting to enclose the remains of the fire, making the interior as dark as possible. 'You must be ready for Inspiration as soon as I return from flight,' said Shoggu. 'Whether for attack or defence.'

Tashi nodded. He could hardly breathe.

They used much of the fresh water from their supplies in the purification ritual – Tashi focused hard on every word – then Shoggu helped Tashi strap on his bindings and Tashi performed some trial moves with the *clathma*, slow enough that sweating wouldn't lose the purification. But it wasn't just effort that made him sweat. Would the *Elohim Gibor* make him charge into gunfire? How much concern would they have for his safety? He reminded himself that only the task mattered. But so far from the Holy Mountain, the same fear assailed him as in the hotel room, that death might cost him more than his life. Would the Lords of Battle ensure his soul reached the Mountain, even across such a distance? He had never heard either way.

Don't doubt.

When it was time, he sat across the embers from his master. Shoggu studied the defiled icon, still streaked with Mrs Fusilli's dried blood.

'I wonder if the magician knew?' he muttered.

Tashi assumed he wasn't expected to respond.

'Do you see any resemblance between this and my scroll-painting?' said Shoggu.

Tashi frowned, perplexed and worried by being asked a direct question, the forgetfulness of ritual it implied. He glanced at the scroll-painting hanging on the shelter's main pole. 'Master, I am not permitted to speak between purification and Inspiration.'

'The purpose of that rule is so you will not tell an inadvertent lie and make yourself impure,' said Shoggu. 'But you are not a child any more. You can tell the difference. And there is a matter that troubles me. You remember I suggested you think about Torrento as a future home?'

'Because you don't think I can be a Watcher,' said Tashi. He'd tried to say it calmly, but the words burned his throat.

'Through no fault of yours,' said Shoggu. 'To investigate the lower world, one must have sunk one's ankles in its filth, and possess a certain craftiness of mind. The pure and innocent, the obedient and steady of service, cannot do so. Of the current novitiates, only Hann is thought to possess the necessary qualities.'

'Hann!'

'And he chafes to explore, I've heard. The irony is that novitiates truly suited to becoming Watchers are also the ones least likely to want to stay, and those who wish to stay we must often refuse. So, yes, in a few years you will probably have to make a home in the lower world.'

Or seek the Mountain.

'But,' said Shoggu, 'we talked about Torrento in particular.'

'Because I might grow rich there?'

'Did you not wonder why I was so against going to that Thangkaran guesthouse?'

'You told me. The charity would have been too easy.'

'Ah,' sighed Shoggu. 'I confess that was an invention. There was another reason.'

Tashi felt as much troubled by the tremble in Shoggu's voice as his confession of falsehood. 'Because Ranga's father won't have monks staying there.'

'I did not know that at the time. But it does not surprise me to find he has not lost his hatred of them.'

'Master…?'

'I never told you,' said Shoggu, 'that I have been to Torrento before.'

Tashi's spine chilled. 'You *know* Ranga's father…?'

'I was once a painter.' Shoggu closed his eyes; his head fell forward slightly. 'Many years ago, I lived in a village at the foot of the Petitioners Road, where I made images of the Holy Mountain and sold them to visitors. By my fortieth birthday, I still had neither wife nor family. I had become dissatisfied, but did not know what else to do. The world was wide, but I feared to explore it. Some others who had shackled themselves to families said how they yearned for the freedom to seek fortunes in foreign lands, but from visitors to the Holy Mountain, I heard of poverty and misery everywhere.

'One day, a young man named Anik came down from Highcloud. He had ended his term as a novitiate, and now had to make a life in the lower world, and was full of bitterness at those who had cast him out after his whole young life of service. He wanted to talk, and I had time to listen. We drank at the village inn, and with the courage of the barley wine, I agreed to accompany him. I even offered to act as his guide, for in my eagerness to be his companion I professed a worldliness I did not possess. He soon surpassed even my pretend experience. In the first town we travelled through, he bedded three women with a gusto even pillows over my ears could not hide me from.'

'No wonder Highcloud cast out such a person,' said Tashi. 'It's a wonder they waited until his graduation.'

'In the end,' said Shoggu, 'we travelled all down through Kurassia to Torrento, Anik being drawn by rumours of licentiousness. In Torrento, I tried to make a living selling paintings, mostly images of the Holy Mountain such as this. But the city was not to my liking. By the time I left to return to Thangkara, Anik had taken a wife.'

'Master? Why tell me all this?'

'Whatever he has done so far, spare Ranga if you come across him. His friendship might be valuable to you, if you decide to go back to Torrento when you graduate.'

'But why should I go there?' Tashi worried at his master's lack of sense, that in old age and the stress of their situation he was becoming confused. 'Just because you once knew his father? Master, this is not helping. It troubles me to speak while purified, and time passes. Much longer, and we shall have to perform the ritual again.'

Shoggu sighed, and nodded his assent. Tashi carefully unwrapped Shoggu's lammager mantle and placed it round his master's shoulders, then threw incense on the embers. As the smell filled the shelter, Shoggu began to pluck at his beads with one hand, gazing with half-lidded eyes at the defiled icon he held with the other.

Tashi sat, trying to keep his thoughts on his master and away from what would come. But with the absence of talk and activity, he found the witch-girl creeping back into his mind, too insistent to be successfully pushed away. The purification ritual had not scrubbed her out, nor did it prevent the internal twitches that came from remembering her.

Why, he wondered dismally, had he protested about his own self being pushed aside, when that self clearly lacked the strength of will to perform his task? He should feel grateful to be occupied by a will that could not be corrupted, even if it came in the form of the voices. If they hadn't spoken to him, would he ever have escaped the witch-girl's enchantment? He could not escape it even now! Even as he castigated himself for it, he couldn't help thinking of her, of how warm and soft her skin would feel; he imagined her pliant, naked body beneath his hand. Shoggu had said that to make a good Watcher, one had to sink one's ankles into the filth of the world. He could sink more than his ankles, and into more than filth.

Too high a price. He must refuse the thought. He was a being of air and fire, of sunlight on snow. The earth of his base form was fired clay. And yet the thought of the slippery heat, the slithery, squelching morass pulling him in, deeper and deeper, forcing him to abandon his will to the mindless bodily grinding and heaving...

He shifted his position, his trapped hardness a discomfort that fed off itself. Shoggu was now fully in trance. He could go outside for a minute. There could be no danger in so short an absence. At Vanessa's house, he had recalled Shoggu easily.

He crept from the shelter. This was not a defeat. It was a kind of hygiene, to put the raging influence of the Witch Mother to sleep – part of the purification ritual, in its way. And Inspiration depended on purity.

By the time he'd gone a short way among the trees, his knees felt weak. He undid enough bindings to take out his erection, pushing away the thought that Gevurah might see him. This island was shut off from Gevurah; it belonged to the Witch Mother, and the girl, the young woman as soft and blood-hot as the skin he now gripped and stroked. He imagined her smooth beauty, and beneath it the bodily horror of coiled bowels and the warm swamp of her sex. It came back to him that he had once wanted to defecate off the Knifebridge. He grew frantic. Maybe Gevurah could see him, he didn't care. The faceless girl fell on him, clasped her thighs around his throat, choked him. It took all his effort to stifle his cries as his body spasmed.

His shamed heartbeat almost broke his chest. He couldn't breathe. He hid his quickly softening penis and scuffed dust over the splashes on the ground. He placed stones on them. It seemed madness now to think that Shoggu wouldn't see them, or smell them, or sense them. His act was now recorded in the Immaterium, in Records, forever. Even now, his master might have detected that something was wrong, and be drawn to this moment.

His master. He should get back to the shelter.

As soon as he ducked under the canvas, he heard the warning signs in Shoggu's breathing. He fought to control his alarm: he had been gone two minutes at most. He made the call-back rhyme, over and again. Five times. Six.

Ten. The background of his mind howled in rising panic. The call-back had worked at Vanessa's, but this was worse. Shoggu looked as bad as he had at Highcloud.

He found the herbs and threw them on the embers. They made no difference. Fifteen times, the rhyme. Twenty.

Yaggit's advanced herb-lore, and all other help, was a thousand miles away.

Thirty.

His master was held by a trap. And he couldn't break it, not unless—

Unless he could kill its maker: Orc.

– *ADMIT US*

'No,' he whispered. 'Please. That inspiration was flawed.'

– *WE GAVE YOU BACK YOUR BLADE*

'I need the true Lords of Holy Battle. I've been purified,' he said, but he heard the weakness in his own voice, the doubt, the guilt.

– *YOU NEED US*

– *ONLY WE CAN DEFEAT THE MAGICIAN*

He knew they spoke the truth. There could be no proper Inspiration now, not with Shoggu in dark-flight. The choice was between letting Shoggu die, and letting them in. And they were still *Elohim Gibor*, of some kind. He had to trust them.

'Master.' His voice shook. 'Forgive me for leaving you again.'

Outside, he picked up the *clathma*. So heavy. He opened himself, surrendered his will and his body. A hard, violent energy spread up the muscles and sinews of his forearm, strained against the compression of the leather. The great sword felt light as a stick.

The end of the island, was his last clear thought before his mind was swamped.

Thera jumped to alertness as the tent-flap jerked open. Her father crossed to the luggage and hurriedly searched through it.

'What's wrong?'

'That Watcher is nearby. The Empyreal cruiser must have landed him yesterday. Now he's searching for me, using something I left as a trap for him before. The fool may as well have sent a telegram. Well, he'll find plenty to keep him occupied…'

He picked up the small case Thera knew contained his scrying bowl and accessories.

'What about maintaining Orc?' she asked. 'Will I be enough?'

'He's far enough under now to do without continuous influence.' Her father paused at the tent-flap. 'Did you part on good terms with Cass yesterday?'

'I think so.'

'She was here a few minutes ago, with the Quallace girl. They're probably now on the trail to the cove. Try to persuade her to come back and take up the priestess role I offered her. If necessary, tell her Orc has been muttering her name. Quickly.'

Half-dazed by her rapid emergence from trance, Thera left the tent and headed down the trail. A few yards along the path, a realisation struck her. When he'd released her from working on Orc, her father had forgotten to take back her focus-stone.

The possibility left her breathless. She could pretend to go after Cass, but in reality go into the forest and scape properly. Talk freely to

Sparrow, for the first time in years.

But the reality of her situation crushed the hope. Her father might grow suspicious, and scry for her: with the large stone, it would be easy. To be seen to betray him, or disobey him, or become less than useful to him, was too great a risk. He had shown her death, had made her live with it breathing on her neck for an hour – enough for a lifetime. She knew the falsehood of all religious consolations. Even Hell would be a consolation next to the truth she had beheld.

The inevitability of absolute nothingness.

Sometimes she almost wished she didn't know. Free of the constant, overpowering knowledge of what extinction truly meant, she might have been brave enough to risk communion with Sparrow. Reality made her a coward, and that made the gap between her and her animath ever wider. Sparrow could afford courage, because she came from a story.

'Though smallest and weakest,' Geist had told her, *'Sparrow was bravest of all. She knew the brand would be heavy for her; she knew the others hadn't made it, for all their apparently greater talents. Fox's cunning: failed. Hare's running: failed. But still she took on the task. And in the end, the very reason the brand was so heavy for her, the very reason she looked certain to fail, was what allowed her to succeed. Her smallness let her through the hole in the sky where the sisters couldn't go. And because of her, we're here now, civilised by fire and all it led to, not grubbing in the dirt for roots to eat.'*

Her inability to take the risk upset her. It made her hate her father, which was pointless. She didn't have the power to make it worth hating him. The subtlety of the magic he'd used to trap Orc that morning had amazed her: all woven on the spur of the moment, yet seeming the culmination of months of planning. That was the mark of a true magician, he'd often told her: creative adaptability, freedom from supposed rules.

Her thought broke off as she saw Cass approaching. The blonde girl's face fell open in surprise.

'Thera!' she said, running up to her. 'Why aren't you with the others? On *Nightfire?*'

'Oh, it was awful!' said Thera. 'I was making fast the ship's boat and it swung and knocked me overboard, and by the time I swam to shore and started making for the cove, the ship had left. I tried shouting, but no one heard me. So Daroguerre said I could help him, because of my skill with Mister Burns.'

She braced herself for incredulous questions. But Cass clearly had other things on her mind. 'I've decided to help him too,' she said. 'Because it might help Martin.'

They walked back to the Spiral together, and reached it just as her father hurried out of the larger tent. He took in the sight of Cass, nodded subtly to Thera, then called for Pisaro and Mord.

'Follow the trail to the island's highest point and strike directly downhill,' he told his men. 'On the northern shore, you'll find a makeshift camp, and the Watcher and his war-puppy.'

'They're here?' said Pisaro. 'On the island?'

'You think me in the habit of giving worthless instructions?' said Daroguerre. 'Kill the Watcher, but subdue the boy if you can. I might have a use for him.'

'Isn't he…' Mord looked at his comrade. 'Dangerous?'

'The novitiate needs the Watcher to Inspire him, and the monk is trapped. Now go, before my patience proves less than the equal of your stupidity.'

As the sailors left with their rifles, Daroguerre turned to Cass. 'Welcome back, Miss Strandborn.'

'What do you want me to do?' asked Cass.

'For now, your mere presence is helpful,' replied Daroguerre. 'We are creating an image or tableau, both in reality and in the psychosphere, one mirroring the other. Tell me, when Orc mistook you for a priestess, what were you wearing?'

'Mistook me for a priestess?'

'He told me it happened a few nights ago, in a hotel bedroom.'

Thera heard Cass's indrawn breath. 'He mistook…? I didn't know.'

'Some kind of nightgown, I assume?'

Cass nodded.

Daroguerre turned, as though to call someone. 'Damn.' He turned to Thera. 'Flash a message to *Tarpon*. When they bring the artefacts up here, they're to bring Miss Strandborn's luggage as well.'

'I'll fetch it.' Esteban stepped from behind the tent. Thera cringed at his stupidity – he'd been ordered to stay out of Cass's sight – but Cass ignored him.

'You want me to wear my *nightdress*?' she asked Daroguerre.

'Your cousin is key to this whole work. Whatever helps him associate you with the officiating priestess would be of benefit.'

Cass looked troubled.

'I'll go down for it,' said Esteban. 'The Sundies will be slow to get here. They haven't brought up the artefacts yet. I'll be much faster.'

Even with a stop to bury your face in it, Thera thought in disgust.

Her father waved him off. Esteban left at a run.

'My apologies, Miss Strandborn,' said Daroguerre. 'He was not to show himself. He'll be punished, I assure you. Now, you're free to wander, but don't touch the artefacts, and be sure not to disturb your cousin. He's in too deep a trance to hear you, but we don't want the psychosphere affected. Thera…?'

He beckoned her to follow him to the tent. 'How did you persuade her?'

'I didn't. She was already coming back.'

'I wonder what she said to the Quallace girl.'

'She said something to me about it being for Seriuz's sake.'

Her father nodded. 'I don't trust her. But she might yet play her role. Resume your work. Remember: seduce Orc, or what was Orc. The goddess is not merely the mask worn by the Serpent Mandala, but every woman he has ever desired. Draw him towards her.'

'I have been trying. It's just… I have trouble with that.'

His smile tightened. 'Why?'

'I don't know how it feels to be… how a man would see me that way.'

'A dowdy bird with a strident, monotonous voice? Is that how you see yourself? Geist did you no favours bonding you with that ridiculous animath.'

'Sparrow isn't ridiculous.'

'But her heart gave out, didn't it?' said Daroguerre. 'She tried to fly to Raven, but the brand was too heavy, the air too thin, and...' He made an explosive action with his hands. 'Poof!'

Her own chest felt suddenly wrong. She couldn't breathe. 'She was shot by a bolt.'

'Is that so?' said Daroguerre. 'Go to your work. Do it as best you can.'

But she was still having trouble breathing. 'It's almost a month,' she said, with difficulty.

'I can't spare the power to replenish you now.'

'I could do my work better. I've been feeling weak. I'd be more effective.'

'You'll last a few days more,' he said. 'Are you refusing me, Thera?'

She shook her head.

Back inside the tent, she settled into her meditative pose. But try as she might, she couldn't forget that sense of her heart about to stop. She feared that this period would be shorter than a month, as her menstrual periods sometimes varied. She worried that her father might delay until too late, or would use her for this one thing and then let her lapse – or deliberately snap the thread that bound her to life, as he'd been compelled to do with Alonso Gregal.

She forced all this from her mind. The only way to keep herself alive was to do her work so well that he would keep her, and his plan would succeed, and he would teach her his secrets of eternal life. And then... but she didn't even dare think it.

She began to sink into her trance.

A cry from outside jumped her out of it.

♋

Ranga's heart sped with the chance before him; his breath quickened through the damp bandage wrapped round his face. Everyone with a gun had left, and the magician, the man whose very existence he had doubted until that morning, held the focus-stone. From his position near the top of the little bluff, Ranga saw the blue crystal clearly. A stealthy creep down to the broken-arch pine, a sprint, a short chase – the man would never run in that robe – and with one thrust of Tashi's sword it would be his. Then he would only have to make his way with his pack to the island's western end, do a half-mile swim to one of the Paps, and wait for his dreams to come true.

The trouble was the others: Cass, and the naval girl in the tent, and Orc. He didn't want to kill them too, but even if they didn't recognise him with his bandage disguise, they would raise the alarm, perhaps even try to follow him. He didn't know their loyalties, but he had to assume they favoured the magician. They seemed to be with him of their own accord.

He seethed with stress. Orc was in some kind of trance, and might not even see him. The naval girl was in the tent and might stay there. But Cass: they'd never been the best of friends, but could he really cut her down from behind as she fled?

Dare he hang on, and hope Cass would leave too? He couldn't wait long: Esteban and the sailors would be back within the hour.

He thought of Vanessa's kiss. That he might lose his only chance through weakness and delay was intolerable. When they were in bed, and her long, loose hair fell around him as she bent her mouth to his, when he was at last able to perform as a man should, then the memories of murder would fade.

For her, his true love, the woman whose life meant more than all others in the world, he unsheathed the sword.

Unexpected noise pressed him to the ground. Feet, running, somewhere back behind his left shoulder – and furious breathing.

A figure ran through the pines, aiming for the stone circle site. It was Tashi, not dressed as before but in tight-fitting black. Ranga's mouth dried at the sight of the sword. Tashi had said it was too big for him to use, but it looked like he was about to use it now.

Maybe, thought Ranga, he wouldn't have to kill the magician after all.

Then he remembered what he'd left out of his note.

30

THE MAGICIAN'S PALACE

Cass gasped as a young Thangkaran ran out through the broken-pine archway, forty yards from where she stood next to Orc. The hate in his features, his complex leather armour, his heavy sword, all stamped themselves on her mind as he veered towards the circle.

Off to her right, Daroguerre cried out. Cass took a step to the left: if the boy was after the magician, she wasn't going to get in his way or anywhere near it.

Then fear raked her. The boy wasn't running for Daroguerre, but towards her.

His feet pounded. She froze. Daroguerre shouted words she couldn't take in; they shocked through her like a tearing vibration. The black-strapped youth sprinted between the stones, sword half-raised, eyes dark holes of fury.

He was going for Orc – and Orc didn't move.

She ran forward, aiming to knock the boy, anything, but a sudden burst of pressure flung her aside and she crashed to the ground, clattering cups and bowls. She rolled, looked back in terror just as the boy swung his sword—

It clanged against a shield, a great round metal disc held by a –

person, a creature, a three-eyed hawk-faced woman *thing* – that hadn't been there before. The two collided. The boy's momentum drove him onto the shield. The hawk-woman stepped back and crouched to take his weight, then sprang her shield forwards and threw him onto the ground.

Cass scrambled up. 'Orc!' she yelled. 'Run!'

He showed no sign he'd heard, no sign of anything. Cass screamed again. The youth had leapt back onto his feet. Daroguerre kept shouting.

The boy swung; his blade clashed against steel. He kicked low, but the hawk-woman chopped her shield-edge at his shin – he jerked back his leg and struck at her exposed shoulder. Hawk-woman ducked, threw herself forward and shield-butted the boy, sending him staggering back, kicking cups. He righted himself, came again.

Cass yelled and pleaded with Orc to wake, to get up, to run. The fight crashed on, the moves too quick to follow. It seemed impossible for Hawk-woman to keep matching the speed of the boy's attacks, but somehow her defence held and he began to slow, the rage on his face joined by exhaustion. Hawk-woman began to strike back. Her talons tore through the boy's arm-strapping; she gashed by his ear, slicking blood down his cheek. But her shield was buckling, its edge more ragged with every hit.

The two moved around Orc, the boy seeking a gap, his loud breaths seething against Hawk-woman's eerie quiet, Daroguerre's chant. Cass stepped away as the youth worked round near her – then he clouted Hawk-woman's shield a two-handed blow that shocked her to one knee, and side-stepped her guard. There was nothing now between him and Orc.

He raised his sword. Cass threw herself forwards.

She snatched hold of his wrist and dropped her weight against it. Her arm wrenched with his stroke, but she hampered him just enough. As the boy's wrist slipped from her grasp and she fell to the ground behind, Hawk-woman caught the sword against her shield and barged against him.

Cass yelled as he kicked back into her. He tumbled over her, his legs slamming hard against her hips. She cried out in pain. Talons swiped: the boy yelped as leather snapped. He thrashed against Cass in a struggle to raise himself. She grabbed for him, to pin him, but too late; he was free – and she was on the ground between the two combatants.

But the youth didn't attack. Cass looked up. He was staring at his sword-hand. It was bright red, red as the bloodied side of his face.

But not with blood, she saw. His skin looked like – metal scales.

'Ah…' he gasped, eyes wide at his hand, chest heaving. 'Ah…'

'Beloved one!' roared Daroguerre.

The boy's head snapped round.

'Isn't that what he calls you? You know that all the time you fight here, men with guns are heading towards him?'

The boy glared at Daroguerre. Rage and anguish tore at his face, and he turned and ran the way he'd come, though less fast, less fluidly than before.

'Thera!' shouted Daroguerre. 'Get on that lamp. Get a signal relayed to Rulanza: thirty marines up here as fast as they can run. Now!'

He came over to Cass, who was shaking too heavily to stand. 'You're hurt. Come to the tent. Thera will look after you when she's finished.'

He helped her up. She couldn't walk properly; her left side had a painful limp. She glanced back just enough to check Orc was all right. She didn't want to see the hawk-faced woman.

'Who? How…?'

'A guardian. Nothing to fear.'

'And that boy? Why?'

'The novitiate I mentioned. Though why he went for your cousin, I don't know.'

To stop the goddess being made. Her legs almost gave way. The monk and the boy must have come on the Empyreal cruiser, trying to stop Daroguerre. And Daroguerre had sent the boy towards Pisaro and Mord and their guns, towards his death. But such a fighter. If she could only find him in time, explain his real target.

She broke from the magician and pushed herself into running, towards the split pine. The bruising didn't stop her, only made it hurt.

412

'Where are you going?' Daroguerre called.

'Toilet!' she shouted back.

It wrenched her to leave Orc. But the warrior boy might be important, and the running, the pain, the action, drove away the chance to think about what had just happened, the madness and terror of it.

Over rocks and roots, around trees and along goat-tracks: the boy had left no obvious trail, but she'd heard Daroguerre's directions to his men. The north coast, where the island was widest. Perhaps a mile from the Spiral. The pines were mostly old and large, and their shade prevented undergrowth – a camp would be easy to spot.

Even downhill, the run was agony on her bruised leg. She wasn't used to running, or judging how far or how long. Down-slope to her right, she glimpsed the sea. Nearly there.

The first gunshot stopped her dead. The second brought a groan from her. The third dropped her to her knees.

From only a short distance ahead, the noise of death kept coming.

♋

Hana focused on her breathing, soothing the impatience that would only delay her. When ready, she visualised the meadow behind the stable at her uncle's farm: before the hay was cut, that time of flowers and warm evenings, the setting for childhood games. Holding away the more troubling memories, keeping an awareness of the tattoos pricking her face, she walked in her imagination barefoot through the long grasses.

Instinct made her turn, to see Hare's black-tipped ears showing above the seed-heads. He raced off, and she ran after him.

They flattened a great ring in the meadow, then a five-pointed star within it, never going over the same part twice. When it was done, Hana sat opposite Hare in the pentacle's centre, and looked into the wide, strange eyes that showed through the holes of his bone mask. Love filled her; a wild thrill of nerves shuddered through her; the world shifted. Taking her eyes from Hare's, she saw a path of darker grass leading away from the pentacle, sign of an underground stream. Hare set off lolloping along it; Hana hurried behind. The grass of her old home changed to maritime pine forest, and soon she saw the Spiral ahead – if it could still be thought of as that place.

A wide chasm now divided it from the surrounding soulscape, a gap crossed only by a bridge of rope and planks. The standing stones lining the chasm's inner edge had become great columns, curving like ribs to meet far overhead. Against the far side of the circle was a building, in marbled shades of purple and red and black, and in front of its portico stood a statue that was clearly Orc. But between this figure and the end of the rope-bridge, Three-Eyes crouched: breasts bared, face vigilant as a hawk.

Hana lowered herself beside Hare. She stroked his trembling haunches, willing him calm. At this distance they were safe, even from that third eye.

'What's happened here?'

'The magician fears attack from the soul-world,' said Hare. 'He protects himself with the chasm and the dome. His palace is built of his pride.'

'Fears attack? From me?'

Hare made a little cough. 'I think not, child.'

Hana looked for another way across the chasm, but it was far wider than she could jump without launching into complete fantasy, which would compromise the reality of the scape and therefore its effects. She peered at the statue. The stone Orc wore a robe, and a crown shaped as the sun's rays, which seemed to confirm what Cass had said. He stared down at something near his feet.

'What can we do?'

'The magician's palace will contain his secrets,' said Hare.

'But how do we get there?' Her previous scaping on the island had been to investigate its distant past; she'd never faced obstacles created by another's will.

'Something comes!' squeaked Hare.

'An idea?' said Hana.

414

'Oh, Mother!' he whimpered.

His tone unsettled her. 'Hare, what—'

'It arrives!' he squealed.

A figure flashed into appearance at the Spiral's edge: red as fire, armoured in scales and mask. It held aloft a huge sword that darkened the air around its blade.

With a many-voiced yell, it struck for the statue of Orc, but Three-Eyes darted to intercept. A whirling battle began. Hana had no idea what was going on, but saw her chance.

'She's distracted. Come on.'

She started towards the bridge, but Hare didn't move. His staring fear of Three-Eyes threatened to infect her again. She couldn't let it – this might be the most important thing she ever did. Steeling herself to punch through her fear, she darted back and picked up Hare by the scruff.

'Unhand me!' he squealed. 'The indignity!'

She ran, hugging him to her chest. Three-Eyes was firmly occupied with the red nightmare. Single-focused, Hana raced across the bridge and onto the Spiral. As she passed the statue of Orc, she saw that the object of its gaze was a tissue-thin picture of a woman's face, which covered a pit of snakes.

All these things needed time to meditate on, but not now. She ran into the palace. The walls of the dim, cold entrance hall were mirrors of stone, lined with statues of Daroguerre. Three doorways pierced the far wall.

Straight away, Hana felt the threat of being observed.

'Check the middle one,' whispered Hare. 'But child, be careful.'

Hana crept beside the second doorway and peered in. Within was an even greater hall. At its far end, on a dais, a robed figure hunched over a bowl. Dread pricked her: the magician's head was a skull, his hands bones. His cloak was made of skins and faces, mouths and eyes wide in fixed, silent terror. Near the hem, one still lived, barely: a young woman in naval uniform.

'His attention is taken by the battle,' whispered Hare. 'We may enter the other rooms, if we are careful.'

The left doorway led to a picture gallery, all its frames empty apart from one resting against the base of the far wall. Hana hunkered to look. The painting showed a mountain of snow and ice, but stained with blood. Peering closer, she perceived the tiny figure of an aged man, flailing helplessly in the red slush. Flies swarmed around him, their buzzing coming faint from the picture. She shifted Hare into a one-armed hold and reached—

'Don't!' squeaked Hare.

'Who is he?' She withdrew her hand.

'This magician sets many snares,' said Hare. 'Quickly: the last room. Time escapes us.'

Within the right-hand doorway was a jumble of crates and boxes, and two cages.

Yes: the larger cage held an otter. The creature lay on the cage floor, eyes opened, but unresponsive. She felt suddenly doubtful. If this were *the* Otter, wouldn't he have a mask like Hare's? But it had to be Orc's: too great a coincidence otherwise.

She tapped the cage bars, without effect. 'Greetings,' she said. Its whiskers twitched. 'Can you talk to it?' she asked Hare.

'In what language?'

The cage had a door, but it was locked. The keyhole was strangely shaped, resembling a three-lobed leaf. Or, it struck Hana, three leaf-shaped eyes that met.

'Have you seen the other cage?' said Hare.

She'd thought it empty, but now saw it held a small brown bird.

'Sparrow…?'

'Quickly!' said Hare. 'The battle ends.'

'Can that be *the* Sparrow?'

'Child, we must leave!'

'Whose can she be?'

'Before we're noticed!'

'Why doesn't she fly out? The bars are wide enough.'

'*Child!*'

'Sparrow!' hissed Hana. 'Fly out – come with us!'

Hare tried to kick free of her arms.

'Hare!' she urged hoarsely. 'It's worth taking the chance. I might have to break myself out of the scape, but I'm not that deep.' She checked, and with little mental shifting felt the Navel's ground under her material body, its air on her skin.

And heard voices.

For a moment she thought they might be in the palace, then realised they were external. She found it difficult to keep aware of them without being pulled from the scape. Two men were walking north through the forest, perhaps fifty yards away, already past the Navel. If they carried on, she wouldn't be seen. Nevertheless, it disturbed her. Rulanza had promised Ferman that his men would use only the cove and the lookout point and the trail between, unless absolutely necessary.

When the voices had faded, she focused back on the room.

'Child,' whispered Hare, 'now the battle is over, we must take great care, or the magician will sense us.'

'As I said, the worst is that I break out.'

'No – if you fail to exit by the proper means, you'll leave a piece of your soul here.'

As Geist had warned her. 'A small piece.'

'But here! If you leave it here, then *he* will have it. Child, you have no idea what he will do with even a small piece.'

She shuddered, suddenly convinced. 'Back to the bridge?'

'If we can.'

She crept back through the hall. Outside, Three-Eyes once again stood at the near end of the bridge, facing outwards on guard.

And yes, a key hung from her belt.

But the satisfaction of seeing it was nothing next to the chill the Precious Night Sister sent creeping into Hana's guts. Despite Hare's warning, she felt strongly tempted to return her mind straight back to her body.

'What do we do? We're trapped.'

'Squeeze me,' whispered Hare.

She cuddled him tighter, his furry heart-beating heat against her skin.

'The warmth of your bosom gives me courage,' said Hare. 'Set me down.'

Trusting him despite her misgivings, she did so.

'One thing to be said for fear,' said Hare from the ground. 'It lends fervour to one's legs.'

Before she could ask what he meant, he bolted straight at Three-Eyes. It was too late to shout. Just as he reached her, Hare swerved aside and brushed the guardian's heels before racing off around the edge of the Spiral.

Three-Eyes leapt into pursuit. The monster would catch him, Hana was certain. Hare had sacrificed himself for her. Appalled, she nevertheless took the chance he'd given her and sprinted for the bridge. She didn't stop until she was well past its other end. Then she made herself turn, terrified she'd see Hare torn apart.

He ran straight past her, zig-zagging across the dirt. 'Quick! Farther!'

They didn't stop until they reached the grassy pentacle. There, Hana took a minute to mentally emphasise her distance from the Spiral, making sure no trace of herself remained there.

'I thought she'd catch you,' she said, when convinced she was safe. 'Was it because she was carrying that heavy shield?'

'No,' said Hare, washing his ears.

'Or was she tired from that battle?'

'She does not tire.'

'Was it because there was only one of her this time, not three?'

'Child,' said Hare, 'we were tricksters all, but some played more subtle tricks than others. Did you truly think those sisters could have caught *me*, even burdened as I was with the fiery brand, had I not let them?'

Hana groaned mentally. Was that a throwaway boast, or something she needed to unpick?

'Since you're so good at subtle tricks,' she said, 'how do we get the key to Otter's cage? I assume that's what we have to do?'

She started at noise. It came again: gunfire, some distance from the hollow. She damped the mental shock so it didn't pull her from trance. The shots came at short, regular intervals. She imagined a rifle being reloaded and fired quickly.

Then six shots with a slightly different sound, more rapid still. Then nothing.

Her heart beat too fast. She struggled to return her focus to the scape. Were the men she'd heard before hunting goats?

No more shots came, and she tried to calm herself back into her previous state. But the noise had so disturbed her, it took minutes of meditation to return properly. 'What can we do now?' she finally asked Hare. 'To get the key?'

'She will not relinquish it,' said Hare. 'And neither of us is nimble enough to steal it.'

'But we can't get it by force. Even that red monster couldn't beat her, whatever it was. Hare?'

He was breathing heavily, haunches like a furry bellows, eyes staring wild.

'Hare...?'

'Mother!' he squealed. 'Something very *ill* is happening! The guns. Child, you must stop it, but beware. *Beware!*'

The first sailor had been killed beside the tent. Cass couldn't tell at first quite what she was looking at, until she realised the man had been cleaved from shoulder to groin. It was Pisaro, who'd escorted her to the cove the day before. Opened. So much stuff kept locked up under pressure.

Don't think. Keep on.

The thin sailor, Mord, was twenty paces up-slope, and so was the Thangkaran boy in black. The sword had cut off Mord's left arm and then embedded itself in his side. Mord's rifle lay discarded among spent brass; his hand still clutched a revolver. The boy lay motionless on his back a few feet away, his vivid red hand out-thrown. Cass was sure it hadn't been red when he'd first attacked Orc, nor when she'd grabbed him.

Not that it mattered now. So much for her hoped-for ally.

Giving Pisaro's corpse a wide berth, she checked the crude shelter. The smoky gloom contained an old, bald man, also Thangkaran, cloaked in feathers. The Watcher. His hands made small movements; he uttered small noises.

A groan made her turn.

The boy was moving. Barely. He lifted his head to look at her, then dropped it back with a sound of pain that was hideous, almost animal.

She went to him, her insides like water, afraid she would have to tend him as he died in agony. His breath seethed between clenched teeth; saliva bubbled over his lips. His outfit made it hard to tell where he'd been shot: it was all black, and large parts were wet with blood. It looked as much an instrument of torture as armour, especially the heavy collar strap.

Her eyes shied from the strange metallic redness of his hand, to his face – the least horrible thing about him, despite the dried blood down one side. No longer contorted by hate, his features would have been pleasant if not twisted by pain: something like Ranga's, but with the slight femininity of male adolescence. It seemed insane to Cass that he could be so young, so far from home, so able to use such a heavy-looking sword.

He hadn't moved again, only breathed. She hoped he'd lost consciousness and would stop living soon. He was beyond help, and beyond helping her.

He groaned again. 'Please…' It seemed to cost all his strength. He swallowed with difficulty, and moved his head – to ease the constriction of his collar, perhaps. She could give him that comfort at least.

She knelt beside him. 'Here.' She took hold of the throat-buckle.

His red hand snapped onto hers. She tried to pull back, but couldn't. '*Help me.*'

'I am,' she said, scared. 'If you'll—'

He moved her hand, forcibly pushing it between two chest-straps, one of them pierced by a bullet hole. The cloth underneath was hot and wet. She was terrified that he would want her to somehow extract the bullet with her fingers, that he hoped she could save him.

He held her hand there, and his other hand came over and pressed down on it. His body squirmed; his back arched, and he let out a long hiss of what she at first thought was pain, but which began to sound almost ecstatic.

'Does that help?' She couldn't keep the tremble from her voice.

He pulled her now-bloodied hand out, and worked it beneath the leather on his stomach. Again he pressed her hand down hard against himself, his abdominal wall frantic with breathing. Again came his disturbing reaction. She tried not to mind, if it eased his passing.

Except that now he sat up: still breathing hard, but no longer in obvious pain. He released her hand. She pushed to her feet and stepped back as he got first onto his knees, then his feet. He crouched over Mord's corpse and wrenched his sword free. She didn't understand how, not with two bullets in him.

'You should rest. You're hurt.'

She jumped back as he casually swung the sword at her. She tripped onto her backside, scrambled up. 'I'm a friend! A friend.'

He didn't press the attack, but his eyes were mad. 'YOU SAVED THE MAGICIAN.'

His voice shocked her, its volume, its throat-tearing harshness.

'I *saved* my – whatever-he-is. Wait!'

He'd started off, stumbling, trying to run.

'You think Orc's the magician?' She caught up, her leg hurting.

'WE SHALL DESTROY THEM ALL.'

'This is mad! You're wrong, it's Daroguerre. And you can't go back: he's ordered thirty men there. You'll be killed.'

'WE ARE THE MATCH OF ANY FOE.'

'*We*—?' He was insane, she realised. And injured. At his halting rate, the Sundarans would reach the Spiral before him. He'd survived two bullets, somehow, but ten, or twenty…

'You have to listen! Daroguerre's the only magician. We can defeat him, together.'

He stopped dead – hit, she hoped, by a bolt of sense – and turned to her.

'YOU MUST TOUCH THIS BODY.'

'What?' She stepped back. 'I just – wait – back there, I just wanted to help you.'

He came towards her. 'YOU ARE THE CONDUIT FOR THE PERFECTION OF FLESH.'

'I don't…' She backed up further.

'EMBRACE.'

She turned and ran, desperately pushing through the pain of her hip. For a few panicked steps the boy sounded only inches behind, then he started to fall back, hampered by his own injuries. Cass had almost reached the tent and the sailors' bodies before she realised that carrying on west along the shore would only take her farther from help.

Bracing her will against the effort, she turned hard up the slope, hoping the boy's sword would slow him enough to stop him catching her.

Fatigue and hurt and the steepness of the climb cramped her pace to barely faster than a walk. Her lungs couldn't cope. A frantic glance showed her she'd gained forty yards.

'Cass!'

She looked wildly. Hana was running down and across the slope towards her. Her clothes looked thrown on.

'Cass, are you all right?'

She pushed herself onwards. 'Boy following,' she gasped, barely able to coordinate speech and breath. 'Attacked Orc, thought he was Daroguerre. He's mad.'

Hana joined her, keeping pace alongside her, looking behind. 'Attacked Orc at the Spiral? What happened?'

'Hawk-woman thing,' said Cass, stumbling on a rock. 'Appeared.'

'*Manifested*? Mother. And that boy's hand, that red one?'

'Don't know,' panted Cass. 'Won't leave me alone. Came on that ship, with a monk – in a tent down there, trapped like Orc is. Daroguerre did it.'

'They're against Daroguerre?'

'Yes, but – he's insane.'

'He invoked something. I saw it.'

Hana halted, turned. Cass gasped to a stop. 'What are you doing?'

'What is it you want?' called Hana down to the boy.

He slowed, as though sizing up an enemy.

'WE KNOW YOU.'

'I don't think so,' said Hana.

'NAKED WITCH GIRL.'

'I… what?'

'YOU SEDUCED HIM, AND SO HIS OLD MASTER WAS TAKEN.' The voice burned with rage. 'BUT WE CURED HIS WEAKNESS AND FEAR. YOUR POWER IS GONE.'

He truly was mad, Cass realised. His words made no sense. She prepared herself for the agony of further running.

'Your master,' said Hana. 'In the tent down there?' She glanced round; Cass nodded. 'We might be able to help, but you have to come back to yourself.'

'HE WILL NOT RETURN TO WEAKNESS. HE WILL ACHIEVE PERFECTED FLESH.'

'You think your master would want you like this?'

'IT MATTERS NOT WHAT THAT AGED WEAKLING WANTS. WE ARE THIS NOVITIATE'S MASTERS NOW, AGELESS AND STRONG.'

'You are not masters here!' Hana held out her palm as though to forbid him. 'This island is sacred to the Mother.'

'NOT OUR MOTHER, WHORE.'

'But his: the boy you inhabit.'

Hideous laughter erupted from his throat. 'YOU WASTE YOUR BREATH. IF HE EVER HAD ONE, HE DOES NOT REMEMBER HER.'

He came faster up the slope. Hana turned and ran past Cass. 'Come on!'

Cass forced her burning legs to move. 'Where?'

'Navel. Energy there might help.'

'No! The cove – Sundarans there, guns.'

'He's on our side,' gasped Hana. 'We have to try.'

Cass almost sobbed with the effort of following. Her mouth was dust, her clothes soaked. Just as she started to think collapsing and awaiting her fate could be no worse than this agony, the slope eased, and ahead were the stones guarding the Navel.

She stumbled down into the hollow to where Hana already stood with her eyes closed and her brows tensed. Cass looked at the cave. If she could get in there before the boy came…

Too late: he stood up there, by the stones. Hana turned to face him.

'Cass, do you know his name?'

'Yes, because of course I asked.' She readied herself to move. Maybe her legs had enough left to scramble up the slope behind her.

Hana drew herself erect. '*This*,' she declared to the now-stilled boy, 'is the place of the Mother. She has the power here. And she has lent it to me.'

Cass thought she sensed, as before, the heaviness of the air in the hollow. Some of it seemed to have got into Hana's voice.

'EMPTY WORDS,' said the boy.

'All words are empty before the truth of the Mother.' Hana's unnatural strength of voice almost matched the boy's. 'She comes from before words. She is the dark warmth your body remembers, even if your mind does not.' She held her arms open. 'This is the place of joining with the Mother. Let my arms be hers.'

What? thought Cass. 'What are you doing?' But the boy spoke over her question.

'YOU SEEK TO SEDUCE HIM.'

'She might have been my age when she gave birth,' said Hana. 'Won't you meet her again, through me? Your journey has been hard on you. You've been hurt and afraid. Those you called into yourself have taken away one kind of fear – but they can't take away your *real* fear, can they?'

The boy's eyes tightened with fury. He started down the slope.

'Run!' cried Cass.

'Keep behind me,' said Hana. 'Far as you can.'

'You're joking! *Run!*'

'Not from him,' came Hana's charged voice.

Cass backed towards the cave. She couldn't leave Hana; she didn't know if her exhausted legs would obey her anyway.

'You have entered the Mother's place!' said Hana, as the boy approached. 'I command your possessors to leave before they harm you further.'

'WE SAVE HIM FROM FEAR AND WEAKNESS, THE THINGS YOU SEEK TO EXPLOIT.'

'It's normal for a child to be weak. There's no shame in a child being afraid.'

'HE IS NO *CHILD*, BITCH MOTHER OF A MILLION MAGGOTS.' The boy raised his sword. 'HE IS A WARRIOR, A NOVITIATE!'

He sprang. Cass cried out, but Hana had already moved; she ducked to one side and threw herself forward to roll beneath and past the boy's charging attack. He screamed in anger. Hana came back onto her feet to face him again.

Hana's agility amazed Cass, but the sword had missed only by inches. And now the boy was between them. He looked at Cass, started towards her.

'YOU MUST PERFECT THIS FLESH.'

'Behind me!' shouted Hana.

Cass ran, stumbling. Hana quickly interposed herself.

'Your body is already perfect,' Hana told the boy. 'It is warm and tender, made to give and receive love. It remembers my touch from long ago.'

He barked out a fractured laugh. 'SEDUCTRESS, YOU ARE BLATANT.'

Hana spread her arms again, her knees slightly bent. 'Your body knows the comfort it needs, as all children do.'

'HE IS *NOT* A CHILD!'

The boy rushed again. Hana dodged left. The boy swung the same way. Cass gasped, but Hana's dodge had been a feint – she threw herself to the right, and the sword struck the ground. With a howl of frustration, the boy turned. Once more they stood face to face, three yards separating them. Hana swept hair out of her eyes.

This time, Cass moved without being told. But the boy seemed to have forgotten her anyway; his gaze was fixed on Hana.

Again, she opened her arms. 'You see? You cannot hurt me. Deep down, you have no wish to.'

The boy kept his sword ready, his face a tight mix of fear and fury.

'I didn't seduce you,' said Hana. 'But if you wish to be held, I wish to hold you.'

He stepped back.

'Don't run,' she said. 'You don't have to be afraid.'

'We don't fear you!' he shouted. 'We are strength!'

Hana stepped towards him. 'You don't need them. You are stronger than their hate.'

'Witch girl! Whore! I *killed* those men! I'll kill you!'

Cass could hardly breathe with the strain on the boy's face. This time Hana looked to have abandoned her preparedness for another strike, and the boy's tension showed every possibility of one. But Cass didn't dare move, in case it broke that tension into violence. The damp air in the hollow clung to her skin.

Hana took another slow step towards the boy. 'They're gone.' Another step. 'You drove them out yourself.' Another. 'In the end, you couldn't bear them to hurt me.'

'I'll call them back!' he yelled, sword raised. 'I *will*!'

His muscles tensed. He looked terrified, but the hate was less, and Cass suddenly remembered his face as he'd been dying, the basic niceness of it.

'Beloved one!' she shouted, as Daroguerre's words leapt to her mind.

'Be true to yourself!'

The moment's silence that followed snapped in a wail of release and horror almost too loud for human voice. The boy staggered back, fell, scrambled up. Still clutching his sword, he ran up the slope and past the guardian stones.

Cass sank down as the last strength in her legs melted.

'Wait!' she cried, as Hana ran after the boy. 'Where the hell?'

Her body hated her for it, but she went after them. Cresting the lip, she caught one glimpse of Hana disappearing between two distant trees down-slope. She was halfway there when a scream froze her. It came again, a howl of anguish.

The barely human cries broke up as she approached their source. She found the two of them kneeling, arms around each other, the boy sobbing into Hana's chest as though his soul were being torn to pieces. His sword, still red with human blood, lay several yards away where he'd flung it.

31

RESCUE PLAN

Cass sat behind a tree and allowed the dam to break on all her tight-wound stress. A rush of sobbing joined with the sound of the boy's hacking misery. By the time it had subsided, leaving her calmer, he'd quietened too. She wondered what had happened, but she made no move to find out before Hana came and found her.

'He's gone back to Shoggu. His master.'

Cass wiped her eyes. 'He's all right? The boy?'

'Tashi, his name is,' said Hana. 'And yes, I think so. For now.' She swallowed. 'Cass, I have to ask you something.'

The tone worried her. 'Uh-huh?'

'Who *are* you?'

She choked down panic. 'What do you mean?'

'Tashi's hand. His skin… it feels like living metal. And I checked the two places he was shot. The same.'

'Oh God,' she gasped. 'That's where—' She didn't dare say it.

'He told me. Where you touched him.'

The fragile equilibrium restored by her release of tears began to crumble. 'But how? What does it mean?'

'You don't know?'

'No!'

'But it's why Daroguerre brought you, isn't it?' said Hana. 'It must be. It's how he regained that lost Zhenaii art. The gods know how, but you can manifest thought-forms.'

Cass shook her head firmly. 'They brought us to dive, to get the artefacts – and the stone. It's the stones that manifest things.'

'Stone?'

'Orc brought it up from the ziggurat. A focus-stone. Daroguerre has it.'

Hana pulled a blue crystal from under her wrist-guard. 'Like this?'

'Yes. But ten, twenty times bigger.'

Hana whistled. 'That's what he was holding?'

'Orc caused a manifestation a few days ago,' said Cass, 'because of his own stone, his small one. And when he went near the elemental on the ship, the thing got bigger.'

'You're sure that was the stone, and not him?'

'The elemental didn't get—' But she checked herself in alarm. What if Mr Burns *had* grown when she'd gone down first? And Thera hadn't told her?

'Sorry, Cass, it can't be the stones, or not just them. You don't have one, but you changed Tashi by touching him.'

'*How*, though?' said Cass, struggling with the horror of it. 'Why would that happen?'

'Because he was possessed, I think. He lost control of an entity he'd invoked, and it tried to force its way through into the world. As to the… science, you're *sure* you've no idea about this? There's nothing you know about that could explain it?'

Cass shook her head helplessly.

'Did Geist, do you think?'

She felt as she had at Amano's farm, in those weeks before Orc's Initiation: the piling on of impossibilities, reality fracturing.

'You're wrong,' she said. 'About me. Maybe he was so possessed it broke through anyway. Maybe the whole world's breaking down, or this island is. One thing I do know, we're not getting anywhere chatting.'

'Hm,' said Hana. 'I said we'd try to help retrieve Shoggu.'

'We have time for that?'

'It'll be worth it if he can help us. Come on.'

As they set off, Cass saw Tashi's sword still lying where he'd dropped it. Nearby were piled the leather straps that had formed his armour. 'So whatever's possessed him is gone now?'

'Maybe not completely,' said Hana. 'But I hope he won't let them in again. He left his sword and armour: that must be a good sign.'

'Not if we need him to fight,' said Cass.

To her relief, Pisaro's body had been dragged away from the tent. Tashi, now wearing a simple grey uniform and with his hand wrapped in a bandage, had opened up the shelter, and knelt before the monk, chanting in a low voice. The old man, Shoggu, still muttered, eyes twitching behind their lids. Cass now saw he held a painting.

Tashi was so focused on his chant, he seemed not to notice their approach until they reached him. Then he broke off and faced them. 'Help him,' he rasped. 'Please.'

'I'll try,' said Hana. 'But it will mean you trusting me. I understand that might be scary.'

'It is the flesh that fears.' He spoke as though parroting a mouthful of broken words. 'I attacked wrongly,' he said to Cass. 'I thought Orc was the magician. I was lied to.'

She said nothing back.

Hana hunkered beside Shoggu, and asked Tashi how this 'dark-flight' had happened. To Cass, some of Tashi's explanation seemed garbled, but the story of how he and Shoggu had found the painting in a Torrento hotel was clear enough. What Daroguerre had done to the museum curator made her recoil inside. She felt unclean to think she'd even spoken with the man.

'She was bleeding from the vagina?' said Hana. 'And the writing on the floor, you're sure it said "The Great Mother of Death"?'

'It is seared on my mind,' said Tashi, sounding almost ashamed.

'In my scape, I saw Shoggu caught in that picture,' Hana said.

'Maybe Daroguerre's used the contamination to trap him: there was blood, and flies. But the blood on it was associated with the Mother, in a perverse way, and I think she might be able to help us.'

'The Witch Mother?' said Tashi, clearly suspicious.

'That's not what I call her,' said Hana. 'But we can stand around arguing theology if you like. A pity Shoggu can't join in.' She indicated where Tashi was kneeling. 'May I?'

He stared at her, took a deep breath, then stood and moved aside. Hana knelt in his place. She reached towards the painting.

'Don't!' whispered Tashi. 'The shock might kill him.'

'He won't feel it,' Hana said, and gently touched the icon with her fingertips. After half a minute of closed-eyed focus, she spoke. 'Mother, this blood, this perverse distortion of the cycle of fertility, was attributed to You, and so was placed within Your power. It was insulting and hurtful to You. Remove its perversion. Clean it, make it natural, in this painting and in all paintings that are this painting, through all worlds that are You.'

After a short pause, she repeated the incantation, though with a few words changed. Then she spoke yet another slight variation – as though she were trying a ring of similar-looking keys in a lock, Cass thought. It felt like some of the damp, pressured air from the Navel had found its way down here. She imagined the surrounding pines listening, judging. She scanned the slope, worried Daroguerre might send other men, either to find out what had happened to Pisaro and Mord, or to find her. 'Tashi,' she whispered. 'If this works, we have to move from here. What do you need to take?'

He nodded at this, and began gathering supplies into a pack, though with half an eye still on Hana. Cass fetched Pisaro's rifle, then went up the slope and got Mord's too, also taking the cartridges she found in the pouch at his waist. With Hana's voice a background murmur, she set about figuring out how the rifle worked, then practised loading and aiming, trying various positions and concentrating on keeping the sight still. Without firing, which might be heard from the Spiral, it was limited as training; but it kept her active and moving, and she needed that, despite her tiredness. She needed to keep from her mind the fact that she could manifest thought-forms. The strain of it was like a spring being wound inside her. And the waiting. If Hana couldn't do anything before noon, she assumed Daroguerre would go ahead, even without herself to officiate at priestess. He might prefer to have her help, but Orc's presence would likely be enough.

The ceasing of Hana's prayer made her turn. The islander stood and allowed Tashi back. The boy started his soft chant again.

Had Hana given up?

Cass shouldered both rifles by their straps and walked back down to Hana. She drew her away a little so as not to disturb Tashi's rhyme. 'Did it work?' she whispered. 'You didn't do your tattoos.'

'I didn't scape, as such,' Hana said. 'I appealed to the Mother to clean the painting.'

'And did she?' said Cass. The image in Shoggu's hands looked as bloodied as before.

'Not literally, of course,' said Hana. 'To be honest, I've never tried anything like this, but the principles are sound. I focused on the Mother removing the associations contaminating the blood, and I think it's those associations keeping Shoggu trapped in the soulscape. In cleaning this one, I'm hoping the Mother cleaned the one in Daroguerre's palace too. Make sense?'

'Not… as such.'

Hana face-shrugged. 'Well, we can but wait.'

'For how long?' whispered Cass.

Before Hana could answer, Tashi cried out: 'Master!'

Shoggu was moving his head, his eyes. Tashi took the painting from him and held the monk's hands.

'Bloody hell,' whispered Cass, and touched Hana's arm. 'You did it. You broke Daroguerre's trap.'

'So it seems.'

'And if it worked with Shoggu…'

'Then Orc has a chance,' said Hana tightly. 'Especially if Shoggu helps.'

Cass drew a deep breath. 'We need to get somewhere safer first.'

It took a couple of minutes for Shoggu to come round to the point where he could grasp what had happened, and their situation. Tashi took off his master's feather mantle, quickly packed it away, then squatted down so the still-weak monk could clamber stiffly onto his back. 'Bring that pack,' he told the others.

Cass and Hana had to carry it between them. Hana guided them westwards and slightly up the slope, to a hollow she knew of: less deep than the one at the Navel, but where they should hear any approach before being seen themselves. While Tashi got his master settled, Cass went back with Hana to collect the shelter. They hadn't quite reached the camp when Hana put her hand on Cass's shoulder. The tension in it stopped her at once.

They crouched, in time to see three Sundaran marines come down the slope from the other direction. One exclaimed loudly, seeing the bodies. The men looked around wildly, rifles raised. Cass couldn't make out the hurried discussion that followed, but it led to the marines retreating towards the Spiral.

'Forget the shelter,' whispered Hana. 'Back to the others.'

'Tashi's handiwork must've given them a scare,' said Cass as they went back, both keeping half an eye over their shoulders. 'Let's hope they stay away.'

'Let's hope Daroguerre doesn't send a whole platoon,' said Hana.

Shoggu got stiffly to his feet as they reached the hollow. 'From what my novitiate has told me, we are not natural allies,' he said. 'But I am grateful for my deliverance. I understand we fight a common foe.'

'We do,' said Hana. 'And the fight's barely started.'

The four of them sat and talked, with Tashi positioned so he could see over the lip of the hollow. It turned out he had already told his master about the hawk-faced woman at the Spiral, and he and Shoggu had assumed Three-Eyes to be the extent of Daroguerre's blasphemous ambition. The revelation that the magician aimed to manifest a goddess-form wrote shock on their faces. Cass described some of her and Orc's place in Daroguerre's scheme, the symbolic roles he meant them to play – but she said nothing about them being keys to the door between the psychosphere and the material world. To her relief, Hana hadn't mentioned it, and Shoggu didn't press to know how manifestation worked. Cass guessed Tashi had told his master nothing about what lay beneath his bandage or his shirt.

When Cass had finished, Shoggu nodded. 'I know something of this ritual that Daroguerre plans. I have seen it.'

'Seen it?' said Cass. 'Where?'

'In dark-flight,' said Shoggu. 'Though I could not escape the travesty of the Holy Mountain on which the magician trapped me, my link to him was never wholly broken, and when his mind was drawn elsewhere, I was able to perceive some of his uppermost concerns. Several times I beheld a clouded vision of what I now think to be a magical tableau. From what I understand, magicians sometimes prepare the ground this way, so that when they finally perform their magic, reality can slip more easily into the pattern already established in the Immaterium.'

Hana nodded. 'And what was in it?'

'The magician himself stood with a priestess, and a king – Cass here, and Orc, as I now know. The magician handed a crystal knife to the priestess, which she then gave to the king. I sensed that to the king, the knife had great meaning: valuable knowledge, but also sacrifice. As soon as he touched it, he was irretrievably lost.'

Cass pressed her hands to her head. 'We knew that already.'

'Not quite, we didn't,' said Hana. 'The crystal knife is the focus-stone, yes? We didn't know Daroguerre was going to make you give Orc the knife. I can see why he wants to: it fits with how the ritual must have been done in ancient times. But it might be his weakness.'

'How?'

'The moment he gives up the stone, he'll detach himself from its powers and lose some of his connection to the psychosphere. That includes Three-Eyes. If she weakens, it'll be easier to steal the key she wears and free Otter from his cage. That might restore Orc.'

'But isn't this all in your imagination?' said Cass, dismayed by Hana's lack of certainty. 'What stops you making the key fly to your hand, or making yourself find it on the floor?'

Hana shook her head. 'Actions in the soulscape are metaphors for the use of power. The key is a symbol for some power Three-Eyes has over Otter – and until I know just what, I have to work with the key as it is. If you don't treat the soulscape as more-or-less real, if you wilfully cheat, then you don't focus your power correctly and won't change anything. I know that much, but I've got almost no experience of working with power. It's a lot more complex than divination.'

'You rescued Shoggu just now, didn't you? And I'm sure he'll want to express his gratitude by helping.'

Hana gasped. 'Cass!'

'Bollocks to tact, there's no time.' She turned to Shoggu. 'Your Holiness or whatever, my cousin is going to get killed at noon. You have to think of a way to help us.'

'He can't fly again,' said Tashi. 'Not after what he's been through.'

'Which *we* rescued him from.'

Shoggu raised his hand for quiet. 'It would be unwise for me to fly again. But where only foolishness hopes to succeed, sometimes wisdom must be set aside.'

'Then you'll help?' said Cass.

'Where I can,' said Shoggu. 'But I have no experience at all in "working with power", as Hana puts it, and only a little theoretical knowledge.'

'But you clearly have psychic ability,' said Hana.

'To divine truth in service to Gevurah is one thing. To use one's own power subliminally, in an attempt to change reality, is anathema to my order.'

'To my college too,' said Hana. 'But when people like Daroguerre try to change the world by manipulating the psychosphere, don't we have to take the fight to them there?'

'That is sorcery,' said Tashi. 'Do not try to seduce a Watcher of Highcloud into such a thing, witch-girl.'

'How the *hell* do you have the balls to talk to her like that?' said Cass. 'She risked her life for you. She almost got cut to pieces – by *you*, remember – and you thank her by calling her names? And how do you think she rescued your master? By magic! Haven't you got that into your thick head yet?'

'He would have been freed with the magician's death.'

'You wouldn't have got near him!'

Tashi's face conflicted between shame and determination.

'You didn't tell me you fought this young woman,' said Shoggu.

'He fights everyone,' said Cass. 'Even if they're helpless.'

'Cass…' Hana touched her shoulder. But Cass ignored her: Hana hadn't been there at the Spiral. She flinched to remember Orc kneeling, as though waiting for the sword.

'I did fight Hana, master.' Tashi looked at the ground. 'The Lords of Holy Battle were enraged by her magic and her seduction.'

Cass snorted, but couldn't speak.

Shoggu looked troubled. 'This was after those two sailors…?'

Tashi nodded.

'And she caused the Lords to leave?'

'She played a trick.'

'I wouldn't call it that,' said Hana. 'And if they were "Holy", then… well.'

'Do not insult them!' said Tashi, his voice cracking with what sounded like suppressed panic. 'You have no right to even speak of them. They are the warriors of Gevurah, the *Elohim Gibor*. It is not for us to judge or understand them.'

Shoggu let out a trembling sigh. 'No, beloved one. She speaks the truth.'

'Master?'

'The tableau wasn't the only thing I learned from my contact with the magician's mind. You were also in his thoughts. Somehow, he knows the nature of what inhabits you. The… true nature.'

Tashi look struck by dread and horror. As though he'd already suspected, Cass thought.

'We will talk when we are alone,' Shoggu said to him.

Tashi nodded, his only movement.

'We'll go,' said Hana.

'If I can think of a way to help you, I shall,' said Shoggu. 'Within my limitations.'

'If there was ever a time to break through our limitations, it's now,' said Hana. 'But if you really can't do any more, at least pray for our success.'

'I shall,' said Shoggu. 'And I shall consider your words. They deserve no less, even coming from one I might have once considered an enemy. I thank you for what you have done for both of us.' He put his hands together before his face, and inclined his forehead to his fingertips. 'Gevurah's strength go with you.'

'Fat lot of use that was,' said Cass as she puffed after Hana, a rifle tight in her grip. 'We save their lives, and what do we get?'

'A warrior wouldn't be any use anyway,' said Hana. 'And we did get something. We found out exactly when we need to act.'

'So Daroguerre's going to give me the stone, and before I have to pass it to Orc, you've got to defeat Three-Eyes and get Otter out of his cage? And we hope this stops Orc sacrificing himself?'

'That's about it. So hold onto the stone as long as you can.'

'And how do you defeat Three-Eyes? What's your plan?'

'That's a bit vague at the moment.'

'*What?*'

'Daroguerre's organised his defences pretty well,' said Hana. 'He's separated the Spiral from the rest of the island: in the soulscape, I mean. There's only one bridge to it, and Three-Eyes guards the end of that bridge.'

'Oh, fantastic!' said Cass. 'I'm just going to shoot the bastard.'

'No!' said Hana. 'Even if we get away, where are we going to hide? What are thirty angry marines going to do to my parents?'

'Then give me some *hope*, Hana!' Her anger was partly at herself, Cass knew. And at Orc. Ever since *Nightfire* had left Torrento, they could hardly have served Daroguerre's interests better if he'd given them precise instructions.

As before, they sneaked onto the bluff that overlooked the Spiral. Perhaps twenty Sundaran marines stood guard just outside the stone circle, facing either the southern side where the trail came out, or the broken-pine arch. A group of others were by the far edge.

Orc hadn't moved. More artefacts cluttered the paving around him now, some still black with tarnish, no doubt those raised from the Great Ziggurat that morning. Esteban sat on a camp-chair by the smaller tent, but there was no sign of Daroguerre or Thera.

'No Three-Eyes either,' Cass pointed out.

'He must have dismissed her back to the psychosphere,' said Hana. 'That won't make my job any easier: it means she can't be distracted by anything happening in the material world.'

'I could just not go back?'

'If you don't take part in his tableau, that might weaken Daroguerre's conjuration, but he still has Orc. If you're not there, he'll pass the stone straight to him, and we've no chance.'

'What do you think the time is?'

'Eleven or so.'

Cass felt sick. An hour left, and they had next to nothing: a known window of opportunity, but no clear idea how to achieve their goal.

'What if I just throw the stone off the cliff when he gives it to me? That would buy us some time?'

'It might buy you a bullet,' said Hana. 'And it wouldn't reach the sea unless you can throw a couple of hundred feet. The cliffs there are too sloped.'

'It'd take ages for him to get it back, though?'

'True,' said Hana. 'I don't know if he'd delay the manifestation until he found it again, or if he has a reserve plan.' She shrugged. 'If it comes to it, it's up to you.'

Cass emptied the cartridges from her pocket and put them beside the rifle. 'You want this?'

'I'll leave it, thanks,' said Hana. 'Ferman tried to teach me to shoot in case of pirate attack, but I nearly did the pirates' work for them, in advance.'

Cass tried for a smile, but it was sucked down the drain in the pit of her stomach. There was nothing more to be said, no more plans to make. Leaving the gun, they crept away to the edge of the trail. They hugged, hard. Cass felt Hana as a mass of strong, solid warmth, and wished that meant something.

'See you when this is over,' Hana said. 'Hard to believe I've only known you three days.'

'Good luck,' said Cass. 'Kick that three-eyed bitch between the legs.'

Hana's eyebrows shaped a query. 'Good luck yourself. And remember, don't give Orc the stone while he's still under. I'll figure something out, I promise.' With that, she launched into a run back towards the Navel.

Cass headed for the Spiral along the trail, claws of dread digging into her lungs and heart. The Sundaran marines at the edge of Daroguerre's camp drew their rifle bolts. Cass approached slowly, arms raised.

'We were told to expect you,' said one.

As she walked onto the open space, Esteban rose from his camp-chair and intercepted her. Clearly Daroguerre's instruction to stay out of her sight no longer applied. That made her want to run.

'Where have you been?' he demanded.

She affected outrage. 'I was *upset!*' She suddenly found she didn't need to affect anything. 'Didn't they tell you what happened while you weren't here? You think I was supposed to just stand around and make small-talk after something like *that*?'

Any reply Esteban might have given was silenced by the flap of the large tent opening. Now she knew he'd ordered the killing and mutilation of a woman, Cass could see it in Daroguerre's face.

'Miss Strandborn. You were gone some time.'

'As I was just saying, I was upset by what happened. I needed to clear my head.'

'Yes, clearing one's head can be useful. Particularly when scrying.'

She tensed, wondering what he meant.

'I do not expect you to know much of such practices,' he went on. 'But did you not remember my saying I possessed such a skill?'

Fuck.

'Perhaps you thought I would be too busy? Indeed, my time would have been better occupied, but your extended "call of nature" led me to fear for your safety. And what did I find when the water in my scry-bowl finally cleared?'

'I don't know,' bluffed Cass. 'I thought divination wasn't reliable?'

'Is that what Geist told you? I have been practising it rather longer than he.'

'Whatever you think you saw, it's not true,' she said. 'I'm not against you. I want to help, for Martin. I was just upset.'

He smiled thinly. 'You should have stayed with your new friends, if you wanted to seriously inconvenience me. It turns out these marines are less biddable than the two incompetents I brought with me, and refused to risk a similar fate. Well, it's of no consequence now, despite your best intentions. The boy and his master have been left weak and ineffectual – they won't risk another Inspiration. And if the Quallace girl returns to that hollow she's so fond of, she'll find a nasty surprise awaiting her.'

Cass's breath caught. 'What surprise?'

'Ah, so she *is* returning there,' said Daroguerre. 'Not that I should be too harsh with her: like you, she's put months of work into aiding me, albeit unwittingly.' He turned to Esteban. 'You now have the tableau role of priestess guard. While Miss Strandborn is the priestess, you will treat her with the utmost respect, if you wish to live. If she behaves in any way unfitting for a priestess, then she forfeits her rank, and you may do with her as you desire.'

Cass chilled. 'Seriuz will kill you.'

'You think he'll throw over his country's adoration for the gratitude of a girl? Hold to that belief, if you wish. It might give you some comfort when—'

'Smoke!'

Cass turned with the others. The cry had come from a small group of marines at the eastern edge of the terrace. One had binoculars raised.

Daroguerre strode across to them. Cass followed, Esteban behind her. Her heart pounded with hope. If *Nightfire* was within sight, then Seriuz could be here in an hour. And whatever he'd done to Yorge and those other fisherman in anger, she was sure he wouldn't let any harm come to her or Orc: he couldn't have known what Daroguerre was planning.

But Seriuz had chased the cruiser north, and the marines were looking southeast.

The Sundaran lieutenant joined them at a run as they reached the edge. He took the glasses.

'What is it?' said Daroguerre, as the officer focused.

Nightfire, please. But there was more than one plume of smoke at the edge of sight, more than one shape on the horizon.

'It looks—' The officer had to clear his throat. 'A dreadnought, and four heavy cruisers.'

'Impossible!' said Daroguerre. 'Seriuz said three days.'

The officer passed him the glasses. 'Curse them to hell,' said Daroguerre, when he'd put them to his eyes. 'It must be coincidence. A naval exercise.'

'If they are here for us, our ships will be like ducks on the water.'

The officer's voice was steady, but Cass caught the tension in it. As Daroguerre kept peering through the lenses, she heard anxiety in the muttering of the other Sundarans.

'We must get a message to Captain Rulanza,' said the officer.

'If the Kurassians approach, his ships are to stay put,' said Daroguerre. 'If challenged, they are to surrender.'

The officer drew breath. 'The Commonwealth navy does not bare its belly like a dog.'

'Then it will be destroyed,' said Daroguerre. '*Barcuda* and *Tarpon* can neither outgun nor outrun a dreadnought.'

The officer spat. 'I do not wish to be held in an Empyreal prison and preached to about their devil's head. And you, magician – you they will execute.'

'You worry unnecessarily,' said Daroguerre. 'Even unopposed, it will take their men over an hour to land and get up here, and by then I'll have the means to destroy them and their ships.'

'To destroy their *ships*? Truly?'

'Every last rivet,' said Daroguerre, with a confidence Cass found terrifying.

The magician handed the glasses back to the officer, and turned to her. 'You and your cousin will soon play a part in a truly historical event, Miss Strandborn: the first destruction of an Empyreal dreadnought. And four cruisers into the bargain. We'll change the balance of power in the Southern Ocean at a stroke.'

Cass swallowed. 'And I'm supposed to think that makes Orc's death worth it?'

'Death? I suspect you of wilful misunderstanding. He won't die.'

'He's a sacrifice, I know that much.'

'There are other sacrifices than that of the body,' said Daroguerre. 'But in any case, the goddess now represents these men's only chance to avoid incarceration or death. Any attempt to sabotage this ceremony will anger them as much as me.'

Cass glanced at the marines, but only momentarily. Their eyes backed up Daroguerre's words.

'Now, enough chit-chat,' said Daroguerre. 'Your bag with your priestly nightdress is in the smaller tent. Don't disturb Thera. When you have changed, go to stand near your cousin, no closer than two paces. Esteban, see she obeys.'

Esteban grunted. Daroguerre returned to his tent. Esteban touched Cass on the arm, making her flinch. 'Do as he says, and no harm will come to you.'

Cold and sick, Cass entered the smaller tent. Thera knelt on a small rug, her eyes closed, in the robe she'd worn in *Nightfire*'s boiler room. The sight of it punched Cass in the stomach. She pulled her nightdress from the bag in the corner and changed behind Thera's back. Then, the garment on, words burst out of her.

'What a piece of luck you happened to be holding that robe when you *fell overboard*.'

Thera's shoulders visibly tensed.

'Do you desert everyone?' said Cass.

'I didn't have any choice.'

'Were you working for him all the time? Pretending to be my friend, what was that for? Trying to find something out about me?'

'Cass, please don't think that.'

'That time you invited me to see the boiler room, that wasn't for me, was it? That was for Daroguerre. Testing us. I bet Mister Burns got stronger when I was down there. But you made out it was just Orc, and because of his stone. Lies, and more lies.'

'You know about the manifesting?' said Thera. 'Look, I don't want you to get hurt. Just do what he says.'

'You don't want me to get hurt, but it's fine for Orc to be killed?'

'He won't be *killed*, Cass.'

'At least you and your boss have got your lies rehearsed.'

'But it's true. Daroguerre needs him alive. Orc will have the best care.'

Something about that phrase struck a chill through her. 'Care, why? What'll happen to him?'

'He won't be dead,' said Thera. 'Isn't that the important thing?'

'To his mind. What will happen to his mind?'

Thera didn't speak.

Irretrievably lost, Shoggu had said. 'Thanks for not denying it,' Cass said bitterly. 'Might be the one genuine thing you've done.'

'That's not fair.'

'Oh, fuck off, "fair".'

She made to leave, but Thera grabbed her. 'You don't understand what he can do,' she said. 'What he'll do to me if I don't please him.' Her voice lowered to a hoarse whisper. 'I can't even kill him. I need him to keep me alive. Please understand, I've never had any choice.'

'There's always the choice not to be a spineless worm.' Cass pulled free and walked out. She couldn't bear to hear any more excuses, whether there was truth in them or not. Conscious of how thin her nightdress was and how little it covered her – she almost cried to think she'd bought it in the hope that she might one day be free to provoke a young man's desire – she avoided the eyes of Esteban and the marines as she walked onto the spiral paving.

Orc knelt, motionless, helpless, amid a litter of ancient treasure he himself had collected, now arranged so as to aid his destruction. Cass felt as though the oppression and humidity of the air were concentrated around him, as though a thunderstorm were about to erupt in that confined space. She seemed to sense the hawk-faced woman from before, even though there was no visible sign of her. But there was also something bigger, vast, an energy that contained the inevitability, almost the *rightness*, of Orc's destruction.

She tried to find hope. But where was hope? Daroguerre had sent men after Hana. And even if Hana found some way to evade them and restore Orc, what then? The Kurassians would arrive, and everyone would be seized.

What would those Kurassians do to Orc and her? And what if the agents of the Kings Behind the World learned of them from official documents generated by their arrest? She'd been stupid to fight Orc's attempt to find their pasts. If those agents existed, they might soon become a very real threat.

'Not so close!' called Esteban from just outside the stone circle. 'Two paces.'

Cass moved back a step. 'Orc, I know you can't hear me,' she whispered. 'But I'm here, anyway.'

It made her feel no better. She felt paralysed in a space from which even the best foreseeable outcome was a life of fear and flight, and the others were all rape or death. She had less than an hour to endure a terrible world, before it got far worse.

32

THE ABYSS

Hana invoked Hare on the way back to the Navel, as she often did when running. Carried as a near-passenger in her suddenly more fluid body, with her increased stride-length and better reading of the terrain, she felt she could win any race against Daroguerre's magic.

But Hare's speed and agility had evolved to evade pursuit, and she picked up his timidity and nervousness too. She'd learned to adjust for this, so when she halted by the twin stones above the Navel and felt a wariness, and a strong reluctance to remove her clothes, she tried to ignore it. There wasn't time to feel scared or wonder if she was being watched.

But the unease worsened as she unfastened her top. Her body tensed with readiness to fight. She pretended to make a slow ritual of her buttons, while her eyes moved side to side.

And she spotted them: two Sundaran marines, hiding behind separate trees on the rim of the hollow. A snare. Her heartbeat told her to flee. But so much depended on her, and the Navel was the only place she might find the power she needed.

Two armed men. At least two.

An answer stuck into her mind like a knife-thrust. It terrified her.

'*One thing to be said for fear,*' Hare had said. '*It lends fervour to one's legs.*'

Her thoughts grasped for an alternative, but there was none. She tried to breathe down her nerves and forced herself to walk into the hollow, popping her waistcoat buttons at long intervals. She guessed the men wouldn't shoot her, for reasons she didn't want to think about. She only hoped they would wait to watch her undress before challenging her.

When she reached the space before the cave, she had one button left, and the men still hadn't made a sound. Uncertain if she would ever see daylight again, she quickly moved to the entrance and sat down in it.

'Stop!' came the shout, just as she pushed herself onto the descent.

No shots came – she'd guessed right. By the time she'd scooted on her backside down to the pitch-darkness at the bottom of the slope, the men's voices were at the cave entrance. She plunged into the next tunnel. Elbows and shins scraped against rocks. Noise came from behind as one marine reached the bottom of the first slope. She prayed he wouldn't spot the tunnel quickly.

Frantic clambering brought her to the Abyss, its edge barely visible in the faint light from across the chasm. She tried to ignore the nothingness that dropped away at her feet. She would need to land on the floor of the far tunnel entrance precisely on the left-hand side, where there was most room – and at a crouch, or she would smack her head. There was no space for a run-up. And only moments to prepare: already a man's voice sounded from the tunnel she'd just come down.

Hare, spring me from the hound's jaws. Let me jump the leap of legend, the leap talked about for a thousand years. Give me your long legs and the strength that comes from fear. Help me—

She stepped to the edge of the fall. She was going to. Her knees bent; she tilted forwards and her muscles snapped into a spring that flung her headlong.

Air rushed. The opposite ledge flew at her. Her outstretched hands struck; her elbows gave to break her weight, her feet overtook them –

446

she bundled into a mass of limbs and struck the tunnel wall. Dazed and shocked, she scooted out of sight, then sat shaking with exhilaration and terror so she couldn't move.

A few seconds later, swearing came from the marine who'd followed her. *Just try it*, she thought. But no plummeting scream came. A minute later she heard the man cursing as he climbed back up, and she dared to think she was safe.

It took another few minutes before she felt calm enough to scape. But there was no smooth floor to crouch on. Just beyond where she sat, the tunnel plunged downwards, then seemed to open out below into the source of the mysterious light. Legs still shaky, her skin grazed and muscles pulled, she crept down the sloping fissure. Spirals and zigzags and serpentine carvings covered every smooth part of the wall. The last section was very steep, a series of irregular slabs like natural steps, which she let herself down one by one. Before she reached the opening, she realised the light beyond was too dim for daylight.

She ducked beneath the opening and stepped onto a wide ledge.

Amazement rooted her. It was daylight, but there was no outside.

The ledge she stood on was high in the wall of a huge cavern. Thirty or forty feet above her, several bright lines pierced the rough domed ceiling. Hana knew them now: cracks in the rocky ground west of the Navel. She'd never connected them with the light beyond the Abyss, nor guessed anything like this lay beneath them. The cave was a hundred feet across, its walls a confusion of buttresses and spires and piers of many-hued rock, all cascading down to utter darkness.

Nerves hampered her breath. The air was heavy with a tingling sense of presence that made her certain this cave was the hidden source of the energy she'd worked with for months. The instinct to be naked was strong; she slipped off her sandals and clothes. People had worshipped here: the ledge had been smoothed, the wall above the entrance carved. And what she'd taken for a boulder at one end of the ledge, where it narrowed to the wall, she now saw as a squat female form, like the stones that guarded the Navel.

As she approached, she saw that starting below it was a larger, rougher ledge that ran further around the cavern. At the far end of that ledge stood another sculpted figure, taller than she was. And then the design revealed itself in full: a pathway of ledges, each with its sculpture, going around and deeper into the cavern.

Thrill and dread shocked through her at the thought that perhaps she alone since the Flood had stood here, perhaps since long before that. The worship here lay deeper in time than the distortions of the ziggurat and the Sun-King. This was a place from before sun, from before even light or form, and the formless darkness of the pit was its source. Looking over the edge, she experienced a faint but chilling desire, and locked her knees. She sensed the silent echoes of the exultant screams of those who'd jumped. The ancient and the primitive swarmed in the air around her. It was male energy, drawn to the Mother in destructive longing. It groped between her legs.

She pushed it away, disturbed. This wasn't the side of the Mother she'd been exploring, not the power she wanted to call on. She had to focus back on her work. And she could scape here.

Kneeling on her discarded clothes, she masked herself, and once in her crouched pose tried to recall her uncle's hay-meadow. But something in the cave's atmosphere wouldn't let her mind relax into that familiar image. After several minutes of trying, a faint animal smell struck her and she raised her head, eyes half-open. There, in the dimness, sat Hare.

'This is different.' She spoke softly, fearful of breaking the trance.

'We are below the world of grass, child,' said Hare. 'We are in that world from which comes the urge of the grass to grow.'

'How do we get across the bridge at the Spiral?' said Hana. 'How do we defeat Three-Eyes and get the key to Otter's cage?'

Hare scratched behind an ear. 'The second might be answered once we have achieved the first.'

'But Three-Eyes guards the only way to the Spiral.'

'Indeed,' said Hare, 'she is the guardian of the magician's schemes. And he has separated his place of power by a chasm, crossed only by a bridge. But is the chasm deep enough?'

Hana struggled to catch his meaning.

'Have you forgotten, child, what you yourself said? "Stone connects." And have you forgotten that I am a lord of tricks? Who would think a proud hare would stoop to burrow like a rabbit? Pick me up. We have a dark journey ahead.'

∽

Thera jumped as a long, ripping shriek sounded in the distance. It ended in a muffled blast, and she realised the dreadnought had fired a shot towards the cove.

No others came. A long-range warning, she guessed. The Sundaran ships would surrender, as her father had told her. The Kurassians would come to the Spiral, and soon.

And if the manifestation failed, and the Empyrean church got hold of her…

She tried to return her will to her task, to project the seductive goddess out onto the Spiral. But all she could think of was Cass.

'There's always the choice not to be a spineless worm.'

It infuriated her that just because Cass had narrowly survived drowning, the bitch thought she had the moral right to condemn anyone who valued their own lives. Cass understood nothing about death. It was one thing to contemplate it after rescue, quite another to be forced to stare into the void, to be encouraged to study final and irrevocable extinction.

She had no cause to pay Cass's words any attention. So why couldn't she put them from her mind?

It was Sparrow. Even without scaping, she sensed her animath through the bond of Initiation: chirping, chirping, wanting to help, to ease Cass's distress, to help her save her tricked, trapped cousin. The bravest one of all.

Stupid little bird. Life wasn't a legend of the Dawn of Time. If *she* died, there would be no return from death. She would be there forever. Except *she* wouldn't, because there would be no *she* to be anywhere.

Pain gripped her chest. Her heart.

The goddess manifestation was her only hope of avoiding execution. Cass and Sparrow could go hang themselves. She couldn't afford any weakness in supporting her father. The only course of action was drastic, and frightened her. But there was no time to agonise over it, and she would never be able to face Sparrow again now anyway.

She gripped her focus-stone, and found the source of the tattoo-mask in her mind, and denied it. She rejected it, she scoured it out, she forgot it. She didn't deserve Sparrow, she didn't want Sparrow, she didn't need Sparrow; she set her free. She visualised Sparrow flying away, to find someone else if she wanted. There was no ceremony she knew for this: she created it out of whole cloth, burning out the relationship between them, killing the bond, willing it dead.

It took minutes of intense mental concentration and anguish, but at the end, she felt calmer. There was no conflict within her now. She had sent away what she knew to be the best part of her, but she could now attend to the task that gave her a chance of survival.

Straight away, settling her mind into focus, she realised there was no point trying to project any seductive goddess. Her father had misjudged her ability. Instead, she understood how she could best use the fear and emptiness inside her.

The goddess's arrival was inevitable because when all was said and done, whatever else she embodied, she was death. And Orc would give himself to the goddess because she was death, and in the end he had no choice. What did a few years matter?

Now bright fiery Sparrow was gone, Thera gave herself up to projecting the darkness that would consume all.

She tried to ignore the irony that she did this in hope of saving her life.

♋

Clutching Hare against her, Hana descended deeper into the darkness. 'It is well that you steep yourself in her,' said Hare. 'But don't forget the magician also draws on the Mother.'

That surprised her. 'He's using *this* energy to create the goddess?'

'As he used it to make Three-Eyes.'

'How can the Mother allow that?'

'She does not care whether her power is put to what we would call good or ill,' said Hare. 'Some uses are more in sympathy with her, some less so. Three-Eyes is closely connected with her, for the Precious Night Sisters guarded the fire from humanity. But returning Orc's self to him is not, so don't expect the Mother's help to come easily. She resents the children who outgrow her.'

They had reached a tunnel leading off from one of the ledges. 'This way,' said Hare. 'We are deep enough now to pass beneath the magician's chasm. The true depths are not for either of us. Not yet.'

The tunnel twisted like the intestines of the earth. Stone chilled Hana's feet, air chilled her skin. At last, when Hare told her it was time to ascend, her feet found stairs. She climbed round the inside of a shaft towards a bright circle of sky, until she emerged from the pit in front of Orc's statue.

Three-Eyes stood by the bridge, facing away from her, while nearby stood the forlorn figure of a priestess. An obvious dark presence infused the magician's palace, while beneath everything she felt the goddess ready to be born, a dark tingle through air and earth. She sensed the truth of Hare's words: it was the Mother's power that Daroguerre drew upon.

She lifted Hare nearer her mouth. The animath was trembling. Three-Eyes' presence jangled Hana's nerves too. 'What now?' she whispered, looking at the key hanging from the guardian's belt.

Hare wriggled. As soon as she set him down, he ran into the palace. Hana followed him into the antechamber and to the right-hand room.

Within, Otter lay in his cage, and—

Sparrow was on the floor: free, and masked. Hana thrilled with excitement.

'Sparrow, can you help us?'

'Fastest and bravest!' chirped the bird. 'Who can defeat us?'

'But child,' said Hare, 'you must be ready. Remember where you have come from, where your body now is.'

'I am in the great cave of the Mother,' said Hana, 'even though I reach here with my mind. Though Daroguerre draws on the same power, he has isolated himself from the rest of the island. I have not – I am joined to it by the intestines of the earth. My power is the stronger.'

'Well said!' exclaimed Hare. 'Let's do some kicking.'

His fear seemed to have vanished. Hana assumed that was good. But she didn't know what they would actually do.

They sneaked back to the palace entrance. 'How will we tell when Daroguerre gives Cass the stone?' Hana whispered to Hare.

'Trust, child,' he said. 'We know when to act.'

'We can take the harridan now!' chirped Sparrow. 'She's asleep on her feet!'

'No!' urged Hana. But Sparrow was off, flying towards the guardian's back.

Hare sprinted after her.

'*No!*'

Three-Eyes turned to meet him.

Hana quailed at the sight. Three-Eyes slashed at Hare with her talons. He sprang aside. Three-Eyes swiped with her shield. Hare rolled backwards. Three-Eyes kicked. Hare jumped over her foot.

'Did you really think those sisters could have caught me, had I not let them?'

He was distracting her, dancing around her, drawing her attention. Sparrow fluttered and hovered at the guardian's back.

But they had moved too soon. Three-Eyes was getting the measure of Hare. Her swipes missed him by less and less.

Then she made as though to strike, but it was a feint. Hare jumped aside, but Three-Eyes' talons caught him in a vicious sweep and flung his small furry body through the air and down into the chasm.

Hana's mind screamed. Three-Eyes looked at her, then stalked towards her.

Rage at Hare's fate pumped through Hana. She gathered that rage and let rip with all the strength of it, the power of the all-consuming earth.

With a loud crack, a chasm opened beneath Three-Eyes' feet. The guardian plunged in, up to her waist. After a moment's shock that she'd caused such a thing, Hana vented her anger, trying to bring the chasm walls together and crush the trapped figure. But Three-Eyes was strong. Casting aside her shield, she put her hands against the edges of the chasm and pushed.

It opened an inch. Hana blasted it with fury, picturing Hare's flung-aside body. Three-Eyes strained, arm muscles bulging, tendons standing out. The chasm opened another inch. Sparrow still flapped behind, occasionally glimpsed.

Hana strove, but her anger was failing her. Doubt crept in. She was a creature of mind, contaminated with fire – she was separated from the Mother, the power from which Three-Eyes was herself drawn.

Three-Eyes heaved, and the chasm opened six inches.

Suddenly the energy changed, as though the air had cleared. Hana glanced to her right.

The priestess held a knife. Daroguerre had handed over the stone.

Just then Sparrow flew up from behind Three-Eyes, holding in her beak the cord she'd pecked through. Tied to it was the key. Three-Eyes howled, but it was a weakened howl.

Hana howled back. She threw away mind and exulted in anger, drawing from the great cave all the power of darkness and ending. The chasm widened. Three-Eyes fell deeper, down to her eyes. Hana squeezed the chasm walls shut again, shut and shut and crushing and closing until with a popping and grinding of rock and bones, blood fountained; she pushed and ground until there was nothing left, only stone slicked with red. It emptied her.

'Sparrow!' she gasped. 'The key.'

Sparrow dropped it into her hand. Pushing away the upset of Hare, Hana raced through the palace, hoping Cass would keep hold of the knife-stone long enough.

Otter was up and masked, worrying at the cage bars. Hana slotted the key, tumblers clicked; Otter almost fell out. Hana ran after him out of the palace. Otter ran up to the statue of Orc, the king, which still stared down into the pit.

Now, thought Hana. *Please, let this work.*

But Otter just ran around, confused. 'Where is it?'

'Where's *what*?' said Hana. 'He's right there – save him!'

'The fire? Where's his fire?' Otter stood on his hind legs, frantically looking about.

'His fire?'

'Did Three-Eyes have it?' said Sparrow.

Hana felt sick. The goddess was growing in power. The conjuration was close.

The priestess, knife in hand, was beside the statue. Hana couldn't move. She had failed.

The priestess offered the knife, and the king's stone hand opened to take it.

33

THE DESTROYER COMES

'You who are the soil that nurtures the wheat, I call you to waken. You who are the rain that waters the soil that nurtures the wheat, I call you to waken. You who are the cloud that bears the rain that waters the soil...'

Daroguerre's performance had gone through its various phases for what Cass guessed had been fifteen minutes already. She sensed the power, and it was swelling.

'... the sword that brings justice, I call you to waken. You who are the rock that yields the iron that makes the sword that brings justice, I call you to waken. You who are the earth that contains the rock that yields...'

The sky to the south was palled with ships' smoke. Farthest east, a cruiser, then the dreadnought, obvious by its size, then the other three cruisers, the two farthest west shown only by their smoke rising behind the tents and trees. None had fired since the dreadnought's single shot half an hour before. Rulanza had clearly surrendered.

Cass knew that meant Kurassians would probably come ashore, maybe to the Spiral. But when?

'... you whose strength makes the ground shake and the storm rage, I call you to waken!' The strength and pace of Daroguerre's voice was increasing. 'You who eat the sun and birth him anew, I call you to waken! You who are the nine moons and the cold eternity and all that lies between, I CALL YOU TO WAKEN.'

Despite the cicadas and the breeze, the Spiral felt hushed.

Daroguerre beckoned her.

Sick with dread, Cass stepped barefoot across hot paving to where the magician stood between two of the circle's standing stones. All through his chant, he'd held two crystals pressed together before his chest: the large focus-stone, and what Cass assumed to be the elemental stone from *Nightfire*. He handed her the former. She sensed the compressed intent within it.

'Give this into the Sun-King's hand,' said Daroguerre.

Hana, whatever you've got to do, do it now. The thread of hope was so gut-wrenchingly thin, it was almost more painful than no hope at all, but she had to keep the stone from Orc as long as possible.

Halfway back to him, she stopped, lifted the stone before her and began to chant.

'You who are the fruit, I call you to waken. You who are the bough that bears the fruit, I call you to waken. You who are the tree that grows the bough that bears the fruit...'

She pretended not to hear Daroguerre's shouted questions.

'... the orchard that contains the tree...'

A hand pulled her round. 'What are you playing at?' Daroguerre looked furious.

'Trying to help,' said Cass. 'Wasn't that what—'

The magician looked like he barely restrained himself from striking. 'Do your task, or I will make good my threat. Esteban is only waiting for the chance.' He turned. 'What do you want?'

A worried-looking marine stood at the circle's edge. 'A runner has come. One of the cruisers looks to be preparing to land men.'

'No more distractions!' said Daroguerre. 'Proceed,' he told Cass as he walked back to the stones. 'And priestess guard, ensure her compliance.'

There had surely been enough time for Hana to act, Cass thought.

If that hope was dead, then the only course left was to delay things enough for the Kurassians to arrest everyone. She and Orc might perhaps survive, no matter what Esteban did to her in the meantime.

She walked slowly up to Orc. She packed her courage into her arm, and pulled it back to hurl the stone as far as she could over the cliff.

A hand seized her wrist. She tried to break free, to throw, but Esteban's grip mastered her.

'Put it in his hand.'

She didn't move. She couldn't. Esteban put his other arm around her and forced her the last couple of feet. She tried to collapse her legs, but he bore her weight.

Orc got up onto one knee.

Hope surged through her: Hana had freed him after all. But relief died as she saw no change in Orc's downward-staring face. He lurched to his feet a sleepwalker, and reached out, requesting the thing that would destroy him.

Esteban forced her hand towards Orc's. Cass strained against the push of his arm. 'Orc!' she called, even though she knew he couldn't hear her. 'Wake up!'

Esteban's hand clamped across her mouth. He pulled her back against him. 'You'll learn to be silent for me,' he hissed in her ear, then thrust her hand into Orc's.

Orc tried to take the stone. Cass made a vice of her fingers. For a moment it seemed enough; Orc acted like someone half-asleep, unable to understand that there was resistance, not putting his full strength into overcoming it.

Then Esteban released her mouth and used both hands on her grip. His fingers were strong and ruthless. He quickly pried two of hers from the stone: enough for Orc to take hold.

'Don't!' cried Cass, as Orc grasped it. Desperate fear gripped her, the sudden clarity that she would lose him forever. 'Oscar!' she shrieked. *'Drop it, you prat!'*

Otter yipped.

Someone had shouted. Hana hadn't caught the words, but where Three-Eyes had vanished she now saw a sun-bright beach, and on it an adolescent boy, a younger Orc, sporting an evil grin and holding out in both hands the slippery mass of a jellyfish.

The moving king-statue had hold of the knife.

Otter darted onto the sand. The beach-vision disappeared in moments, but Otter was already running back, a bright flame between his open jaws. Just as the king put the knife to his own throat, Otter's fiery mouth bit the statue's ankle.

Stone skin shattered. Fragments rained down, chunks and flecks and dust. Within was nothing.

The priestess too had disappeared, and the pit.

'What happened?' said Hana. 'Did it work?'

No answer came; Otter and Sparrow were gone. But the energy of the goddess-in-waiting still filled the air and the earth. It had not dissipated, and was shot through with anger.

♋

The focus-stone lay on the paving where Orc had tossed it. Daroguerre's ranting drowned all other noise. Cass wrenched herself free of Esteban's slackened grasp and seized Orc.

His legs gently gave way. She lowered herself with him, then turned as footsteps sounded.

Daroguerre's face was iron. He snatched the stone from the ground.

'Give me your gun,' he told Esteban.

'No!' cried Cass. 'Please…'

'You promised her to me,' Esteban said.

'I'm not going to shoot *her*, idiot.' Daroguerre held out his hand. 'And I won't ask again.'

Horror tore through Cass. Daroguerre was still going to sacrifice Orc, but with a bullet. 'Stop him!' she shouted at the marines. 'Can't you see this is wrong?'

A few looked away, but none moved. Esteban took the revolver from the back of his trousers and handed it to Daroguerre, who stepped back and took aim – but not at Orc.

Esteban's face paled. 'You saw – there was nothing I could do.'

'What you do now will be of help,' said Daroguerre. 'Your death will be magically useful, as well as gratifying.'

'Please!' he cried. 'You said I could kill Seriuz! He murdered my family! And the goddess – I'm her true worshipper. Please, I'm only—'

Cass jumped at the shot. She jumped at each of the next three Daroguerre fired into Esteban's fallen body. Orc's arms crushed the breath from her.

'Be thankful you two are more valuable,' said Daroguerre.

He went back and put the gun on the flattened top of one of the stones. Cass clutched Orc harder. She wanted not to see Esteban's corpse. She wanted to try running, but marines blocked all routes from the Spiral, and she didn't think she could move.

'What's happening?' whispered Orc. Cass didn't know how to start.

'Be sure they go nowhere,' Daroguerre told his men. He raised both stones high and breathed deeply, quickly, several times.

'And thus once more is she denied her rightful sacrifice and receives only the unworthy!' he cried. 'In anger she spreads death across the land, and an ocean of blood cannot placate her. In rage she arises. All she once birthed she hungrily devours in plague and fire. The balance of light and dark is consumed by night everlasting. The destroyer comes. Skalith *comes*. SHE COMES!'

Without pause, he performed the incantation again. And again. He kept repeating it, increasingly frenzied.

'I can feel her,' moaned Orc.

Cass hugged him tighter. This short time might be all they'd have.

'Cass, I'm sorry. I was an idiot.'

'Me too.'

'It was a trap. I should've realised. I didn't learn anything—'

His words cut off at Daroguerre's shriek. The freezing ululation, on and on, raised the hairs on Cass's neck. Finally the magician bent his knees to squat, and struck both crystals against the ground.

A shock went through Cass like from a silent explosion. She tasted metal.

At the edge of her vision stood a large dark figure that hadn't been there before.

She had to look.

Fire lit Skalith's eyes as she surveyed the Spiral from twice the height of a man. Her emotionless face was a black mask, her teeth white and sharp. Snakes writhed in the goddess's hair; two larger serpents, rooted in her shoulders, twined around her arms. She wore only a skirt made of ropes of shrunken skulls. Her left hand grasped a stone sickle edged with fire.

Cass felt paralysed, sure she was about to become prey. Struck by the impossible solidity and power of the sight, it seemed in a moment that her whole life had been futile, that all life was futile, that however hard life tried to escape, this thing would catch up from the nightmare of its beginning to claim it again. The world had reached its end.

She gagged as a foul reek swept over her. Stasis broke: one of the marines shouted, then others. In three strides Skalith reached the nearest man. Snake fangs grasped his head. His scream ended as the sickle swept through his neck, flinging blood.

'Cease!' cried Daroguerre. 'There are greater enemies!' But his voice was barely audible as the marines pushed to escape. Orc jumped up and pulled Cass with him, staggering after the Sundarans towards the trail. But Cass realised that if everyone was running that way, that was direction the goddess would most likely chase.

'This way.' She tugged Orc's arm, guiding their flight to the broken-pine arch north of the bluff. Off the paving of the Spiral, running became agony; roots and stones and fallen twigs hacked at the soles of her feet.

Orc slowed, gasping. Out of sight now, they sank behind a tree. The cuts on Orc's feet had opened again. Daroguerre's chanting had resumed, but Cass couldn't catch the words.

'What's going to happen?' she said, barely able to speak. 'Do you know? From when you were under?'

Orc shook his head.

'He called her without you. How?'

'Not the same,' said Orc. 'This is the aspect angry at being denied.'
He was shaking, Cass saw. So was she.

'How long can she exist for? Can he control her? Can she be
stopped?'

'I don't know.' Orc's eyes were wet. 'He's made Death, in the flesh.
There might not be any escape.'

'Don't say that.' But he was right: the goddess could easily catch up
with them.

'I can't walk,' he moaned. 'I can't do anything, except fuck things up.
I should've listened to you and left that stone where it was.'

'No, you shouldn't. I was wrong – we need to know our pasts.'

He looked at her. 'Even…?'

'I changed my mind,' she said. 'Whatever we did, we need to face it,
not run. But *now* we need to run. I'm not going to die before I find out
who you are.' She stroked his bare arm, pressed the muscle of it, warm
and alive. 'Come on, we should get deeper in. Lean on me.'

With his weight on her shoulder, she helped him limp onto the
spine of the island, heading for somewhere deep among the pines.
Maybe she should be looking for Hana or Shoggu, rather than finding
somewhere to hide. But what she'd said to Seriuz, about being so used
to death that she no longer feared it, now seemed stupid. If anyone who
survived wanted to call her selfish and a coward, good luck to them.
She was going to look after the person she had started this life with. It
was other people's battle now.

Distant gunfire told her it was already under way.

☾

Thera stood by the tent, having thrown on her uniform. For all her
mental preparation, the figure standing near the headless corpse of the
marine threatened to strip her mind of rationality. Instinct wanted her

to run after the Sundarans. But she couldn't leave the man she needed to keep her alive, nor could she tear herself from the sight.

Death was no longer formless extinction: it had a shape, even a horrific beauty. The goddess's skin was polished jet, her eyes burning coals, her teeth wet and white. The serpents coiled about her arms were patterned in subtle colours; lustrous scales shifted over restless muscle. Skalith was occupied with licking the rapidly decaying flesh from the marine's head. She reeked of rot, and, on a more subtle level, stank of power.

As Thera crept towards the stone circle where her father stood in concentration, a loud buzzing heralded a swarm of insects streaming from beneath the goddess's skull-skirt. Thera prepared to run, but the swarm settled on the marine's corpse to form a heaving mound of glittering wings. She claimed the revolver from the top of the stone. Glancing southwards, she saw the Empyreal ships for the first time. She recognised the dreadnought as *Iron Tiger*, second only to *Empire's Peace* in the arsenal of the Kurassian navy. She guessed those in the crow's nests of the dreadnought and the two visible cruisers were now watching the goddess. It crossed her mind to wonder how they were reacting.

Skalith attached the marine's bared and somehow-shrunken skull to one of the ropes that made up her skirt. The insect-mound seemed to have collapsed in on itself. As the swarm began to rise back under the goddess, Thera saw the marine's body had vanished.

'What do we—'

'Hush!' said her father. 'I'm readying an exhortation.'

Thera wondered how much influence he would have without the link provided by Orc's imprisoned will. Her insects having returned, Skalith looked about her.

'Vengeful destroyer!' cried Daroguerre. 'Hear one who serves you!'

The dark goddess regarded him with fire, as though caught between listening and killing. Her head-snakes writhed.

'I know the reason for your wrath,' said Daroguerre, maintaining his loud voice as though to convince the goddess that he was her equal. 'I know the sun refused you, refused to be swallowed and reborn, setting himself blasphemously apart from you. I know that men listened to the sun's detestable proclamation and called him a god, and so each believed himself to be a little god, also set apart from you. This is why you return in wrath, you who are the consequence of that denial, you who are plague and famine and the fire that sweeps through dried and withered fields.'

He flung an arm towards the Empyreal warships. 'And there are your enemies! There are the ones who worshipped the sun and turned him wholly into a man. There are those who derogate you with false names and deny your power. They *must* be *destroyed*!'

The goddess ululated a shriek, far worse than the one Daroguerre had used to call her. She ran to the southern cliff and jumped from view.

Thera hurried with her father to the edge.

'What can she do?'

'What can she not?' said Daroguerre, his voice still exultant. 'She is the fire that sweeps through dried and withered fields – thus she encompasses the power of your elemental stone. She is all-consuming. None shall stand against her. Look!'

Thera gasped. Skalith had become visible again, far below, running over the sea as though it were land, and heading straight for *Iron Tiger*.

Gunfire flashed along the dreadnought's flank: twelve-pounders, her close-defence system. But the water-bursts were always behind the goddess – she moved too fast. The sparks of rifle and machine-gun fire came from everywhere on the side of the ship. Klaxons sounded faintly over the distant murmur and crackle.

Either nothing was hitting her, or Skalith shrugged it all off.

She had almost disappeared, dwarfed by the ship. But impressive as she had been close up, she was only the height of two men, and the dreadnought had eight-hundred of those. Thera wondered how the goddess could achieve anything. Was she going to behead and slowly consume everyone? How would she even get aboard?

A shell screamed overhead. Thera threw herself down. It hadn't been big, but big enough: a twelve-pounder from one of the dreadnought's escorting cruisers.

'Get down!' she cried. 'They've seen us – they think we control her!'

'Their defiance is futile!' yelled her father. 'They shall all die.'

Other shell-shrieks ripped the air, but Thera quickly realised the danger was less than she'd thought: the ships' guns were much lower than the Spiral, and couldn't shoot at a steep enough angle to arc a shell onto it.

'What hope the machinery of men against a million years of rust?' Daroguerre held the stones high, shouting as though he truly were the goddess's worshipper. Sweat dripped from him. 'What hope iron against the death of the earth from which it came?'

Noise exploded. Smoke and powdered rock showered upwards from below the edge of the cliff. None of the debris hit them: the shell had struck too low. But Thera realised that if one landed even slightly higher, it might be fatal. 'Back!' she pleaded, grabbing her father's arm. 'You can still see from the circle.'

He came reluctantly, all the time keeping up his exaltation. The howling of shells was near-constant. More began to hit the cliff-face, the smaller explosions from the twelve-pounders now joined by the cruisers' main guns; the ground trembled even at the circle. Thera looked back at *Iron Tiger* – the dreadnought's rear turret had turned to face them.

Its guns flamed. Seconds later, the double scream overhead almost deafened her.

What was Skalith doing? She couldn't see any sign of a battle, no more flashes from small-arms.

'Is the goddess killed?' she shouted.

'The destroyer is the end of all things!' cried her father. 'How can she herself be ended?'

But Thera heard doubt. *That's it*, she thought. There could be no survival now. *Iron Tiger*'s main guns blazed again. Thera tensed, ready. Seven seconds took an hour.

The blast-shock tumbled them both to the ground. A mass of rock and stone fragments erupted from below the cliff-edge, powering up into the sky with a thick cloud of smoke and dust. Several feet of the edge of the terrace slid out of sight with a roar, but the shells' impact was far enough below the edge for only a few fragments to land near them, carried in a cloud of breeze-blown smoke that stank of chemicals and burnt earth.

Even with the breeze, it took half a minute for the dust to clear. Long enough for the dreadnought to have fired its big guns again. It hadn't.

Thera got to her feet. Through the thinning haze, the ship looked different. It was listing towards her, its stern lower in the water than it had been.

'For she is the mother of all seas!' her father cried. 'All those who try to stay above her delude themselves, for she will draw them down into her silent deeps.'

Thera couldn't believe it. One of the world's greatest war machines was being destroyed before her eyes. She tried not to imagine the panic below decks, the desperate, too-late sealing of bulkhead doors with sailors trapped behind them. No, they didn't deserve her pity: they had tried to kill her. And failed. It seemed almost nonsensical – a mighty battleship against her and her father, and the battleship had lost.

Her near-laugh died as the ship threw out a mountain of smoke in all directions, a roiling eruption of darkness within which a fireball broke upwards, flickering red and gold amongst the clouds of black. Seconds later, a shattering peal rolled over the world.

'For she is the mother of fire!' exulted her father. 'Saeraf tried to take it from her, but she has consumed him.'

One of the magazines, Thera realised. Smoke rolled and billowed on the water while a plume of it reached ever-higher into the sky, borne on the heat of tons of ignited cordite. She couldn't swallow. That smoke hid hundreds of deaths. Hundreds. There could be no doubt.

'She can't survive that?' Her voice trembled.

Her father just laughed, near-hysterical at his own success.

'There is your answer!' He pointed towards the cruiser a half-mile west of *Iron Tiger*'s smoke-shrouded grave. Explosions burst up from the sea as the ship's guns fired at something approaching across the water, too small to be seen.

Thera flinched with the implication. If that explosion hadn't destroyed Skalith, then how many more ships? And when they were all gone…

'When will she stop?'

'Perhaps never.' Her father was focused on the sea. 'But my influence will improve with practice, and you can be taught, and we might recruit others. Our Lady of Destruction might yet do in place of the ruling goddess I was denied.'

His voice had recovered its rationality, to Thera's relief. No shellfire had come their way for several seconds. *Iron Tiger*'s smoke had almost hidden the cruiser to the east, but Thera could see the ship swinging about.

It was fleeing. The others would do the same – even if the goddess were to vanish, the Kurassians would no longer have the advantage over *Barcuda* and *Tarpon*.

She touched the sleeve of her father's robe. 'We've done it. We've won.'

'I shall ignore the implication that you ever doubted me.'

The power, she realised. The power of being the daughter of the man who ruled the world, and who needed her talents, who needed her alive.

'Nothing can touch us,' she said.

'Nothing,' said her father, 'and no one. Let my former masters shiver in their desert bolthole. It shall not be their new world that rises from the old, but mine.'

And mine. She would create a world too. She would get her father to teach her his magic. Now she was no longer a shaman, bound to one dowdy little bird, she would master a thousand gods, and the technique of extending her life, and then the magic of holding another's life by a thread as her father held hers.

She would force Cass to look into extinction: that would stop her blathering about 'spine'. She would make everyone in the world understand the nothingness that awaited them. Awaited *them*, but not her. Not any more.

The westward cruiser was now listing. She prepared for the explosion.

A foot scuffed behind her.

She span and brought up her gun.

The youth stopped dead five paces away. She recognised him: he'd fought Three-Eyes, though now he wore grey and carried a shorter sword. That blade had been meant for her and her father, she realised with a chill – at their moment of triumph, only the scuff of a foot had stopped him stealing their lives. The boy's eyes fixed on hers, filled with the knowledge that he'd blundered, that his own young life was over.

Her finger tightened, but didn't pull. It was as though some part of her needed him to attack before she could get it over with. She didn't understand her own hesitation. She had so much power now: how could she not use it?

The boy slipped his left hand inside his shirt.

'Second one down,' said her father, still facing the sea. He hadn't noticed.

And she'd missed seeing the cruiser go up. Annoyance burst in her, and she indulged it as she now had the right to indulge anything. She pulled the trigger.

34

THE HIGH SNOWS OF TAMFANG

For a long time after Hana and Cass disappeared up the slope, Tashi sat and waited for Shoggu to tell him what he already knew, and tried not to listen to the voices inside his head.

– he will lie about us, he fears us, he knows our strength

But Shoggu only sat frowning at his hands. Tashi wondered how long a speech he was preparing.

'They are Qliphoth, master. That's what you can't face telling me.'

– the magician planted the lie in the old man's mind

Shoggu's hands ceased moving. 'Of some kind.'

'How can I be rid of them? Did the magician's thoughts tell you that?'

– you do not want rid of us

– we are all that gives you strength

'They did not, beloved one.' Shoggu let out a long breath.

'Then what can we do?'

'We must hold out here until *Archon* returns. Perhaps we should move to one of the smaller islands.'

'What about the magician? And that three-eyed creature?'

'It might be that Hana can dispel the magic.'

Hana, who had called him a child. She had told him his possessors could not take away his real fear. Had she known what it was?

'If she cannot,' Shoggu went on, 'there is nothing we can do. Despite her urging, I have neither the learning nor the moral authority for anything more than prayer.'

– he has no authority at all, look at him

'Quiet!'

'Tashi?'

'Nothing, master. Except – an enemy has returned we have waited thousands of years to fight, and you say we must sit on our hands?'

'You think I *should* attempt to aid Hana magically?'

'No!' *– he is tempted to use magic, he is weak and corrupt*

'Then what else is there? You said you couldn't defeat the three-eyed monster before, and that was with *their* strength.'

'I attacked the wrong target. If I kill the magician, the monster might vanish.'

'We cannot know that. And the risk! You mustn't exposed yourself to the stresses of combat. They will take you over again.'

'They will do so anyway! Their voices will drive me mad.'

– when you accept us, when we speak with one voice, there will be no conflict

'Voices?'

He nodded, ashamed.

– what are you afraid of

'You must calm the emotions they feed on.' Shoggu looked intently into Tashi's eyes. 'Those emotions come from fear, and you have no more reason to fear. All will be well. We have already succeeded in our task.'

He frowned. 'How so, master?' *– the old weakling gives up, he does not serve the lord*

'We have witnesses to the magician's powers and ambitions. Even if Daroguerre hides his activities from the Immaterium, the record of those young women's words will be accessible to the Abbot.' – *another weak old man* – 'He will readmit us to Highcloud, and then you shall be cured. He will know how.'

'That idiot?'

'Tashi!'

'How will I last long enough to get back there?' Desperation threatened to break him. 'How will I sleep, with demons shouting at me?'

'We shall pray each evening, beloved one.' – *empty words* – 'And perform the cone of protection as often as we can.' – *you do not deserve it* – 'It might weaken them.' – *beloved by whom*

'Can we pray now?' – *the lord of strength and righteous anger does not love weaklings*

Shoggu frowned. 'It might be wiser to move the camp first.' – *the storm on the mountain despises the meek child*

'Master, please.' – *we know what you are afraid of*

– *what you most fear*

Shoggu sighed, and relented.

Tashi answered every line of the catechism, as he had many hundreds of times before; but it only partially quieted the voices of the Qliphoth. After what seemed like an hour, Shoggu's voice became weak – *he is old and frail and he lacks the holy strength* – and he instructed a period of silent prayer.

In the silence, the Qliphoth grew stronger.

This would be the way of it, Tashi thought. Unlike his master, or himself, the Qliphoth would not tire. They could wait. They already had a hold on his body. They had burned away his rotting flesh in the hotel room, and he had now beheld the external manifestation of its replacement. It was lucky the Kurassians had supplied two medical kits with bandages: Ranga had taken one, but that had still left Tashi the other to swathe his hand. He didn't want Shoggu to see it, nor beneath his shirt. – *no blade or bullet can pierce you there, when we have you fully you will be the greatest warrior*

They ached, those parts of him. Not like pulled muscles: it was both an ache, and numbness. It felt deeper than his flesh. – *perfect flesh feels no pain, it feels wrong only because we do not have all of you, the weak parts of your body fight with the strong*

The body was only a tool, he had always been taught, not a part of his true self. But now that it was being taken from him, he feared to lose it. Another fear to add to the many, and to what he now realised had always been his greatest.

♋

Otter and Orc had been gone only moments when visions began to assail Hana, mind-pictures she tried in vain to refuse: death and blood and bones piled in mounds, swords and sores and plague-blackened skins, the sun darkening to a cinder and falling to earth. The atmosphere was shot through with a terrifying anger.

Wondering if she should leave, she looked at the bridge. Something hurtled across it towards her.

'Hare!'

The masked animath scuffed to a halt. 'By many strange paths, before you ask.'

She laughed with relief. 'I thought I'd lost you.'

'Was it not always more likely that I allowed Three-Eyes to defeat me so your reaction would be provoked?'

'Is that what happened?'

'What matters is that I have returned from death,' said Hare. 'And I run in advance of its coming. Child, we have succeeded in one task, but we risk failing in the bigger one.'

'Daroguerre can still manifest the goddess? Can we disperse this energy? Am I strong enough?'

'We shall need help,' said Hare.

'Shoggu? If I can persuade him to join forces…' She'd already thought of a possible means of contacting the monk.

She crept into the palace, Hare shivering alongside. From the central room came waves of energy, an incantation. In the left-hand room, the small painting was now free of blood, cleaned by her earlier prayer to the Mother.

'Can we use this?' whispered Hana.

'Do not ask: act!' said Hare, and leapt into the picture.

Hana was perplexed to see him run around on the snow, his fur now pure white. 'My northern cousins have lent me a coat,' he said. 'Follow.'

Hana prepared herself, and imagined herself through the frame. She landed almost knee-deep in freezing snow, high on a mountainside.

'Carry me, child,' said Hare. 'I shall keep you warm.'

Holding his furry heat against her chest, Hana slogged through the snow, the air thin and hard to breathe. The severe cold felt far removed from the island, and from the Mother energy with which she worked. But that might be a good thing, if Daroguerre was tapping the dark side of that same power. She might struggle to ally with the energy of the mountain, but it should prove strong against Daroguerre's magic.

But where was Shoggu? There was no trace of him.

'Climb,' said Hare.

Yes, thought Hana: what mattered here was the desire to go ever higher, away from the living world. So she did. The air thinned further. Her legs ached. The vision of the towering peak appalled her – but the reverse would be true for the Thangkarans, she understood. This was the home of their ideal. She thought of Tashi, with no warm mother, only this terrible spire of cold.

Looking up at it now, she saw a figure toiling ahead of her, his robe a slash of red against the snow. He clutched the hand of what seemed to be the ghost of a child. Hana fixed the vision of him in her mind's eye, and ran.

⊙

Shoggu had been in silent prayer for some minutes. Tashi watched, concerned. It had been less than two hours since Shoggu had been pulled from dark-flight, and even in prayer, he might slip back into it. When his master's face twisted, Tashi leant forward and started the call-back chant. To his relief, Shoggu joined in almost at once.

'The magician tried to trap you again?'

'No, I think not,' said Shoggu. 'I believe I had some contact with Hana, wherever she is.' – *the temptress, the whore* – 'She encouraged my thoughts to the magician's place of working. I beheld…' He breathed. 'The abomination.'

'The goddess?' said Tashi, shocked. 'He's truly made it?'

– he befouled the world while you sat here

– the old man did nothing, he serves the magician with his weakness

Shoggu nodded. 'The blasphemy exists.'

'And now there are two monsters.' Tashi got to his feet.

– you must make war on him, you are the only one who does not serve him

'Beloved one, what are you doing?'

'I have to destroy him.'

'You cannot fight! The Qliphoth—'

'So we return to Highcloud with our *proof*,' said Tashi. 'How many more abominations will he create in the meantime? The women failed, as I knew they would.'

'But even if you manage to resist them, you will die!' said Shoggu, aghast.

'Then I'll die a novitiate of Highcloud.' Desperation choked him. 'What else am I for? I have only five years remaining in this body anyway.'

'Don't say so. You can make a life for yourself—'

'I *cannot*, master! I can't live in the lower world. It's too much for me.' Bismark, Torrento, the heat-swarming island, Hana naked, his semen: the memories merged, surrounded his embattled self, compressed it. 'It's different for you. You came from here.'

'So did you,' said Shoggu. – *listen not, he seeks to weaken you*

'Even if that's true, I don't remember it. I belong to the Mountain, and only to there: to Highcloud, and the task for which it was built. How many times have you reminded me what that was?'

'Because I was obsessed.'

'Because you were *right*!'

Shoggu moaned. 'Beloved one, listen: there is a reason I was so attentive to the Zhenaii threat, when the other Watchers had lowered their guard.' – *do not listen, he is weakness* – 'I came to Highcloud not to be a Watcher, but because of nightmares I'd suffered when travelling with Anik. I perceived the Zhenaii's hidden influence everywhere; I believed their evil was only waiting to re-enter the world. The Watchers discovered I had the talent to join them, but found no truth behind my dreams; and ever after, I heard it whispered that I gained my place through delusions or falsehood.'

– the whispers were right, he is deluded and false and old and weak

'For years, I longed to validate the warnings of my dreams, to prove myself right,' said Shoggu. 'I persuaded myself that mine was a holy goal, because it was the reason for the Watchers' existence. But now I see things truly. Pride drove me more than rightness. That accursed bargain with the Prelate – how could I have entered into it if I had been pure of purpose? How could I bear it now if that corrupt obsession led to your death?'

'But your fears spoke the *truth*, master! Daroguerre *has* reclaimed the Zhenaii evil. Whatever drove you, you were right to bring me here.' He let out a deep breath. 'I'll try to make it back. But I have to fight. There is no one else.'

'And the Qliphoth? You risk your soul...'

'I risk it by doing nothing. Do you think Gevurah will admit me to the Land Beyond Sky if I shirk the only fight that ever mattered? Don't worry: I won't let them take me. I know what they are now, and where they come from. They come from fear. But not fear of injury or death. They come from my fear that I'm not... that I don't deserve...' He swallowed.

'Beloved one?'

He shook his head, suddenly unable to speak. But he had to try.

'We novitiates are told we are called "beloved one" because we are especially beloved of Gevurah, for our purity of service.'

'Which is true.'

'But I have never felt… I do not know if I was ever…' His heart cramped in his chest.

'He does love you,' said Shoggu softly. 'And He would not want you to sacrifice your life to try to gain his approval.'

'That is not why. I must fight because there is evil. I only wanted to explain where the Qliphoth came from. They come from my need for strength, my fear of my weakness, my fear that I was not good enough. But I know now the strength they offer me is a cheat, because it does not come from Him.'

– it is the only strength that will save you

Shoggu looked away, but Tashi had already seen his eyes were wet. 'Gevurah give you strength, beloved one.'

– only we can

Tashi nodded. 'Pray for me, master. It will help to know you do so.'

Shoggu picked up the bloodstained icon of the Mountain. He slit round the inner edge of the frame with a knife, and gave the oil-paper to Tashi. 'Take this.'

'It was fouled with magic.'

'The magic was cleaned.'

'Itself by magic.'

'By a person who loves you,' said Shoggu.

'Hana?'

'She risked her life to free you from the Qliphoth. That could not be done without love.'

– she wanted to seduce you, corrupt you, degrade you

'Why would she?'

– she wanted you to bestialise yourself

'It is not for me to judge why any woman does anything. But she did. Pakundran theorised that Qliphoth are created when a deed or word or thought is made in the absence of love.' *– we are not them, we are holy –* 'Maybe the presence of love can hinder them. Take it, please, that some good might come of my having painted it all those years ago.'

Tashi slipped it inside his shirt.

'You have the Mountain within you, beloved one. Do not give in to them, fearing that in death they will drag you to Hell. Trust me that if your time comes, even here, you will find the Mountain nearer than you think.'

Something in Shoggu's voice pricked Tashi's mind with suspicion. 'Master, tell me you do not intend to aid me in any way other than prayer?'

Shoggu smiled weakly. 'The focused exercise of power, you mean? Like Hana? That would endanger my own soul, would it not?'

Tashi nodded. He stepped close to Shoggu and embraced him, briefly. The old man felt frail in his arms, a bundle of warm sticks.

There were a thousand things more to say, and none. Tashi turned and jogged, awkward and stiff, up and along the slope in the direction of the Spiral. As he reached what he thought would be the last place from which he could see the hollow, he halted and looked back, but it was already out of sight.

He ran through the forest, breathing hard through the tight hurting of his muscles. The Qliphoth encouraged him; they offered to remove the pain if he admitted them fully. He hoped he would be able to keep them at bay.

When his route brought him to where his *clathma* and bindings lay, he wondered if the Qliphoth had guided his steps.

   – take them, without them you cannot win, you don't want to die

But the big sword and his bindings didn't belong to him. They belonged only to his Inspired strength. *– the strength you need to win, our strength, have we not perfected your flesh*

It ached where they'd changed him. *– because your former weak flesh resists it*

   – take the sword, strap on your armour

   – you deserve nothing from him if you are weak

'Silence.' Nevertheless, he had halted. 'I know what you are.' *– to fight without strength serves the enemy*

   – your human body makes you a tool of sin

   – the lord will love you only for the magician's destruction

'Gevurah made me as I am, no stronger.' – *he sent us to aid you, to refuse us is to deny him*

– *he made you strong but the witch-world weakened you*

– *you cannot believe he will love a weakling*

'I know who I am,' Tashi said. 'I will not give my will to another.' But no word, no thought would calm them.

– *you will die and the lord will not even notice*

– *you are nothing without us, with us you are the greatest warrior, his greatest mortal servant*

– *his most beloved*

– *which lord would love a worm above a lion*

– *take the sword, even if you do not admit us you will need a weapon*

He couldn't deny that. A single blow might achieve something if he could reach the magician himself, and for even a single blow he would need a sword. His own strength might be enough to swing the *clathma* once.

He adjusted his bandage so he could grip the hilt. He refused to look fully at his changed fingers. As he picked up the sword, its blade streaked by the paths of deflected bullets, he sensed the Qliphoth crowd round.

Hana had loved him more as a worm than a lion. – *because she needed you weak, to corrupt you* – She had unfastened and removed his armour, strap by strap. But if the Qliphoth took him again, she would not be with him to drive them out.

He jumped as a shriek cut through the air, somewhere east. Another whistled right over his head. Shells from a warship's guns, they must be. He wondered what could be happening.

– *hurry, every wasted second serves evil*

He went as fast as he could. The missiles kept flying, trailing their screams. Explosions came from ahead, minor at first, then joined by heavier ones.

Exhausted with pain, he saw the trees end ahead, the arch of the split pine. He didn't run through it this time, as he had when he'd attacked Orc. He climbed the slightly higher ground that overlooked the Spiral. From some distance away came the heaviest explosion yet. It sounded as though the sky had cracked.

He crouched beside the pine nearest the cliff-edge. To his surprise, the Spiral was almost deserted. The magician – the *real* magician this time – stood just southeast of the stone circle, with a shorter, uniformed figure. They looked out to a sea heavy with smoke; a plume of it boiled into the sky. There was no sign of any goddess, nor the three-eyed shield-bearer. By itself, that meant nothing: the three-eyed one had appeared from nowhere the time before, and might do so again.

But if he could creep up before the magician could call her…

– rush him with the sword, this is no hopeless fight, you can win

– but you will need our strength, our speed

The shellfire had stopped. He would no longer have the noise as cover. But there was hope.

– you cannot wield that weapon without us

– you will fumble the blow

– the lord will loathe you for it

As he turned to go back to the split pine, his eye caught a glint at the base of a neighbouring tree. In a hollow amongst roots, something had been partly covered with fallen twigs.

He moved the twigs aside, and his heart stumbled over what he saw.

His *dughra* lay there, and a knapsack.

Amazed with relief, he dropped the heavy *clathma* and took up the short sword. The Qliphoth howled at the exchange.

'I accept my weakness,' he whispered.

– that knife will achieve nothing, it is too small

– it serves the enemy to choose puny weapons

– the lord will despise you as a traitor

Only when it was in his hand did he think what its presence here might mean. He peered around, but saw no sign of Ranga.

He went back off the rise and through the natural gateway of the split pine. The two figures still stared south at the roiling mass of smoke. Tashi crept around the stone circle to come up on the magician directly from the rear.

Fifteen paces. The Qliphoth were so insistent, the voices so near-constant, he feared Daroguerre would hear them. But he and the short-haired young woman both looked absorbed. The sound of gunfire came from a ship out to sea, to the right of the mass of smoke.

Five paces.

His foot scuffed. He froze. The woman turned, her gun up.

– admit us now, we are all that can save you

She'd made no noise. The magician still didn't know. *– admit us and you can rush him –* She might miss. The gun might jam. *– admit us just enough –* He might survive the bullet and be able to strike.

He slid his left hand into his shirt, to touch the image of the Mountain.

The ship silently erupted in smoke.

'Second one down,' said Daroguerre.

The woman's eyes filled with hate.

Her finger tightened just as the magician turned.

Daroguerre snapped out his arm. The gun barked. Tashi jumped from noise, expecting pain, but the magician had knocked the woman's shoulder and the bullet went wild.

'What are you doing?' she snarled.

'Keep your aim on him,' said Daroguerre, and then the sound of an explosion rolled over the sky. 'But await my word,' he added as the thunder faded, leaving in Tashi's ears only the thunder of his own desperate blood. 'I wish to talk with him.'

He held two stones, Tashi saw now, held them pressed together, his face tight with concentration.

– admit us, it will take but a moment

– no bullet can pierce perfected flesh

– this has been made a place of transformation

He didn't know what to do. The thought of being shot again scared him.

'You and your master have caused me a great deal of trouble,' said Daroguerre. 'Because of you, I was forced to flee Torrento, rousing suspicion and cutting off possible retreat. Because of you, we were nearly killed at the ziggurat. And had it not been for one of my creations, you would earlier have killed a young man of great importance to me.'

Tashi didn't know whether to speak. He tried to stay calm. Hate would feed the Qliphoth that now clamoured for release.

'But none of that matters, in the end,' Daroguerre continued. 'Had you not brought an Empyreal ship to follow me, Seriuz would still be here, interfering. I might have been forced to stick with a plan others had made. Had you not caused that dreadnought and its cruiser squadron to come here, I would not have had the chance to test out the full destructive power of my great work.'

— he talks, the woman has relaxed her guard

— admit us now and destroy them

— his thoughts call the blasphemy back to him, you must act now

'You have tried to hinder me,' said Daroguerre, 'but you have only achieved the reverse. Everyone works for me in the end, whatever their intent. So why not make it formal? I can give you something you could never otherwise hope for. I can teach you to control the power that resides within you, to exercise its strength without surrendering your will. And using the Strandborns' ability to catalyse manifestation, you can learn to switch between the Qliphoth's more powerful form and your normal body. You see, I understand what you are host to. I know what they are.'

'They are the offspring of sin,' said Tashi.

— the lie the magician told your weakling master

'In a way,' said Daroguerre. 'But they are not the demons you believe. They can be tools. All gods, all goddesses, all demons, are tools. Dangerous tools, sometimes, but even a simple saw is dangerous to the untrained child.'

— he lies

— we are the holy will of the lord

— he insults the lord with his claim, kill him

Daroguerre raised the stones before his face. 'I command you Qliphoth to silence!'

Tashi gasped. With a feeling like a sudden gust of wind through his mind, the voices had almost gone. Only the quietest trace remained.

The magician smiled. 'You see? They are biddable to one with power. You have a foot in the psychosphere, and I rule that sphere, as I shall shortly rule the physical world. The fighting ability you exhibited earlier is nothing compared with what you can achieve with full control. I am building a new world. I shall require a means of enforcing my will. And as a reward, I can grant you the means to live forever. To never die.'

'You speak with the tongue of King Serpent,' said Tashi, shaken. 'Such a thing is not yours to give.'

'Thera? Tell him.'

'It's true,' said the woman. 'He knows how.'

'And I speak with no tongue but my own,' said Daroguerre.

'And if I agree?' said Tashi. It felt wonderful to have his mind free of voices again, as clear as sunlight on ice. He touched his shirt, feeling the crinkle beneath. *The Mountain is within me.*

Daroguerre smiled. 'I didn't doubt that you would. You stared into the face of death, did you not, in Torrento? No one who looked hard enough into that face would refuse my offer.'

Tashi kept his thoughts to himself. He licked his lips, nervously preparing, then peered towards the tents thirty paces behind his enemies. He adopted an expression of puzzlement. 'Are those your men?'

They looked – and in the moment of their distraction, Tashi threw his sword.

He'd done it in Bismark when Inspired; he thought his muscles remembered how. But the *dughra* turned in the air and hit Daroguerre hilt-first in the stomach. The magician doubled over but the woman had already turned back – she cried out, aimed. Tashi threw himself to one side.

Impact punched his shoulder with the gun-crack. He twisted, fell hard.

He couldn't move. The ground was white, the sky above somehow both blue and clouded. He couldn't work his body. The voices rushed back. – *NOW you need us, NOW you have no choice* – The woman was still trying to shoot, but there was no noise, no flash.

The magician stood bent over, winded. He'd dropped the stones; they lay on the ground next to the *dughra*.

Get up, get up. Tashi's left arm felt awkward, wrong. His left shoulder ached, with that same ache as where he'd been changed before.

'No…' – *again we save you, we are all that can save you*

Even without Cass's touch, another part of him had altered. He sensed it sending out threads of command, damping shock, powering response. And the ground was white. The Mountain?

He pushed himself up, his legs feeling barely real. The woman pulled the magician away towards the tents. The man had picked up his stones but left the sword. Tashi staggered to retrieve it.

– seize it, kill him, destroy them both

The *dughra* was barely back in his hand when he caught movement at the southern cliff. Over its edge a giant figure hauled itself. It could only be the goddess. She stood, backed by the wrack of smoke, her dark skin gleaming in the sunlight through the now-breaking clouds.

– ADMIT US

She was the most appalling thing Tashi had ever seen, with the snakes in her hair and on her arms, her sharp teeth, her flaming eyes.

– ADMIT US OR YOU WILL FAIL

He tried to swallow his fear. Fire edged the sickle in the goddess's left hand. She started forwards, fangs shining with venom.

– ADMIT US NOW

'No,' he whispered. Breathing hard, he tried to gauge distance and timing. It was already too late; the sight of the goddess had stalled him; he couldn't make it to the magician without being intercepted. And he would not run away. He was a novitiate of the Holy Mountain, about to give battle to the evil the monastery had been established to guard against. His battle would stand testament in Records. The Mountain was within him. He felt its pure cold around him; he had seen the snow-white ground when the magician had dropped the stones.

Gevurah was with him.

His mind shook with demonic clamour.

The goddess was now only yards away. Tashi moved to meet her, heart racing, pulled muscles flaring in pain. A stink came from her like hundreds of rotted bodies.

 – *ADMIT US*

'No!'

She hulked over him, bloated with death, slowed by her bulk. Her sickle swept. Tashi ducked and flung up his arm. Sparks showered; his *dughra* turned her sickle, but the impact bore him down. He twisted out of the blade's path, heat lashing his arm. He darted under her reach and sliced hard across her leg, then a snake's jaws snapped in front of him and he flinched from it and fell to the ground.

 – *ADMIT US*

He rolled from her foot as she stamped. He stabbed her ankle; his blade glanced off. She kicked; he rolled again. He threw himself between her legs as the sickle came down. The air beneath her was like an oven.

He scrambled out behind her, flashed with sweat from her heat. She turned, the air shimmering around her. The sleeve of his sword-arm was charred. He hurt with the cold-pain of his burns – but already the pain was changing to that dull ache of wrongness.

 – *ADMIT US*

'No!' he gasped. 'I accept my weakness.'

 – *YOU WRETCH, SHE WILL NOT STOP WITH YOU*

 – *YOUR MASTER, YOUR PRECIOUS WITCH GIRL*

 – *THEY WILL DRINK FROM HER DUGS OF DEATH*

 – *SHE WILL ADD THEIR SKULLS TO HER SKIRTS*

The goddess came again.

He readied his trembling muscles and darted beneath her reach, slashing hard at her leg. The strike jarred his arm as though he'd hit stone. Something caught at his back and he stumbled, crashed to the ground. He pushed to his feet, screamed as pain ripped his shoulder blade.

It raked deep into his back, and the goddess was behind him, and he couldn't stop the Qliphoth: already the damaged flesh was being transformed.

He glanced to his left. The magician stood by the tents, once again holding the stones pressed together, his face taut. The battle had put Tashi between the man and his creation.

Panting hard, he faced her. The leg he'd hit showed no sign of injury. His sword had done nothing. And the goddess would not tire. Her fiery eyes and fanged mouth showed no emotion.

– *ADMIT US* – He didn't know if killing Daroguerre would make any difference to the goddess, but it was all he could try.

He bent his knees and angled as though to move right, then sprang to his left as hard as he could and drove himself into a run towards the magician.

A blow smashed into his leg and sent him flying, the sword clattering from his hand. He struggled up and his leg folded under him, pain spearing through the bone. His sword was too far away. The air grew suddenly hot, loud with footsteps. He turned to face the goddess. She was already on him, over him, and he couldn't get to his sword, couldn't run.

She picked up the sickle she'd thrown. He tried to back off but his leg wouldn't work. This was it, this was it. She brought the weapon down at him. He threw up his hand and caught the blade. The red skin resisted its edge but the force drove him against the ground. Bandage flamed and blackened. Heat lashed his front, charring, searing, and still pressure bore him down; he couldn't get out from it. Her other hand gripped him. Serpent fangs sank into his shoulder. She held him, burning. He choked on the stink of crackling skin. Smoke tore at his lungs and throat in a violence of coughing, screaming. The Qliphoth howled for release. He pressed all his shredded will against them. He willed himself to die quickly, to accept his weakness, to keep the Qliphoth from taking any more of his rapidly destroyed body.

He could no longer feel the Mountain. The picture against his chest was in flames; his clothes were on fire, his skin gone. His mind was a howling of pain and demand. He had to die unclaimed. He had to believe he could find the Mountain, but he couldn't feel it. His master had promised him. His master; he could see Shoggu's face, and suddenly everything, the monastery, the Abbot, the Knifebridge, the cell in High Place, Hann, Aino.

Home.

'Find it, Brother. I'll be on the bridge to salute you.'

He couldn't bear it, it was taking too long, and with that crack they swarmed in and agony became a dark euphoria.

– *WE WILL REMAKE YOU*

Burned skin hardened; torn muscles knitted into flesh that was not flesh; unendurable pain became the ache of what should not be, the Cry of Sin, and the will of that flesh raced through his body to his mind, pushing him back.

– *YOU CANNOT DIE, YOU WILL NOT DIE*

He was transformed, his flesh perfected in the crucible of pain, his self burnt down to the purity of rage and hate.

– *YOU ARE OURS AND THE WORLD IS OURS*

His eyes were going dark.

– *YOU ARE OUR INSTRUMENT*

His grip closed harder round the sickle. He wrenched it from the goddess's hand and hurled it aside. His left arm twisted out of her grasp and he punched hard upwards as a blade extruded from his knuckles. His body-weapon sank deep into the goddess's stomach. She staggered back shrieking, and as she pulled herself off the blade he carved it to one side. Black putrid offal slithered from her, steaming, smoking; a million dead insects fell to the ground.

Another blade formed from his right hand as he stood. The goddess flailed at him. Her serpents lashed, snapped. He struck off one head, then the other, precise blows through scale and spine, sending them thudding to the ground in sprays of dark blood. More blood came as he swiped off the goddess's right hand. He wanted to see all that was in her. She was no person, but a monster; it made it easier to relish dismemberment, repayment for his near-death, his body's death, his irreversible transformation.

He plunged and slashed, a surgery of fury. She was bloated and slow, and her fire couldn't touch him now, couldn't burn him, couldn't make him scream. He sliced off her other hand, then her forearms, he cut through the tendons behind her knees and when she fell he decapitated all the snakes of her hair. He carved and sliced while her howls of rage filled the sky, then he put out her eyes, slit her bowels open and hacked off her head.

Her fanged mouth gaped at the sky, silent. The fire in her died.

Now for the others. He retracted his blades: they were too unsubtle for the agonies he would inflict on the magician and his accomplice. The nails of his right hand became razors and picks; the two middle fingers of his left hand became shears.

His head searched for the humans, and seemed to find them gone. He sensed annoyance. He sensed the consideration of Ultimate Form; but even now, the transformation had not gone far enough. An attempt to achieve Ultimate Form would too greatly deplete the available energy.

He sensed these thoughts, but they weren't wholly his. He'd been made an observer again, less present in his body even than before. He couldn't see. He sensed his head was staring towards the tents, but he saw no tents. When fighting the goddess, he had been focused only on her, and hadn't noticed as the rest of the world had been closed off from his senses. There was nothing now, the ground only a whiteness, and overhead blue.

He sensed walking.

Stop, he told what had been his body.

– *YOU CANNOT STOP US*

Again, he focused his will into that command: *Stop*.

– *WE ARE UNCEASING*

– *WE SHALL EXTERMINATE THROUGH YOU*

– *WE SHALL BUILD THE NEW WORLD*

Their voices battered him. But he sensed frustration, stasis. He held them in check. This time, he had fought against their possession, and now, by concentrating with all the mental force left to him, he could at least keep the body from moving.

– YOU CANNOT RESIST US

– ALL FLESH SHALL BE OPENED TO JUDGEMENT

– ALL FORMS OF THE WITCH SHALL BE SLICED WITH CLEAN EDGES

It was so great an effort. His will eroded in the face of such untiring hatred. He sensed movement again in the body that had once been human, once been his.

– IT BELONGED TO THE WITCH

– IT DISEASED YOU

– WE HAVE REMOVED YOUR GENITALS

– THERE SHALL BE NO BREEDING

– THERE SHALL BE NO LIFE

– OUR MANIFESTO IS ABSOLUTE AND PURE

Gevurah, he pleaded. *Help me.*

– YOU MAY NOT INVOKE THE LORD AGAINST US

– WE SERVE HIS TRUE DESIRES

No, thought all that was left of Tashi. *He cannot want my Self taken from me. He gave it to me. It's His, I am His, I AM HIS.*

In that sudden truth, that pure burning understanding of himself, the whiteness clarified. All around him was snow. High above reared the peak of the Holy Mountain, blazing with sunlight against the blue. Hope leapt in him. Shoggu had been right: the Mountain had been with him all the time.

He willed himself to run up the slope.

Iron weight held him. The voices of the Qliphoth dragged at him. He couldn't move a leg, not even an inch.

Lord Gevurah.

He stared up at the peak, fixed what was left of his mind on its brightness, its purity. It hurt to look at. He could get no closer, but the vision strengthened his will. Focusing on it held back the Qliphoth as much as any denial; the Mountain's towering statement of ice and rock quietened their voices. They would not give up, but neither would he. Exhaustion was a thing of the body, and he had no body now. He was a spark of will and life, holding in check a monster of death.

Forever. He understood that, but couldn't let the horror overwhelm him. Too much depended on his endurance, his willingness to pay this price. All he could do to prevent a slaughter was to stare half-blinded in pain at his true and eternal home, the blazing peak he had yearned for his whole life, but would never, now, reach.

35

THE END OF THE DREAM

When no sound had come from the world beyond the pines for half an hour, Orc said, 'We should move. We can't stay hiding forever.'

Cass looked less than happy. 'I didn't go to all that effort just so you could stick your neck in trouble again.'

'We need to find out what's happening. Let's get to that trail, at least.'

With her supporting him, they made their slow, wincing way down through the quiet forest. Orc thought the air felt less oppressive. Above the trees, the cloud-cover was starting to break.

Soon the dusty path showed a few yards ahead.

'Are your shoes at the Spiral too?' said Cass. 'I can go and see if there's anyone there.'

'No you won't,' said Orc.

'We need them. You can't even walk.'

'And you can't run if there *is* anyone there.' Orc sank to the ground. 'We wait here and see if anyone comes by. If there's anyone still alive.'

They sat just back from the trail, out of clear sight. They'd already talked through what Cass had done and discovered that morning. Now only questions remained, too many to start on. But Orc found sitting in silence worse. He kept wanting to shift nearer Cass; the need to hold her, the urge to feel the heat and softness of her skin, was almost overpowering. And if he gave in to that, he would be in danger of losing all restraint, whatever the consequences. He thought he could feel the same in her, too. She was the tautness of the whole forest.

He moved so she wouldn't see the effect she had on him. He scraped a pine twig over the ground between them. 'What you said, about how we make things manifest. The Zhenaii used to do it, right? That's what caused the Flood.'

'So Hana said.'

'And didn't you say there was a city being flooded in your dreams?'

Cass frowned at him. 'Go on.'

'That's as far as I've got.'

'I didn't make the link. But what could it mean?'

'No idea,' said Orc. 'But it's the only connection with our pasts that's come out of this whole mess. I wonder if Geist knew. He did try hard to find out who we are. Maybe he suspected something about us, and never let on.'

'But if we were that important to him, why did he go off and leave us at Amano's?'

'I guess he expected us to stay put,' said Orc. 'But I have an idea why he went. I think he's like a man with more than one wife.'

Cass snorted a laugh.

'I'm serious,' said Orc. 'There's me and Hana, and now I know about her, I wouldn't mind betting there are three others somewhere: Fox, Eagle and Sparrow. He was with us more than a year. Maybe he thought he needed to give the others some time. Did Hana say when he taught her, or when she last saw him?'

'We didn't get round to talking about him,' said Cass. 'I hope she's okay.'

Orc heard something. 'What's that?'

Footsteps sounded from the direction of the cove. More than a few men. Orc and Cass crouched closer behind a large pine and watched the trail. First to appear was an officer without a jacket.

'Martin!' cried Cass before Orc could stop her.

The men shocked to a halt; rifles went up. Juneau held a pistol, and lacked his usual smile. Trailing the two Kymerans came a Sundaran officer with about twenty marines.

Orc followed Cass out, furious with her recklessness. He hated to see Seriuz's arms enfold her thin-clad body. There was less obvious warmth from Cass as the two embraced, but that didn't make Orc feel much easier. She might still have thrown away their whole escape.

'You've no idea how glad I am to see you both alive,' Seriuz said.

'I have a very good idea,' said Cass, as they released each other. 'But… you know what's up ahead?'

'Lieutenant Forgas here told me what happened,' said Seriuz. 'But there's been no sign or sound for some time, neither of Daroguerre nor his creation. I'm sorry I wasn't here.'

'Me too,' Cass said.

'I had no idea about that dreadnought and her cruiser squadron,' said Seriuz. 'They must have left Torrento well before *Archon* contacted them. I still can't understand why.'

'And what would you have done if you had been here?' said Cass. 'Fought them?'

'Have they gone?' said Orc.

'Sir…' said Juneau.

'We'll talk later,' Seriuz said. 'Are your clothes there? I'll bring them back if I can.'

'You know Thera's up there?' said Cass. 'Or she was. I think she's been working for Daroguerre all along. Martin, you can't trust that man. He didn't give a damn about your orders. He gave the stone to Orc so he could sacrifice him to make the goddess while you were away. He threatened me with Esteban if I wouldn't help. I don't think he was doing it to bring peace to Kymera.'

Seriuz nodded, his gaunt face grim. 'Juneau, stay with them.'

After Seriuz and the marines had gone off towards the Spiral, Juneau got them a few yards into the trees and sat with them, pistol readied, while he told them what had happened. *Nightfire* had tailed *Archon* to the port of Carnega, but without Thera they couldn't approach the cruiser with enough speed to evade her guns, nor get close unseen at night. After staying off Carnega an hour, *Archon* had then steamed back towards the Hollow Isles, but on nearing them had diverted towards smoke on the horizon, which had turned out to be three Empyreal cruisers heading east.

'We came straight here, of course,' said Juneau, 'dreading what we'd find. And what we found wasn't what we'd feared, but it wasn't much better.'

He told them about the goddess's work, the smoke and wreckage and bodies, all that remained of *Iron Tiger* and the heavy cruiser *Relentless*. The pitifully few survivors, abandoned by their own navy, were still being rescued by *Makhral* and *Tarpon*.

'And where's the goddess now?' said Orc.

'That's what the captain's finding out,' said Juneau. 'Gods keep him safe.'

Twenty sombre minutes later, two marines returned with their bags. One of them used a first-aid kit to treat Orc's feet. Clothed and shod at least, but both still limping, Orc and Cass accompanied Juneau and the marines back to the Spiral. The marines wouldn't say what they'd found. Orc assumed the goddess had disappeared at least.

But she had not. Her body lay dismembered on ground stained dark with her blood. A few Sundarans stood looking at the monstrous corpse, a respectful distance upwind.

Several more surrounded another lying figure. Orc glimpsed red. 'Oh no,' said Cass, and hobbled over.

'What the hell?' said Orc, when he saw it.

It was a man, not a large man, wearing bizarre, form-fitting armour whose red metal sections seemed to join in seams rather than overlap. The helmet's mask was a terrifying face, as blood-red as the armour: a grotesque demon snarling in rage, but with eyes closed. Most unsettling of all, a variety of horrible-looking instruments protruded from the fingers of both gauntlets.

Over some sections of the armour were scraps of grey cloth, many blackened. Orc swallowed as he looked closer. Unless the armour were flexible, and not steel at all, he didn't see how it could let the wearer move. It was more like a reptile's hide, but made of sections of plate and chain links as well as scales. And why would a helmet include a mechanism to close the eyes?

Seeing the tears on Cass's face, a cold shock went through him. He remembered the story she'd told, and realised who this must be.

'This is my fault,' she said.

'No,' he said, 'it can't be. How?'

She didn't answer, but walked to one of the standing stones of the circle and sat at its base, staring between her knees. As Orc joined her, he saw the sky to the south filled with the smoke of burning wreckage.

'You said it was just a couple of places, where you touched him?'

'But that must have started it,' said Cass. 'Hana said he was possessed. What I did must have given the thing inside him a foothold. Hell, Orc, we're living disaster zones. Is he dead? Or unconscious? I didn't see any breathing.'

'You're not asking the right person.'

'Maybe Hana will know. Or Shoggu. God, I don't want to be here when Shoggu sees what's happened to him.' She put the heels of her hands in her eyes. 'We ran. We left it up to others.'

'What could we have done?'

'Yeah, I know. Nothing, not against the goddess. But what if we could have stopped Tashi becoming that thing? He was here, fighting, on his own. We should have been here, Orc.'

'Hey...' He rubbed her shoulder, then looked up.

'The captain wants to see you both,' said Juneau. 'He's in the larger tent, with Mister Daroguerre.'

'That's easy then,' said Orc. 'No effing way.'

'Daroguerre's no danger,' said Juneau. 'He's been shot.'

'Dead?' said Cass.

'No, a flesh-wound.'

'Who by?' said Cass.

493

'Who do we send the reward to?' said Orc.

'You can ask him yourself,' said Juneau.

In the tent's dim interior, Seriuz slumped in a camp-chair; Daroguerre lay on a sleeping-roll, his head propped on Thera's lap. The left sleeve of the magician's robe had been cut off, and the upper arm heavily bandaged. His face was pale, his hair dishevelled. He met Orc's gaze briefly, then closed his eyes.

'What happened?' said Cass.

'He's been wounded, can't you see?' said Thera.

'I don't care about that,' said Cass. 'I mean about Tashi.'

'The boy who tried to kill Orc?' said Thera. 'I'd have thought you'd be glad to see him gone.'

'Answer her,' said Seriuz.

'He completed his transformation by himself,' said Daroguerre weakly. 'The very fabric of this place must have been altered. I didn't know that possible.'

'Is he dead?' said Cass.

'I suspect so,' said Daroguerre. 'When I was shot, he was still human, about to die. Then he changed. He destroyed the Skalith manifestation, but his transformation must have been too much for him to survive. Fortunately for us.'

'For everyone, by the look of him,' said Seriuz.

'Is that it?' said Thera. 'Can Mister Daroguerre be left to recover now?'

'No,' said Seriuz. 'I still need to get to the bottom of what happened between you four in my absence.'

Orc barked a laugh. 'What, you left us to play nicely, and now you want to know why we were fighting when you came back from the shops? Might've been something to do with your mate trying to turn me into a vegetable.'

'I tried no such thing,' said Daroguerre. 'After your symbolic sacrifice, you would have been recalled. You agreed to that yourself.'

'That was a trap,' said Orc. 'Give me some credit.'

'Thera admitted it,' said Cass.

'I did not!' cried Thera.

'No?' said Cass. '"He'll get the best care"? Remember that?'

Thera looked at Cass with seething hate.

Cass turned to Seriuz. 'You know she deserted you?'

'We've discussed that. I'm still thinking what to do about it. Mister Daroguerre maintains he couldn't have succeeded in creating the goddess without Thera. Much as I dislike using ends to justify means, it can't be denied that we might all be in a very black spot without his manifestation – yourselves included. Had the Kurassians arrested you and learned of your talents, I dread to think what they might have done.'

'Our talents?' said Orc. 'So you know about that?'

'I do now. I always knew you were needed for more than your diving skills, but Mister Daroguerre has only just appraised me of the full truth.'

'And why is it?' Cass asked Daroguerre. 'Why do we have this "talent"?'

'I am not privy to that knowledge,' the magician said. 'But I can help you find out.'

Orc snorted. 'No thanks. We'll learn it some other way.'

'We're not going anywhere with him,' Cass told Seriuz. 'You realise that?'

'I doubt the captain will ditch his ambitions so hastily,' said Daroguerre. 'Think what has happened here today. I have proven manifestation possible: not just a lowly elemental bound to a specific crystal, but a fully functioning, physically solid entity, and with extraordinary powers. We still have the artefacts, and I can build upon the knowledge and experience gained here. Even with the stone gone, I might succeed.'

'Gone?' said Orc.

'It was stolen,' said Thera. 'And we need to get it back.'

'Stolen by whom?' said Seriuz.

'The "winner",' said Thera sullenly. 'That's what he called himself. The one who shot Mister Daroguerre.'

'But who was it?' said Orc.

'His face was bandaged. Tall, quite young I think. Dark hair. Civilian clothes.'

'Who the hell could that be?' said Cass.

'Unfortunately,' said Daroguerre, 'I'm in no state to scry for him, or the stone. You,' he said to Orc. 'You held it. It might be that you can locate it through that past connection. The thought-form of the guardian sister has been dispelled, which means your animath has been released. You must scape for that stone: we must recover it if possible.'

The man was mad, thought Orc. He talked as though they were allies.

'If you can uncover the thief, all well and good,' said Seriuz. 'But the Sundaran ships need to leave now to have a chance of running the Straits tomorrow night, and I don't have the men to search the island or go chasing hunches.'

'Why go anywhere?' said Thera. 'We'll find the stone, and create another goddess. Let the whole Empyreal Navy come. There won't be a suicidal Thangkaran brat to stop her next time.'

Daroguerre shook his head. 'The build-up of Mother energy has been consumed; much of the power behind Skalith's manifestation came from that. We cannot risk being caught here. If the stone is gone, so be it.'

'You still have the firestone, at least?' Seriuz asked Thera. She nodded.

'That was the master-stroke,' said Daroguerre. 'Incorporating the fire element. And that can be done again, Captain. It can all be done again, in Sundara. Your dream need not die.'

'We're not going anywhere with that man,' said Cass. She backed towards the tent entrance, but Juneau moved to block it.

'Sir?'

Seriuz frowned.

'Is it all to be in vain?' Daroguerre asked him, visibly struggling with pain. 'The Strandborns are essential. The dreadnought's destruction will bring war closer. Yet it is likely still some way off, and the Kurassians will be terrified of another goddess. If I can manifest another such being, in Sundara or elsewhere, the war might still be prevented. If that chance is denied me, then the crew of *Iron Tiger* will be the first of many, Kurassian and Sundaran and Kymeran – the Southern Ocean and the lands about will turn red.'

He raised himself on one elbow. 'Captain, you instigated this project because of the threat you saw to your country. If you let these two go, you make that threat a certainty.'

Orc tensed. The man was right. Seriuz couldn't afford to release them.

Seriuz studied his hands as though searching them for advice. His scarred face looked weary, as if from days without sleep, years without peace.

'When I was a boy,' he said at last, 'I saw the face of Argantas in the knots and grain of a piece of board in my grandmother's house. I made corn-stalk figures of Jonastas; I went with my friends to drink illicit wine in caves dedicated to Puristo. I wanted all those gods to come to life. When I saw *Nightfire*'s elemental, I was entranced. But a creature visible in shifting flames is not so far removed from one seen in pine-knots. At some level, one is still able to pass it off as imagination.

'I wanted the gods of my childhood to live; but now I realise I wanted to be able to put them away again, back to statues and corn-stalks. I want no part in any more manifestations. I believe nothing but evil will come of them.'

'Then you are a fool,' said Daroguerre.

'A little less of one than I have been, I think. I have woken from a dream I should never have had.'

'Millions will rue your decision, Captain,' said Daroguerre. 'They will rue it with their blood – and all for the sake of two vagrants no one will miss. I need them. I insist. I command you, you cannot let them go…' He broke into coughing.

Seriuz rose from his chair and walked outside, beckoning Orc and Cass after him.

'I command you, I said!' came the choked call as they left. 'I commanded a *goddess*. You are nothing, a mere public servant, a disgrace…'

Seriuz took Orc and Cass out of earshot, to stand near the edge of the cliff overlooking the smoke and debris where *Tarpon* had finished rescuing the few Kurassian survivors.

'Thank you,' said Cass.

'What'll you do with him?' said Orc.

'Do with him?' said Seriuz. 'Take him to Sundara. He might go on from there, or make his talents available to the Shahanate. But if he chooses to stay with me, and tell me a hundred times a day that a million innocent people will regret my decision, it's hardly less than I deserve. I can't foresee he'll be proved wrong.'

Orc wanted to ask why Daroguerre wouldn't be punished, but kept quiet. There was still time for Seriuz to change his mind about them; he didn't want to risk antagonising him.

'You shouldn't trust him, though,' said Cass. 'He is evil.'

'Any more than I?' said Seriuz.

'At least your motives were understandable,' said Cass. 'What *were* his, even? He didn't know the dreadnought was coming, so why didn't he wait for your return?'

'I might pry that from him, given time,' said Seriuz. 'But if he had no sympathy with my aims, why ally himself with me at all? He was the one with the magical ability, and the knowledge of your particular qualities. If his own plans didn't involve a popular rising, then what was I to him? Merely a means of transport? No, he has a long association with the League. I trust him so far, at least. Now, you should return to the cove. I've advised the Quallaces to leave the island by nightfall. I'll ask them to take you to the mainland.'

'Do you know where Hana is?' said Cass.

'She wasn't at the cove,' Seriuz said. 'She'll be around somewhere, I'm sure,' he added, but Cass looked worried. 'You'd better go.'

They walked as fast as they could comfortably manage to the trail junction. Cass took the path to the Navel, and Orc went down to the cove alone. He passed some of Seriuz's crew with stretchers, and Bouran with a medical bag.

The stacks of the Sundaran warships were pouring smoke, and so was the single stack of *Aurora*. The Quallaces and their servants were carrying boxes on board. Stefanie asked if he'd seen Hana, and he told her Cass had gone to look.

Cass arrived, breathless, ten minutes later, and called to Ferman for rope. The two were soon gone again, leaving Orc to sit on the shore and curse his injured feet.

Soon the marines came down from the Spiral, and within minutes the three Sundaran warships had steamed off. *Nightfire* could remain well into the night, Orc guessed, and still catch up with the Sundarans before they ran the Straits. But the departure of the battleship and cruiser left the island virtually undefended if the surviving Kurassian ships chanced a return.

Cass and Ferman were gone a long time. Stefanie paced. Orc toyed with his focus-stone. He thought of finding somewhere quiet and scaping; but there was no certainty of getting enough time and privacy, and he wanted a break from magic altogether. It wouldn't hurt for his reunion with Otter to wait: Daroguerre's words, and a vague memory of teeth biting his ankle, assured him his animath would come next time.

As for learning where the large stone was, he already had his suspicions.

Next down the trail were two men carrying Daroguerre on a stretcher, with Thera walking alongside. The bearers carried Daroguerre onto the jetty and laid him down. Thera was helping the magician up as Orc reached them.

'Mister Strandborn,' said Daroguerre, his voice slurred. 'Now is the test of your maturity. Leave the events here to the past. You have genuine talent, but need a teacher. The opportunity remains.'

'What, to be used again?'

'You might find it better to be used by me than by others.'

'Even Geist didn't try to flush my mind down the drain.'

'I wasn't talking about Geist,' said Daroguerre. 'I cannot speak more fully now. But if you and your cousin put aside childish pride and imagined grievance, and work with me as partners, the rewards will be great.'

'No chance.'

'Think!' said Daroguerre. 'Wealth uncountable, and information – in time, the means to acquire *any* information. You understand?' His voice was edged with what sounded to Orc like fear. 'The situation is more complex than you think.'

'Seems pretty simple to me,' said Orc. 'You tried to turn me into a vegetable. Ergo, fuck off.'

'Seriuz will guarantee your safety.' Daroguerre spoke tightly, in pain and exhaustion. 'Don't throw this chance away.'

'Okay, then,' said Orc. 'To show you mean it, give me the big stone.'

Daroguerre's brow clenched in apparent confusion. 'Stolen.'

'We told you,' said Thera.

'And I don't believe you,' said Orc. 'No one on the island fits the description you gave, unless one of those marines changed into civvies, or Ferman slimmed down and put on a wig. You gave me fake details to throw off any scaping I did.'

'Then what do you think happened to it?' said Thera.

'You're hiding it,' said Orc.

She laughed. 'From you? Why bother? It's ours.'

'I fetched it up. I've got more right to it.'

'If you believe that, your mind's already been trashed,' said Thera. 'It's no good,' she said to Daroguerre, who nodded. She turned to the sailors. 'Take us on board.'

'No, hold on,' Orc told them.

'Ignore him,' Thera said, then turned to him. 'You have no command over these men, wretched boy. What's more, they hate you. You two have brought the captain's plan to ruin and condemned his whole crew to exile. May you rot in the pits of Naganos. May you never find the truth of yourselves. May you give each other syphilis. Now go away.'

She returned to her task. The stretcher bearers gave Orc an

unfriendly look. Orc felt shaken as he walked off the jetty. Thera was right: the same men who'd applauded them for finding their lost anchor would have found his life small price for the chance to return home as saviours of their country.

And what was *his* country?

'We should have been here, Orc.'

He watched *Nightfire*'s boat being rowed out. The large stone was beyond his reach now, but maybe, in the end, that was no bad thing. It had brought nothing but trouble. At least he and Cass were reconciled, and shared the same aim again. There had to be another way of finding their pasts, and at least they had some idea of a new way forward.

An hour later, Cass reappeared with Hana and Ferman and everyone who'd been left at the Spiral. They carried luggage, and two stretchers bearing shrouded bodies: Tashi and Esteban, Orc assumed. All the living were grim-faced, but Cass and Hana looked especially upset, and Hana was filthy.

While Seriuz and Ferman talked to Stefanie, Hana accompanied the stretchers. Esteban was transferred to *Nightfire*'s boat, but Tashi was left on the jetty. Then Hana led the bearers of one of the stretchers back up the trail.

'You found her, then?' Orc said to Cass.

'In the cave.' She seemed distracted, more interested in the boat.

'They're taking the bodies?'

'Seriuz will have Esteban buried at sea,' said Cass. 'Tashi's coming with us.'

'He is?'

'Hana did a scape, or a meditation, or something. She thinks his real self might still be in there, very deep down. We might be able to help him, maybe change him back, once we know more about what changed him in the first place. Hana thinks you're right: Geist probably did know something about manifestation, and us.'

Orc nodded. 'We need to find him.'

'Hana saw him a few months back. Must have been just after he left us.'

'Saw him where?'

'Some college she belongs to. We can ask later. Right now, she's too cut up.' Cass looked at Tashi. 'It's weird, he couldn't accept who she was or what she did or what she believed in, but it's like none of that matters to her. I thought he was a dogmatic little prick. But there's no denying he was brave as hell. We owe him a lot, and Hana. And there's someone else we owe, too, and he'll be easier to pay back. There's only one thing he wants now. Come with me.'

She led him to a half-ruined building used as a tool shed. She handed him a spade, and took one herself.

'Six feet long,' she said. 'Deep as we can.'

She chose a patch of ground near the vegetables. Digging hurt Orc's foot, but he didn't complain. Cass wouldn't say who it was for. 'You never met him,' she said. 'You'll find out soon.'

So he dug for those who'd happened to die, while he happened to live. He dug because it was the job of the living to bury the dead, whether or not there was any justice in who had ended up each side of that dividing line that was both as thin as a thread and as wide as all the world. He couldn't see that he deserved to still be here. He had recklessly committed himself to his own destruction, and had been saved by words, by memories, by connections – which was to say by magic, something no more substantial than luck.

And by determination, and love. He felt unworthy of it.

He and Cass had managed a grave three-feet deep by the time Hana returned. The shrouded body on the stretcher looked too small for a full-grown man. Orc had already worked out who it might be, from the story Cass had told after they'd escaped the Spiral. A gap in the rough-cut shroud showed red cloth.

'What happened?' he asked.

'Shot,' said Hana. 'In the back. That bastard Daroguerre must have sent more marines after them than we thought. But Shoggu was still alive when the abomination was destroyed, I'm sure of it. What a bloody waste, to be killed when the fight was already over.'

'The Sundarans have gone,' said Orc. 'If it was one of the marines...'

502

Hana nodded. 'I know. Too late.'

The bearers used sheets to lower the body into the grave.

'I'm afraid I'm ignorant of the Thangkaran ceremonies,' said Ferman.

'It wouldn't be right for one of us to perform it anyway,' said Stefanie.

'Should I say a few words?' said Seriuz.

'No, I will,' said Hana. 'As he said to me, we weren't natural allies, but we were united against a common foe. And you were that foe, Captain.'

She stepped forwards. 'None of us knew Shoggu well, and only two of us even met him. He arrived in secret to prevent a great evil, and thanks partly to him, that evil was destroyed. I believe I worked with him at the end. I sensed his attempts to project his holy mountain to where Tashi fought, and I tried to join my power with his. He'd been taught that working with energy like that was witchcraft or magic or sorcery. But he put aside those beliefs, and perhaps in his own mind even risked his soul, to help someone he loved. Shoggu, I will do my best to help him too.

'Whoever shot him, the man ultimately responsible is known to us all, and may he suffer for it. Shoggu's suffering is at an end. He was a brave man, true to his beliefs but willing to compromise, and he deserves to go to whichever rest he would have wanted.'

After a silence, Ferman said, 'Perhaps we can contact his monastery, and ask what they would like as a marker, or a memorial. We'll be back at some stage, I've no doubt.'

'I regret having to rush this,' said Seriuz, 'but we should all be off this island by dark.'

The stretcher bearers shovelled earth on top of Shoggu. Even though Orc had never met the old man, it felt too hasty, as though everyone was running away from the consequences of everything they'd done.

We should have been here, Orc.

When the grave was filled, Hana found a piece of rubble with a sharp corner, and placed it at the head of the grave to look something like a mountain peak.

The sun had already gone from the cove, screened by the shoulder to the west. Tashi on his stretcher had been taken on board *Aurora*.

Nightfire's boat now waited at the jetty for Seriuz and the others.

'So, Miss Strandborn,' said Seriuz. 'Another goodbye. And this time, I don't expect to see you again, even if all goes as well as it can. Try not to get tangled up in what's coming.'

'You're going to Sundara?' said Cass.

He nodded. 'My family is in Makassal; we'll pick them up on the way. I should have liked to bring Tetana back to Torrento with the threat of war lifted and a goddess uniting its people, but now it'll be exile for her and Robert too. And then… gods, I did this to *prevent* a war.'

'It would have happened anyway, sir,' said Juneau. 'That's the point.'

'I need to ask you something,' said Cass.

Seriuz looked as uncomfortable as Orc felt. 'You're sure of that?'

'Would you have stopped it?' she asked. 'If you'd been here, and Daroguerre was able to create your perfect ruling goddess by trashing Orc's mind, would you have said no?'

Seriuz glanced at Juneau. Orc couldn't read the look that passed between them.

'Before I knew what horror Daroguerre would unleash, you mean?' said Seriuz. 'You ask whether I would have gone ahead with my plan if it only required the sacrifice of your cousin? Let me turn the question around – would I have risked thousands of lives in a needless war, just to spare him?'

Cass visibly swallowed. 'That's what I'm asking, yes.'

'The "if" is too big. I wasn't here.'

'That's not an answer, Martin.'

'No war is clean,' said Orc. 'Not even a war of liberation.'

Seriuz's eyes narrowed at him, as if trying to work him out, then he gave the smallest of nods and turned to Cass. 'Don't harbour any regret at not seeing me again,' he told her. 'The regret should be mine alone.'

He shook her hand – she looked unhappy – then offered his hand to Orc. For a moment, Orc felt like refusing; then he saw in Seriuz's expression that this was not an attempt at friendship or to cancel grievance, but a loser acknowledging a victor. Or whatever. He was tired of conflict. He prepared to squeeze hard in case Seriuz tried to overpower his grip, but the man shook with no more than normal firmness.

Orc and Cass watched, not speaking, as the boat was rowed out. Juneau raised an arm in farewell as they rounded the mole, but Seriuz had his back to them.

'We'd better move ourselves,' said Ferman. 'We don't want to hit the Paps in the dark.'

Cass looked around. 'Where's Hana?'

'Already on board, with our passenger,' said Ferman. 'Do you really think he's… safe?'

'Mister Quallace,' said Cass, 'I have more faith in Hana than in anyone I've met. If she thinks Tashi's stable, that's good enough for me.'

He nodded, looking as though he were half-convinced and willing to live with the other half. 'Come on, then. Time to leave.'

Nightfire was already steaming eastwards by the time *Aurora* left the cove. Ferman turned the yacht in the opposite direction, with the aim of skirting the Paps before heading north towards the mainland.

Down in the saloon, Orc found the drinks cabinet, and poured brandies. He and Cass sat on a padded leather banquette by a porthole, which gave a last view of the ruined settlement.

'We should have been here,' he said, half to himself.

'Orc?'

'You were right, what you said. But not just at the end. When you brought me back from Daroguerre's trap, it felt like I'd been moved in between. Like I'd woken up somewhere completely different to where I went to sleep.'

'How do you mean?'

His mind agitated, trying to grasp it. 'When I went into that scape, everything was just us. The rest of the island didn't matter, let alone the rest of the world. And when I came back – bam! – Empyreal warships, the goddess, Esteban getting shot, soldiers. It wasn't the world I went to sleep in, but it *was*. It was always that world. I just didn't see it before, because I didn't look. I couldn't look anywhere except you and me.'

Cass gave a small nod.

'We've never really been here,' said Orc, 'not since we came round on that beach. That briefing Seriuz gave us – as soon as I worked out the stone was here, everything else got pushed out, the war and everything. But we're part of it. It was always our mess, even if it wasn't our fault. You told Seriuz we don't belong anywhere. But we belong in the world, don't we? It's time to act like it. Hey, why are you laughing? I'm being serious.'

'I know you are,' said Cass, now clearly trying to suppress her smile. 'And you're right, every word. About both of us.' Her face softened, saddened. 'But where's this bold determination to belong in the world going to get you when you need to find Geist and help Tashi? You're going to be spending more time scaping than ever. Hana too.'

'Yeah, we'll both need you to keep our feet on the ground.'

Cass laughed. 'I don't think *she* will. But what I do think is that we've found a friend, at last. A real one, this time.'

Orc hoped so. He thought of the possibilities: someone who knew the world, and magic, and who might actually be on their side. Someone who could help them find Geist, and everything that might follow from that. 'That's a good thing to find. Better than a stupid stone.'

'And we've found something else: your name.'

'I don't want it back till we find yours too.'

'We'll put it by, then,' said Cass. 'Except I might tease you with it.'

Orc put down his brandy. It was time. 'Something I've found.' He breathed in, then touched Cass's forearm and slid his hand down into hers; and though he thrilled at her skin, this wasn't about that. 'Some words,' he said, trying not to sound as shaky as he was feeling.

'Go on,' she said, eyes as serious as anything.

'Whatever we are to each other, and whatever I'm allowed to mean by it...' But his heartbeat was too powerful and he knew if he went further it would shake him apart.

'What?'

He shook his head in dismay. Couldn't go further, but couldn't bear to abandon it.

Cass burst out a kind of snorted laugh, but he could see from her face that she was trying not to cry. 'That's a messy way of saying it,' she said. 'Or not saying it.'

'Sorry.'

'Me too,' she said. 'And more important.' She squeezed his hand. 'Me too.'

He bit his inner lip to keep his jaw from trembling.

'And messy suits us.' She sighed, half-happy, half-tired. 'Oh, come here…'

She leaned into him. Arms enclosed.

'Whatever it means,' she said into his neck.

'Whatever it means,' he said into her hair. She smelt of sweat and dirt, but he didn't care; it was her smell, and he could hardly smell clean himself. And the boat would have a shower, maybe even a bath: a boat's engine made endless hot water.

The thought of a bath was almost impossible after all that had happened. He couldn't believe they were safe. For a few days, at least, truly safe.

They sat against each other as the yacht chugged along. They didn't stir except to take sips of their drinks, until, passing to the west of the second of the Paps, Orc ducked his head to peer up at the summit through the porthole. For a moment, he thought he saw the light of the setting sun strike something pale, something that almost might have been the shirt of a seated figure. But when he blinked, he couldn't make it out again.

'Something wrong?' mumbled Cass. She was half-asleep, exhausted. Orc moved his gaze from the porthole, and shifted slightly to press closer against her.

'For once,' he said, 'no.'

36

THE WINNER

By the time the steam-yacht had disappeared over the northern horizon, the sun was a ball of molten gold in a rust-coloured haze. Ranga went back to the only level bit of bare rock he'd found, and the bed he'd made from pine-branches overlaid with a blanket. It was still damp from his swim across from the main island, even though he'd tried to protect his gear by lashing it to a crude raft of fallen wood. He was a poor swimmer, and there had been times during the crossing he'd thought he might not live to clamber out the other side.

That would have been too cruel, to drown with his long-sought prize in his possession, and an even greater prize only days away.

How many days, he didn't know. He had hoped Vanessa would arrive this evening: unrealistic, but he really didn't want to spend a night here, alone. He would have traded years of his future to keep the sun in the sky.

He checked his old tobacco tin, to make sure the blue crystal jammed diagonally between its corners hadn't gone anywhere – he kept fearing the thing would disappear – then lay back on his lumpy blanket. The first stars showed through breaks in the thinning cloud. They lanced him with beams of ice. He verged on shivering.

Perhaps there was no one else left on the three islands. No one, and no lights. The main island was now the Isle of the Dead, fled by the living, leaving only ghosts.

Which didn't exist.

He concentrated on the good things to come. He imagined candlelight, a bottle of fine wine, Vanessa's gaze intense with admiration.

He would have to adapt the story, of course.

'That's what I do. I'm a liar.'

It would be best to skirt the luck of Cass leaving the carbine not ten yards from where he'd lain hidden. He could say he'd had the gun all along, that he'd persuaded a sailor on *Archon* to give him one. But even that might not be enough to make him seem like a man with a plan, a resourceful, driven hero. 'Why,' Vanessa might ask, 'did you not shoot the magician as soon as he'd sent the monster out to sea?'

Would she be so picky? Still, there had been excellent tactical reasons. 'I knew that if I missed,' he could answer, 'the magician and the naval girl would reach the cover of the tents before I got off another shot, and it would be dangerous to follow – I had to assume the girl's revolver still contained two bullets. And there was the chance the magician would call his monster back to land as soon as I fired. I judged it better to wait for another opportunity.'

'Better?' he imagined her querying. 'Or safer?'

'If I'd been interested in safety, my Lady, I would have run as soon as he'd created the thing.'

Intelligent, if not dashingly heroic. But it still wasn't the image he wanted to present, that of someone in control. The real opportunity to get the stone hadn't come from something he'd done, but from another piece of good fortune: Tashi's arrival.

And Tashi's inclusion in the story would itself bring problems.

'He was still alive?' He envisaged her frown. 'You were to make sure of them both as soon as you reached the island. Was my safety from persecution and death of no importance?'

He began to sweat. What could he tell her? That he *had* shot the magician as soon as he'd sent the monster out to sea, and that the creature had been destroyed out there? What if someone came to the island and found the monster dismembered, and whatever Tashi had become, and Vanessa read about it in the newssheets – how would he explain it?

But who would know the red creature *was* Tashi? He could say it was something another magician had pulled from thin air to fight the goddess. It made no less sense than what had actually happened.

Yes, that could be his story: a titanic struggle between magician-made monsters. And during that struggle, he'd seen his chance, and made his shot. And when the monsters had killed each other, he'd descended from the place of his long, clever concealment...

His palms sweated against the wood of the loaded carbine as he approached the tents, alert for any movement from the slaughtered she-monster and the keeled-over figure that had once been the Thangkaran novitiate. The sea was full of smoke and ships, the surviving vessels now some distance away. Gun ready, Ranga rounded the corner of the tent. The magician, pale-faced, was slumped in the arms of the naval girl. She grabbed for the revolver beside her.

'It's empty,' said Ranga, speaking loudly through the breath-sodden bandage that concealed his face. 'I can count to six.'

She retracted her hand. 'Who the hell are you?'

'I'm the winner of this game we've all been playing. Your monster's dead, and I'm here for my prize.'

'Prize?'

'The blue stone. Hurry!' He twitched the end of the carbine.

'You shot him for a *stone*?' she cried. 'You've killed us both, you bastard.'

Ranga aimed at the magician. 'He doesn't look too bad. Want him to stay that way?'

He'd never seen such an ugly expression. It scared him, the hate in it: for a panicked moment he thought the girl might become a monster herself. She grabbed the blue stone from the magician's grasp, despite his feeble protests, and threw it at Ranga's feet.

'There!' she screamed. 'May it bring you misery and death.'

'Sorry to disappoint you,' said Ranga, 'but what it will actually bring me is the love of the world's most beautiful woman.' He slipped the stone into his pocket, then, still covering her one-handed with his carbine, he collected her revolver and hooked it in the back of his trousers. The girl's eyes burned.

'Go away, thief,' she said. 'Leave me to look after him.'

There was no way to deflect that hate, or turn it back on her. Ranga tried a nonchalant shrug, and left. He should feel elated, he knew. But he'd never shot anyone before, and it had upset him. Though the magician likely deserved death, he couldn't see himself as an executioner.

And he hoped, hoped…

On the bluff, he collected the bag of supplies he'd taken from the camp. Tashi's big sword still lay there. Ranga wondered why the boy had claimed to be unable to use it when he'd done so with apparent ease against the three-eyed creature that morning. Almost as puzzling was how Tashi had survived the distant gunfire that had afterwards come from the direction of the camp.

The camp Ranga had to visit now.

Hoping, hoping…

He retraced the steps he'd taken at dawn, feeling his pocket every so often to make sure the stone hadn't fallen out. After half a mile he winced, seeing red movement between the pines down-slope. He'd hoped Shoggu had died in the earlier gunfire; he'd hoped Tashi's suicidal assault on the magician and his monster had been out of grief. But no, Lady Luck had pleasured him with one hand and crushed his balls with the other.

On shaky legs now, he descended to intercept the labouring monk. Shoggu carried nothing except a canvas scroll, held in his bony right hand. Ranga unwrapped his bandage disguise. As their eyes met, the monk's thin lips tightened further.

'What happened?' he asked.

'He killed the monster,' said Ranga. 'I assume you knew about the monster?'

'I felt…' Shoggu's free hand scraped at his chest. 'Is Tashi…'

'He didn't make it,' said Ranga.

Shoggu swayed on his feet and Ranga moved quickly, steadied him. 'You want to sit down?'

'No. It is not… a surprise. May he find the Mountain.'

'You would have been proud. He was a real fighter.'

Shoggu nodded. 'I was always proud. But I was not enough, I think.'

Ranga assumed the monk had meant to say *it* was not enough, but there was no time to clarify. Insensitive though it might be to hurry past Tashi's death, there was something he needed to find out.

'I assume you got the note I left?' he said. 'Explaining who I am, and my lie about Vanessa being a magician?'

Shoggu glanced up at him, wetness in his eyes. 'Oh, I suspect the only lie about Vanessa was the one in that note.'

Ranga's heart almost failed him. He tried to sound amused as he said, 'What makes you think that?'

'Your confession on *Archon* made too much sense.'

'It made no sense at all!' said Ranga. 'It might have *seemed* to make sense, but that's me, that's what I do. I'm a liar. That's what we secret service agents do: we tell lies. And we make them convincing.'

'It rang true with what I sensed about her, but didn't realise at the time.'

'Of course it rang true,' protested Ranga. 'She's in on it too. That's what we *wanted* you to feel, so you'd fall for my lie. Listen: you know my sudden reverence for Gevurah was a lie, or why would I have left you this morning? But if I wasn't really a convert, and Vanessa was really that important to me, why would I implicate her? It makes no sense. What could I possibly have gained that was important enough to take that risk?' The tobacco tin dug into his hip. 'I tell you, Vanessa's high up in the service too, and if you go around molesting her, you'll make serious enemies.'

'As you say,' said Shoggu. 'A liar.'

'You'll find out when you get back there.'

'As you say. If I get back there.' Shoggu started his slow walk again, heading towards the place of the battle.

'You can't!' said Ranga. 'Wait – you wouldn't want to see him.'

'On the contrary,' said the monk. 'I want very much to see him. I pray that I am found worthy to follow after him.' He took another two steps, his back bowed. Ranga's hands gripped the carbine. His heart pounded. Then Shoggu half-turned, as though afraid to face him directly.

'You must give my apologies to your father.'

Ranga swallowed. 'Apologies?'

'Tell him I came back, and took a secret of his. Something of his, but not of your mother's. He will know what I mean.'

He set off again, his steps desultory, as though in mere pretence of walking.

You gave me no choice. Ranga raised the carbine. The monk looked like he was tensing his shoulders. The gun-sight shook. *You made me do this.*

More steps, and more and more.

The twitch, the sound, the shock. He almost dropped the gun. Shoggu fell like a puppet whose strings had been cut, collapsed within a red shroud that settled around him.

He woke beneath a nightmare moon, soaked in sweat. He found the tobacco tin under the blanket and checked the stone, then stared at the face of his pocket-watch until its markings sank in. One in the morning. But he wasn't going to risk sleeping again.

He would have to sit there, and think.

He did a lot of sitting and thinking over the next two days. He thought about what would happen after Vanessa picked him up. He thought about what would happen if her boat had sunk. He thought about whether he should swim back to the main island, just for variety. To see if the bodies were still there.

He thought about the two bullets he'd fired.

The first had been difficult: he hadn't used a rifle in four years. Revealing his carefully concealed existence had been full of risk, and foolish, because he'd seen no hope of the goddess being defeated. At the time of his shot, Tashi had been held in her grasp, screaming as his clothes and skin burned away. The sight had boiled Ranga to the point where he'd had no choice but to shoot the man who seemed to be directing the horror.

It hadn't been heroic; he couldn't claim that. But it had been driven by a hatred of suffering and cruelty. It had been driven by something good.

It balanced the second bullet, a little.

You stupid monk. Why couldn't you believe me?

Sleeping at night brought bad dreams, but lying awake brought a horrible sensitivity to imagined noises, whispered words among the pine needles, vengeful laughter among the cricket-song. Napping during the day was easier, but he couldn't sleep for an hour without starting awake, terrified Vanessa's boat had come and gone.

He did a lot of staring at the horizon.

At three each afternoon he performed the ritual Vanessa had hurriedly taught him, holding the stone and concentrating his will upon it. He'd never attempted anything magical before, and would have no way of knowing if he was doing this right, until she came.

If she came.

He thought a great deal about how to butcher and cook a goat.

Late afternoon, two days after he'd gained the stone, a boat appeared to the northeast. At dusk, Ranga watched men reefing sails a quarter-mile offshore. In the purpling dimness, a light flashed.

He abandoned shoes and shirt at the water's edge, jammed the tobacco tin deep into his pocket and the empty revolver deep in his waistband, and swam. With horrifying slowness, the boat grew to loom above him: a sleek fifty-foot yacht, with a narrow stack whose smoke streamed against the star-crowded sky.

The crew lowered a ladder at the stern. As Ranga hauled himself up onto the deck, he saw Vanessa by the wheel. He'd never imagined her in culottes and a blouse, yet she looked utterly beautiful in them, a goddess both disguised and revealed by modern ordinariness. Her companion, clearly the yacht's owner, was heavy-set and about fifty, his head thick with curly, oily hair on which was jammed a ridiculous naval-style cap. Ranga itched to shout at him to get away from Vanessa, but her obvious tension kept him silent.

He pulled the tobacco tin from his pocket, and her eyes widened fractionally.

'Not here,' she said. 'Marcello,' she said to the man, both hands on his shoulder, 'be so good as to commence our return.'

'Right now, my sweet?'

'This might not be a sensible place to linger.'

She beckoned to Ranga, and descended a steep stair. Dripping, Ranga followed. The owner gave him a nasty look. Ranga held back a smug one.

Seated behind a table in the saloon, Vanessa extended a slender arm and held out her hand. Ranga took out the stone: four months' work, his yearning adoration crystallised and compressed into one sharp-edged flake. Wet and half-naked, his drenched trousers dragging at his hips, he felt like a Sundaran skin-diver presenting history's greatest pearl to a legendary empress, who would shortly bestow upon him a kiss worth more than a mountain of gold.

'Quickly,' she snapped.

He sat, awaiting her verdict, while sailors' calls and the sound of winches came down from the deck.

'This is in truth a focus-stone,' Vanessa said. 'And such a size. This is a master-key to all the locked doors of Records, a knife to cut through any shroud.'

'Your delight makes it all worthwhile, my Lady.'

'And the Watcher and his boy?'

Ranga flinched from the memory of the gunshot.

'Ranga?'

'They won't trouble you.'

'Speak plainly. Are they dead?'

'Yes, my Lady.' It confused him that he still felt compelled to call her that, even though they would now become lovers.

'Good,' she said. 'You are a sweet and loyal friend.' Her words set his heart alight. 'You have been of more service to me than any number of rich men with their yachts and carriages. I look forward to hearing of your exploits as we make our tedious way back to civilisation.'

His chest tightened. But he had his line ready. 'My Lady, how I got this for you is of no consequence. All that matters is that I did so.'

'You're too modest,' she said. 'Or is there something you seek to hide?'

He tried to laugh. 'I've already confessed to murder. What else could there be?'

'You would not have lied to me, about the Watcher?'

'No! He's dead, I swear it.' For a moment it angered him that she might doubt the sacrifice he had made, the last of his innocence.

'You will not have forgotten,' she said, 'that this stone will allow me to view everything that happened on the island? I have brought my scry-glass.'

The blood drained from him. 'I fear you'll be rather bored.'

'The timbre of your voice suggests otherwise.' A smile curved the edge of her luscious mouth, but it mismatched her eyes. 'I'm intrigued. And uncovering your exploits will be good practice in using the stone, before I turn to its real work.'

'Its real work, my Lady?'

'Not so fast, Ranga. If you have something to confess, you had best do it now.'

He bowed his head, for the first time feeling the cold of his damp skin and hair, his wet trousers. 'I didn't kill them straight away. I thought they might be useful.' That at least he hoped she couldn't disprove. 'Without Tashi, I could never have got the stone.'

'You disobeyed me.'

'It was a difficult situation. I had to be adaptable.'

'Oh, Ranga,' she said. 'I wanted to trust you. After so many years of pain, I finally felt ready to give my heart to a man, if I could but find one worthy of my faith. The stone is a large credit in your ledger, but this revelation… what use would the stone have been to me if the Watcher had escaped to persecute me? Did you not think of that?'

He didn't know how to answer her. He couldn't tell her that Tashi had reminded him of his sister. He realised now that Vanessa had seen the removal of the Thangkarans as a higher priority than the stone itself. He'd blown it. Distraught at the magnitude of his failure, the loss of his dream, he put his head in his hands. There would be no kiss now, nor anything else.

'I can make it up to you,' he said, trying not to let his voice reveal how upset he was.

She sighed. 'Perhaps. Third time saves all, they say.'

'Anything, my Lady.' Any shred of hope, he would cling to.

She met his gaze, her dark eyes beautiful even in electric light. As she studied him, his heart burned with the need to prove himself worthy of her love. Finally she nodded.

'I shall tell you why I need this stone,' she said. 'Some years ago, a man stole something of mine. I have often scryed for him, and sometimes sensed him from afar, but he keeps a shroud woven about himself. Enhanced by this stone, my scry-glass will at last uncover his location.'

'What did he take?' It must have been something spectacular, Ranga thought, for her to have gone to such efforts.

'That need not concern you.' Vanessa sighed. 'Know only that my life has been darkened ever since. That's why I so wished to find a man I could have absolute faith in.'

'I won't fail you again. I'll find him and kill him.'

'No,' she said. 'You'll bring him to me, whether of his own will or by force.' She studied the stone in her hands, continually changing its angle, as though each rough facet held rare and precious knowledge. 'I must confront him face to face, in my own house. And you might have to bring him some distance. He was ever a traveller, a wanderer.'

There was a look in her eyes Ranga hadn't seen before. It only made him yearn for her more. So complex, so much to discover.

'Wherever the rogue hides, I'll come back with him – and the thing he took, if he still has it.'

'Oh, he still has it,' said Vanessa, 'for all that he has done his best to lose it.' Her grip tightened on the stone, her knuckles whitening. 'And I shall ask him, at last, whether he wants it or not – and if he does not, then the world will have seen the last of Corvan Geist.'

G: There is no cause for congratulation. This was nearly
       a disaster.

A: Nearly is no matter. Two powerful warships destroyed
       by a manifested entity, with many witnesses to the
       destruction. Twelve hundred dead, well in excess of
       what we might have achieved releasing the goddess
       in Torrento. The energy was enough to arrest all
       deterioration.

G: A Torrento event would have caused greater public
       horror and awareness.

A: Word will filter out. Sailors talk.

B: I must bring something to your attention.

G: And the Sundaran involvement? That was supposed to
       be secret. It was a mistake.

A: We will turn it to our advantage. What of Scarab?

F: His protections will not avail him long. His
       disloyalty will be scoured from him.

C: And I have some new techniques I would like to try out
       on him.

B: There is a matter I must raise.

A: And the monk's boy?

F: Scorpion has been tasked with his destruction.

B: This channel might have been compromised.

A: What?

B: I looked again at the sending of the dreadnought.
       The telephone call to naval intelligence was made
       by a party passing on information from a telegram
       received that same night. I have not been able to trace
       that wire other than its city of origin, Makassal.

A: Is that surprising? There are Empyreal agents there.

B: But with knowledge of the three bears? Yes, alone
       it means nothing, but listen. I have also reviewed

some of the island material, now the obfuscating
energy has been discharged. On the night of our
party's arrival, a device for detecting psychosphere
voices was mentioned, a so-called clairaudioscope.
The researcher claimed it had been invented by his
brother. I traced his brother. To Makassal.

G: Holy fuck.

F: These dialogues?

A: Revert to secondary communication. All acknowledge.

D: Acknowledged.

E: Acknowledged.

C: Acknowledged.

G: Acknowledged.

B: Acknowledged.

H: Acknowledged.

F: Acknowledged.

I: (Weak) Acknowledged.

J: Acknowledged.

K: (Weak) Acknowledged.

L: (Distortion, transcriber felt nauseous)

M: Acknowledged. And you who listen, this is the last you
will hear. But guard against your dreams, if you can.

About the author

Bryan Wigmore escaped from accountancy in his twenties, and has been on the run ever since, hiding out in nature conservation, survey processing, and writing. He lives in West Sussex.

Acknowledgements

I owe a huge debt to Jane Middleton and Jeff Richards, who gave excellent advice and support from the beginning, and to many other members of the wonderful *SFF Chronicles* online community who have helped shape and polish this story. Also to Simon Burgan, a tireless sounding board, and to Carol Kemm, without whose practical support this book might not exist. Lastly, thanks to Susan Cooper, Ken Wilber, Grant Morrison and Hiromu Arakawa, for striking the sparks that set fires in my brain.

The Fire Stealers sequence continues in

THE EMPYREUS PROOF

Read a taster...

She bit back a scream as a presence touched her mind, like a long needle sliding behind her eyes. A cold wind tugged; she braced herself and let it pull her through the gap in the wall of dust, to where darkness and empty air surrounded her. She stood atop a tall column, on a space so narrow that she would fall if she didn't hold herself dead still.

'I am here, Hana Quallace,' came a voice behind her.

She shuffled herself round, and quailed at the sight.

The being shone against the blackness. His mask was pure gold, but its brilliance was nothing next to the light that came through the eye-holes and mouth: the light that penetrated her clothes, her flesh, her bones, to the marrow of her bones, and found there only food for worms. The hair of the Shining One was coils of gold wire; his robes were dense with gold thread, so heavily woven that few of the images shimmering there could be made out. Mighty gold-feathered wings flashed behind him in an effortless beat, keeping him in place without disturbing the dead air. But though the Shining One seemed unaffected by gravity, Hana sensed she herself was not. The drop all around her felt horribly real: if she fell, the psychic shock of the landing might kill her. She had entered a realm under another's control – and that, she was suddenly sure, had not been wise.

She fought to assert herself. 'You know my name, sir. How should I call you?'

'You might call me "Lord".' The words were not easy to define; his speech seemed to come from the back of her own mind as much as from behind the mask. 'Or you might call me "A".'